shortlisted for the 2007 Crime Writers' Association International ...
for *The Savage Altar*, and in 2012 for *Until Thy Wrath Be Past*.

LAURIE THOMPSON is the distinguished translator of novels by Henning
Mankell and Håkan Nesser. He was editor of *Swedish Book Review* between
1983 and 2002.

"A superior example of Scandinavian noir" JULIA HANDFORD, *Sunday Telegraph*

"Another enormously successful Swedish import, Larsson is a remarkably good
writer who has been well served by her translator" JESSICA MANN, *Literary Review*

"The growing friendship between Mella and Martinsson is one of the best things
about Larsson's novels, which grow in confidence with each book"
JOAN SMITH, *The Sunday Times*

"Among the current female Scandi crime authors, I think that Åsa Larsson is one
of the best . . . I look forward to the next Åsa Larsson novel, as she really is 'the
one to watch'" KATHERINE ARMSTRONG, *Shotsmag*

"This book reminds me of Ruth Rendell's psychological thrillers . . . Overall this
series is really amongst the cream of recently translated Scandinavian crime
fiction" LAURA ROOT, *Eurocrime*

"A breath of fresh cold air in the seething squad of Swedish sleuths . . . This
double act has a dangerous edge to gladden fans of Lisbeth Salander"
BOYD TONKIN, *Independent*

"Larsson's laid-back style makes her unflinching probing of the icy depths of
the human heart all the more chilling" JAKE KERRIDGE, *Daily Telegraph*

"The new Larsson is to be followed with the most minute attention"
BARRY FORSHAW, *Independent*

Also by Åsa Larsson in English translation

Åsa Larsson

THE SECOND DEADLY SIN

Translated from the Swedish by
Laurie Thompson

MACLEHOSE PRESS
QUERCUS · LONDON

First published in Sweden as *Till offer åt Molok*
by Albert Bonniers Förlag, Stockholm, in 2012
First published in Great Britain in 2014 by MacLehose Press
This paperback edition published in 2015 by

MacLehose Press
an imprint of Quercus
55 Baker Street
7th Floor, South Block
London W1U 8EW

ISBN (MMP) 978 0 85738 998 5
ISBN (Ebook) 978 0 85738 997 8

2 4 6 8 10 9 7 5 3 1

Typeset in Minion by Patty Rennie
Printed and bound in Great Britain by Clays Ltd, St Ives plc

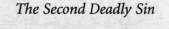

The Second Deadly Sin

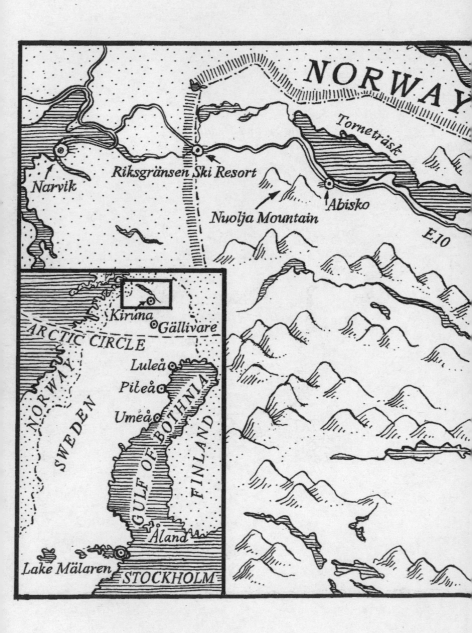

NORWAY

Torneträsk

Riksgränsen Ski Resort

Narvik

Nuolja Mountain

Abisko

E10

Kiruna

Gällivare

ARCTIC CIRCLE

NORWAY

SWEDEN

Luleå

Piteå

Umeå

GULF OF BOTHNIA

FINLAND

Åland

Lake Mälaren

STOCKHOLM

AUTHOR'S FOREWORD

I am reading Leviticus. God is furious, and is reeling off all His laws and the punishment in store for those who fail to obey them. He is spewing forth menace and anger. In Chapter 20 the Lord says that anyone who sacrifices a child to Moloch "shall surely be put to death: the people of the land shall stone him with stones". God will direct His wrath at him and isolate him from his people. How can that happen when the culprit has already been stoned to death, I ask myself. But if people turn a blind eye to a man who has sacrificed a child to Moloch, all his family will be subjected to the wrath of God.

I read a little about Moloch. It seems that he is a god who can provide riches, bountiful harvests and victory in battle. Was there ever any god who failed to promise such rewards? Children were sacrificed. Hollow statues of Moloch were made of copper. His embrace was voluminous. Fires were made inside the statue, making it red-hot. Then a living child would be placed in Moloch's lap.

I thought about that as I wrote this book. Sacrificing a child in order to prosper, in order to achieve earthly glory.

How can a dog possibly scream like that? Samuel Johansson has never heard a dog make such a noise before.

He is in his kitchen, making a sandwich. His Norwegian elkhound is on a running leash in the back yard. The calm before the storm.

Then the dog starts barking. Loud and angry at first.

What is it barking at? Certainly not a squirrel. Johansson recognises the way his dog barks at a squirrel. Surely not an elk? No, elk barks are less strident, more substantial.

Then something happens. The dog screams. Shrieks as if the gates of hell have just opened up before it. It is a sound that fills Johansson with cold terror.

And then silence.

Johansson races outside. No jacket. No shoes. No clear thoughts.

He stumbles his way through the autumnal darkness, towards the garage and the dog kennel.

And there, in the light from the lamp over the garage door, stands the bear. It is tugging at the dog's body, trying to drag it away, but the dead dog is still attached to the leash. The bear turns its blood-stained jaws towards Johansson and roars at him.

Samuel steps back somewhat unsteadily. Then he summons up superhuman strength and runs faster than he has ever run before, back to the house to fetch his gun. The bear stands its ground. Nevertheless, Johansson seems to feel the beast's hot breath on the back of his neck.

He loads the rifle with his wet hands before cautiously opening the door. He must keep calm and shoot accurately. Otherwise it could be all over in a flash. A wounded bear would take less than a second to pounce.

He creeps through the darkness. One step at a time. The hairs on the back of his head are sticking out like nails.

The bear is still there. Gobbling down what is left of the dog. When Johansson cocks the gun, it looks up.

Johansson has never trembled so much. There's no time to lose now. He tries to stand still, but it is impossible.

The bear shakes its head threateningly. Snarls. Huffs and puffs like a pair of bellows. Then it takes a deliberate step forward. That is when Samuel shoots. There is an explosive blast. The bear falls. But quickly it stands up again. And disappears into the darkness.

It has vanished now into the pitch-black forest. The light over the garage door is no help at all.

Johansson walks backwards to the house, aiming the gun left and right as he does so. Ears pricked, listening for sounds from the forest. That bloody bear might come bounding towards him at any moment. He can only see for a few metres.

Twenty paces back to the door. His heart is pounding. Five. Three. He's inside.

He's shuddering now. His whole body is shaking. He has to put his mobile down on the table and hold onto his right hand with his left in order to push the right numbers. The leader of the local hunters responds after only one ring. They agree to meet at first light. There's nothing they can do in the dark.

As dawn breaks all the men from the village gather outside Johansson's house. It is -2°C. Tree branches white with frost. Leaves have fallen. Rowan berries gleam rust-red among the grey. Something feathery is floating through the air – the kind of snow that never settles.

They stare at the devastation in and around the dog kennel. More or less all that is left, attached to the running leash, is the dog's skull. The rest is blood-soaked slush.

It is a hard-boiled collection of men. They are all wearing checked shirts, trousers with lots of pockets, belts carrying knives, and green jackets. The young ones have beards and a peaked cap on their heads. The older ones are clean-shaven and wear fur hats with ear flaps. These are men who make their own motorised carts for dragging back home the elks they have shot. Men who prefer cars with carburettors, so that they can mess around with the engines themselves and are not dependent on service garages where they nowadays just attach computer cables to the cars.

"This is what happened," the hunt leader says, as the more gnarled members of his team stuff new wads of chewing tobacco into their mouths and glance furtively at Johansson, who is having difficulty in controlling the tics in various parts of his face. "Samuel heard the dog howling. He grabbed his gun and went out. We've had bears prowling around here for quite some time now, so he realised that might be the problem."

Johansson nods.

"Anyway. You go out with your rifle. The bear is gobbling away at the dog, and turns to attack you. You shoot it in self-defence. It was coming towards you. You didn't go in and fetch your gun, you had it with you from the start. No messing about in this case. Nobody's going to be prosecuted for breaking hunting laws, right? I rang the police last night and put them in the picture. They had no hesitation in classifying it as self-defence."

"Who's going to hunt it down?" somebody wonders aloud.

"Patrik Mäkitalo."

That piece of information is followed by total silence while all present consider the implications. Mäkitalo comes from Luleå. It would have been good if somebody from their own local hunting team had been commissioned to track down the bear. But none of them has a dog as proficient as Mäkitalo's. And deep down they wonder if they are proficient enough themselves as well.

The bear is wounded. And so highly dangerous. It is essential to have a dog that dares to hold the bear at bay, rather than panicking and running back to its master with the ferocious beast hard on its heels.

And the hunter must not get cold feet either; when Teddy comes crashing through the undergrowth he might have no more than a second in which to react. The lethal target area on a bear is no wider than the base of a saucepan. And the hunter is aiming without a rifle support. It's like shooting a flying tennis ball. If he misses it is by no means sure that he will get a second chance. Hunting bears is not something for anybody with shaky hands.

"Speak of the devil," the hunt leader says, looking along the road.

Patrik Mäkitalo gets out of his car and greets the assembled group with a nod. He is about thirty-five. He tends to screw up his eyes; his beard is long and narrow, like a goat's. A Norrbotten Mongol warrior.

Mäkitalo doesn't say much, but listens intently to the hunt leader and asks Johansson about the shot. Where exactly was he standing? Where was the bear? What ammunition did he use?

"Oryx."

"Good," Mäkitalo says. "A high residual weight. With a bit of luck it might have gone right through the beast. That would make it bleed more, and make it easier to track."

"What do you use?"

It is one of the older hunters who plucks up the courage to ask.

"Vulkan. It usually stops just inside the skin."

Of course, the old-timers think. He doesn't shoot to wound a bear. Killing it outright means he doesn't need to track it down. And he's keen to preserve the bearskin in good condition.

Mäkitalo cocks his rifle and disappears into the trees. He returns after only a minute or so, with blood on his fingers.

He opens the tailgate. His hunting dogs are in a cage, their tongues dangling out of broad doggy smiles. They have eyes for nobody but their master.

Mäkitalo asks to see a map. The hunt leader fetches one from his car. They spread it out on the bonnet.

"This no doubt shows the route it took," Mäkitalo says. "But it's heading into the wind, through newly planted woodland, so there's a risk it might have veered off over here somewhere."

He points to the beck that flows down into the River Lainio.

"Especially if it's a mature varmint that's learnt how to outwit dogs. You'd better make arrangements for a boat that could come to meet us, if necessary. My dogs aren't afraid of getting their feet wet, but their master isn't as hardy as they are."

Everybody summons up a smile, signalling their empathy for the task ahead.

The hunt leader gets down to practicalities and asks, "Do you want to take somebody with you?"

"No. We'll follow the trail and see where it leads us. If it takes us over here and towards the marshes, it would help if you could go and stand guard here and there." He gestures at the map. "But let's get some idea first of where it's gone."

"He ought to be easy enough to find, if he's bleeding," one of the men says.

Mäkitalo doesn't even condescend to look at him when he replies: "I dunno about that; they often stop bleeding after a while and then they hide away in the thick undergrowth and tend to double back and creep up on whoever is following them. So if I'm unlucky it could be him who finds me."

"Too bloody right," the hunt leader says, giving the colleague who spoke out of turn a withering look.

Mäkitalo sets his dogs loose. They disappear up the hill like two brown streaks, sniffing at the ground. He follows them, G.P.S. device in hand.

Full steam ahead. He looks up at the sky and hopes it will not start snowing in earnest.

He is making rapid progress. He thinks briefly about the hunters he has just met. The type that sit around boozing and snoozing when they're supposed to be on the lookout. They would never be able to move as quickly as he does. Never mind track down the prey.

He crosses the dirt track. On the other side is a sandy slope. The bear seems to have run straight up it, legs wide apart, making heavy weather of it. He puts his hand in the obvious footprints.

The people in Lainio are already on edge. They know the bear has been around now and again. Dung next to an overturned rubbish bin, steaming in the cold morning air, as red as a mushy porridge of blueberries and lingon. There's been a lot of bear talk. Old stories have been dusted down.

Mäkitalo examines the clawmarks in the ground where it has dug its paws deep in order to thrust itself up the hill. It must have a claw the size of a knife in each toe. The villagers have measured the prints, placed matchboxes beside them and taken pictures with their mobiles.

Women and children have been kept indoors. Nobody has dared to venture out into the wood to gather berries. Parents collect their children by car from the school bus stop.

It must be a pretty big varmint, Mäkitalo thinks as he examines the tracks. An old carnivore. That's no doubt why it took the dog.

Now he comes to a pine forest. It's flat and the going is easy. The pines are tall, widely spaced, a colonnade, straight trunks, no branches, the wind sighing in the crowns high above. The moss that usually crackles underfoot in the summer is damp, soft and silent.

Good, he thinks. Nice and quiet.

He crosses an old boggy meadow. In the middle is an ancient barn that has collapsed. The rotten remains of the roof are scattered around the skeleton. It has not been cold enough for the ground to freeze. His feet sink deep into the swampy turf; he is becoming very sweaty. There is a smell of mud and iron-rich water.

Soon the trail veers away towards the coppices and brushwood in the direction of Vaikkojoki.

A few ravens croak and caw in the distance through the grey morning air. The vegetation is growing more dense. The trees are shrinking, fighting for space. Spindly pines. Messy grey spruce twigs. Stunted birches: most leaves have blown off, those remaining range from yellow to dull green and grey. He can see no further than five metres in any direction. Barely that.

He is down by the beck now. Has to keep brushing away twigs with his arm. He can only see a couple of metres ahead.

Then he hears the dogs. Three loud barks. Then silence.

He knows what that means. They have tracked down the bear. Disturbed it, forced it to move away from where it was lying wounded. When they detect the pungent smell coming from such a hideaway, they usually bark.

After another twenty minutes he hears the dogs barking again. More persistently this time. They have caught up with the bear. He checks his G.P.S. One and a half kilometres away. They are barking while on the move. Barking and chasing the bear. Best to keep plodding on. No point in getting too excited yet. He hopes the young bitch doesn't get too close. She is rather excitable. The other bitch works more calmly. Good at standing still a safe distance away, holding the hunted animal at bay, barking. She seldom goes any closer than three metres. A wounded bear is not a patient bear.

After half an hour they start barking from a stationary position. Now both the bear and the dogs are standing still.

Typical! Just where the vegetation is at its thickest. Nothing but undergrowth and no view at all. He keeps going, and is now only two hundred metres away.

The wind is coming from the side. Not a problem. The bear should not be able to smell him. He cocks his rifle. Presses on. His heart is pounding.

It's O.K., he thinks. He wipes his hand on his trouser leg. A bit of adrenalin goes with the territory.

Fifty metres to go. He peers into the undergrowth where the barking is coming from. Both dogs are wearing jackets that are luminescent green on one side and orange on the other. To distinguish them from the bear in circumstances where that is necessary. And also to see what direction the dog is facing.

Now he sees a glimpse of something orange up ahead. Which of the dogs is it? Impossible to tell. The bear usually stands between the dogs. Mäkitalo screws up his eyes, peers into the undergrowth again, moves as quietly as he can to one side. Ready to shoot, reload, shoot again.

The wind veers again. At the same time he catches sight of the other dog. There are about ten metres between the two of them. The bear must be in there somewhere, but he can't see it. He must get closer. But now the wind is coming from diagonally behind him. That is not good. He raises his rifle.

Then he sees the bear. Ten metres away. No clear view for taking a shot. Too many tree trunks and too much undergrowth in the way. It suddenly stands up. It must have got wind of him.

It charges at him. It all happens so quickly. He hardly has time to draw breath before it is almost upon him. There is a creaking and crashing and snapping of branches.

He shoots. The first shot makes the bear swerve to one side, but it keeps on coming. The second shot is perfect. The bear collapses three metres short of him.

The dogs pounce on it immediately. Bite at its ears. Chew its fur. He lets them do whatever they want. That is their reward.

His heart is slamming like an open door in a storm. He tries to get his breath back in between praising his dogs. Well done! There's a good girl!

He takes out his mobile. Rings the local huntsmen.

That was a close shave. A bit too close for comfort. He thinks briefly about his little boy and his partner. Then he banishes any such thoughts from his mind. Looks at the bear. It is big. Really big. And almost black.

The local huntsmen arrive. The air is heavy with autumn chill, pungent bear and admiring respect. They truss up the body of the bear with ropes and attach straps running over their shoulders and under their arms so that they can drag it to a clearing not far from a track that can be accessed by their four-wheel drive pick-up. They work like slaves, and agree that it is a hell of a big beast.

The inspector from the county council arrives. He inspects the place where the bear was shot to make sure that no laws have been broken. Then he takes no end of samples while the hunters are recovering from their efforts. He clips off a clump of fur, cuts out a skin sample, cuts off the testicles, prises out a tooth with his sheath knife so that the age of the bear can be established.

Then he cuts open its stomach.

"Shall we check what Teddy's been eating?" he says.

Mäkitalo has tied his dogs to a tree trunk. They whimper and strain at their leashes. It's their bear, after all.

Steam rises from the contents of the bear's stomach. And the stench is awful.

Some of the men take an involuntary step back. They know what's inside there. The remains of Johansson's Norwegian elkhound. The inspector knows that as well.

"Ah well," he says. "Berries and meat. Fur and skin."

He pokes around in the slushy mess. His face suddenly assumes a suspicious expression.

"But for Christ's sake, this isn't . . ."

He falls silent. Picks up a few pieces of bone with his right hand, which is protected by a plastic glove.

"What the hell is this it's been eating?" he mumbles as he pokes around in the slush.

The huntsmen come closer. Scratch at the back of their heads so that the peaks of their caps slide down their foreheads. One of them takes out a pair of glasses.

The inspector straightens up. Quickly. Takes a step backwards. He's holding a piece of bone with his fingers.

"Do you know what this is?" he asks.

His face has turned grey. The look in his eyes sends shivers down the spines of all the others. The forest has fallen silent. There is no wind. No birdsong. It seems that it is refusing to reveal a secret.

"It's not a dog in any case. I can assure you of that."

SUNDAY, 23 OCTOBER

The autumnal river was still talking to her about death. But in a different way. Before, it was funereal in tone. It used to say: You can put an end to it all. Run out onto the thin ice, as far as you can before it breaks. But now the river said: You, my girl, are no more than the blinking of an eye. It felt consoling.

District Prosecutor Rebecka Martinsson was sleeping calmly as dawn began to break. She was no longer woken up by angst poking away at her from the inside, digging into her, scratching around. No more night sweats, no more palpitations.

She no longer stood in the bathroom, staring into the mirror at black pupils and wanting to cut off all her hair, or to set fire to something – preferably herself.

It's good now, she said instead. To herself or to the river. Sometimes to another person, if anybody dared to ask.

And it *was* good. Good to be able to do her job again. To tidy up her home. Not to feel her mouth constantly parched, not to break into a rash after taking all her medicine. To sleep soundly at night.

And occasionally she even laughed. While the river flowed past as it had done for generation after generation before her, and would continue to flow long after she was no more.

But just now, for the blinking of an eye she would be alive, she could laugh and keep her house tidy, do her job properly and occasionally smoke a cigarette in the sunshine on her balcony. Then she would be nothing, for a very long time.

That's the way it is, the river said.

She liked to have the house clean and tidy. To keep it as it was in Grandma's time. She slept in the alcove in the varnished sofa bed. The floor was covered by rag mats made by her grandmother. Wooden trays hung from wall hooks in embroidered slings.

The drop-leaf table and chairs were painted blue, and worn and shiny wherever hands and feet had rested. Crammed onto the metal ladder shelves were volumes of low-church pastor Laestadius's sermons, hymn books and thirty-year-old copies of magazines from another time – *Hemmets Journal*, *Allers* and *Land*. The linen cupboard was full of threadbare mangled sheets.

Lying at Martinsson's feet was the puppy Jasko, sniffling away. The police dog handler Krister Eriksson had given it to her eighteen months ago. A handsome sheepdog. He would soon be lord of all he surveyed – at least, that's what he himself thought. Raised his leg high when he peed, and almost fell over. In his dreams he was the King of Kurravaara.

His paws twitched and trod in his sleep as he chased after all those annoying mice and rats that filled his days with their tempting scents but never allowed themselves to be captured. He yelped and his lips twitched when he dreamed about clamping his teeth into their backs with a satisfying crunching noise. Perhaps he was also dreaming about all the local bitches responding to all the bewitching love-letters he peed onto every available blade of grass during the day.

But when the King of Kurravaara woke up, nobody called him anything but the Brat. And no bitches queued up outside his door.

Martinsson's other dog never lay in her bed. Never sat in her lap as the Brat frequently did. Vera the mongrel might allow herself to be stroked very briefly, but there was no question of longer spells of tenderness.

She slept under the table in the kitchen. Nobody knew her age, nor her pedigree. She used to live with her master in the depths of the forest, a hermit who made his own anti-mosquito balm and pranced around naked in the summer. When he was murdered, his dog ended up with Martinsson. If she hadn't taken her in, she would have been put down. Martinsson wouldn't have been able to cope with that, and so she had taken Vera home with her. And she had stayed there.

In a way, at least. She was a dog who knew her own mind. Who left it up to Martinsson to track her down when she wandered off along the village road, or went off to explore the potato patch down by the boathouse.

"How on earth can you let her wander off like that?" said Martinsson's neighbour Sivving. "You know what people are like. Somebody will shoot her."

Please look after her, Martinsson prayed. To a God she sometimes hoped existed. And if you can't do that, let it happen quickly. Because I can't stop her. She's not my dog in that sense.

Vera's paws never twitched when she was asleep, nor did she go hunting after tempting scents in her dreams. What the Brat dreamed about, Vera did while she was awake. In the winter she would listen for sounds made by field mice under the snow, pounce down upon them and break their backs just as foxes do. Or stamp down with her front paws and kill them off like that. In the summer she would dig out mouse nests, gobble up the naked youngsters and eat horse dung in the pastures. She knew which farms and houses to avoid. She would run past those places, skulking down in the ditches. But she knew where she would be treated to cinnamon buns and slices of reindeer meat.

Sometimes she just stood there, staring into the north-east. On such occasions Martinsson would get goose pimples. Because that was where the dog's original home was, on the other side of the river, up in Vittangijärvi.

"Do you miss him?" Martinsson would ask on such occasions.

And was pleased that only the river could hear her.

Now Vera woke up, sat on the floor next to the head of the bed and stared at Martinsson. When Martinsson opened her eyes, Vera started wagging her tail.

"You must be joking," Martinsson groaned. "It's Sunday morning. I'm asleep."

She pulled the covers up over her head. Vera lay her head on the edge of the bed.

"Go away," Martinsson said from under the covers – although she knew it was too late now: she was wide awake.

"Do you need to pee?"

Whenever she heard the word "pee", Vera usually sat down next to the door. But not this time.

"Is it Krister?" Martinsson asked. "Is Krister on his way here?"

It was as if Vera could feel when Krister Eriksson got into his car in Kiruna, fifteen kilometres away from the village.

In reply to Martinsson's question, Vera walked over to the door and lay down to wait.

Martinsson collected her clothes that were hanging over a chair back next to the sofa bed, and lay on them for a few minutes before getting dressed under the covers. It was freezing cold in the house after the minus temperatures of the night, and you couldn't just leap out of bed and put on icy cold clothes.

As she sat on the lavatory, both dogs assembled in front of her. The Brat put his head on her knee and insisted on being stroked.

"Time for breakfast now," she said, reaching for the toilet paper.

Both dogs dashed out into the kitchen. But when they noticed that their food bowls were empty, it seemed to dawn on them that the alpha-female was still in the bathroom, and they raced back to Martinsson. By now she had flushed the toilet and washed her hands in cold water.

After breakfast the Brat went back to the warm bed.

Vera lay down on the rag mat next to the hall door, settled down with her nose on her front paws, and sighed deeply.

Ten minutes later a car drew up outside.

The Brat shot out of the bed in such a rush that the covers were scattered in all directions. He dashed under the dining table, raced up to Martinsson, then to the door, then to the bed and repeated the same operation. The rag mats were sent flying, he slid over the varnished wooden floorboards, and kitchen chairs fell over.

Vera had stood up, was standing there patiently and also wanted to be let out. Her tail was wagging away, but she didn't overdo things.

"I really don't understand what you're trying to tell me," said Martinsson innocently. "You'll have to explain yourselves more clearly."

And the Brat whimpered and yelped and stared pleadingly at the door, running up to it and then back to Martinsson.

Martinsson walked extremely slowly to the door. In slow motion. Looked unremittingly at the Brat, who was shaking and trembling with excitement. Vera just sat there, anticipating the inevitable. Martinsson turned the key and opened the door. The dogs bounded down the steps.

"Oh, was that what you wanted?" she exclaimed with a laugh.

Eriksson the police dog handler parked his car outside Martinsson's house. Even from a distance he had noted that there was a light in her kitchen window on the upper floor, and his heart gave a little leap of joy.

Then he opened the car door just as Martinsson's dogs came rollicking down the steps.

Vera was first. Her hindquarters were swinging from side to side, and she hunched her back in sheer pleasure.

Krister's own two dogs, Tintin and Roy, were two hard-working, handsome, well-disciplined and pedigree sheepdogs. Martinsson's Brat was Tintin's son. He was destined to be a super-dog.

And so Vera, a vagrant with no pedigree at all, had become a member of the gang. As thin as a rake. One of her ears stood straight up, the other was limp. And she had a black patch around her eye.

To start with he had tried to train her. "Sit!" he had said. She had looked him in the eye and put her head on one side. If I could understand what you meant, well, maybe – but if you're not going to eat that tasty-looking bit of liver, then perhaps . . .

He was used to dogs obeying him. But her he could not charm.

"Hello, you scruffy little mongrel!" he said, tugging gently at her ears and stroking her head. "How can you be so slim when you spend all your time gobbling?"

She allowed herself to be stroked, then made way for the Brat. He was running around like a cat with a firework up its bottom – between Eriksson's legs, all over the place, couldn't stand still long enough for Eriksson to stroke him, then lay down totally submissive – then up again, stood up with his paws on Eriksson, lay down once more on his back, twirled around, then ran off and fetched a pine cone that they might be able to play with, dropped it at Eriksson's feet, licked Eriksson's hand then yawned – one way of getting rid of some of those feelings that had become too much to cope with.

Martinsson appeared in the porch. He looked at her. Beautiful, beautiful. Her arms crossed and her shoulders up by her ears to keep in the warmth. The contours of her small breasts were visible through her military-style vest. Her long dark hair was slightly tousled in a just-out-of-bed way.

"Hello!" he shouted. "I'm glad to see that you're an early bird."

"Early bird, my foot," Martinsson shouted back. "It's that confounded dog. You two are in cahoots in some mysterious way. She wakes me up whenever you're on your way here."

He laughed. Joy and pain arm in arm. She already had a boyfriend, a lawyer in Stockholm.

But I'm her man here in the forest, he thought. I'm the one who looks after her house and garden and takes care of her dogs. When she goes to see him, admittedly. But still.

I take whatever I can get, was his mantra. I take whatever I can get.

"That's a good girl," he whispered to Vera. "You carry on waking her up. And give that bloody lawyer a bite in his leg."

Martinsson looked back at Eriksson, and shook her head pensively. He hadn't said straight out that he was in love with her. Nor did he impose himself upon her. But he always gave himself the pleasure of gazing long and hard at her. He sometimes smiled and looked at her as if she were a miracle. Without asking first he would come and visit her, and go for walks through the forest with her. As long as Måns wasn't staying with her, of course. When he was, Eriksson would give them a wide berth.

Måns did not like Krister Eriksson.

"He looks like something from outer space," Måns used to say.

"Yes," Martinsson would say.

Because it really was true. Eriksson had been badly burnt as a young boy, and his features were permanently damaged. He had no ears, and his nose was not much more than two holes in the middle of his face. His skin was like a shrivelled map in pink and brown.

But he has a strong and nimble body, she thought as she watched the Brat licking his face. The dogs knew what that dry skin of his felt like.

"Just so that you know," she said with a little smile, "he spent all yesterday afternoon in Larsson's dunghill, digging up old cowpats and wolfing down all the white maggots he could find."

"Huh!" Krister said, pulling a face and trying to thrust the Brat to one side.

Vera raised her head, looked towards the road and gave a bark.

Eriksson's dogs also started barking in his car. They obviously thought everybody had been having fun for ages, except them.

The next moment Sivving the neighbour appeared down by the letter boxes.

"Hi there," he shouted. "And hello, Krister – I thought I heard your car."

"Oh my God," Martinsson mumbled. "Only a few minutes ago I was having a nice quiet Sunday morning . . ."

Vera scampered off to greet Sivving. He was walking as fast as he could, but that was not very fast at all. The left side of his body was unable to do what he wanted. His left foot was dragging behind him. His left arm hung helplessly at his side.

Martinsson watched as Vera pulled off Sivving's mitten then circled slowly round him – just sufficiently slowly and close to him that he was able to grab it back.

"Bloody bitch!" he exclaimed, his voice full of warmth.

Vera never plays with me like that, Martinsson thought.

By now Sivving had reached them. He was still a big man. Tall. A dauntingly large belly and a shock of white, fluffy hair looking like the puffball head of a dandelion.

"Can we drive out to Sol-Britt Uusitalo?" he asked without beating about the bush. "I've promised to go and see how she is. They rang from her workplace and were worried about her. She lives out at Lehtiniemi."

Martinsson groaned inwardly.

There's always something he wants me to do for him, she thought. He promises people things, then comes here to me even though it's early on Sunday morning.

But Eriksson opened the car door on the passenger's side.

"Jump in," he said to Sivving, pushing back the seat so that it would be easier for him to sit down.

He's nice, Martinsson thought. Kind and thoughtful. She felt a prick of conscience.

"Ann-Helen Alajärvi – I expect you know who she is, Gösta Asplund's girl," said Sivving, struggling to fasten the safety belt over his large stomach. "She works as a breakfast waitress with Sol-Britt at the Winter Palace. She rang and was worried about her: Sol-Britt ought to have been at work at six o'clock this morning. I promised to call in and check up on her. I was just going to go out for a walk with Bella, but then I saw that Krister had turned up. It's good that you're here as well, in case we need to break the door down."

He smiled at them. A prosecutor and a police officer.

"That's not the way we work," Martinsson said.

"Oh yes it is," Eriksson said with a laugh. "That's exactly how we work. Rebecka climbs up onto the roof and swings her way in through the window and I barge down the door."

They set off for Lehtiniemi.

"Is she a friend of yours, then, this Sol-Britt?" Eriksson asked.

Martinsson was sitting in the back seat with Vera and Sivving's German pointer Bella. The Brat had to share the dog cage with Eriksson's dogs.

The car reeked of dog. Bella tended to get carsick, and long strands of dribble were dangling from her mouth.

"Well, I wouldn't go so far as to say she's a friend," Sivving said. "I mean, she lives some distance away. And she's younger than I am. But Sol-Britt has always lived here, and so obviously we have a chat whenever we meet. She had a bit of an alcohol problem a few years ago, and so at that time it was nothing unusual if she sometimes didn't turn up for work. Her workmates knew all about it. She once appeared on my porch and wanted to borrow some money. I said no, but I offered her some food. But that wasn't what she wanted. Anyway, three years ago her son was run over and died. He was thirty-five, worked at the ice factory in Jukkasjärvi; he was a promising skier as a young lad, won the Junior District Championship when he was seventeen. He left a little boy, only about three or four years old. What's his name, now . . ."

Sivving fell silent and shook his head, as if that would make the boy's name come tumbling out. You could not tell a story without knowing all the names.

My God, does he never stop talking? Martinsson wondered, gazing out of the window.

It came in the end.

"Marcus! That's it! Thereby hangs a tale as well. His mum had moved to Stockholm a long time before that. She'd found a new man, and had two kids with him. Pretty quick work. She ran off to Stockholm just after Marcus's first birthday. She moved in with the new bloke straight away and had new kids. And she wasn't very interested in looking after the lad. Sol-Britt was really pissed off. Mind you, she was pleased to have Marcus staying with her. And it was like a new start for her. She joined Alcoholics Anonymous and stopped drinking altogether. I asked Ann-Helen this morning when she rang if she thought Sol-Britt might have had a relapse, but she said no way. So no doubt she's right. All kinds of things could have happened. People slip on mats and hit their heads on tables. It can be days before anybody finds them."

Martinsson pulled a face that said *I call in on you at least once every day*. She noticed Eriksson looking at her in the rear-view mirror.

"Anyway, have you been picking cloudberries this year yet?" he said.

"It's a bad year for cloudberries. Nobody seems to have found any. Too few insects. I have a few bogs over at Rensjön where I usually go picking. There's always some about – but not this year. I spent several hours looking, and I didn't even get enough to cover the bottom of the bucket. There's a sort of strip of birch trees along the edge of the lake. I went down three or four years ago, when it was a very good year for cloudberries, and I thought there was bound to be loads: but there wasn't a single one. And so this year, when there wasn't a cloudberry to be seen anywhere, I thought I'd better check that strip of birch trees even so – and it was full of them! It was like an orange carpet wherever you looked! No more than about fifteen metres wide and a hundred metres long. I spent a couple of hours picking, and I got seven or eight litres. But that was all there was."

"Wow!" Eriksson said, duly impressed.

Martinsson took the opportunity to allow her mind to wander. Good that Eriksson was on form and interested. So that Sivving could chatter away to his heart's content. Dogs weren't the only things that needed to be exercised.

"Mind you, it's not that easy nowadays, with my arm as it is," Sivving said. "You should have seen us in the old days, when Maj-Lis and I used to go picking blueberries in Pauranki. Could it have been '95? In eight hours I picked 145 litres of blueberries. They were growing everywhere. At the edge of bogs and on dry land and in clearings. They were so heavy that the stalks were bent over – at first all you could see was greenery, and you had to lift them up in order to get at the berries. Great big ones. Sun-drenched and incredibly sweet. Here we are! You don't need to drive into the parking area. Just park at the side of the road."

At last, Martinsson thought.

Sivving was pointing at a house by the side of the road. Made of wood, two storeys. Painted yellow. Built at some time in the first half of the twentieth century. An iron balcony over the front door seemed to be in such a state that you couldn't walk on it. There was no porch. Two wooden duckboards, one on top of the other, led up to the front door. Presumably the original porch had been dismantled, but nobody had got round to building a new one. There was no lawn; the house was standing on soft pasture-land on a sandy-soil base. A sundial and a flagpole with paint flaking off it stood in the middle of the garden, looking lost. Hanging on an outdoor drier were some duvets and pillowcases, frozen stiff – a sign that the frosty nights had already arrived.

"I wonder if it wasn't that same year that I picked so many cran-berries," Sivving said, enjoying all his berry memories and reluctant to stop recalling them. "I was out picking in the late autumn. You had to wait until the afternoon because the night frosts meant that the berries would be frozen fast into the turf by morning."

Martinsson shuffled around on the back seat. Why couldn't he get out now and find out what had happened to Sol-Britt, so that they could go for a walk in the forest?

He no doubt needs to carry on remembering until there's nothing left for him to say, she told herself. Let him finish off.

"One day I picked twenty-four litres," Sivving said. "I gave two litres to Maj-Lis's sister in Pajala. Some Finnish relatives came to visit her, they went out and picked five litres and were thrilled to bits. Gunsan said: 'I know somebody who picked twenty-four litres.' 'Sitä ei voi,' they said. 'Nobody can do that.' 'He can,' Gunsan said."

He broke off and looked at the house. Everything was quiet.

"I'd better go and check," he said. "You'll wait here, won't you?"

Sivving opened the front door without knocking, as was the custom in the village.

"Hello!" he shouted, but there was no answer.

The entrance hall led into the kitchen, which was neat and tidy. The stainless steel sink was bright and shiny: the draining board had a little cloth in the middle with an empty vase on it. The plate rack was empty. The white glazed tiles were decorated with stickers, every other one with a four-fruit pattern, and those in between with large flowers in yellow and brown.

He paused for a moment. His thoughts went back to his wife Maj-Lis: she too had never left even the smallest glass on the draining board. Everything had to be finished and done with, dried with the tea towel and put away in its cupboard.

He remembered occasions when he had done the washing up. No matter how careful he thought he'd been, she had always followed him round with a cloth, wiping and polishing.

Things are not the same without Maj-Lis, he thought.

It had never occurred to him that she would die before he did. They were the same age, after all. All that confounded research showing that women lived longer than men . . . Why should he and Maj-Lis be the exception?

When she died he had ironed tablecloths and picked flowers to put in vases all around the house. Heather and wild rosemary and globeflowers. But the house had not seemed to be alive. It was as if it did not want to be alive.

He could not face the prospect of selling it. Nor could he bear to carry on living there among all that emptiness. The best solution had been to move downstairs into the boiler room in the cellar.

Less cleaning to do, he told anybody who wondered what was going on. How could he possibly explain the real reason to people who would not understand?

Now he looked around Sol-Britt Uusitalo's kitchen. Curtains with tie-backs. Ornaments and flowers on the window ledges.

But all the doors of the lower cupboards were standing open.

Odd, he thought. Why on earth were they open? Perhaps she heard a mouse gnawing away, and tried to find it. Or had she been looking for something else? Cleaning stuff that she had misplaced? Or something like that.

The bedroom door was ajar. Not a sound from inside. Should he go in?

"Hello!" he shouted again. "Sol-Britt!"

He hesitated. Should he really go into a woman's bedroom without being invited? Perhaps she was lying there drunk.

Drunk, half-dressed, unconscious. He didn't really know her, and even if Ann-Helen didn't believe she could have had a relapse, nevertheless . . .

He felt more and more uncomfortable. It would be best if Rebecka went in. She was a woman, after all.

Outside in the road Martinsson and Eriksson had got out of the car. The dogs were all lying peaceably – soon they would be able to go running around in the forest.

Eriksson took a tin of chewing tobacco out of his pocket. He pressed some to form a wad and inserted it under his top lip.

He noticed a faint trace of disapproval in Martinsson's look.

"I know," he said.

"Have your baccy if you want," she said with a smile. "It's just that it's not my thing. I tried it once and I don't think I've ever felt so ill."

Eriksson put the tin back into his pocket. Then he took it out again.

"I'm going to give it up," he announced.

"Why?"

He looked down the hill.

She said nothing but looked down the hill as well.

Then his face lit up again and he pointed at his upper lip.

"My last wad of baccy."

He hurled the tin of chewing tobacco as far as he could into the trees.

Sivving emerged from the house.

"She's not in the kitchen," he shouted, looking back over his shoulder. "But I didn't want to go into her bedroom. She might be lying there asleep, then all of a sudden she wakes up and finds a man standing there . . . God only knows what might happen. Or what do you say? Do you think I should go in?"

"Her car is parked here," Martinsson said to Eriksson.

They looked at each other. It does happen that people pass away in their sleep. It is not all that uncommon.

Tintin barked loudly, and started scratching at the bars of her cage.

"O.K., I'll go in," Martinsson said.

Eriksson grabbed hold of her arm.

"Hang on a minute!" he said, looking at Tintin.

The dog was standing up on her hind legs, sniffing in all directions. She barked again, and scratched at the cage bars.

"She's making a point," he said in a low voice. "There's a smell of

35

death in the air. She's caught on to it very quickly. The air here must be like a sea of blood."

"Sivving," Martinsson shouted. 'Wait. Don't go back into the house. Krister and I will go."

Martinsson went in through the door with Eriksson close behind her. She shouted, but still there was no response. The open cupboard doors looked as if they wanted to say something, but they did not manage to produce a single word.

A heart attack, Martinsson thought as she approached the bedroom door. She has fallen and smashed her skull.

But what if she is not dead? Maybe she is lying there injured.

In fact Sol-Britt Uusitalo was lying on her back on her bed. Her head was turned to one side. Her eyes were open, as was her mouth. Her tongue was halfway out. One arm was hanging down from the bed.

She was wearing only a pair of knickers. The duvet was on the floor beside the bed. All over the corpse were little brown wound marks.

"What on earth . . ." Martinsson began, but stopped short.

Eriksson went up to the bed and just to be sure placed his fingers against the woman's neck. A few sluggish flies flew up from the corpse to the ceiling. He nodded to Martinsson.

Martinsson observed the dead woman. Thin trickles of dried blood from some of the wounds. She searched inside her own body for feelings. Something approaching agitation, perhaps? Horror?

But she felt nothing.

She looked at Eriksson: he was serious, but calm. It was only on television that police officers threw up at the scene of a murder.

"What's happened?" she said, noting her objective tone of voice. "Has somebody stabbed her?"

"Are you still there?" Sivving shouted from outside.

"She's here!" Martinsson shouted in reply. "Stay where you are."

"Look at her face," Eriksson said, leaning over the body. "Here, on her cheekbone. It looks as if somebody has peeled away the skin."

"We must leave her as she is," Martinsson said, "and ring for the forensics boys and the pathologist."

"Look at the wall," Eriksson said.

Somebody had written something on the wall over the headboard. WHORE, it said, in large black letters.

Martinsson turned on her heel and left the house. Sivving was standing outside the front door, worried stiff.

"What's happened?"

"Oh, Sivving," Martinsson said.

She stretched out her hand to touch him, but stopped halfway through and let her hand drop.

She was so fond of him. Her parents were dead. Her grandmother as well. Sivving was closer to her than anybody else in the world, but they never touched each other. That was not their way.

She felt just now that she ought to have made touching him a regular habit.

I could have touched him just as Grandma used to touch me, she thought. Casually. Just a little pat on the back or a stroke on the arm as she passed by me in the kitchen. When she helped me to zip up my jacket, or to put my gloves on. When she brushed the snow off me on the porch.

If she had done that sort of thing with Sivving, perhaps it would not have felt so awkward now. She longed to hold his hand, but could not bring herself to do it.

"What's happened?" Sivving said. "Has something awful happened? She's dead, isn't she?"

Eriksson had appeared behind Martinsson's back. He looked at Sivving.

"Didn't you say that she lived with her grandson?" he said in a low voice. "Marcus, was that his name?"

"Yes," Sivving said. "Where is he? Where's the boy?"

Police Inspector Anna-Maria Mella looked in surprise at her youngest son, Gustav. How could there be such a lot of chat in so small a body? He started talking the moment he opened his eyes in the morning.

Now he was standing in the doorway of his parents' bedroom while she was rummaging through a drawer, looking for a pair of tights with no holes in them.

It was the birthday of Robert's sister in Junosuando, and Mella thought she should wear a skirt. How was it possible to have a whole drawer full of tights, but none of them without holes?

Besides, her skirt was too tight. It was astonishing that just an extra kilo could make such a difference. It used to fit her snugly around the waist. Now it crept up higher and higher so that the waistband reached her ribs the moment she moved. It became too short, displaying half her thighs.

I look like a spring chicken, she thought as she examined her reflection despondently in the mirror.

"Mum, do you know what? Malte's big brother has 'The Legend of Zelda: Phantom Hourglass'. Me and Malte were allowed to watch him play, and he got really really far. There's a cave. And in it there's a door, and do you know what you have to do to get through it? Mum? Do you know?"

"No."

"You have to talk to a plate on the door and then you write on it

– I can't remember what you have to write, I'll have to ask Malte, but anyway . . . Are you listening?"

"Hmm."

"Then the door opens and you cross over a bridge and there's a sword there. Oh, I'd love to have a Nintendo D.S. Can you buy me one?"

"No. Go to your room and put your clothes on. They're on the chair."

Hole after hole, she thought, flinging another pair of tights to the floor. I have such hard, cracked heels, they make holes in all my tights.

Gustav was still in the bedroom doorway, but now he was on all fours, shuffling away.

"Look, I can stand on my hands, look now when I—"

"Now listen here, young man. Off you go to your room. On with your clothes. This very minute!"

He slunk off to his room.

Ah, at last, she thought, running a pair of tights over her hand to examine them more easily. Not a hole to be seen!

She began to wriggle her way into them. As she pulled them over her bottom a large hole appeared . . . The next pair were no good either. And the following pair acquired a hole as she pulled them over her knees.

She rummaged through the drawer again. An untidy mess of knickers, socks and tights. The dust made her sneeze.

"Oh, bugger it!" she exclaimed.

"What's the matter?" her husband Robert said as he came in, newly showered.

"I've peed myself," Mella said, sitting down on the edge of the bed. "I was searching around in my dusty underwear drawer, then I sneezed and bloody well peed myself. I'm a wreck."

"A lot?"

"No, of course not. Just a little drop. But still . . . I give up. I thought I'd wear a skirt as your sisters always look so smart, but it'll have to be trousers and an incontinence pad."

"Oh, darling. Come here, let me have a feel."

"What? If you so much as touch me I'll turn my police pistol on you."

She stood up, took a pair of cotton knickers and some socks from the drawer, and put them and a pair of jeans on inside thirty seconds.

I don't care, she thought. I can't compete with them in any case.

She stuck her head into Gustav's room. He was on his bed, standing on his hands.

"I thought I'd told you to get dressed! How many more times do I have to tell you? Get dressed, get dressed, get dressed! . . ."

"Just one more time – I need to beat Lovisa at school, we have a competition to see who can stand on their hands longest, and she always wants to do it again and again because I always beat her. She says her record is thirteen seconds. It's so hard doing it on the bed because it's so soft. Take the duvet and the pillow off. Did you hear, Mum? Take the—"

"Put this jumper on NOW before I lose my temper."

Mella pulled her son towards her and fitted the jumper over his head. She ought to have ironed it. His hair was too long as well. Robert's mother was bound to point that out. Gustav was still jabbering away non-stop from inside the jumper.

"Mum, surely you don't believe that Lovisa's record is thirteen seconds, when she can't do it for any longer than three seconds at school. And Mum, do you know what? Have you seen my wish list?"

"Thousands of times. And there's a long time to go before Christmas Eve. Put those socks on."

"But you haven't seen the new list! I wrote loads of things on it only yesterday. And you can buy all the things from Ellos dot com. And then there's my Lego list. I've got a Lego list as well. Ouch! My eyebrow! Aaargh!"

"I'm sorry."

A boy's head emerged from the jumper. She helped him to find the armhole as well.

"There are so many Lego sets I want. For instance—"

"Here! It says on my wish list that you have to put your underpants and socks on."

"What? Is that all you want for Christmas? Great. But Mum, I still want to go to Ullared. Linus in my class has been there, and there are sooo many things you can buy there. And can you guess how many traffic signs I know now? About a hundred, mebbe. How about this: if there's a blue round thing with an arrow pointing somewhere. Dead easy. I got that straight away. No problem. I didn't even have to ask you or Dad. It mines you have to drive to there – to where the arrow's pointing. And if there are arrows inside a round circle. Do you know what that mines?"

"Trousers! Now!"

"Yes, I'm putting them on. It mines a roundabout."

"Means," said Petter, who was passing his little brother's room on his way to the kitchen.

Mella managed to get Gustav's trousers on and dragged him into the kitchen while he went on and on about various traffic signs and the lessons in swordsmanship that Link gets from Oshus when he has left the cave. She sat him down in front of a bowl of sour milk and muesli and an open sandwich while making a now-you-can-take-over-before-I-do-him-an-injury sign behind his back to her husband. Robert was already sitting at the breakfast table, focusing all his attention on the *Advertiser*.

Their sixteen-year-old daughter Jenny was hunched over her physics textbook. Mella had long since given up any hope of being able to help her with her homework. The death blow had been a test on Euclidian geometry.

Petter, the eleven-year-old, was staring at his bowl of sour milk and muesli with a helpless expression on his face.

"I haven't got a spoon," he said.

"But you've still got legs, I assume," Mella said, pouring coffee into her mug and sitting down with a thud.

"Mum, do you know what?" Gustav said, having been quiet for five seconds since his mother had shovelled a spoonful of sour milk into his mouth.

"Can't somebody shut him up?" Jenny hissed. "I'm trying to revise. I have a test tomorrow."

"Be quiet, you," Gustav said indignantly. "You interrupted me!"

"I forbid you to talk to me," Jenny said, putting her hands over her ears.

"If I get a Lego Mummeleo Falko for Christmas I'll be quiet for a whole month. Can I have it, Mum?"

"It's called a Millennium Falcon, you nitwit," Petter said. "Mum, do you know what it costs? Five thousand nine hundred and ninety-nine kronor."

"Come off it!" Mella said. "Who pays six thousand kronor for a Lego set? It's not on."

Petter shrugged.

"It's you who's a nitwit," Gustav shouted.

Petter made a rapid series of gestures with his fingers: first at his face, *face*; then up to the heavens, *up*; then two fingers, *to*; then he waved them in a fuck-off gesture, *fac*; then held his left index finger upright with his right one horizontally across the top of it, *t*; and finally drew a letter S with his right index finger. Face up to facts.

"Stop it now," Gustav yelled, with a sob in his voice. "You should face up to the fact that you are a fat nitwit!"

"For God's sake shut up now, all of you!" Jenny screamed. "That does it! I'm not coming with you. I've got a test tomorrow, can't you understand that?"

Gustav gave his elder brother a shove. Tears came flooding into his eyes. Petter laughed scornfully. Gustav set about him with his fists.

"Ouch," Petter squeaked in a loud, unnatural voice.

Robert looked up from his newspaper.

"Put the dirty stuff in the dishwasher now," he said, apparently unmoved by the world war that had just broken out.

Jenny stood up, slammed her book shut and yelled, "I'll do it!"

At that point Mella's mobile started ringing. Where on earth had she left it? Not too far away, judging by the volume.

"Be quiet now, everybody," she shouted. "Can anybody find my phone?"

She struggled to her feet and followed the noise, ending up at a pile of clothes on the chair in the hall.

Silence had fallen in the kitchen. Her family was observing her. It was not a long call.

"Hello," she said. "What the hell . . . ? I'll be there right away."

"What's happened?" Jenny asked. "Come on, Mum, you know we won't tell anybody."

"Has somebody died?" Gustav said. "I bet it's somebody I know."

"No, it's not somebody you know," Mella said.

She turned to Robert.

"I've got to go. You'll have to . . ."

She finished the sentence with a hand gesture covering the breakfast and the mess in the kitchen and the children and Robert's family and the car trip to Junosuando and back with all the youngsters.

She could feel a flush spreading over her cheeks.

Stabbed with a thin, pointed weapon, she said to herself.

Her heart was beating calmly in her chest now.

Multiple stab wounds, maybe a hundred. And in Kurravaara of all places!

"Give my love to Auntie Ingela," she said to the children.

She turned to Robert, with an expression she hoped looked like disappointment.

"And to Grandma," she said. "I'm really—"

"Cut it out," Robert said.

He pulled her close and kissed her hair.

Sivving could not stand still. He was swaying from side to side, gazing towards the forest.

"You'll find him," he said to Eriksson. "I know you will."

They were still outside Sol-Britt Uusitalo's house. Forensics officers and pathologists were on their way. Eriksson glanced at Martinsson. She was talking on her mobile.

They were still looking for the boy. The bed in his upstairs room was unmade. They had checked the woodshed and the old barn, and searched the area around the house. Shouted for him. No Marcus.

Eriksson muttered an inaudible answer as he put the working jacket on Tintin, Sivving was still swaying from side to side behind him.

Eriksson was used to this. There were always people shuffling about behind him – the parents of children who were lost in the forest, grown-up children whose senile parents had wandered off and lost their way. Everybody who hung around listlessly behind him always wanted a happy ending. He and Tintin were their big hope.

But Tintin had no feelings of worry or anguish. She was whimpering away, eager to get started. Full of canine enthusiasm and desire to start work.

Eriksson suddenly felt gloomy. He was not looking forward to finding the boy dead. There was so much that could have happened to him. His imagination provided him with so many alternatives to the happy ending.

Somebody is carrying the boy out to a car. He's kicking and wriggling in his captor's arms. He has a bleeding wound in his head, and a rag stuffed into his mouth. Another scenario: a madman stabs a woman to death in her bed. The boy wakes up and is also stabbed, but manages to escape into the darkness. Staggers along for a short while, then dies a solitary death in the forest.

The plan had been to go for a stroll through the forest with Martinsson and the dogs today. It would be one of the last days when walking in the forest would be possible. The snow would soon be here.

At least the boy hadn't been lying in his bed, stabbed to death. There had been a jumper lying on the floor. Black, with a pattern that could just be made out despite all the many washings. Presumably he had been wearing it the day before.

Eriksson let Tintin sniff at the jumper, then gave her the command: seek! They began by circling the house. The lead was stretched tightly. At the back of the house she branched out, sniffing at the parched autumn grass. She continued through the rowan trees with their masses of blood-red berries and into the coniferous trees, down into the ditch, up again, past an old bathtub sunk into the moss. They passed a pile of sawn planks covered by a green tarpaulin.

Then she raised her nose. The scent in the air was very fresh. They must be close now. She led him through the pine trees, along a narrow path. Now they were out of sight of the house.

And there, not far ahead, was a children's playhouse.

If you could call it that. The decrepit cabin was made of plywood sheets, painted with Falun red paint, and had a roof of tarred cardboard. The window had been broken a long time ago, and was covered by a piece of transparent plastic sheeting.

Eriksson paused for a moment. Tintin strained at her leash, whimpering.

He had discovered dead children before. He recalled a twelve-year-old girl who had taken her own life. That was up near Kalix. He shut his eyes tightly in an attempt to obliterate her image. She had been sitting under a tree, and it had looked as if she were asleep: her head had not fallen to one side.

Tintin had found her after a search lasting for three hours. And as Tintin is not a fan of doggy treats and wasn't even especially hungry at the time, Eriksson rewarded her the way he always did when she had carried out a task to his satisfaction: he played with her. That was the best reward she could possibly wish for. And it was important that she should feel that a successful end to a search was something to celebrate with a bit of fun.

The dead girl had remained sitting under the tree while Eriksson larked around with Tintin only a few metres away, shouting: "There's a good girl! Now I'm coming to get you, what a lovely girl you are!"

Meanwhile two colleagues had turned up at the scene. They looked at the dead girl, then they stared at Eriksson as if he wasn't quite right in the head. Eriksson put Tintin back on her lead and led her away in silence. He made no attempt to explain why he did what he did. Why should he? They would never have understood. But no doubt all kinds of rumours about him circulated around Kalix.

The boy was lying there in the playhouse. Eriksson was almost certain of that. Tintin was whimpering, tugging at her lead and wanting to go there. No point in hanging about. He must investigate without delay.

There was an old flowery mattress lying on the floor. Lots of empty bottles were standing on a rickety table. Somebody – perhaps several people – used this playhouse as somewhere to relax and sink a few beers. But just now there was a little boy lying on the mattress, under several blankets and rather a dirty and tatty cover.

"Well done, my lovely!" Eriksson said.

Tintin swaggered around, bursting with pride.

Eriksson moved to one side the blankets and cover. Placed his hand carefully on the boy's neck. His skin was warm. There was a pulse. Eriksson examined the white jumper and the bare feet: no blood. He seemed to be uninjured.

The relief was so massive that Eriksson shuddered, as if from the cold. The boy was alive.

At that very moment he opened his eyes. He stared at Eriksson, his eyes wide in horror.

Then he screamed.

Sivving circled round the car once more, dragging his crippled limbs after him.

He'll fall down at any moment, Martinsson thought. I'll never be able to get him up again.

"Shouldn't you sit down?" she said.

"It's pretty obvious that she hasn't had a man about the place for a while," Sivving said, seeming not to hear her. "Just look at that fence. The snow will bring it down next winter. How do you reckon he'll get on?"

He gestured in the direction that Eriksson had headed, together with Tintin.

Martinsson looked at the fence, which was leaning in all directions. The posts were rotten. She refrained from observing that her own fence was solid and upright, despite the fact that there was no handyman in the house, and that there were several layabouts in the village whose fences had given up the ghost long ago.

"Did you say that her son was run over?" she said instead.

"My God, yes," Sivving said, standing still for a few moments. "Poor little sod. First his mum runs off to Stockholm. Then his dad gets run over. And now his grandma . . ."

"How was he run over?"

"They don't know. It was one of those hit-and-run affairs. Maybe you're right and I should sit down for a bit. Is that allowed? Won't it leave all kinds of traces to confuse the scene-of-crime boys?"

"You can sit in the car. I'll pull back the driving seat and we can leave the door open. And you can tell us all you know about Sol-Britt."

Sivving sat down and mopped his brow. Martinsson almost felt like doing the same.

"Anyway, when her son died. Inevitably the locals wondered if somebody in the village might have done it. Everybody knows there's a few blokes who drive when they're drunk. They might have panicked and driven off. Or not even noticed."

Bella and the Brat were scurrying about in the dog cage – they'd been told they were going for a walk in the forest. Vera lay on the back seat, sighing.

"And then there was Sol-Britt's dad last year," Sivving said. "But you know all about that, no doubt."

"No, I don't."

"Come off it, of course you do. He was mauled by a bear. Oh, for God's sake, when was it? My memory's useless! Yes, the beginning of June! It was in the newspaper! He was old, they thought he'd got lost. And then, it can't be more than two months ago, they shot a bear not far from Lainio. It had killed and eaten a guard dog that was tied up on a running lead. And in the bear's stomach they found bits of the old man, Frans Uusitalo, Sol-Britt's dad. The bear had spent the whole of the summer gobbling him up, bit by bit. Ugh!"

"Ah yes, I read about that. So that was Sol-Britt's dad, was it?"

Sivving looked accusingly at her.

"I've just said it was. Have you forgotten already?"

He sat quietly for a while. Martinsson wandered off into a world of her own. She remembered the man mauled by a bear in Lainio. When they found a bone from one of his hands inside the belly of the bear, they started searching the area. They eventually found the body. Or what was left of it.

It did happen occasionally that people were mauled by bears up in these parts of the far north. If they found themselves between a female bear and her cubs. Or if they had a stupid dog that chased after the bear and then came hurtling back to its owners with the beast at its heels.

"And his mum as well," Sivving said. "Sol-Britt's grandma, that is. She was murdered too."

"What?"

"She was a teacher in Kiruna. When was that, now? Er, she must have arrived just before the First World War. My uncle had her as a teacher. He always used to say she was as sweet as a sugar lump. Nice to the children. She had a little boy, although she wasn't married. He was Sol-Britt's dad, the one that was mauled by a bear. She was murdered when he was only a few weeks old. A horrific story. She was beaten to death in her own classroom one winter evening. But that was a long time ago."

"Who killed her?"

"Nobody knows. Her friend looked after the little boy and brought him up as if he'd been her own child. It wasn't so easy in those days."

He glared accusingly at her as he said that.

Martinsson thought about Sivving's mother, who was widowed early on and had to bring up the children by herself.

I know I'm very lucky, she thought. I could have children and we'd survive without any problems. They would have a roof over their head, food in their bellies and they could go to school. I wouldn't need to give them away.

She looked at Sivving. She knew he had stared real poverty in the face. "We could easily have ended up in a children's home," he sometimes used to say.

Not everything was better in the good old days, she thought.

It is 15 April, 1914. Schoolteacher Elina Pettersson is on the train from Stockholm. She's going to Kiruna. The journey takes thirty-six hours and twenty-five minutes, according to the timetable – but there is a delay due to all the snow on the lines. She has spent two nights on the train, and her backside is giving her hell after having to sleep in a sitting position: but soon she will reach her destination.

When she looks out of the window she sees an endless expanse of stunted trees, laden with snow. Snow-covered bogs and lakes. Herds of reindeer, staring wide-eyed but apparently without fear at the huffing and puffing, squeaking and clanking train belching out smoke. Over and over again the carriages have to be uncoupled while the engine backs, then charges with its plough at the drifts of snow, and struggles to clear the lines.

So much snow, and so much forest. It is incredible how big Sweden is, how far north it stretches. She has never been so far north before. Nor has anybody she knows been so far north.

The sun gushes in through the windows, pools of brilliant light form on the mock-leather seats and trickle back and forth over the green-and-blue patterned plush. The light is so brilliant that it is difficult to keep one's eyes open, but she does not want to draw the curtains. It is all so beautiful.

She is free. She has just celebrated her twenty-first birthday, and she is on her way to Kiruna! The world's newest town. That is where she belongs. In this new age.

In just a few decades Sweden has raised itself out of poverty. It is not long since vaccines, peace and potatoes enabled the population to start increasing. With a big bang. All those poverty-stricken people . . . Now that they did not simply die off, they somehow managed to survive. Gave birth to more poverty-stricken children, hollow-cheeked. How would they survive? Continue to dig even more ditches, or work as milkmaids? No. The last century had no place for them. The towns were still ridiculously small. Instead, people emigrated from Sweden. Young people, inspired by a new feeling of strength and dreams, headed for America. The authorities stood by and watched it happen, incapable of action, and merely preached patriotism and contentment.

The journey out of poverty began as it usually does for the poorest: by means of natural resources. Iron ore. Forests. And then, as the twentieth century dawned, the exploitation of creative genius really began in earnest. Patents were taken out on inventions, new companies were formed left, right and centre.

Now people began migrating into towns, where there were industries making wood pulp, telephones, machine guns, agricultural machinery, adjustable spanners, pipe wrenches, dynamite, matches. The new Sweden was beginning to become rich.

She stretches her back and thinks it is time she ventured as far as the refreshment car. She really must get a little exercise. Soon, very soon now, she will be in Kiruna.

The whole town has an electricity supply – bliss! Street lights and household electricity. And there is a swimming baths, a bandstand and a library.

She looks out at the snow, glistening in the sun, and smiles. Her face is not used to smiling. She runs her fingers over her mouth, and feels what it is like to smile. Only now, when she has left the countryside behind her, abandoned Jönåker, does she realise that she has been miserable for two whole years.

It is like waking up from an unpleasant dream and hardly being able to remember what it was about. She will forget the village school. All those characterless children of crofters, farm labourers, smallholders, shepherds, maidservants, hands for hire. The sort of children who know they will never be able to continue their studies once they have completed the six years of schooling demanded by the law. By the age of twelve they will be sufficiently grown-up to make a living. But they can never desert their father, mother, siblings. Something has been extinguished inside them. You can see it in their eyes. When it is raining or snowing outside, the air inside the classroom reeks of the stench of cowsheds, filth and wet wool.

And then there are the sons of the gentleman farmers. They can travel by road and rail now, they can even fly. Fat and prosperous, up-and-coming country squires already, they can behave however they like when they come into contact with their classmates, and even their teacher – after all, their father owns the whole village, and the surrounding forests and fields. Any teacher who wants to keep her job handles the boy indulgently. She gives him high marks, to make sure she does not miss out on her Christmas present: a barrel of rye, ham and sausages, not to mention some fodder for her own cow. Oh yes, be nice to the boy, and remember who his father is.

The village priest – at last she can be rid of him!

I hope he fries in Hell, she thinks.

He was also chairman of the board of school governors. They fell out at the very first meeting. She had been in favour of spelling reform and her head was full of the feminist writings of Ellen Key. He considered Ellen Key to be immoral, Selma Lagerlöf unwholesome, Strindberg a lost soul, Fröding a writer of pornography. Tears came into his eyes when the pupils sang about daffodils dancing in the meadows of Sweden, but in between times he was incapable of removing his gaze from her breasts. If she ever found herself alone in a room with him, she could never be sure where his fat fingers might end up. And he often found an excuse to call in at the school after the children had gone home. Such visits always ended up in a race round the teacher's desk, with her in the lead and him in pursuit.

It will be different in Kiruna. Her head is full of dreams. Her heart, full of hope, is beating in time with the pounding of the rails.

She is like a spring-cleaned house. The floors have been scrubbed. There is a smell of soft soap and wind and sunshine. All the windows and doors are wide open, and the rag rugs are hanging out to dry on lines stretched between the birch trees.

She is ready to fall in love. And he boards the train in Gällivare. The man who will capture her heart.

The boy screamed in sheer terror. Tintin barked.

Eriksson ordered Tintin to be quiet, backed out of the playhouse and stood outside the door, out of sight.

"I'm sorry," he said. "Did we frighten you? I know I look pretty scary."

The boy stopped screaming.

"I'll stay here, outside," Eriksson said. "Can you hear me?"

There was no answer.

"I'll tell you why I look like I do. When I was a little boy my house burnt down. When I came home from school it was on fire. My mum was inside it. I ran in because I knew she would be lying on the bed, asleep. I was very badly injured. That's why I don't have any ears and no nose and no hair and funny skin. But I'm nice and friendly on the inside. And I'm a police officer, and I've been looking for you with my sheepdog, Tintin, because we were worried that something might have happened to you. Are you afraid of dogs?"

Silence.

"Because if you aren't, maybe Tintin can come in and say hello to you. Would that be O.K.?"

Still no response.

"I don't know if you are nodding or shaking your head, because I can't see you. Do you think you could answer me using your voice?"

"Yes."

He sounded very faint.

"Does that mean yes, Tintin can come in?"

"Yes."

Eriksson let go of Tintin, who scurried inside but soon came out again.

Bloody dog, he thought. Why couldn't you have stayed there with him?

"Oh dear, that was a quick visit," he said. "Did you have time to stroke her?"

"No."

"She's one of those dogs who only make a fuss of their master. And that's me. But I know another dog you would like. Her name's Vera."

"I know her. She comes to visit me and my grandma, and Grandma usually makes some pancakes and then when Vera has eaten one or two with us she goes back home. It's Sivving's dog."

"Yes, Sivving sometimes looks after her, that's true – but in fact she's Rebecka's dog. Do you know who that is? No, I don't suppose you do, but I sometimes look after her as well."

Eriksson couldn't help laughing out loud.

"Vera, that is."

"You can come in now if you like. I'm not scared of you."

"O.K., here I come. There we are. Oh dear, it's pretty cramped in here now. Shift yourself a bit, Tintin! Well done, girl! You've done an excellent job. She tracked you down, followed your scent all the way from the house, and now she's feeling very proud of herself."

"She has a nice soft tongue. We used to have a dog as well."

There was a smell of mould in the playhouse. Time to withdraw.

"Don't you feel cold? You haven't got any shoes or socks on. Did you run here in your bare feet?"

The boy suddenly looked serious. He nodded briefly, but kept his eyes on the dog's soft ears that he was trying to reach so that he could stroke them.

"It would be great if you could tell us a bit about that later, but just now I'd like to carry you to my car. It's parked outside your house. I think you ought to put some warm clothes on. Sivving is there. You know him, don't you?"

"Can I play with Vera?"

"If you want to."

But she's not the kind of dog that likes being played with, Eriksson thought. A pity we don't have a Labrador handy. A stupid, happy-go-lucky dog who lies still when kids want to have a ride.

He took his jacket off and put it on the boy. Marcus answered his questions, but avoided looking him in the eye.

It was very rare for Krister Eriksson to touch another human being. He thought about that as he picked the boy up and carried him back through the woods, through the rowan trees, and over the lawn to the front of the house. After a while the little body began to shake a bit as the warmth came back into it. The boy had his arms round Eriksson's neck, and wasn't heavy in the least: he was breathing against Eriksson's cheek and his vertebrae were sticking up inside his skin.

Eriksson had to suppress an impulse to hug him tightly, to hold hard onto him as a worried parent would have done.

That's enough of that, he told himself. What you are doing is the job you're paid to do.

Sivving struggled out of the car, thanked the Good Lord, and looked as if he were about to start crying in relief. Martinsson was also there, gave him a quick smile and looked him in the eye. He also felt like crying without knowing why – probably due to the relief of having found Marcus alive.

"What happened to your mum when your house burnt down?"

Marcus whispered in Eriksson's ear when Martinsson went into the house to fetch some shoes and clothes.

"Oh," Eriksson said, hesitating for a moment. "She died."

"There's Vera."

The boy pointed to the edge of the trees as Vera came scuttling out.

"I had to let her go for a little run," Martinsson said.

Vera scampered up to Eriksson. She had something in her mouth.

"What's all this?" he wondered.

Then he burst out laughing. He stopped immediately. He couldn't stand here laughing when Marcus's grandma had . . .

"What's the matter?" Martinsson said.

"It's Vera. She's found my chewing tobacco box that I threw away."

And boy, do I need a wad, Eriksson thought. But it will have to be the last one.

Inspector Anna-Maria Mella stood in Sol-Britt Uusitalo's bedroom together with prosecutor Rebecka Martinsson and her colleagues Tommy Rantakyrö, Fred Olsson and Sven-Erik Stålnacke. They had put police tape all round the house and grounds.

"The villagers will soon be turning up to gape," Stålnacke said. "And in ten minutes, maybe a quarter of an hour at most, we can expect the local newspapers. And the national evening papers as well, come to that. They'll send their nearest hacks, and it won't take long. An hour from now we'll be able to read all about the murder on the net."

"I know," Mella said. "Eriksson can take the boy with him and get him away from here – it's great that he's willing and able to take care of him."

Eriksson can sit in on the interrogation later, she thought. So that the boy feels secure.

"Will you be taking care of that?" Stålnacke said. "Talking to the little lad, I mean."

"Assuming none of you is desperately keen to do it?"

Her colleagues all shook their heads.

"Surely it can't have been the lad who did it?" Rantakyrö said. "That's the kind of thing that only happens . . . somewhere else."

Mella made no comment.

They looked at Sol-Britt's body, spotted with blood, and the word on the wall over the bed.

All those wounds, she thought. Would a seven-year-old have the strength? Would he know how to spell "whore"? Does he know what the word means? Out of the question, out of the question, she concluded.

Mella took a deep breath.

"O.K.," she said. "Who would call her a whore? Somebody in the village, perhaps? Has she been threatened? Is there some old flame? Or maybe a new one? Sven-Erik, will you do the rounds? There aren't any neighbours within sight of the house, but talk to the ones along the road. Have they seen or heard anything? Talk to her work-mates as well. Who was the last to see her alive? Has anything special happened lately? You know the kind of thing to ask."

Stålnacke's thick moustache shifted perceptively to one side. He knew exactly what she meant, and had no objections.

Good, she thought. Sven-Erik is good with people. He makes himself at home at their kitchen table. Sips coffee and gossips away. Makes them feel that he is a relative paying a call. Come to think of it, he is nearly always like that. In a fanciful sort of way, he really is related to everybody. Or went to the same school. Or remembered their youthful sporting triumphs.

Sven-Erik would be due to retire before long. Then she would be the oldest member of the team. It seemed impossible to imagine. It was only the other day that she celebrated her twentieth birthday after all – the same age as Tommy Rantakyrö. He was the young pup of the team. Wads of chewing tobacco as big as pine cones under his lips. As restless as a teenager with creepy-crawlies under his skin. Always checking up on what the others were doing. Always the last to be given duties to perform. Always expected to be dealt the joker. And usually got it.

"Freddy," she said, turning to Olsson. "No doubt you know what to do?"

"Incoming and outgoing calls," he said without hesitation. "Text messages. Computers. At home and at work, I assume. Have I permission to go and look for her mobile?"

"There's an open handbag in the hall. Take a look inside, the forensics team will accept that. She didn't have her mobile beside her bed in any case. But we can't start poking our noses in all over the place. That would send them round the bend."

Olsson went out into the hall. He soon returned with a mobile in his hand.

"I'll check it," he said.

"It's odd that all the kitchen drawers are shut, but all the cupboards are open," Stålnacke said. "As if somebody was looking for something. Something big."

"The murder weapon?" Olsson guessed.

"Tommy," Mella said. "Will you have a word with Marcus's teachers? The headmaster and his staff. And after-school activities, if he attended any."

Rantakyrö smiled wryly.

"What shall I ask them about?"

"What sort of state is he in? Is he normal? Is he not well? Is everything . . . Was everything well at home? We must get in touch with his mother."

"No doubt Sivving knows what she's called. I can contact her," said Martinsson.

"Good. Do that right away. Some journalist or other will be ringing her at any moment now. Has Sivving had anything else to say about Sol-Britt?"

"She was working at the Winter Palace as a breakfast waitress, but this morning she didn't turn up for work – that was why Sivving wanted to drive out here. She had alcohol problems before, but since her son died three years ago she stopped drinking and looked after her grandson. Marcus's mum is alive, but she lives in Stockholm and has a new family, and prefers to have nothing to do with him."

"What's the matter with some people?" Stålnacke bellowed in disgust. "What kind of a mother abandons her child?"

Mella didn't know what to say. There wasn't a sound to be heard in the room. Martinsson's mother had abandoned her family when Rebecka was a little girl. Not long afterwards she fell under a lorry – nobody knew if it was an accident or not.

The same thought had struck Stålnacke. Nobody could think of anything to say. Stålnacke cleared his throat.

Martinsson did not appear to have been listening. She was gazing out of the window. Outside in the garden Marcus was throwing a tennis ball. It looked as if he was urging Vera to fetch it. In vain, of course. Vera had never played fetch in her life. She just stood there watching the ball until Marcus gave up and fetched it himself. He tried throwing it over and over again. Sometimes Eriksson ran after it. It was only Vera who remained motionless.

"That boy out there," Martinsson said, pointing at Marcus, "does he understand that his grandmother is dead?"

They all looked at Marcus.

Children could be so upset or so detached when it came to grief, Mella thought. She had seen it all before. A child crying over its dead mother one moment, then spellbound by a cartoon film the next.

"Yes," Mella said finally. "I think he probably does."

Mella had been on a course about interrogating children, and on several occasions she had interviewed children when there had been suspicions of domestic violence in the family. It was a very specialised topic, but she did not really think it was all that difficult. If only her family knew how calm and patient she could be when it was necessary . . .

It's only at home that I ask questions and don't bother to listen to the answers, she thought with a wry smile.

"So, we'll meet again at three o'clock at the police station," she decided. "I suppose we'll have to have a press conference, but that won't be until eight o'clock tomorrow morning. Not a minute earlier, no matter what. Tommy, will you drive back to town and fetch the video camera, please? I must have a chat with Marcus before he . . . as soon as possible."

"Look!" Martinsson said. "Look at the dog! She's playing!"

Vera had suddenly started scurrying after the ball, bringing it back and dropping it at Marcus's feet.

"She's never done that before," Martinsson said.

Then added, as if to herself: "Not with me, at least."

He's the type who gets bullied at school, Eriksson thought when Mella switched on the video camera. Like me, but he's nice.

Marcus had long, fair hair, was on the small side for his age with a pale face and dark shadows around his eyes. But he was clean and his nails were neatly clipped. His clothes had been kept in a chest of drawers in his bedroom, folded and ironed. The pantry and the refrigerator had been full of wholesome food, and there had been fresh fruit in a bowl in the kitchen. Sol-Britt had evidently taken good care of her grandson.

Now the boy was sitting on Martinsson's kitchen sofa. Vera was lying by his side, and enjoying being patted and stroked. Eriksson was sitting on the other side, taking it all in with a somewhat astonished smile.

That confounded dog, he thought.

If it had been himself or Martinsson sitting there, stroking Vera, she would have jumped down and gone away ages ago.

"Do you know what?" he said to Marcus. "I took Vera with me to visit some friends of mine in Laxås not all that long ago. They had a cat that had just had kittens, and she refused to leave her brood, not even for a second. She was as thin as a rake, because she didn't even allow herself time to eat anything. But when we got there, she ran off and left her kittens with Vera. The kittens crawled all over Vera, and bit her ears and her tail."

And sucked her titties dry, he thought. Poor old girl.

"The cat mother was away for over an hour," he said. "No doubt she made use of the time to eat lots and lots of mice. But she trusted Vera."

Kittens and a lonely boy, he thought. Vera has endless patience with them.

"So, let's get started," Mella said. "Can you tell me your name, and how old you are?"

"My name is Marcus Elias Uusitalo."

"And how old are you?"

"Seven years and three months."

"O.K., Marcus. Krister and Tintin found you in a hut in the forest today. Can you tell me how you got there?"

"I went there." Marcus moved even closer to Vera. "Will Grandma come to fetch me?"

"No, your grandma . . . Don't you know what's happened to her?"

"No."

Mella looked at Eriksson, hoping for help. Hadn't he explained? Hadn't he told Marcus anything?

Eriksson gave a subtle nod. Of course he had told Marcus. But she must put the brakes on – he had barely sat down. She ought to talk about something else first.

"I'm afraid your grandma is dead, my darling," Mella said. "Do you know what that means?"

Marcus looked at her, a serious expression on his face.

"Yes, like my dad."

Mella said nothing. She looked uncertain. She contemplated the boy, her eyes narrowed.

He seemed to be calm and collected, if somewhat subdued. He was stroking Vera's soft ears.

Mella shook her head, almost imperceptibly.

"She's a nice dog," she said.

"Yes," said Marcus. "She likes to eat pancakes with me and

Grandma. Once she came to school with me on the bus. She just jumped on board even though she didn't have a ticket. But dogs don't need one. She sat next to me. Nobody minded, not even Willy. Everybody wanted to stroke her. And my teacher – she was only a supply teacher, but she phoned my grandma. And Grandma phoned Sivving, and Vera ended up going back home in a taxi. It wasn't all that expensive, because Sivving works as a volunteer on the patient ambulance service. But Grandma says that Vera is the only one who has ever taken advantage of the free rides."

"Tell me how you came to be in the playhouse in the forest."

She's still going too fast, Eriksson thought. He tried in vain to make eye contact with Mella.

"We had a dog as well," Marcus said. "But it disappeared. Maybe it was run over."

"Hmm. How did you get to the playhouse, Marcus?"

"I walked there."

"O.K., do you know what time that was?"

"No, I can't tell the time."

"Was it dark or light outside?"

"Dark. It was night-time."

"Why did you go out to the playhouse in the middle of the night?"

"I . . ."

He paused and looked confused.

"I don't know."

"Think about it. I'll wait here while you think it over."

They sat there in silence for ages. Eriksson tapped Marcus on his arm. Marcus was lying across Vera. He whispered something into the dog's ear. He'd forgotten what the question was.

"Why didn't you have any shoes on? And no jacket?"

"You can jump out of my bedroom window. You land on the roof of the porch at the back. And then you can climb down the ladder."

"Why didn't you have any shoes on?"

"My shoes are in the hall."

"Why did you jump out through the window? Why didn't you go out through the door?"

The boy said nothing.

Eventually he shook his head,

Time to pack up, Eriksson thought.

Didn't he remember? The questions piled up inside Mella's head. They all wanted to come tumbling out at the same time. Why did you wake up? What did you see? Did you hear anything? Would you recognise . . . ?

He just sat there, stroking the dog. Seemingly unconcerned. Mella didn't know what to say.

"Do you remember anything?" she said in the end. "Anything at all? Do you remember when you went to bed that evening?"

"I have to go to bed every night at half past seven, Grandma says. Every night. It doesn't matter what's on the telly. I always have to go to bed very early."

I must stop now, Mella thought. I'm pressing him too much. He'll soon start inventing things. That's what they kept emphasising on that course. Children like to keep their interrogators happy. They'll say anything in order to keep you happy.

"I wake up when anybody comes to look at me," said Marcus to Eriksson. "When you and Tintin came I woke up almost straight away. Do you think I was sleepwalking?"

But a few minutes ago he told us how he jumped out through the window, Mella thought. This just isn't working. I'm making a mess of everything. We'll have to call in a real pro.

"The conversation with Marcus Uusitalo is concluded," she said, switching off the video camera.

"We'll ring your mum," she said to Marcus. "But she lives in Stockholm. That's a long way away. Is there any grown-up you know who lives around here that you would like to stay with?"

"My mum never wants to talk to me. Can't I go home to my grandma?"

Mella and Eriksson exchanged looks.

"But . . ." she began, then broke off. She was incapable of completing the sentence.

Eriksson put his arm round Marcus.

"How about this, my friend?" he said. "Shall you and I and Vera and Jasko – that's also Rebecka's dog . . . Jasko . . . but do you know what we call him? The Brat! How about all of us, my dogs as well, driving home to my place for some breakfast? You must be starving!"

Marcus ran out into the garden with the dogs. Eriksson followed him, and in the doorway almost crashed into Martinsson. She took a step back and smiled. He found it difficult not to embrace her. The dogs all jumped up at her in greeting.

"I've spoken to his mum," Martinsson said.

"And?"

The wind made its presence felt on the porch. Raised a few strands of her hair. Her eyes were the same colour as the grey sky and the tall, sand-coloured autumn grass. He was forced to take a deep breath. His heart started beating faster.

Calm down, he told himself. I can stand here and look at her. We're becoming friends. I'll have to be happy with that.

Martinsson exhaled deeply, a sure sign that her conversation had been far from easy.

"What can I say? She was horrified about what had happened, of course, but explained that she wasn't in a position to look after Marcus. Can you believe that? She said that she and her partner had a few problems, and that he would leave her if she were forced to take care of Marcus. That her man could hardly cope with his own two children just now. That he was an egotistic bastard. That he had problems at work. But that you had to sympathise with him even so. And that I ought to sympathise with her as well. That she never thought about herself, it was nothing to do with that. Blah blah blah."

She pulled a face. Pursed her lips. Narrowed her eyes. Averted her gaze.

"Are you alright?" he asked.

"It's not about me," she said.

Now, he thought: his hand reached out and he caressed her. First her cheek and her ear. Then her hair.

She did not draw back. She looked as if she was about to burst into tears. Then she cleared her throat.

"Is Anna-Maria still here?"

He nodded. He wanted to embrace her. Press his lips against her skin. His nose into her hair. There was a kind of electric charge between them. Was it possible for her not to feel it?

"Did you get anywhere?"

He shook his head.

He made a big effort and managed to recover his voice.

"I'll take him home to my place," he said. "I didn't know when you were coming back, so I was going to take Vera and the Brat as well. The young lad has really taken to Vera. She makes him feel safe. I'm not going to let him be taken away by welfare ladies he's never seen before. Mella can bring in some pro to interrogate him, but until then he's staying with me and the dogs."

"Excellent," she said with a smile. "That sounds great."

Anna-Maria Mella said yes please to the blueberry porridge and coffee that Martinsson offered her.

"I'm only too pleased to see it finished off," Martinsson said. "My freezer's crammed full with berries."

She smiled at Mella, who was tucking in like a genuine mother of several children, shovelling in the porridge at high speed and swigging the coffee as if it were juice. Martinsson reported on her conversation with Marcus's mother. Mella reported on her interrogation of Marcus.

"He seemed so unaffected," she said, demolishing a crispbread sandwich as if her mouth were an industrial grinder. "And he seemed completely unable to grasp the fact that his grandmother was dead. I got no sense out of him at all – you can check it out on the computer. But he must surely have seen or heard something. That's obvious, don't you think? Why else would he jump out of his bedroom window and hare off to the playhouse? He must have been scared stiff."

"I talked to Sivving," Martinsson said. "He told me that Sol-Britt didn't have any relatives in Kiruna – apart from a cousin who lives here in Kurravaara on a temporary basis because her mother is in hospital. We must speak to her in any case. Perhaps Marcus can live with her for the time being? No harm in asking. Sivving didn't know if she and Sol-Britt saw much of each other."

"Do you think you could have a word with her?"

"O.K."

Mella looked down at her clean plate with a smile, and made an appreciative gesture with the palms of both hands pointing up towards the heavens.

"Thank you. I haven't eaten blueberry porridge since I was a little girl."

Mella looked round Martinsson's kitchen. She felt at home there. The polished wooden floor was strewn with rag rugs. The cushions on the blue-painted sofa had been made by Martinsson's grandmother out of cloth she had woven herself. And they were stuffed with the feathers of seabirds Martinsson's grandfather had shot.

Bouquets of dried buttercups and cat's foot were hanging over the wood-burning stove alongside a capercaillie's wing that Rebecka used to wipe crumbs off the well-ironed and embroidered tablecloth. And the thin white curtains were starched, as was the custom in Martinsson's grandmother's day.

The kind of thing one has time to do when one does not have any children, Mella thought.

All the tablecloths she had inherited were lying unironed in a cupboard at home, giving her a bad conscience for some unknown reason. Her kitchen table was covered by an oilcloth that had turned grey thanks to all the ink from countless copies of the *N.S.D.* and *Annonsbladet.*

"Go and speak to her, then we can meet at Pohjanen's office at two o'clock. I want to hear what he has to say before the run-through at three."

Lars Pohjanen was the pathologist. Martinsson nodded. She knew that Mella had invited her to be present at the meeting with Pohjanen and at the run-through so that she didn't feel excluded, rather than because she felt she needed any help.

People are odd, Martinsson thought, recalling how things had been the last time she had been in charge of the preliminary inquiries and Mella in charge of the police investigation. Relations had been somewhat strained, and Martinsson had felt excluded. But now that Mella was going out of her way to include Martinsson, she could not help feeling a bit uncomfortable.

Nobody is ever satisfied, she thought. She has asked me to join in the game, and there's no need for me to worry about her motives. Whether she really does want me to be on board, or is just trying to be nice to me.

"I'll be there," she said. "And you're welcome to the meal. Grandma always used to make blueberry porridge for me when I was a girl."

"By the way," she said as Mella was lacing up her boots in the hall, "Sivving told me that Sol-Britt Uusitalo's grandmother was murdered too."

"What?"

"Yes! She was a schoolteacher in Kiruna."

Hjalmar Lundbohm, managing director of L.K.A.B., the mining company that dominates Kiruna, joins the train in Gällivare on 15 April, 1914. He is tired and dejected. Feels old and worn out. It is as if he has a birch-bark knapsack on his back, crammed full of people and worries. Workers seething with anger. Constantly waving clenched fists in the air, chanting trade union slogans, looking for trouble. Palms of hands being slammed down onto tables, demanding an immediate end to all this damned oppression.

All those trade unionists and hotheads who have been sacked by the sawmills in Västerbotten for being too revolutionary, then move up to Kiruna. Kiruna needs every man and woman it can find who can put up with the cold and the darkness. But then he's the one who has to tussle with them – agitators, socialists, communists.

Also crammed into his knapsack of woe are over-zealous civil servants and over-confident engineers who bicker and argue and all want more than they are entitled to. And the Stockholm politicians, and the Wallenberg family who demand profits no matter what. The iron ore must be mined. Dug out of the mountain. All that investment in the railway and the municipal community of Kiruna must be rewarded.

Right down at the bottom of the knapsack are the mine's victims – the injured, the maimed. The widows of dead miners, and the little fatherless children staring poverty in the face.

A knapsack full of granite. The slag from the iron ore.

How on earth will he be able to satisfy everybody? Take the housing situation: how can he possibly produce accommodation for everyone who needs it? He wants to create a real town. Kiruna will not become like Malmberget. Must not. Malmberget, the mining town a hundred kilometres south of Kiruna, is a real Klondike. Teeming with debauchery and drunkenness and whores. He doesn't want anything like that. He wants schools and bathhouses and adult education – as in Pullman City in the U.S.A. and Henry Ford's Fordlandia in South America. Those are models to live up to.

It must become a genuine town, and it must look good as well: but that will take time. Meanwhile, people must have roofs over their heads. Overcrowding is a problem. Every square inch of floor space is used at night for sleeping on. Unauthorised house building is another problem: they can shoot up in a single night. They have to be demolished, and then women stand there surrounded by their homeless children, sobbing.

Food is a constant problem. As is the water supply.

He simply cannot cope. He cannot manage to help everybody in need of assistance.

He has just had a meeting with the managers of the mines in Malmberget. They are outraged because they consider the Kiruna mines have access to too many railway wagons. They also want to transport their iron ore.

Just as he boards the train, a gust of wind blows over the railway station. Snow whirls up and every single flake glistens like a hovering diamond.

If only I could paint, he thinks. If only I could paint instead of having to slave away with all these insoluble problems.

The train shudders and clatters, and starts to move. He heads straight for the restaurant car.

There is only one person sitting there. The moment he claps eyes on her, all his oppressive thoughts vanish in a puff of smoke. He feels the need to rub his eyes, and assure himself that what he sees is not a mirage.

She has chubby pink cheeks, big enchanting eyes with long eyelashes, a snub nose like a potato and a sullen-looking mouth like a small red heart. She looks like a child. Like one of those coloured prints featuring a little girl walking along a footbridge over a beck, blissfully unaware of all the dangers of the world.

But the most fascinating thing about her is her hair. It is blonde and curly. Lundbohm thinks it must reach down as far as her waist when she lets it hang loose.

He notices that her shoes are well cared for despite being somewhat the worse for wear, and that the edges of her overcoat are trimmed in order to conceal their threadbare nature.

Perhaps that is why he asks if she does not mind him sitting down at her table. The fact is that he is surprised to find her sitting there on her own: she ought to be surrounded by navvies and miners desperate for female contact. He looks around, half expecting to see suitors hiding behind the heavy curtains or under the tables.

She says in a friendly tone, albeit somewhat shyly, that of course he may join her. She also glances around at all the empty tables in the restaurant car.

He feels the need to excuse his pushy behaviour. After all, he is wearing his working clothes, as it were, and looks just like everybody else: she can't possibly know who he is.

"Whenever I see a new face, I like to find out who it is on the way to my Kiruna."

"Your Kiruna?"

"Oh dear, you mustn't pay too much attention to the words I use."

He sits up straight. He wants her to know who he is – for some reason that seems to be very important.

He holds out his hand, ready to be shaken.

"Hjalmar Lundbohm. Managing director. I'm in charge of the mine."

He makes the claim with a little wink, an attempt to signal his modesty and to distance himself from his exalted office.

She looks sceptical.

She thinks I'm flirting with her, he realises, feeling awkward.

But luckily for him, at that very moment the waitress arrives with coffee. She notices the sceptical look on Elina's face.

"What he says is true," she says, pouring out a cup of coffee for the managing director and topping up Elina's. "He really is the managing director of the mine. If he didn't insist on shuffling around in his working clothes, he could dress himself up like the upper-class gentleman he really is! He should have a nameplate round his neck."

Elina's face lights up.

"Good heavens! So you are the one who appointed me. I'm Elina Pettersson, the schoolteacher."

From then on the four hours between Gällivare and Kiruna simply fly past.

He asks about her training and previous appointment. She explains how she attended a private college for the training of primary school teachers in Göteborg, that the school in Jönåker where she worked had thirty-two pupils, and that her salary was three hundred kronor per year.

"And how did you like it there, fröken Pettersson?" he wonders.

For some reason she plucks up enough courage to say "Well, I got by . . ."

There is something about the way he listens that opens up her heart. Perhaps it is his half-closed eyes. His heavy eyelids give him a sort of thoughtful, dreamy expression that somehow loosens her tongue.

Words come gushing out of her, describing all the dull, tedious experiences that have dogged her these last few years. She talks about the children, her pupils, that she had dreamt about and longed to meet while she was at college. She tells him how depressed she was when she discovered that nearly all of them were so unwilling to learn anything. She hadn't expected that: she had thought they would all be ravenous to learn and read books, just like she had been when she was a little girl. She tells him about the vicar and the gentleman farmer who was a member of the school governors and seemed to think that reading from the catechism and counting with the aid of an abacus was quite sufficient, and that there was "no reason to agree" to her request for a wooden blackboard with easel and chalk for a total price of five kronor, in order to improve the children's writing and spelling. Nor would they allow her to buy three copies of a Selma Lagerlöf reader.

"What makes you think things will be any different in Kiruna?" Lundbohm says.

He raises his head slightly, and looks her in the eye.

"The fact that you are a different kind of man," she says, meeting his gaze until he turns away and orders another cup of coffee.

She becomes aware that she has some kind of hold over him. He is so much older than she is, so she hasn't thought about him in that way while they have been conversing. But of course, he is a man after all.

She is not unaware of her good looks, and sometimes she has taken advantage of them herself. It was her hair and her trim waist that led to the repairing of the roof of the teacher's house very cheaply by a couple of local farmhands two years ago.

But more often than not her beauty has been a confounded

nuisance. It is a pain, constantly having to hold would-be suitors at bay; but now, when she sees Lundbohm averting his gaze because he is afraid that it might betray his thoughts, she feels her heart give a leap of pleasure.

She has a hold over him. Over the man Rudyard Kipling calls "the uncrowned king of Lapland".

She knows that he is acquainted with a lot of remarkable people – Prince Eugen, Carl and Karin Larsson, Selma Lagerlöf. But who is she, compared with people like that? Nothing, a mere nobody. But she still has her youth and her beauty, and that combination has given her this experience. She thanks God from the bottom of her heart. If she had been ugly, she would never have found herself sitting here with him.

Now he is looking at her again.

"If you find that anything is missing from your classroom that ought to be there," he says, "readers, blackboard and easel, slates for the pupils – just let me know. Personally."

Their conversation moves on to the importance of education. She says that Kiruna is a mining town, and hence she is well aware that everything is going to be different from what she has been used to. She thinks that the best thing about the labour laws passed in Sweden in 1912 is the protection given to young children that prevents them from being exploited by industry. There are no such laws preventing them from being exploited in the interests of agriculture.

"How will children be able to educate themselves in school if they are already worn out by hard labour? The desire to learn is snuffed out in their heads. I've seen this happen with my own eyes."

Now she starts talking about her beloved Ellen Key and *The Century of the Child*. Her cheeks glow as she preaches the gospel according to Key, how all a child's bodily and spiritual energy until the age of fifteen should be concentrated on its education in school, indulging in sport and play, being encouraged to perform tasks at home and in vocational schools – but certainly not exploited by being forced to work in industry.

"Nor should children have to perform exhausting work on farms and in farmhouses," she says, lowering her gaze as she recalls the way in which young boys and girls were made to slave away as housemaids or farmhands by the gentleman farmer.

Lundbohm is infected by her enthusiasm.

"As far as I'm concerned, industry and other similar activities are merely the means, not the goal," he says.

"So what is the goal?"

"The goal is always to enable people to lead the most rewarding life possible. Also on a spiritual level."

When he says this, she looks at him with such veneration that he feels obliged to add, almost in embarrassment, "Besides, the most efficient workers are always the ones who have been through school."

He explains that they have also reached this conclusion in Russia, where standards of general education still leave much to be desired. Workers who can read and write always receive higher wages than those who can't: illiterates always end up doing the most onerous and debilitating work. And the reason why German industry has progressed further and faster than its English counterpart is that German citizens are better educated. And just look at the productive and intelligent American workers. It's all down to schooling.

Lundbohm feels exhilarated. Happier than he has felt for a long time. That's the blessing bestowed by travelling. For several hours one has nothing better to do than to get to know a fellow human being.

And when it's a fellow human being like this one! . . . Ravishing. And intelligent with it.

There is a shortage of beautiful women in Kiruna. The women are young, to be sure. Kiruna is a newly built town populated by young people. But life is hard up there in the far north; it takes its toll and the drudgery marks their faces. They lose their apple-red cheeks. They dress in men's overcoats and woollen shawls in an attempt to keep out the cold. It's true that the engineers' wives retain their healthy glow, but they don't want to go out walking or jogging as women would do in Stockholm. No, in summer there are too many mosquitoes, and in winter it's too cold. So they stay indoors and lounge around and put on weight.

Their conversation hops around from one topic to another.

They talk about the Mona Lisa, which had been stolen and disappeared for two years before reappearing at the Louvre just before Christmas. A crafty art gallery owner in Italy lured the thief out of his lair and pretended to be interested in buying the painting.

They agree to differ when it comes to votes for women – but Elina insists that she is no suffragette, and Lundbohm jokes that if she were to become one, he would personally force-feed her in prison. Elina asks him to talk about Selma Lagerlöf and her visit to Kiruna when she was writing her book about Nils Holgersson and his marvellous journey all over Sweden: and he does so. They discuss Strindberg's posthumous reputation, his bitterness and his funeral. And they talk about the *Titanic*, of course. It is exactly two years since the catastrophe took place.

Then, before they know it, they arrive at their destination. Such a disappointment. The train shudders to a stop, doors open, people jostle in their attempts to disembark with all their luggage.

Elina has to go back to her compartment.

Lundbohm takes his leave, wishes her all the best, and encourages her again to get in touch with him personally if there are any problems or any equipment missing in her classroom.

She hardly has time to blink before he vanishes.

She is surprised. She thought they would at the very least get off the train together, perhaps walk along the platform together. Then she feels angry. If she had been an upper-class lady no doubt he would have accompanied her to her compartment, carried her suitcase and helped her off the train. Offered her an arm to lean on as she stepped down onto the platform.

When she is standing outside the station building, waiting for her two trunks to be delivered, her anger is replaced by shame.

What on earth had she expected? That they would become friends? Why should he have been interested in that?

And she had gone on a bit. Thinking back, she could not help but blush. He must have thought she was the most presumptuous and self-centred little schoolmistress he had ever come across. Her inflammatory speech about Ellen Key – to somebody who actually knew her.

A youth appears with her trunks on a wheelbarrow. They are very heavy – one of them in particular. It is very difficult, wheeling them through the deep snow.

"What have you got inside these trunks, Missus – bricks?" he asks with a grin. "Are you thinking of building a house?"

Another youth appears and offers to help, but she has difficulty in hearing what they are saying.

The station is teeming with people. Loading and unloading is going on wherever you look. Outside the station building are queues of horses and sledges waiting for passengers. A girl is standing by a large pot of coffee over a small gas stove, selling mugs of coffee and buns.

A flock of thrushes are singing in a birch tree laden with snow. That is all she needs to rekindle her high spirits. The shame she had been feeling melts away. He is only a man, after all, and there are thirteen to the dozen of those. How beautiful it all is, thanks to the snow and the sunshine. She wonders what it will look like in the evening, with the mountain lit up and all the street lights aglow.

Kiruna – the name sings inside her mind's ear. Kiruna. The name comes from the Sami word *gieron*, which means ptarmigan.

*

Lundbohm hurries off the train. He has no time to spare as he has had an idea about the accommodation provided for the new school-teacher. It has to be arranged at once, so that she doesn't realise that he has changed what was planned, for what he thinks will be for her benefit.

He doesn't want to give her the impression of being an old man pestering her, but he wants to meet her again. And if his little plan comes off, he will certainly be able to do that. Often.

Sol-Britt Uusitalo's cousin was called Maja Larsson. Martinsson leaned her bicycle against the woodshed, and looked around.

It was Larsson's mother's property. It was obvious that an old person who had run out of steam had been living there for a long time. The house was clad with pink Eternit panels, and several of them had come loose. The gutter was also hanging loose. The window frames needed repainting. The porch seemed to have sunk and was at an angle outside the front door. Several large, straggly bushes – Martinsson guessed they were currant bushes – were growing on the south side of the house. Remains of the homemade trellis that used to support them were lying on the ground, rotten and covered in moss.

Martinsson knocked on the door as the bell didn't seem to be working.

Larsson answered it, and Martinsson almost took an involuntary stride backwards. What a beautiful woman! She was not wearing make-up, and the wrinkles on her face gave her a weatherbeaten look. Her cheekbones were high, and she stretched her long, slim neck when she saw Martinsson. A regal movement – perhaps that was what almost made Martinsson take that step backwards. She seemed to be about sixty. Her hair was pure white, and had been braided to form lots of long, thin plaits which were collected in a large bun at the back of her head. Her hair was snake-like. Her eyes were light grey, her eyebrows thick and blonde. She was wearing a pair of men's trousers which hung around her hips, and a V-necked brown woollen jumper, patched at the elbows.

"Is something wrong?" she said.

Martinsson realised that she was staring. She introduced herself and explained why she was there.

"It's your cousin," she said. "Sol-Britt Uusitalo. I'm afraid that she's been murdered."

Larsson looked at Martinsson as if she was a little girl selling Christmas magazines. Then she sighed deeply.

"For Christ's sake . . . I expect you want to come in and talk. Yes, of course you do – come right in."

She led the way into the kitchen. Martinsson kicked off her shoes and followed her. She sat down on the rib-backed settee, declined the offer of coffee and took a notebook out of her pocket.

Larsson opened a kitchen drawer and dug out a packet of cigarettes.

"Let's hear it, then! Would you like a fag?"

Martinsson shook her head. Larsson lit one for herself and sent the smoke spiralling out through her nostrils. She stood by the stove and pulled a metal chain which opened a ventilation flap in the ceiling.

"Somebody stabbed her while she was asleep."

Larsson closed her eyes and lowered her head. As if she were trying to take in what Martinsson had just said.

"Please excuse me if I seem . . . It's my mother. She hasn't much longer to live. I'm only staying here so that I can be close to her as the end approaches. I sometimes feel as if I don't have any emotions left in my body."

She looked intently at Martinsson.

"Marcus?!"

"He's O.K.," Martinsson said. "Uninjured."

"Have you come to ask me to look after him?"

"I don't know. Could you?"

Larsson's face hardened.

"Huh, I assume that means his little mum said no. Had she injured her back, perhaps? Or had a pipe just burst in her kitchen? Did she even bother to ask how he was?"

Martinsson thought how Marcus's mother had gone on about the probability of her partner walking out on her if she agreed to look after her son. She had not asked about how he was.

"I'll take care of him," Larsson said. "Of course I will. If there's nobody else. It's just that my mother is so . . . I'm away at the hospital nearly all the time. I don't know if I'd be able to manage it. He doesn't know me at all. I don't live here – as I said, it's just now, when my mum . . . And I must admit that I'm crap when it comes to handling children. I never had any myself. Oh God, oh God . . . I think the world has gone mad. But I'll look after him. Of course I'll look after him."

Martinsson opened her notebook.

"Who might have called her a whore?"

"What do you mean?"

"Somebody had written that on the wall above her bed."

Larsson stared hard at Martinsson. Like a fox standing motionless in the trees at the edge of the forest, trying to decide if the approaching stranger is friend or foe. In the end she responded. Her voice was low and soft. The silver snakes were wriggling on top of her head.

"I know who you are; you're Rebecka Martinsson. Mikko's and Virpi's daughter. You've moved back here. I didn't know what you look like nowadays – I only met you once when you were a little girl. Well, Rebecka, you know what it's like here in the village."

"No, I don't."

"Perhaps you don't. You're a prosecutor after all. People daren't muck you about. But it was different with Sol-Britt . . ."

She shook her head. A gesture that suggested she didn't have the strength to spell things out.

"Tell me."

"Why? People in this village are a lot of bastards, but they wouldn't murder her. If I spill the beans and you then go round asking questions, they'll know I've snitched on them. And I'll have stones thrown through my windows."

"Somebody stabbed her to death," Martinsson said sternly. "Not just once. A hundred times. I saw her. Are you going to help me?"

Larsson placed her hand on the back of her neck and glared at Martinsson.

"You're good at what you do," she said.

"Yes, I'm good at what I do."

"I knew your mother. We used to go out dancing together. She was good-looking. She had loads of admirers. Then she met your dad and they got married and I moved away, so we lost contact. Sol-Britt used to come with us sometimes, although she was younger than we were. But she was my little cousin after all. Then she got a bun in the oven, and had her little boy, Matti, when she was only seventeen. The father did a runner before Matti was a year old. I don't even remember what the bastard was called anymore. He moved away, and things went pretty well for him. He got a job with Scania as a lorry driver. Anyway, Sol-Britt met somebody else, but then that didn't work out either. So she found another man, but he drank too much. He used to bring his mates back home with him, and they kicked up a row until all hours. So she kicked him out. And that was that. Matti's schoolmates used to tell him that his mother was a whore and a drunkard."

"Did she drink?"

"Yes, she did. Far too much. But do you know what: lots of people drink too much. Still, she ended up as somebody all the other bloody losers could think they were better than. All the women in this village who think they are pretty well off. I think they feel it's a bit more bearable living with an idiot of a man if you make up your mind that the worst thing that can happen to you is having to live without one. So they can say everything in their garden is lovely – and they can drink with a good conscience as well, because they've all decided that Sol-Britt drinks more than they do. And when she wanders round the village after having downed a glass or two, she's drunk and a pain in the neck. All the others chat and pretend to be normal, no matter what state they're really in. Sol-Britt was one of those people men went to visit when they were drunk, when they'd had a row with the wife or been left on their own. They would stagger round to her house. And she would serve them coffee. That was all. I know that for a fact. Not that I think it matters, but that's the way it was. Then they would stagger back to their wives or to a neighbour or to one of their mates, and boast that they'd screwed her. All bloody lies. Wishful thinking. Anyway, quite a few people called her a whore. I don't understand why she carried on living here. And I don't understand why you've come back here."

Martinsson looked out of the window. Was it snowing? A few isolated flakes were floating around in the air, as if they couldn't make up their minds whether to fall or to go back where they had come from.

She did not want to listen to all this. She did not want to hear about her parents. And she did not want to hear the truth about a Kurravaara that was not the one she knew.

It is easier to keep all that at arm's length, now that I'm grown up, she thought. I do not need to have anything to do with people like that. It was different when I was small. And we were all in the same class. You did not have a chance in those circumstances.

"Was there anybody threatening her?"

"Marcus gets bullied by some of the youngsters in the village. They all share the same school bus into Kiruna. Sol-Britt took that up with the headmaster. The other parents were up in arms. With Sol-Britt! Because she dared to accuse their children. Sol-Britt stood her ground and stuck up for herself when Louise and Lelle Niemi turned up at her front door and started shouting and screaming. They did the kind of things the police can't catch them for. Like switching on full headlights to dazzle her. And yes, they called her a whore. Mouthed the word whenever they met her in the shops in town. And Marcus begged his grandma not to do anything or say anything because that only made things worse for him. And so their little boy would push Marcus into the ditch or into snowdrifts whenever he bumped into them. Pinch his things. She bought him three new rucksacks last year. Marcus said he had lost them, but he doesn't just lose his belongings."

She lifted all the dirty crockery and cutlery out of the sink, put the plug in and started running hot water as she put plates, glasses and cutlery into the foaming hot water.

"I don't know why I'm telling you all this. They're idiots – but they didn't kill her."

She washes up in the old-fashioned way, Martinsson noted. She rinses everything in a plastic bowl, rather than under a running tap – it's important to save hot water.

"Where do they live?"

"In the big yellow house further up the creek. Are you saying you didn't know that? Don't stir up trouble with them and their gang. That's my advice if you want to carry on living in this village."

Martinsson allowed herself a wry smile.

"I've stirred up trouble with people before. I don't let people scare me."

Now it was Larsson's turn to smile, just as wryly. A hasty smile. It didn't last long, frightened off by something – sorrow and death, perhaps.

"That's true. I've read about it. And heard about it as well, of course. There's a lot of talk about what you do. You killed those pastors – that was not far from here, in the Kurravaara district."

And somewhere in Sweden those children are growing up, Martinsson thought. Without a father. Hating me.

She looked down at her empty notebook

"Is there anything else you want to tell me? About Sol-Britt. What sort of state was she in when you last saw her? Was there anything she was worried about?"

"No. Or rather, to be honest, not that I know of. I wouldn't have noticed if there was. I sit with my mother and try to feed her. Keep an eye on her. She did a few jobs here not long ago. Mending things and cleaning."

She looked around the room.

"But now she's just a little bird. You are like your mother."

Martinsson felt herself stiffening.

"Anyway, thank you for your time," she said in a friendly voice, giving nothing away.

Larsson stopped washing up and turned to face her. Martinsson felt the woman's gaze penetrating deep inside her.

"Oh, so that's the way it is, is it? But your mum wasn't a bad person. And your dad wasn't a victim. If you ever want to talk about it, you're welcome to call in for a coffee one of these days."

"I don't understand what you mean," Martinsson said, rising to her feet. "We'll be in touch about Marcus."

She looked at the clock. It was time to go to the post-mortem.

As always it was very cold in the autopsy chamber. Martinsson and Mella made no move to remove their outer garments. The faint smell of decomposing bodies and the more evident smell of strong cleaning materials and surgical spirits were relegated to the background by the tobacco smoke produced by the Dr Pohjanen.

He was sitting on his working chair, a cigarette in one hand and a dictaphone in the other. The chair was made of metal and had small wheels – a sort of skeleton desk chair without a backrest. Mella assumed that he rarely stood up nowadays. She had heard that he had given up driving last year – excellent! No doubt he was highly dangerous in traffic. He seemed always to be tired out, and spent at least half his working day lying on his back on the sofa in the coffee room. Less and less Pohjanen, more and more cancer. She found herself feeling angry with him, for some reason she could not identify.

Underneath his unbuttoned green smock he was wearing a T-shirt with a picture of Madonna. The image of the fit-looking singer wearing a top hat over her blonde hair provided a sombre contrast to his own lifeless skin. The rings under his eyes were dark, almost blue.

Mella wondered how on earth Madonna had found her way onto his body. No doubt he had been given the T-shirt as a present. By his daughter. Or maybe his granddaughter. She couldn't believe for the life of her that he had the least idea who Madonna was.

Sol-Britt Uusitalo was lying on her back on a steel bench in the middle of the room. Pohjanen's bloodstained latex gloves were lying beside the opened-up corpse.

A few metres further back an assistant, Anna Granlund, was sawing through the skull of another dead body. The sound from the motorised circular saw made Mella shudder. She gestured to Granlund, who gestured back: she would soon be finished. Sure enough, after a moment she switched off the saw, removed her protective goggles and greeted the visitors.

She's the one who does everything now, Mella thought, looking at Anna Granlund. Everything apart from the actual thinking.

"What's all this?" Martinsson said as soon as the saw had fallen silent. "Smoking in here? You'll get the sack."

Pohjanen managed a raucous "ha ha" by way of reply. Everybody knew he could have taken early retirement years ago. He was allowed to do whatever he wanted – provided he stayed on for at least another day.

"Are you thinking of grassing me up?" he croaked, with a self-satisfied smile.

"I hoped you might be able to give us a few details," Mella said, nodding towards the dead body.

"O.K., O.K.," he muttered.

He waved his hand, indicating that they could cut out the obligatory song and dance that ensued whenever she came and started asking him questions before he was ready. All the fussing around because he was annoyed by being interrupted and unable to work in peace. And then she would flatter him, and he would allow himself to be appeased.

"At first I thought it might be a nail gun," he said, "I've seen a couple of cases of that, and the nails generally disappear underneath the skin. And there's very little bleeding, as in this case. Assuming that some of the first shots were fatal. But there are no nails in the wounds. And so . . ."

He put on another pair of latex gloves and produced a tray carrying skin samples cut into thick slices. Mella thought it might well be some considerable time before she ate bacon again.

"Here," he said, pointing, "you can see the penetration in the surface skin, and then the tiny holes in the corium and below that – very little damage to the tissue. And look here: the surface penetrations are quite round, and they go deep."

"An awl?" Mella wondered.

"Close."

"A nail through a piece of board?" suggested Martinsson.

Pohjanen shook his head.

He pointed to Sol-Britt's body with his left index finger and his right thumb and index finger, so that the fingers reproduced three holes in a row in several places.

"Orion's belt, Orion's belt, Orion's belt," he said, pointing out several similar places. "You don't notice it at first because there are so many wounds."

"What, then?" Mella said.

"A hayfork," Martinsson said.

Pohjanen gave Martinsson an approving look.

"Yes, that's what I think as well."

He lifted up Sol-Britt's hands.

"No wounds due to attempts to protect herself. And as there was so little bleeding, I'm inclined to think that the very first stab was fatal."

Martinsson frowned. Pohjanen glanced at her, and explained.

"If you die, if your heart stops beating, no blood is pumped into your body. If there is no blood being pumped into your body, you don't bleed. Jesus on the cross is an example of that. It says in the Bible that the soldiers broke the bones of the others who were crucified beside him, but they didn't break Jesus's bones because he was already dead. Then they stabbed a lance into his side. And blood and water came gushing out. Which means that he wasn't already dead, but probably died at that moment. I've had a lot of discussions with churchgoers about that: they want to believe that he gave up the ghost when the Bible said he did."

"Churchgoers don't like people like you," Mella said in order to cheer him up. "Only the other day Mari Allen at the Rudbeck Laboratory revealed that the skulls of Saint Birgitta and her daughter Katarina in the shrine at Vadstena are not related."

Pohjanen chuckled in satisfaction – which sounded like an engine that was reluctant to start.

"And not only that, there was an age difference of two hundred years between the skulls," Mella said.

"Huh," Pohjanen said. "Throw the holy bones to the dogs."

"She looks to be at peace," Martinsson said. "Do you think she was asleep when she was killed?"

"All dead people seem to be at peace," said Pohjanen drily. "No matter how painful their death was. Before rigor mortis sets in, all their muscles, including the muscles in their face, relax."

Martinsson shifted fractionally. Pohjanen noticed it at once.

"Are you thinking about your father?" he asked. "Forget it. If you look peaceful, the odds are that you were at peace. That is a possibility, believe it or not. Anyway. Lots of blows are fatal."

He pointed to a wound between Sol-Britt's navel and her pubic bone.

"This stab penetrated her aorta. That's where the samurai used to strike when they committed *seppuku*. She has a bleeding in her pericardium, and if you want me to guess I would say that could well have been the first blow. I examined the wound and found traces of rust – I'm almost certain of that. I can send it for analysis if you like."

"An old hayfork, then," said Martinsson.

"I don't suppose there are any new ones – does anybody use a hayfork nowadays?"

"And she was lying in bed . . ." Mella began.

"Yes, quite definitely. We haven't started turning her over, but there are some stabs which went right through her body – this one here above her collarbone, for instance. There is matching damage to the mattress."

"The murderer must have stood on her bed, over the top of her," Mella said. "Or at the side of the bed. It must have been hard."

"Very hard," Pohjanen agreed. "And he was stabbing through bone as well. But if you try something like this – it seems such a reckless thing to do, somehow – then your body is going to be full of adrenalin. A state of mad fury, or perhaps ecstatic elation. And note that the murderer didn't stop, but went on and on long after the victim was dead. That often indicates mental derangement."

"Obviously, we'll check whether any of the mental hospitals have released any loonies lately," Mella said.

Oh, shit! She could have bitten her tongue off. Shit, shit, shit! Why was her mouth always quicker than her brain? Martinsson had been sent to a mental hospital – she had been in such a state that they had to give her electric shock treatment. She had been hallucinating and screaming. That was after Gunnar Vinsa had shot himself and his son. Mella had never spoken to Martinsson about that. It had been beyond her comprehension. She had not even known that they still gave electric shock treatment. She thought that was what happened in prehistoric times. As in "One Flew over the Cuckoo's Nest".

"That's enough of that," Pohjanen growled.

At that very moment Mella's mobile rang. She answered, relieved to have been given an escape route. It was Stålnacke.

He didn't beat about the bush. "I thought we were going to have a press conference tomorrow morning," he said.

"That's right," said Mella.

"Really? Then why is von Post chatting with a gang of journalists in the conference room at this very minute?"

Mella refrained from exclaiming, "What the hell are you on about?"

"I'll be there right away," she said instead, and hung up.

"You're not going to like this," she said to Martinsson.

We meet again, thought District Prosecutor Carl von Post when he saw Inspector Anna-Maria Mella and Rebecka Martinsson getting out of their cars. You bloody idiots.

It was several years now since Martinsson had arrived in Kiruna to poke her nose into his investigation concerning the murder of Viktor Strandgård. The moment she stepped off the plane, she thought she was somebody. A successful lawyer with Meijer & Ditzinger. As if that was of any significance. Her boyfriend was a partner. He, von Post, had no difficulty in understanding how she had got the job – but the media, all those damned journalists, had worshipped her. Once the murder had been cleared up, you could read about her everywhere. He had been presented as the idiot who had arrested the wrong person. He had thought he would have been rid of her after that – but oh, no. She had floated up to the surface again and started work as a prosecutor. She and that dwarf of a police inspector Mella had somehow blundered their way through the investigation into the murder of Wilma Persson and Simon Kyrö. It was a miracle that the murderer was caught, but the press – these bloody journalists again – had described her as a Modesty Blaise.

For years he had been spending his time on cases involving drunkenness, thefts of snow scooters and assaults. On the whole. One murder, though. A bloke from Harads who killed his brother of a Saturday evening.

Carl von Post was stuck as a prosecutor working on minor cases up in Lapland. And it was all their fault. Modesty Bloody Blaise and that policewoman she had on a leash. He did not have a snowball's chance in hell of landing a job in a decent-sized law firm in Stockholm. But he had made up his mind. Things were going to change. It was his turn now to come into the spotlight, be written about. A spectacular murder like this one was just what the doctor ordered. She did not need it. And now he had made sure it was going to be his case. That pair were not going to get it back again, and he was about to make that clear to them.

Carl von Post turned to face the assembled journalists. They were all keeping an eye on their iPhones, and scanning Twitter and Flashback in search of something extra. Microphones had been switched on. The national evening papers *Expressen* and *Aftonbladet* had sent their usual freelancers. Reporters from local papers *N.S.D.* and *Norbottens-Kuriren* were hovering in the corridor a little further away, in the hope of collaring somebody they knew. The hacks from Swedish Television and T.V.4 were each wielding a gigantic camera. And then there were people he did not know from Adam. They were all trying to talk him into allowing them a few minutes of extra time afterwards.

"Five minutes," he said, gesturing at the rows of chairs in the conference room, then hurried out in order to make sure that he could talk to Martinsson and Mella out of earshot of the reporters.

Mella strode purposefully towards Carl von Post. He slowed down so as not to give the impression of being stressed – but she had seen through the glass doors how he had almost run to the exit. Martinsson was lagging behind.

"Hi," von Post said with a smile. "Good that you could come. I heard you'd been to see the pathologist – perhaps you could brief me on what he had to say, so—"

"Now listen here," Mella interrupted. "I'm about to have a heart attack. I hope you can utter a few well-chosen words that will calm me down . . ."

"What do you mean?"

"What do I mean?!"

Mella thrust her arms up into the air, then her hands landed on the top of her head as if to prevent it from exploding.

"You've called a press conference. Now. I'd already called one. Tomorrow morning at eight o'clock."

Von Post folded his arms.

"I'm sorry that things developed rather quickly. I ought to have let you know that things had changed, of course. I'm in charge of the preliminary investigation, and I think the sooner we talk to the press, the better. You know what can happen otherwise. Our own minions will be bribed to leak information about the state of the investigation – the press will stop at nothing in order to sell a few more copies."

"You don't need to tell me how to handle the press. In charge of the preliminary investigation? Don't make me laugh. Martinsson is in charge of the preliminary investigation."

Von Post looked at Martinsson, who had joined them and was standing beside Mella.

"No, she's not," he said coldly. "Alf Björnfot has appointed me."

Alf Björnfot was the chief prosecutor. When Martinsson moved back to Kiruna and stopped working as a lawyer in Stockholm, he was the one who had persuaded her to join the local prosecution service.

Mella opened her mouth to say that he would never do anything as bloody stupid as that, but closed it again. It was obvious that von Post would not simply take over on his own initiative. He wasn't an idiot. Or rather, he was an idiot: but not quite as stupid as that.

Martinsson nodded, but said nothing. There was silence for a few seconds, until von Post broke it.

"The basic fact is that you are too close to the dead woman. Alf asked me to take over."

"I didn't know her," Martinsson said.

"No, but you lived in the same village, and sooner or later someone you know will turn up as a witness. It's a sensitive situation. You must recognise that. Björnfot can't allow anything like that to happen. There's too big a risk that we would lay ourselves open to being challenged."

He looked hard at her. She did not move a muscle.

She must have a bit of brain damage, he thought. A slight handicap.

Martinsson managed to keep her face expressionless. The strain made itself felt in her forehead, but she was pretty sure that her face betrayed no hint of it. They had swept her aside as if she were nothing more than old rubbish. And Björnfot had not even rung her to explain the circumstances.

Don't show any signs of being hurt, she told herself.

That would be a bonus that von Post would really appreciate. He would gormandise on her wounded self-esteem like a vulture on its prey.

"And then, of course, he's a bit worried about you," von Post said in a gentle tone of voice. "After all, you have form when it comes to illness, and a case like this one can be rather trying."

He leaned his head on one side, and stared at Martinsson.

Don't say a thing, Martinsson said to herself.

Von Post sighed, and scrutinised his iPhone.

"We'd better get started," he said. "What did the pathologist have to say? In a nutshell."

"I don't have time," Martinsson said. "I have to go and fetch the dogs."

But she made no move. Simply stood there.

"He said nothing," Mella said. "He hadn't even started."

Both women crossed their arms. They stood there without moving for a while. Then Martinsson dropped her arms, turned on her heel and left.

Von Post watched her get into her car and drive away. So that's that, he thought.

One little nigger boy less, he thought.

He found it hard to suppress his smile.

Only one little nigger boy left now. And that bitch Mella had better not get it into her head that she can stir things up.

"I'm not prepared to put up with any crap from you, Mella," he said. "Either you can tell me what he said, or you're off this case."

Mella stared at him in disbelief.

"I mean what I say," he said, continuing to look her in the eye. "A police officer who doesn't keep the person in charge of the preliminary investigation informed has serious problems when it comes to cooperation. And I can assure you that if you behave in that way, I shall have you transferred to traffic duties at the drop of a hat. The chief constable of the province is a mate of mine – he rents my summer cottage at Riksgränsen."

He eyed her with raised eyebrows: how would she react?

"But he didn't have much to say," Mella said.

Her cheeks were bright pink.

"She had probably been attacked with a hayfork. She died more or less straight away. There were an astonishing number of stabs. Or blows, or whatever you want to call them."

"Good," von Post said, tapping her on the shoulder. "Let's get going. It's time for the press conference."

"Is there always as much snow here as this?"

Fröken Elina Pettersson is gazing out over Kiruna from the elevated driver's seat. She is alone up there, because the young driver has jumped down from the sleigh and is leading the horses, which are panting and steaming after their exertions.

"No," he said. "There's always a lot, I suppose, but we've had a snowstorm lasting for three days. And then this morning there was a sudden change, and it's been fine and warm. That's a lesson you can learn straight away – you're in the mountains now. The weather can change at a moment's notice. Last Midsummer's Eve we youngsters were at a dance out at Jukkas. It was warm and very pleasant. The leaves had just begun to come out. And at about eight o'clock in the evening it started snowing."

The memory of it makes him laugh.

The whole town seems to be covered by a feather duvet. All the buildings have long white skirts. The snow has drifted up high against the walls. Young boys are shovelling away on the roofs for all they're worth. They are naked from the waist up, but they're wearing heavy winter boots.

"If they don't do that, the roofs will collapse when the thaw comes," the young driver said.

The street lights are wearing Cossack hats, the mountain with all the mine shafts is covered in snow and could be any old mountain. The birch branches are sagging down under the weight of the snow, forming fairytale doorways that glisten in the sunlight flowing through them. She is dazzled by the intense light, and finds it hard even to screw up her eyes and peep through the narrow slits. She has heard that one can become snowblind – is this what that means?

"You're supposed to wait in the school," the driver said. "Somebody will come and fetch you. I'll leave all your belongings on the sleigh, and take them down to where you'll be living later."

So she sits waiting on her own in the school. It is Sunday, and the place is deserted. Strangely quiet. A thin veil of dust dances upwards in the beams of the sun shining in through the windows.

There is a blackboard – excellent – and a lot of posters and wall-charts, motifs from the Bible, maps, pictures of plants and animals. She can already hear herself telling her pupils the most exciting stories from the Old Testament: David and Goliath, of course, Moses in the bulrushes, the heroic Queen Esther. She wonders how many of the plants and animals pictured can be found this far north. The children will press flowers for themselves, and learn about the flora and fauna in their own environment. There is a harmonium, and a guitar hanging on the wall.

She wonders how long she will have to wait, for she feels very hungry. She has not eaten anything since finishing off the last of the sandwiches she had taken with her for the journey – and that was around two o'clock the previous day, almost twenty-four hours ago.

She hears the sound of somebody closing the outside door, then stamping off the snow from his or her shoes out in the corridor. Then the classroom door opens and in comes a woman of about her own age. No, on second thoughts, even younger. Elina had been misled at first by her dumpy body, her ample bosom and rounded bottom. She is still young enough for it to be considered puppy fat, but this young girl will soon become a stout matron. She is attractive, though. It occurs to Elina that they are similar in some respects

– snub-nosed and round-cheeked. Although the new arrival has dark hair. Her brown eyes are inquisitive and expectant: she looks as if she is expecting Elina to tell her some good news.

"Fröken Elina Pettersson?"

She holds out her right hand. It is a little red and dry. Hard skin and very short nails. The hand of a hardworking woman.

Like my mother's, Elina thought, feeling guilty about her own soft, upper-class hand.

"I'm Managing Director Lundbohm's housekeeper, Klara Andersson. But you can call me Lizzie, like all my friends do. Busy Lizzie! I mean, there's no point in being formal if we're going to be sharing the same lodgings. Come."

She takes hold of Elina's arm and leads her out into the snowy sunshine. The pace is fast, and Elina finds herself almost having to jog. Lizzie chatters away as if they have been friends forever.

"At last, that's all I can say. I've told the Managing Director a hundred times that what I want is a place of my own. I've been sleeping in the maids' dormitory in the boss's house until now. But with all the guests he always has as well! Artists and businessmen and mine managers, and lots of those adventure-loving tourists who really must explore the mountains and get lost and have to be rescued. First you have to make sure that they can eat and drink and be waited on – and that can be at any time of day or night: the boss's little mother did a terrific job of spoiling him when he was a kid. And then, when you can collapse into bed at last, knowing that you'll have to be up again, slaving away after only an hour or two's sleep, the drunken overnight guests stagger in and start scratching and growling like dogs outside your bedroom door! Ugh! Disgusting dirty old men! The door's locked and bolted, of course, but you don't bloody dare to sleep! Not Lundbohm, I hasten to say – he has never . . . Anyway, I have a place of my own at last."

She dangles a key in front of Elina's nose.

"I expect you're used to having a place of your own. But there's a shortage of accommodation in Kiruna. You have to share here."

She clings onto Elina's arm.

"And I'm delighted to share with you. I could see that the moment I met you!"

The place is called B12 – short for building number twelve. It's a so-called tin box. It's almost impossible to see that the walls are green, as they are covered by ice and snow. The tin roof is red, Lizzie informs Elina.

"Just wait and see how it gleams in the summer, thanks to the midnight sun! It's so beautiful here!"

Their flat comprises a large kitchen and a living room upstairs. No furniture. A simple wooden floor.

"A stove!" exclaims Lizzie. "A real iron stove with an oven!"

She inspects the Husqvarna stove. The hotplates seem to be in working order, as is the ash door. And there are two special baking plates.

Lizzie turns to look at Elina with a broad smile.

"We can bake every morning. And sell stuff to the labourers who work in the mine or at the ironworks during the week. If you and I sleep down here in the kitchen, we can rent out the living room – there's enough space there to sleep four people. During the day we can stand their mattresses on end and make sufficient room for a drop-leaf table with two chairs. So you can read and work there, or have sessions with your pupils. I mean, the tenants won't come back home until eight or nine o'clock at night. Maybe a bit earlier if they have their dinner here – that would give us a bit of extra income. But if we only give them bed and breakfast, we would earn eight kronor a week from them. And then we'd earn a bit more from selling bread as well."

Having heard all this talk about bread and breakfast and dinner, Elina has to sit down – she's so hungry. She flops down onto the firewood bin. It dawns on Lizzie the state she's in.

"What an idiot I am!" she exclaims, taking hold of Elina's head with both hands and kissing her on the forehead. "I ought to have realised."

She instructs Elina not to move from the spot – she'll be back directly.

While Lizzie is away, Elina feels her body filling up with happiness. It is as if the early spring sunshine is flowing through her veins, a stream of gold. She has acquired a friend, she can feel it. A cheerful, irrepressible, lovely friend. Who has hurried away because Elina "must get something solid in her belly"!

Elina looks around. That's where the kitchen sofa must stand, the wooden bench that converts into a double bed. There must be rugs on the floor, and the walls need painting – white, obviously. Everything must be simple but tasteful, just as Ellen Key recommends. And there must be geraniums on the window ledges in the summer, of course.

She recalls all the lonely evenings and Sundays she has endured over the last three years. Never again.

Lizzie comes back, accompanied by a young girl who works as a housemaid. They are laden with cleaning equipment: aprons, buckets, scouring cloths, soft soap, a big cauldron for heating up water, and brushes. She has some sandwiches for Elina, and a piece of dried, salted reindeer meat. She takes a knife and cuts the almost black meat into thin slices.

"It tastes a bit different if you're not used to it, but it warms the cockles of your heart. Try a bit. You've only got your posh travelling clothes, but I thought I could give this place a thorough clean . . ."

Elina bursts out laughing. Does Lizzie think she is so posh that she doesn't know how to do the cleaning? Her clothes can be washed, after all. If Lizzie would be so good as to hand over an apron, she will soon see what her new friend is capable of!

Lizzie laughs as well, and says that she has not yet come across anybody who is better than she is at cleaning. The housemaids can look after Lundbohm this evening. She has produced a steak from the larder and no guests are expected, so she and Elina can brush and scrub away until midnight, no problem.

Then they start cleaning. There is only the kitchen and a living room, and with some help from the housemaid it is all done in no time. They go out into the garden and fill the cauldron with snow, then heat it up on the stove. They use a mop to clean the ceiling, dust the walls and doors, and get down on their knees to scrub the floor. The neighbour from the flat downstairs comes up to inform them politely that it has started raining in the room down below, so could they please take it easy with all the water. They go over everything again with lots of cloths and a modicum of clean water, then polish the window panes with newspaper. Steam is gushing forth from the floors and the cauldron – the little flat resembles a sauna. They open all the windows wide, and the fresh air mixes with the smell of soft soap. All the time they are singing at the top of their voices: hymns and folk songs about mothers who murder their children, unhappy love, and poverty-stricken children who die of an endless stream of afflictions.

In the afternoon two removal men arrive with Lizzie's furniture: a kitchen sofa bed exactly as Elina had envisaged it, with mattresses, covers and pillows; a small drop-leaf table, two Windsor-style chairs, a commode, a washbasin and a water jug. A large pile of rugs and tablecloths. Two chests full of goodness only knows what.

Lizzie and Elina sit down on the firewood bin, each of them with a traditional wooden mug of hot coffee. Every muscle in their bodies is aching after all that carrying and scrubbing. Their skin is covered in a thin layer of salty, evaporated sweat.

But they both know exactly how to spruce themselves up and flirt with the removal men: they toss their heads, stroke their hair to one side, offer them coffee and cakes – and hey presto! The men produce a wide plank of wood and various pieces of timber with which they construct a couple of trestles that the plank can rest on to make a bench for the lodgers to sit on in the kitchen when they have their breakfast; and it all fits neatly under the kitchen sofa when they are not being used.

As the removal men walk down the stairs, they meet the young sleigh driver and a friend who are carrying up Elina's luggage.

The chest is so big and heavy that it's almost impossible to manoeuvre it up the stairs – the young boys nearly let it slip and end up underneath it. The removal men give them a hand.

"What on earth have you got in there?" Lizzie wonders.

Everybody looks at Elina.

"You didn't need to bring a chest full of iron ore," says one of the removal men. "We've got plenty of that here already."

"It's books."

Lizzie's eyes bulge like those of a squirrel.

"Books? My God! Where the devil will we put them?"

"I thought we could have a bookcase."

Lizzie stares at Elina as if she has just suggested that they should keep tigers and elephants in the flat. A bookcase! Only the gentry have anything like that.

The removal men roar with laughter, and promise that they will soon be back with appropriate bits of wood and nails – but in return Lizzie must offer them a meal: they have heard about her reputation as a cook. She nods without smiling, unable to avert her eyes from the chest.

Chief Prosecutor Alf Björnfot looked at the display on his mobile. Martinsson. He cursed to himself. He ought to have phoned her. He was tempted not to answer the call, but he was not that much of a coward.

"Hello Rebecka," he said. "Damn and blast—"

"Had you intended to ring me?" she said, interrupting him.

"Yes," he said, taking a deep breath. "But the day simply flew past – you know how it is."

Don't ask her to forgive you, he told himself.

"Go on, then," she said in a calm voice. "That'll be best, as I really don't know what to say."

"Well," he said. "Von Post came to me and . . . er, he offered to take over responsibility for the preliminary investigation. She lived in Kurravaara after all, and you live there as well and so . . . No doubt you can see the problem."

"No."

"Oh, come on, Rebecka. Surely everybody in the village knows everybody else? Sooner or later there was bound to be a hell of a difficult situation."

"But my living there doesn't stop me from taking on other crimes in Kurravaara, does it? Breaking the snow scooter speed limit, thefts of boat engines, burglaries . . ."

"But this murder is getting one thousand per cent media coverage. They'll have us for breakfast if we put a foot wrong. You know that."

Silence.

"Hello?" he said at last.

"It's best if I don't say anything," she said.

She sounded upset. He wished she had sounded angry.

"What ought I to have done?" he asked.

"Maybe you should have trusted me. Relied on my handing over to somebody else if that kind of problem arose. Just as in any other case. Instead of taking the coward's way out because the media are in full cry. It was my murder. And you simply gave it away without even phoning me."

He ran his hand over his face and tried to muffle the sound of his frustrated sigh, which sounded to him like the trumpeting of a blue whale.

Why had he not telephoned her? he asked himself. She was far and away the best prosecutor at his disposal. He was the one who had begged her to come and work for him. He ransacked the innermost depths of his conscience.

Von Post had come to see him. "It's my turn now," he'd said. Then he had raised the possible problem of people in Kurravaara being interrogated by somebody who lived in the same village. It had seemed reasonable at the time. Then he admitted in all humility that a tax evasion scam he had been helping Björnfot with was beyond his capabilities. He suggested it was something that Rebecka could take on instead. "Something for her to get her teeth into," von Post had said. "Nobody knows more about tax laws than she does."

And so Björnfot had said yes. But why had it not occurred to him to phone her at once? Because somewhere deep down inside himself he knew he had done the wrong thing. He had chosen to avoid conflict with von Post. He had given the dog a bone. Taken it for granted that it was no big deal as far as Martinsson was concerned.

Thought that she might have fun sorting out that tax scam. Van Post was so bloody dissatisfied all the time. He had thought that . . . Well, he hadn't really thought at all.

"Anyway, that's the way it is now," he said.

He sounded grumpy. He could hear that himself, and tried to change course.

"Anyway, I have a tax scam in Luleå that I need somebody competent to get involved in. Would you like to take it on?"

He regretted it the moment the words had passed his lips.

"You must be joking," Martinsson said slowly. "Don't you even have the sense to be ashamed of what you've done? No, I am not prepared to pick up the crumbs from a rich man's table. But I *am* owed seven weeks' holiday. I'm going on leave as from now. You or von Post can take over the criminal case I'm supposed to be dealing with in court tomorrow, and all the rest of the stuff that's lying on my desk."

"You can't just—"

"Don't you dare say no," she growled. "Or I'll resign."

He became angry.

"Don't be childish," he exclaimed.

"I'm not being childish," she barked. "I'm grown up and pissed off. And so damned disappointed in you. You coward. Whoever would have thought you'd end up sucking von Post's cock?"

He gasped for breath. He seemed to have a steel band clamped around his chest.

"What the . . . That's more than enough . . . I'm hanging up," he roared back. "You can ring me when you've calmed down."

He slammed his mobile down onto his desk. Stood there for a few moments looking at it. Hoping that she would ring him back. Then he would tell her that she should pull her socks up.

"You'd better pull your damned socks up!" he yelled at the mobile, pointing menacingly at it.

He sat down and started rummaging through his papers. He couldn't remember for the life of him what he'd been doing before the call came.

Who did she think she was? How did she dare?

His administrative assistant came in and asked about the following week's court timetable. It took them half an hour to run through it, by which time his anger had ebbed away. He wiped his brow with a handkerchief and sat down on the edge of his desk.

He almost wished that he was angry again. The calm after the storm revealed a mirror in which he could see his own reflection. He was not happy with what he saw.

He should not have handed the case over to von Post. He hadn't been thinking straight. He had simply said: "O.K., take over." And now he found himself in a right pickle. But what was done could not be undone. He did not want her to be angry with him.

"It was wrong," he said out loud to himself.

He pinched his nose and breathed out through his mouth.

And there is no need to start thinking in terms of damned gender roles.

At ten o'clock on the evening of her first day in Kiruna, Hjalmar Lundbohm comes to visit her.

"I saw that the lights were still on," he says by way of explanation. Lizzie curtseys and invites him in.

She and Elina have just washed themselves with the last of the water in the cauldron. Earlier, Lizzie roasted a pork joint American style with a divine onion sauce for the removal men who returned to build the bookcase. So much has happened that Elina feels giddy and bewildered: it seems to be at least a week since she got off the train feeling embarrassed after Lundbohm had marched off with no more than a curt goodbye.

Now she wishes she had put on a rather more elegant blouse, but it had never occurred to her that he might come to visit them.

Lundbohm has come for a specific purpose, of course. He wants Lizzie to have the guest list for dinner the next evening. Lizzie looks surprised. He tends to give her advance notice only when a large-scale gathering has been organised, and not always even then. She curtseys again, and gives Elina a knowing look.

"I expect that fröken Pettersson is used to having a flat of her own," Lundbohm says. "But we're short of space in Kiruna, so it's usual to share."

For God's sake don't make me have to live on my own again, Elina says to herself, but what she actually says is, "I've no doubt the arrangement will work very well. Would you like a cup of coffee?"

Lundbohm would love some coffee, if there is nothing stronger on offer.

And so they drink coffee from traditional wooden mugs. Elina notices that he does not seem to mind that. He is evidently the type who eats simple Lappish food on wooden plates one day, then dines with royalty the next.

He admires the rag rugs, and compliments them on making the flat so snug and homely. He sits on the wooden bench that converts into a double bed at night, and Lizzie says they'll do some painting tomorrow, and hang up some wallpaper. She informs him that the bookcase will be painted blue.

"What are you going to put into that?"

"Books, of course!"

She points at the trunk.

"The new teacher has brought a whole library with her."

Lundbohm looks long and hard at the new teacher. Then he asks if he might be allowed to take a look at the books.

Elina's hands are shaking, but what choice does she have?

And at the same time, she also welcomes the opportunity to show who she is.

When Lizzie sees all the books, she needs to sit down.

"That's amazing," she says. "Have you read them all?"

"Yes," Elina says, with a trace of bravado in her voice. "And I've read some of them several times!"

Lundbohm produces a pince-nez from his pocket.

"Let's have a look, then," he says, and Lizzie takes books out of the chest one by one. They are lovingly packed between linen towels and sheets of tissue paper. Lizzie folds the tissue paper meticulously and piles it up. Lundbohm reads the titles out loud.

Elina just sits there and lets them get on with it. There are so many emotions surging through her. So many voices.

I'm so tired, she thinks when a lump in her throat signals that she is close to tears.

Voices. The women in the village back home who insist on telling her mother that the girl will be driven mad as a result of reading all those books. Who say that she's an idle layabout when she sits there concentrating on her school homework. Snatch the pen out of her hand and tell her she should be helping her mother with the washing up. It is her mother who puts her hand on her daughter's shoulder and prevents her from standing up. Who puts the pen back into her hand and says: "My girl is going to read books. As long as I have the strength to keep going, my daughter is going to study." She recalls her schoolteacher sitting at the kitchen table back home, talking to her mother. "If Elina proceeds to higher education, I'll pay whatever it costs. I don't have any children of my own to pay for."

Lundbohm picks and chooses from among her books, commenting on the ones he has read and asking about the ones he has not.

Elina tells him what he wants to know. She keeps it simple. After all, how could she explain to a man like him that books can save your life? He's no doubt never been more than an arm's length away from the theatre, literature, studies, travels.

But she smiles, and it feels better. She is soon speaking without inhibitions, and whenever she picks up one of her books she is only too happy to make its acquaintance again.

She is also sitting on the kitchen bench that converts into a bed, and soon she has a pile of books on her knee. Unfortunately there is a pile between her and herr Lundbohm as well.

There are books for children, of course – both she and Lundbohm prefer *Huckleberry Finn*, but there is also *Treasure Island* and *The Strange Case of Doctor Jekyll and Mr Hyde*, although Elina explains that the latter is not really for children, and outlines the plot for Lizzie, who shudders in horror but rather likes the feeling. Then

Elina digs out Mary Shelley's *Frankenstein*, and announces that they will be reading aloud from that book every evening.

Lundbohm reads a few paragraphs aloud from Jack London's *Call of the Wild* and *The Sea-Wolf*. Kipling's *Kim* is wrapped up in a towel together with Nobel Prize-winner Rabindranath Tagore's *Song Offerings*.

English and German novels, Selma Lagerlöf, Ellen Key and August Strindberg.

Lundbohm and Elina pass the books to one another, and sometimes, for just a few moments, they are both holding the same book. She leans forward and reads the same text as he is reading. He smells of soap.

He must have washed himself before coming to visit us, she thinks. Does anybody really do that when they are just going to call in on their housekeeper and tell her how many guests there will be for dinner?

Lizzie makes some more coffee, then waves her magic wand and produces some sugar lumps and the special cheese that people up here in the north dip into their coffee. They all drink the sweet coffee, then fish up the lumps of cheese that make crunching sounds as they chew them.

Down at the very bottom of the chest are some books wrapped up in brown paper tied with string.

"Because these books are not all appropriate for being looked at by one's employer," Elina explains with a stiff upper lip.

"Let's see how much this employer can tolerate," Lundbohm says with a laugh, opening the packages one after the other.

First up is the *The Penholder* by Elin Wägner.

"Wägner and Key . . ." Lundbohm says.

"Yes," Elina says. "And Stella Kleve."

They both know what the other is thinking. The teacher sympathises with authors who believe that love is more important than a marriage certificate.

And she buys books, he thinks. That's why she wears worn-out shoes and a scruffy overcoat.

He is possessed by a desire to buy some clothes for her. A pretty blouse. With lace trimmings.

In the next parcel is Fröding's *Splashes and Spray*. No wonder that collection of poetry was wrapped up in brown paper. Fröding was even taken to court for one of his poems.

Elina loves Fröding. How can anybody think that what he writes is obscene? All those poems about loneliness and the longing for love and tenderness. How often did Fröding console her when she sat there in the schoolroom, all alone? He was always even worse off than her, always more of an outsider.

"He didn't die, actually," she says.

Lundbohm closes his eyes as he sits there and recites from memory:

> I sat down there with well-filled glasses,
> drinking all day and all the night,
> dreaming away as well I might
> of alcohol and lovely lasses.

There follow several seconds of silence. Elina is lost for words. A man quoting Gustav Fröding. He did so with the perfect level of restraint in his voice, not too much emotion. He made a short pause between "dreaming away" and "as well I might", so that one almost had the impression he was creating the poem himself, searching for the right words, searching for everything she was searching for herself. Anything that can douse the fever that sometimes takes possession of her – the feeling of restlessness, loneliness.

Lundbohm sits there in silence, his eyes half-closed as if he is dreaming.

I ought to kiss him, she thinks, and is astonished by the reaction of her heart.

She immediately tells herself that she is being stupid. She has only just met the man. He is so much older than she is. And he is fat.

But when she looks at those weary, half-closed eyes and those lips that only a few seconds ago curled slightly to express a stab of pain as he recited somebody else's words that embodied his own longings, she sees a young man in him, even a young boy. She wants to get to know him. To become familiar with all his ages. She wants to know everything about him. She wants to kiss him. To own him.

"Good Lord," Lizzie says. "'Dreaming away of alcohol and lovely lasses'. That's just what my Johan-Albin used to do. Before he met me. He's given up booze now. But I can tell you that I've got some books as well."

She takes out her contribution to the bookcase from one of her suitcases.

Lundbohm comes back to life in delight when he reads titles like *Behind Closed Curtains* and *The Sweetness of Sin*.

He puts on his pince-nez, thumbs through the pages at random, then begins to read:

Leopold slowly put his arm round her, and sent hundreds of white rose petals floating down onto her neck. "My lovely," he whispered and gazed longingly into her eyes. Then he kissed her – one long, passionate kiss.

Now it's Lizzie's turn to close her eyes and listen as if she is sitting in church.

"Lovely!" she says when he has finished reading.

Lundbohm smiles in amusement.

"Aha," says Elina. "So you smile at sentimental novels, do you? I have quite a few of those as well."

She unpacks several brown paper parcels containing cheap paperbacks. There are crime novels featuring Sherlock Holmes and Nick Carter, and the Swedish writer Samuel Duse's books about his detective Leo Carring; also adventure tales, romantic fiction set in the wilds of northern Sweden, mystery yarns, and love stories by the Swedish bestseller Jenny Brun.

The air is now filled with formal dress balls, inheritances, murder by poisoning, crofters' daughters who become wealthy socialites, ghosts, opium dens, gold-mining communities, pirates, grave desecrators, thwarted love, forbidden love, shattered dreams, spies, jealousy, pangs of conscience, baby farmers, swindlers, revenge, sheikhs in the desert, seducers, mysterious strangers, innocent victims, hypnotists, car chases, polar bears, man-eating tigers, charming doctors, unscrupulous criminals, desert islands in the Pacific Ocean, North Pole expeditions, dangers, despair and happy endings.

They read aloud from the blurbs, and admire all the stylish covers.

"What a lot of immoral pornography!" Lundbohm says, smiling at Elina.

She puts her head on one side and indicates that she is a hopeless case.

Lizzie yawns loudly and ostentatiously. Lundbohm stands up at once, as if she has made a trumpet call.

"I'll come and inspect the rest of the books in the near future," he says, pretending to be censorious as he points to the rest of the brown-paper parcels at the bottom of Elina's chest.

They look out of the window and see that it has started snowing in earnest.

"Not again!" Lizzie says with a sigh.

Lundbohm takes his leave. Lizzie and Elina convert the kitchen bench into a bed. As soon as they have put on their nightdresses, they collapse into it.

"I'm so pleased to discover that you are very good at cleaning and laughing," mumbles Lizzie into Elina's ear. "You're just what the doctor ordered."

Then they both fall asleep.

Lundbohm walks home through the snow. There is no sign of life in the streets. He is in remarkably high spirits. He has not had so much fun for a very long time. Albeit with his housekeeper and the new teacher.

He says her name out loud. He's feeling that childish. The sound doesn't travel far. The dancing snowflakes swallow up his voice.

"Elina," he says. "Elina."

Rebecka Martinsson knocked on Krister Eriksson's door. He lived in a brown-painted four-roomed detached house in Hjortvägen. It was good of him to look after Marcus. She wondered how things had gone. A chorus of barking dogs could be heard from inside the house.

She went in, squatted down and greeted them all. Tintin stood there with great dignity, all four paws on the floor, and allowed herself to be tickled under her neck while curling her lip in the direction of young Roy, making it clear that he would have to wait his turn. The Brat was unworthy of her attention, and she ignored him as he crawled and slithered around Martinsson, whimpering and trying to lick her face. His mistress, his lovely mistress – where had she been all this time? Vera said a brief hello, but then returned to the kitchen. Krister was frying thin slices of reindeer meat, which were spitting and crackling in the pan.

Marcus came crawling up on all fours.

He was wearing a jumper that was a little on the large side.

Newly bought, Martinsson thought.

The boy's fair hair was hanging down over his eyes. His arms and legs seemed thin and spindly.

It's not easy to deal with children, Martinsson thought. You could ask a grown-up how he was. If you could do anything to help. Express your sympathy. But what can you do with a young boy who comes crawling up to you on all fours?

"Hello, Marcus," she said in the end.

He barked eagerly at her in response.

"Well, well," said Martinsson to Eriksson with a laugh. "Have you found yourself a new dog?"

"I certainly have," Eriksson said, also laughing. "It's a wild dog Vera found wandering about in the forest. Isn't that right?"

"Wuff!" Marcus said, nodding his head.

"He hasn't got a name yet," Eriksson said. "What do you think?"

Martinsson stroked Marcus's head and caressed his back.

Terrific, she thought. At least I understand dogs.

The boy crawled off into the living room, and returned with a tennis ball. It was too big for him to hold it in his teeth, so he held it in one hand in front of his mouth.

"There's a good dog! Fetch!"

She threw the tennis ball away. The Brat and Marcus scampered after it.

When Eriksson put the question, she said she would love to stay for dinner. Reindeer meat with preserved raw lingonberries, mashed potatoes and a brown sauce. Marcus ate his dinner out of a bowl on the floor. Vera sat patiently beside him, hoping she would be given the remains.

After dinner Marcus went out into the garden, which was enclosed by a wire Gunnebo fence. While waiting for the coffee water to boil, Eriksson started the washing up.

"He seems thrilled to bits, sleeping in the kennel outside," he said. "I reckoned that if he wants to be a dog, and is happy pretending to be one, then why not?"

"Why not indeed? A police officer from Umeå will be coming tomorrow: she's apparently very good at interviewing children. Maybe she can get Marcus to remember things?"

"Who's going to look after him? Has that been decided yet?"

"His grandma's cousin will take him. Maja Larsson. She's living in Kurravaara at the moment – her mother's in hospital. I'll give her your number."

Eriksson nodded.

"He's welcome to stay here. One extra dog doesn't make much difference . . . I heard about that von Post business . . ."

Martinsson squashed some crispbread crumbs on the table with her fingernails.

"I've been sidelined," she said. "Björnfot has handed the investigation over to von Post."

"Good Lord! But why?"

"He says it's because we could lay ourselves open to objections due to the fact that I live in the same village as the murder victim. But I think it's mainly because von Post is desperate to take the case on. And that Alf simply . . ."

She shrugged rather than finish the sentence.

"Have you spoken to him?"

"Rather briefly."

She waited until Eriksson had put a mug in front of her and filled it with coffee before continuing.

"I called him a cocksucker."

He burst out laughing.

"Well done! It's good that you haven't let it get you down."

Martinsson grinned and blew into her mug.

"You mustn't take these things personally," she said, trying to sound reasonable. "I drew a heart round his behaviour and tried to see it from his point of view"

"The cocksucker's point of view."

Eriksson looked at Martinsson. He had put her in a good mood. He wanted to do that always. Cheer her up when she was out of sorts. She was smiling broadly. He could see her tongue. Her lips were red.

Without warning his head was filled with images. He was forced to turn away from the table and start fiddling with the washing up. Did she have to keep moving all the time? Shaking her head. Raising her shoulders so that the movement of her breasts was visible under her jumper.

"I don't know what got into me," she said. "I was so angry. And it all happened so quickly. But now . . ."

She shrugged, and looked sad and tired.

"That's not so surprising, I'd have thought," Eriksson said. "It's natural to be hurt and angry. If you're badly treated."

"Yes. But I've no intention of turning up while they are investigating the murder. I'm going to take all the leave that's owing to me."

She took a couple of gulps of her coffee and tapped at the mug with her fingernail.

"What do you think happened to her?" she said.

"I don't know," he said softly, as if he were afraid Marcus might hear even though he was outside. "All that pointless stabbing, over and over again. Maybe somebody in the village who lost his rag. Sol-Britt was an outsider, after all. People gossiped about her. Some loony might react to that. The type that murders a celebrity, or somebody the village calls a whore."

"Guilt," Martinsson muttered. "A whole village has been sitting at their kitchen tables calling Sol-Britt Uusitalo a whore. Pointing the finger. And then somebody loses control. Picks her as the one to stab to death. Who's guilty? The whole village? Me? Because I live there and preferred not to know about such things, not to see?"

Eriksson did not answer. Martinsson was staring fixedly at the bottom of her coffee mug, as if the truth could be found in the dregs. Then she gave a start. Remembered that she was supposed to be doing something for Sivving, for Christ's sake. She got a grip on herself and thanked Eriksson for the meal.

Then she left. Took the Brat with her, but left Vera behind for Marcus's sake.

Eriksson remained standing in the kitchen. Feeling a bit confused. As always when she tumbled into and out of his existence.

He wondered if the Wild Dog might perhaps fancy some ice cream for afters.

Anna-Maria Mella sat at her kitchen table, eating a cold pancake. Her knife and fork lay undisturbed at the side of her plate, and she was eating the pancake as if it were a sandwich – without even bothering to heat it up in the microwave. Robert and the children had spent the whole day at his sister's. She was able to think about whatever she liked, in peace and quiet.

What a bloody mess!

She put her elbows on the table. Lingonberry jam dripped down onto the tablecloth. She scraped it up with her index finger, which she then licked clean.

Ought she to have told von Post to go to hell today? Should she have been loyal to Martinsson?

She realised that there was nobody she could ask about this.

There was no point in talking to Robert. She knew what he would say. "Oh, come on! You were not the one who removed Rebecka from the investigation. Why should you turn awkward squad because somebody else had her replaced? You should just carry on doing your job. I don't understand your problem."

Some people were able to talk to their mothers. She had never been able to do that. Her parents lived down in Lombolo, and they only met about once a month. She couldn't force Jenny and Petter to accompany her anymore, so they hardly ever met their grandma and granddad. And in any case, her mother was not all that interested. She liked babies: they were good fun and easy to cope with. But older children were a nuisance, kicked up a noise and ran about all over the place. Especially Mella's children. Mella's brother lived in Piteå, and her mother used to go on and on about his children – how well they were doing, and how nice and calm and clever they were. And as for Mella's father . . .

She sighed. Her father used to go for walks, and kept a close check on the weather. That was his life. Why had her parents sold their house? When they had it he could spend hours pottering about in the house and garden, but now all he did was go for endless walks. He would be most upset if his daughter started going on about problems at work.

And I don't have any girlfriends, she thought as she started taking clean crockery out of the dishwasher.

But is it really my fault? She made a threatening gesture with a fork before putting it away in a drawer. I work full-time and have four children. How could I make time for girlfriends? Or the strength to cope with them? If we were ever to arrange to have a beer at Ferrum or to go to the gym together, you can bet your life that one of the children would fall ill. And after a while folk get tired of that sort of thing. They find other people to go to the cinema with.

Mella closed the dishwasher and picked up a tea towel to do some drying.

The kitchen looked quite tidy now. Admittedly the tea towel smelled of old napkins, but there was no unwashed crockery lying around, no obvious dirt traps. If only the family would go and visit relatives more often, she would be able to make their home neat and tidy.

Then Jenny came into the kitchen. She filled a glass with water, took an apple and leaned against the bench.

"How's it been today?" Mella said.

"O.K.," said Jenny in a tone of voice that suggested this wasn't a time for discussing matters.

I could ask her, Mella thought. If I dared.

Jenny would no doubt be disappointed. Would have thought that her mother should obviously have supported a colleague she liked who had been sidelined.

She's so young, Mella thought in self-defence. Everything is black or white as far as she's concerned. Or else she's right. Probably she's right.

Jenny suddenly stood up and looked at her.

"How are you, Mum? Louise wrote on Facebook that she saw you on the telly today."

Without warning she threw her arms around Mella – the apple in one hand, the glass of water in the other.

"You need a hug," she said with her mouth up against her mother's shoulder.

Mella stood stock still. Held the smelly tea towel as far away as possible, so that the stink wouldn't scare Jenny into beating a retreat.

Life goes by so fast – a hundred-metre runner who laughs at her as she flies past.

It was not all that long since Jenny used to lie in Mella's arms, sucked her breasts. Who was this long-legged, made-up young woman?

Stop, time! Mella commanded, closing her eyes.

But the moment had already passed. Mella's mobile rang in her pocket. Jenny let go of her and left the kitchen.

It was Fred Olsson.

"Sol-Britt Uusitalo's mobile," he said without beating about the bush.

It sounded as if he had food in his mouth.

"I've worked my way through it. Retrieved her erased text messages as well. I think you ought to see them."

Kiruna was a black silhouette against the graphite-grey sky: the huge granite terraces on the mountain where the entrances to the iron ore seams were located; the skeleton-like clock tower of the town hall; the triangular church perched on the mountainside like a Lappish shack.

There was a ring on Krister Eriksson's doorbell.

"Maja Larsson," the woman said, holding out her hand. Eriksson shook it.

"I'm Sol-Britt Uusitalo's cousin," she said. "I'm supposed to collect Marcus."

She was good-looking. About sixty, he would say. Her hair tumbled down from her head in a thousand silver plaits.

He noted that she did not react to his own appearance. Some people would stare hard into his eyes as they spoke, making sure that their gaze didn't happen to fall onto his burnt skin or his mouse-like ears. And when he looked away, or was busy with something else, they were unable to tear their eyes away from his face.

He noticed nothing of that sort with Maja Larsson. She looked at him as his sister did, or as people who knew him so well that they had forgotten how different he looked.

"Would you like a bite to eat?" he said when they came into the kitchen. "There's still some of the dinner left – I can pop it into the microwave if you fancy something."

She said yes please, and duly ate what she was given. She seemed tired. For a moment he thought she would fall asleep at his kitchen table. She blinked slowly, like a child.

"I heard that your mother is ill," he said. "I can look after Marcus if you like."

She looked grateful for that suggestion.

"Perhaps we can share him?"

After the meal they went out to the dog kennel. It was dark, but Marcus had equipped himself with blankets, a torch and some comics. Vera was also lying inside. When Eriksson asked him to come out, the only response was a chorus of loud barking – and it wasn't Vera.

"He's a wild dog," Eriksson said.

"Is he dangerous?"

"No, I think he's very friendly."

No matter how much they tried to persuade him, the Wild Dog refused to come out. He yelped and growled after everything they said.

"He doesn't know me at all," Larsson said quietly. "He seems to feel safe in there. Perhaps he saw something when Sol-Britt . . ."

"He's welcome to stay here," Eriksson whispered.

"Are you sure? Thank you very much."

She then said aloud, "Even if he is friendly, I don't think I dare take that wild dog with me. Maybe I can come back and stroke him tomorrow?"

"What does the Wild Dog have to say to that?" Eriksson said. "Is that alright with you?"

"Wuff!" was the response from inside the kennel.

Larsson said thank you for the meal. Eriksson said it was a pleasure – there was food left over after all: Martinsson had not eaten very much.

She gave him a quick smile. She's one of those people who can read a man's thoughts, he told himself after she had left.

He felt he had been unmasked. She realised that he enjoyed letting her know that Martinsson had been there.

Fred Olsson sat down in Mella's visitor's armchair, and handed over a printout to both her and von Post. Von Post was sitting on the edge of Mella's desk.

"These are the erased text messages I extracted from Sol-Britt Uusitalo's mobile. I've marked the ones I think might be of interest. It might be possible to dig out a few more, but to do that we'd have to send the handset to Ibas."

"What's that?" Mella said, shifting her desk chair so that she could see Olsson. Von Post had been sitting in the way.

"It's a company that specialises in retrieving data. In the Iraq war some gang or other had shot and destroyed a hard disk with an A.K.5 – three bullet holes, all the way through. The Yanks sent it to Ibas and they were able to rescue ninety-five per cent of the contents."

"Wow!"

"Mind you, it didn't contain anything of interest. It was just a flight simulator. Hardly worth the three hundred thousand they had to cough up for it."

"Very good," said von Post. "It's a bonus to have an I.T. wizard in the team. Have you thought of applying for a job at the National Forensic Laboratory?"

Olsson caught Mella's eye: they were on the same wavelength. Then he stared down at the document and said nothing.

If only I were a bit quicker on the uptake, Mella thought. Grin and make a witty reply instead of just sitting there, long-faced and silent. I'd have had a seat on the National Police Board by now. Or at the very least a job in Luleå.

"*Come on round then, if you're feeling randy*", Sol-Britt had written to somebody. "*Marcus is asleep.*" "*It's not on – Maja is here.*" "*Mmm, you're welcome to try that on me.*" "*Me as well.*" "*Kiss and goodnight.*"

Under the heading "INBOX" four messages attracted her attention. "*Is it O.K. if I drop in?*" "*Can't wait! What about you?*" "*She's away with the fairies – can I call in?*" "*Fancy a shag?*"

"So she had a boyfriend. Who sent these messages?" Mella asked.

Olsson shrugged.

"It's a Telia number. I looked it up, but it's one of those pay-as-you-go cards. And it's not registered, so . . ."

He shrugged again.

"But one good thing is that you can check up on which transmitter the message was sent by. So you know to within a radius of two kilometres where he was at the time. If the text message was sent from Lombolo in the evening, it's a fair guess that he lives out there. If it was sent from the mine during the day, well, it's reasonable to assume that he works there."

"Excellent," von Post said. "Good work."

"And I think," Olsson said without taking his eyes off Mella, "that Telia sells bundles of pay-as-you-go cards to retailers. So that should mean we could track down who sold him the card, and when it was activated."

"Somebody might well remember something," Mella said, nodding her approval.

Von Post agreed.

"But what about this?" Mella said, pointing to a text message. "It was sent the day before yesterday. To her cousin Maja Larsson."

I must send him packing, we can't go on like this, it said.

Von Post stood up.

"Surely Martinsson spoke to Maja Larsson, didn't she?"

"Yes, of course," Mella said.

"But she didn't discover that there was a lover involved! And that Sol-Britt evidently broke off the relationship! What the hell did they do, then? Drink coffee?"

Probably, Mella thought. God only knows how much coffee we get through . . .

"Right, we must go there," von Post said. "Now!"

It took half a second for Mella to realise that he meant they should call on Larsson and not Martinsson.

"Who are you going to send there?" she asked.

"I want to talk to her myself. You're all welcome to come as well. Let's go there all together."

Mella stood up. It was gone eleven at night. Larsson might well have gone to bed. Dragging people out of their beds made them scared, sometimes aggressive. The police became enemies.

But Sol-Britt Uusitalo had been in a relationship with somebody. And Larsson knew about it.

It's always somebody they know, Mella thought despondently. A man they were close to. Somebody they were madly in love with.

Olsson seemed hesitant.

"Do I really have to come as well?" he said.

On her second day in Kiruna, Elina Pettersson puts on her best blouse and tries to convince herself that it is because this is her first day at her new school. She is going to meet her pupils, and the two other teachers.

But she thinks about herr Lundbohm as she pinches her cheeks to give them a rosy glow, and bites her lips to make them really red.

There is no sign of him, not at school during the day nor at home in the evening when she thought he might turn up to inspect the rest of her books wrapped up in brown paper.

Not the following day either. Nor the day after that.

Almost two weeks pass.

Elina cannot stop thinking about him. She tells herself to stop being so silly, but it does not help.

She thinks about him when she reads aloud for the children from *Huckleberry Finn*, making them laugh out loud, and when they sit there open-mouthed, enchanted by the account of Engineer Andrée's hot-air balloon expedition and its mysterious disappearance. This would be a good time for him to march into the classroom and say, "No, no, don't let me disturb you," tell her to continue reading about Andrée and sit there with the children for a while.

She thinks about him when the sun shines over the snow and she is being followed by a gang of handsome young workmen who are keen to invite her to a cup of coffee and offer to carry her books. If only he were to come walking towards her and see that she was never in danger of sitting around all by herself – if that's what he thought!

She thinks about him when she and Lizzie switch off the electric lights in the evening, and she feels a pang of pain in the region of her heart. She and Lizzie have so much fun together, but it is a strain to have to share a bed with her. Elina lies there awake, throbbing with emotion and longing as she feels Lizzie's warm breath on her skin as a sort of reminder, a knocking on the door of her desire. For him.

She tries to concentrate on her work. The pupils are pretty awful up here as well.

Ellen, Ellen: Elina prays to her Ellen Key. When will all these young children see an improvement in their living conditions?

But at least in Kiruna they have shoes to wear so that they can walk to school; the poor relief authorities see to that. Needless to say the classroom smells of dirt and wet wool and soaked reindeer-skin shoes, but at least it doesn't smell of the cowshed. And the windows can be opened. When the sun is shining, it's possible to have fresh air in the classroom.

She and Lizzie attract four lodgers. And they start baking bread in the mornings to sell to the miners. Lizzie never seems to feel tired. She is the one who wakes Elina up in the mornings with a wooden mug of coffee, by which time she has already made the dough.

"It's not even five o'clock yet, and we're already ten kronor richer," she says, and they sit for a while on the edge of the bed, dunking yesterday's bread in the hot coffee.

Elina makes an effort not to seem all that interested in what Lizzie has been doing at work. Nevertheless, she is informed about what Lundbohm has had for dinner every day – and thank goodness, it seems that his guests are usually men.

Didn't he feel anything? she wonders. When their hands touched.

Was she the only one who felt a warm, throbbing stream flowing through her veins?

Love is like a noose. At first it hangs slack around her neck. But then, the further away he goes, the tighter it becomes.

If only he had fallen for her like a ton of bricks. If only he had courted her assiduously. Then she might not have felt the need to think about him every minute of every day.

Men! she thought angrily. There are thirteen of them to the dozen.

Then, almost a fortnight after their evening with the books, he suddenly appears in the doorway of her classroom. The pupils have all gone home, and she is genuinely surprised to see him.

"Good Lord, it's the managing director!" she exclaims, and a hint of a smile appears on her lips.

A smile that is exactly right for a senior teacher, a chairman of the school governors, a headmaster or a managing director of a mine.

But then she falls silent because her heart is bouncing around inside her chest, despite her strict orders for it to be still. He is carrying an oblong-shaped parcel wrapped in brown paper under his arm.

"I've got a present for you," he says, and hands over the parcel.

"Thank you," she says.

Then she abandons her feigned indifference, sets her heart free and allows it to scamper around wherever it likes. She looks him shamelessly in the eye.

"Would it be safe to open it here and now?"

"I would advise strongly against it," he says, and smiles at her like a little boy. "But perhaps you might like to consider drinking a glass of port wine at the house, and opening it in peace and quiet?"

She says amen to that, and they walk side by side to the mine's administrative area. Every time they happen to touch one another, she starts trembling. It's almost unbearable.

The managing director's residence is a simple blockhouse with a fairly recent extension.

"It was a bit on the modest side to start with," he says, "but that's the way I wanted it. It should blend in with the countryside around here. And with the workers' houses."

Yes, that is something she knows about him already. His modesty. She has heard it being discussed in Kiruna. How Lundbohm goes around wearing a red working-man's shirt, and is mistaken for a nobody when high-ranking gentlemen come to visit the town. And how he mixes with the Lapps, and sits in coffee bars chatting to people. And she has heard that he has a big heart. But she also knows that the residence is reminiscent of Anders Zorn's country house and Carl Larsson's Sundborn, since both those artists were consulted and gave advice to the builders.

So much for modesty, then, she thinks.

He is in fact a snob, although he tries hard to give the impression that he does not care about outward appearances. But that is just how she wants him to be. This character weakness simply makes him more human, and fills her with tenderness. Who can love perfection? No, love requires solicitude, and solicitude requires the loved one to have faults, requires wounds, frailty. Love wants to heal. Perfection has no need of healing. Perfection cannot be loved, merely worshipped.

He invites her into his study. An open fire is crackling away in the hearth, and there is a tray with cold cuts – smoked reindeer meat and ptarmigan breast. Goodies that Lizzie or one of the maids will have prepared and carried in.

They eat, and he asks her about how she is settling in, and her first impressions of the remote far north.

Then it is time to open the parcel. She fiddles with the ribbons, unwraps the brown paper, and finds herself holding Sigmund Freud's *Die Traumdeutung*.

She has heard about that. About the interpretation of dreams. Our dreams are not in fact messages from our forefathers or from the gods, but they reveal our forbidden desires.

Freud has many disciples, she knows that. But no doubt most people still dismiss him as a dirty-minded Jew.

The forbidden desires are to do with sex. She doesn't dare open the book with him standing by her side.

"Thank you," she says. "How did you know that I can read German?"

"You had Goethe in your trunk."

Ah, yes: of course she did. She feels so warm. Perhaps it's the open fire, she thinks. And the wine.

She starts laughing. Says thank you again. And on the spur of the moment she kisses the book's front cover.

"There you are, you see. A forbidden desire," he mutters, and looks at her from behind his half-closed, dreamy eyelids.

Then she puts the book down on his desk.

I must make the move, she thinks.

I'm too young, too pretty. He would never dare.

She puts her arms around his neck, kisses him, presses herself up against him.

For a whole second he does nothing, and she just has time to think: oh my God, I've got it wrong, he doesn't want me at all.

Then he puts his arms around her body. His tongue finds its way into her mouth. They are breathing hard, sweating already.

And she feels so happy. She has to hold him off for a moment so that she can laugh. And as she laughs she feels she could just as well cry. Because he does in fact want her. Because they both want the same thing. And everything is so lovely and so right.

They undress each other – or at least, open up. So that what is going to happen can happen. They unfasten buttons and belts. Up with skirts and down with trousers.

His fingers are exploring her already. She is sitting on the edge of his desk, and thinking in some far distant part of her brain that she mustn't get ink stains on her skirt as she couldn't afford to deal with that.

But then she stops thinking, and he penetrates her. He has more staying power than she had thought.

He looks her in the eye all the time, never looks away, his feelings are genuine. This really is love.

And he is skilful. So much so that afterwards, when he leans his forehead gratefully on her shoulder, she has to try not to think about where he has learnt such skills, who has taught him.

"So you're not going to work tomorrow, then?"

Sivving spread out a newspaper – an old issue of *Norrländska Socialdemokraten* – on the table and handed over a tin of boot-leather wax and a nylon stocking to Martinsson. When she came with the food provisions he had ordered, he had instructed her to go back home immediately and fetch her winter boots.

"If you didn't wax them last spring, you really must do so without delay," he had said when she protested. "It'll start snowing any day now. Maybe tomorrow! There's no time to lose!"

And so she had trudged back home and fetched her winter shoes and Prada boots. She would have preferred to lounge in front of the television in splendid isolation . . . But instead, they were sitting on either side of the Perstorp-laminated table in Sivving's boiler room, waxing boots.

"No," she said, buffing up the leather with the nylon stocking, "they'll have to get by without me. Björnfot or von Post will have to take over my cases."

Bella was lying on her back on the sofa beside her, fast asleep with her back legs outstretched and her ears inside out.

The Brat had been allowed to borrow Bella's elk horn, and was lying at Martinsson's feet, chewing away at it. A crackling, scraping sound. It was hard. But tasty. Occasionally he paused, his head leaning on the bowl-shaped horn, as if it were a pillow.

"Good," Sivving said, heaving himself to his feet in order to fetch some glue he thought would be just the thing to stick down a sole that had come loose from the shoe he had just been waxing. The front of the shoe looked like an open mouth.

"In that case you can help me to carry in firewood."

She nodded. Last spring they had piled up some newly chopped wood in a neat circular heap with the bark pointing upwards, so that it would dry out in the sun. There must be at least three cubic metres to carry into the woodshed, but that was O.K.: she was looking forward to the effort involved. Then going to bed with aching muscles and a tired back.

"Have you eaten?" he said.

"I had a meal at Krister's."

Sivving looked extremely pleased, though he did his best to disguise the fact.

"Maybe he can help us with the wood as well," he said offhandedly.

No doubt he would love to, Martinsson thought.

Eriksson and Sivving liked to pretend that all three of them were part of the same family. Sivving needed help with various things. Eriksson often called on him to replace a broken kitchen tap, or to shovel snow, or to fix his computer. Then they would invite Martinsson round for a meal. Or ask her to look after the dogs while they drove into Kiruna to buy some valves or some superglue, or God only knows what. As if Sivving was her aged dad.

She did not worry about it. They were welcome to get on with it, if it kept them happy. Måns didn't like it at all, of course. If Krister and Sivving were around when Måns rang, she would move to another room. Sometimes she would say: Sivving and I are doing this or that – without mentioning Eriksson. But Måns was suspicious and would ask: "What about that policeman from outer space – is he there as well?"

She didn't know why it had to be like that – she had nothing to hide.

Well, not all that much, in any case. She sometimes thought about his hands. And the fact that he was in such good physical shape. She sometimes thought about how he made her happy.

It occurred to her that she had left her mobile in the car. Maybe Måns had tried to ring her. She ought to go and fetch it. But decided not to. She never used to leave it lying around. Always had it with her, even when she was in the bathroom. She was always expecting him to phone her.

"How's Marcus?" Sivving wondered.

"I don't know. He was pretending to be a dog all the time he was with Krister. He seems to be somehow oblivious."

"Poika riepu," Sivving said with a sigh. "Poor boy. Both his dad and his grandma dead. He has nobody left. They really are an accident-prone family."

"They certainly are," Martinsson said, feeling something stirring deep down inside her.

Like a grass snake swimming in still waters.

"And then there's Sol-Britt's dad," she said. "He was devoured by a bear."

"By Jove yes, those hunters must have had a shock when they found the remains of Frans Uusitalo in the bear's stomach. Did you hear, the bear was so big they had to call in Patrik Mäkitalo from Luleå. And that dog of his."

I hate coincidence, Martinsson thought.

While she was an articled law clerk in Stockholm, she had met a police officer who used to say that as a sort of mantra. He was dead now. But the mantra had stuck with her. I hate coincidence.

If the whole family is wiped out . . .

But then, the old man was devoured by a bear, she thought. Not murdered.

But she couldn't stop thinking about it. There had been too many deaths in that family.

144

Sivving contemplated his shiny winter boots with the feeling of satisfaction that only genuine shoe care can endow.

"My mum used to say that Hjalmar Lundbohm was Frans Uusitalo's father," he said.

Martinsson sat up and paid attention.

"What? The managing director of the mine? With that teacher who was also murdered?"

"Yes," he said, taking a deep breath. "I recall my mum saying that a lot of people thought he ought to have settled down when he'd fallen in love. But nothing came of it."

"Because she was murdered."

"Yes. Or maybe they split up before that. I don't know. Nobody said anything about it afterwards. I know my mum sort of bit her tongue after she'd told me about it. Sol-Britt knew, but she never spoke about it either. She told me once when she was – well, let's say, not completely sober, and on a war footing with men in general and with one of hers in particular. But you had to turn a blind eye to it. Pretend that you weren't even born when it happened."

Martinsson could see Hjalmar Lundbohm before her very eyes. A portrait of the man who built up Kiruna and was managing director of the mining company from 1900 to 1920: he always seemed to be overweight with heavy, drooping eyelids. Not a good-looking man.

"I gather he never married?" she asked.

"That wasn't because he had anything against women – according to what I've heard, in any case."

Sivving looked hard at her.

"Anyway," he said. "Shall we have a little nightcap? And then it's time for you to go to bed. You have to be up early tomorrow in order to carry wood for me. Don't forget that."

Martinsson promised.

Winter is beating a retreat. Hjalmar Lundbohm and the school-teacher Elina Pettersson fall madly in love.

The late winter snow is sighing and dripping tears. Icicles as long as church steeples. The streets are covered in mud and slush. Trees are trembling as they long for spring. The snow is still a metre or more deep in the forest, but the sun is warming everything up. Nobody needs to feel cold for a while, at least: spring is on its way, God bless it!

They make love with wild abandon. Tell each other that they have never felt like this before. Think that nobody could ever have felt like this. Believe that they were made for each other. Compare their hands and find that they are almost identical.

"Like brother and sister," they say, placing the palms of their hands together, and feeling that they want to remain in Lundbohm's bedroom for evermore.

"I'll lock the door and swallow the key," he says when she gets up in the early morning so she can slink away without being seen.

But like everybody who is madly in love, they are careless.

Lundbohm sends a messenger boy to the school. He knocks on the classroom door and hands over an envelope.

Elina can't wait to open it, and reads it to herself in front of the class as her cheeks become bright red.

"Dear Schoolma'am," it reads, "on the advice of my doctor I have stuffed my underpants full of snow. It doesn't help."

She writes a reply while the boy waits.

"Herr Lundbohm," she writes, "I'm standing in front of a class of children. This must stop."

If anybody else reads this, they'll think we're short of chairs, she thinks.

In May the nights start to become light. They lie awake, talking. Making love and talking. Making love again. She can talk to him about anything at all. He is interested in everything. He is curious and educated.

"Tell me something," she sometimes says. "Anything at all."

Outside in the light of the night male ptarmigans are running around over the snow, laughing away in ghostly fashion. Pygmy owls and hawk owls are hooting. Arctic foxes sob like babies as they listen for field mice beneath the covering of frozen snow.

They sometimes tiptoe down into the kitchen. Eat leftovers of ptarmigan breast, artic char, reindeer fillet with cold sauce and jelly, jam, white bread. They drink full-cream cow's milk or beer. Making love makes you hungry.

The people in Kiruna are not used to seeing the managing director around so often. He travels a lot. He spends most of his time in Stockholm. But he goes abroad as well. To Germany, America and Canada.

He is never normally to be seen in Kiruna during the summer, for instance. He could no doubt face up to it snowing at midsummer, but he would have problems with all the mosquitoes and gnats, those blood-sucking pests.

But in the summer of 1914 he astonishes the citizens of Kiruna by staying at home all the time. People think this is because of the war. On June 28 Archduke Franz Ferdinand and his consort are murdered in broad daylight in Sarajevo. That sparks off a whole series of declarations of war. It means business for the mine in Kiruna. The King of Lapland is in excellent spirits.

But that is not because money is rolling in. He is in love. That is why.

Martinsson walked home through the dark. She was thinking about what Sivving had told her about Sol-Britt's family. Her father had been mauled and eaten by a bear. Her son had been run over. Her paternal grandmother, the schoolteacher who had an affair with the one and only Hjalmar Lundbohm, had been murdered. And Sol-Britt herself had been stabbed to death with a hayfork.

She collected her mobile phone from her car. She had missed a call from Måns. He had left a message: *Hi there, it's me. Ring if you have time.*

That was all.

What do you mean, "ring if you have time"? she thought, and was filled with a mixture of guilt and anger, and a need to defend herself against an accusation he would deny he had made.

She could write a whole essay on that message.

He seems to be trying to get his own back, she thought as she walked up the steps.

The Brat ran up the steps in front of her. Stood wagging his tail outside the door to the suite of rooms on the upper floor. Just as pleased and expectant at the thought of coming home as of going out.

Getting his own back for what? she thought as she listened to the crackling sound from the dry birch bark as she lit a fire in the stove in the bedroom.

She washed her face and wiped away her make-up. The Brat had already settled down in her bed.

Because she hadn't rung. Because she hadn't answered her phone. She ought to ring him now. But she didn't want to. "If you have time" squeezed all the positive feelings out of her.

Damn it all, she thought. Why can't he simply write "I'm longing to be with you"?

She sent him a text message: *Tired worked all eve bed time now g.n.*

Then she changed "g.n" to "goodnight". She wondered if she ought to add "love you", but decided not to. She sent the text then switched off her mobile. Disconnected the landline as well.

And she did not set the alarm clock either – she was not going to go to work the next morning.

Her thoughts turned to von Post and her boss, Björnfot. It was dereliction of duty not to take on the cases she was supposed to do.

But they can go to hell, she thought angrily.

She closed her eyes, but couldn't go to sleep. The Brat was too warm, jumped off the bed and lay down under the kitchen table.

Sol-Britt's family. Rather too much bad luck, too many accidents.

After a while she felt for her mobile and phoned Sivving.

"What actually happened in that hit-and-run case?" she said.

"What?" Sivving said, half asleep. "Has something happened?"

"Sol-Britt's son. That hit-and-run case. What actually happened?"

"Good God! What time is it? Nobody knows. As I said, they never caught whoever did it. One of those bastards . . . Just left him to die at the side of the road. It was some time before they found him. He'd been flung behind some osier bushes."

I hate coincidence, Martinsson thought again.

"Now listen here, young lady," Sivving said brusquely. "Think about that tomorrow. Goodnight!"

Martinsson had barely registered that he had hung up when the mobile rang again, and she answered.

It was Måns.

"Hello," she said in her most seductive voice. Her irritation was all gone now.

"Hello," he responded. His voice was teddy bears, warm blankets, a cup of tea and foot massage.

Silence ensued.

Who was going to start? It was as if they were proceeding with caution now, a reluctance to make the first move. "I'll be damned if I'm going to", or "Why is it always me who has to?" Perhaps also a worry that the other one would not respond with the same degree of vulnerable affection.

It was Måns who played his cards first.

"How are you, my diddle-diddle darling? I've been following the news today – but it wasn't somebody you knew, was it?"

No complaints because she hadn't phoned him. Just affectionate solicitude.

"No, but I've had an . . . interesting day. I don't know where to start."

"Come on, tell Daddy all about it."

"Huh," she said, pretending to be reluctant as always.

Then she told him. About the murder. About how she had been swept aside from the investigation. About her row with Björnfot.

He laughed at the thought of her quarrelling with her boss.

"That's my girl," he said.

Måns said nothing about how he would happily wipe his arse with documents lying on the desk of a chief prosecutor in the far north of Sweden. He said nothing at all.

Martinsson melted. She was well aware that if she had continued working for Måns at Meijer & Ditzinger, one of the biggest firms of solicitors in Sweden, she would have been earning three times as much as she was making now. She knew that Måns thought she was wasting her talents as a prosecutor in the far north of the country, that she might just as well be working on the checkout at a local supermarket, and that he very much wanted her to go back and be with him in Stockholm. She knew that. But she was pleased that he hadn't raised the matter.

"That's great," he said instead, in his sexiest voice. "You can come here and lie in my bed waiting for me to come home from work. At last we can get our relationship back on track."

"I can take a holiday," he said after a moment's thought. "How about a trip to somewhere exciting? The West Indies? South Africa? I have a mate who sells fantastic themed holidays in China and India – I could have a word with him. Shall I do that?"

"Yes, do that," Martinsson said.

She didn't want to travel anywhere at all, but she didn't have the strength to argue with Måns as well. One major row a day was quite enough.

She knew what Måns was like. He did things so quickly. He was quite capable of booking a holiday for the pair of them in the West Indies while they were still talking on the telephone. But if he was going to have a chat with his friend, that gave her a little respite. Her mind was in turmoil. She would have to pack a suitcase. Otherwise: ahoy, Captain, stand by for a major storm. Only a few seconds ago she had felt so good, talking to him: but now she found herself trapped in a corner.

"I love you," she said, although that was not how she was feeling just now. "I must go to bed."

I'm out of my mind, she thought. One moment I'm in love, the next I'm running away. How on earth does he put up with me?

"Goodnight," he said. His voice was different now.

He didn't tell her he loved her. She could hear him thinking: *I'm certainly not going to. Why am I the one who always has to?*

They hung up.

*

Måns Wenngren concluded his call to Rebecka Martinsson. He felt restless, not in the least tired. If only he'd had somebody to go out with, he'd have gone to Riche and ordered a vodka martini or two.

He regretted having made the call.

I ought to hold back, he thought. Trying to love her is like trying to squeeze a handful of sand.

Bloody woman, he thought, examining himself in the mirror.

Handsome top dog? Old man? He would go to Riche anyway, and have a glass or two. Just sit there, observing beautiful women. Much better than gaping at "Mad Men" on the telly, all alone in his flat.

Martinsson looked dejectedly at her mobile.

Take no thought for the morrow, for the morrow shall take thought for the things of itself, as it said in the Good Book.

Her mobile ting-a-linged yet again. She thought it would be a text message from Måns, but it was from Eriksson.

The Wild Dog, Roy and, believe it or not, Vera are racing around here for all they are worth, making deep scratches in the parquet floor. Tintin thinks animal welfare should take all the others into custody. I hope the Wild Dog will soon be domesticated.

All her depression faded away in a flash.

She could see in her mind's eye how Vera and Marcus and Roy were chasing each other round the living room table, while Tintin sat in the kitchen, staring accusingly at Eriksson.

Marcus is really enjoying himself. Eriksson is doing a great job. Kind and playful and . . .

She fell asleep with her mobile in her hand.

District Prosecutor von Post and Inspectors Mella, Stålnacke, Olsson and Rantakyrö drove to Kurravaara to interview Maja Larsson.

Von Post had explained why it was necessary for there to be so many of them. It was not to scare her. But Larsson should not assume that she could get away with keeping quiet or telling lies this time. That was why there had to be several of them. That was why the interrogation would take place in her home.

What a load of bollocks, Mella thought. Of course he wants to frighten her, and he likes to have an audience. That's his personality reduced to its basic characteristics. A real bastard.

The type who takes the credit for work done by others. Trims his sails to every wind and saves his own skin. If he praises you, you'd better watch out because you know he wants something from you. But he considers himself to be socially competent.

He had gone out of his way to learn the names of her children, and always asked after them. She hated responding to his faked interest and squirmed in embarrassment when she told him about Jenny's pony-riding or about Petter's progress at school.

Now he had decided to make use of the fifteen-kilometre journey to Kurravaara where Larsson was staying by giving his fellow passengers a crash course in interrogation techniques.

"It is absolutely essential to gain the trust of the witness. She must have confidence in the interrogator."

You don't say, Mella thought.

"An experienced interrogator interprets all the signs – body language, for instance."

Somebody in the back seat grunted. Stålnacke blew his nose.

"An uninhibited conversation. That's what we try to achieve. What we are working towards. We don't ask any direct questions. We simply talk about things. In that way an experienced interrogator can . . . can get to know absolutely everything."

Now Olsson seemed to have something stuck in his throat.

Thank God it's dark inside the car, Mella thought. She joined in the grunting.

Maja Larsson opened the door with her arms full of dirty washing. The thousand silver plaits were dangling down over her neck.

Incredibly beautiful, thought Mella, who had been living for almost half a century without a man ever turning his head to look at her.

And she didn't seem put out in the least by the prosecutor and his crew.

"Will it take long?" she asked wearily. "Can I sling this stuff in the machine?"

"Well," von Post began – but by then she had already turned on her heel and disappeared into the bathroom. After a while they heard the washing machine starting to turn.

Mella noted the look of irritation on von Post's face as she and her colleagues took their shoes off in the hall. He kept his shoes on.

Only country yokels walk around in their stockinged feet, Mella thought. The upper classes always have a servant to clean up after them.

"Örjan!" Larsson shouted to somebody at the top of the stairs. "The police are here."

They all looked up and saw a man in his sixties looking down at them. Mella couldn't see much more of him than his hair. No defor-estation there. He stared down at the gathering in the hall below.

"What the hell have you been doing? Robbing a bank?"

Larsson shrugged.

So much for trust in the interrogator and uninhibited conversa-tion, Mella thought, the whole of her body gripped with squirming embarrassment.

Her colleagues traipsed into the kitchen after von Post. It took some considerable time. Everyone was trying to be last, hoping that there wouldn't be enough room for all of them so that the luckiest could wait outside. Back to their schooldays . . .

When they had all ended up in the kitchen, they looked at each other. Von Post and Larsson had sat down on either side of a tape recorder that he had placed between them.

I can't possibly join them in there, Mella thought from the doorway. I'd be much too close. How big can a kitchen be? In the end she decided to join her colleagues. They were lined up, leaning against the sink. They stood there, shuffling from one foot to the other, clearing their throats, contemplating the decorative fringes of the rugs, wondering what on earth to do with their hands.

"Anyway, fru Larsson," said von Post loudly and clearly, "when Rebecka Martinsson spoke to you, you didn't mention the fact that your cousin Sol-Britt was in a relationship. Can you tell us about that now?"

Larsson sat there for a few seconds that felt like an eternity. Then she lit a cigarette and inhaled twice before answering.

"I thought she was the prosecutor in charge of the investigation?"

"Not any more she isn't. I thought you said you were prepared to cooperate with us. Your cousin has been murdered. I don't know, but isn't it a bit odd that you don't seem to be prepared to help the police?"

God help us all, Mella thought.

"You look young," Larsson said. "How old are you?"

"Forty-five. We're just trying to do our job, as I'm sure you understand."

Von Post leaned forward and placed his hand on Larsson's side of the table. She leaned back.

"Who was she having a relationship with?"

"You look younger. Much younger."

Larsson moved her head back and forth, in a figure-of-eight shape, staring hard at his face.

"You haven't had an operation, but you must be using Restylane – right?"

Von Post withdrew his hand. He glanced sideways at the row of police officers.

"Certainly not, but . . ."

"There's nothing wrong with that. Looking after your appearance. Why shouldn't a man . . . ? Especially if you're keen to make a good impression in the media. And your fingernails are shit hot – if I could afford it I'd have mine looked after by manicure professionals as well."

Von Post opened his mouth, then closed it again. In the end he said, "Why did you lie?"

"Have I lied?"

"You didn't say that Sol-Britt had a lover. Martinsson must have asked you about that, surely?"

Mella gasped for breath. It had dawned on her what von Post was after. He wanted Larsson to say that she hadn't lied, and that Martinsson had never asked. He wanted to have Martinsson's error in black and white. She realised now why von Post had insisted on recording the interview, and having a transcript. He wanted everybody to know that Martinsson had boobed.

Larsson said nothing.

"Huh," she said eventually.

Von Post raised an eyebrow.

"You really are driven by all the wrong motives, aren't you? My cousin is dead. She has been stabbed to death. You want to become a celebrity and put your colleague in the shit. You want me to say . . ."

She turned to look at Mella and her colleagues.

"How did he manage to get Martinsson sacked from the investigation? I'd like to know that."

Nobody spoke. Von Post leaned back on his chair and crossed his arms. As if to signal that he wasn't going to allow himself to be provoked. That he had all the time in the world. That they could remain sitting here until sunrise tomorrow if necessary.

"You're wearing expensive clothes as well," she said. "Just look at those shoes that you didn't condescend to take off before stamping around on my mother's woven carpets. You couldn't afford those on a prosecutor's wage. So you must have a wife who earns more than you do. I can see that it can't be easy to cope with that. Given the way you are. My guess is that you either beat her up or screw somebody else in your office because you hate her and are so het up about the injustice of life."

It was now so silent in the kitchen that the ticking of the wall clock sounded like thunder. Everybody knew that von Post's wife worked in a bank and earned much more than he did. It was also common knowledge that he bedded young would-be prosecutors, district court clerks and the occasional witness. Olsson contemplated his cuticles and Stålnacke was stroking his moustache.

Larsson was now going for the kill.

"I'll bet you anything you like that your dad had the same job as you. But that he was more successful. A lawyer, I expect? Or was he a senior doctor?"

Von Post was looking pale. His father was a Justice of the Supreme Administrative Court.

"Are you refusing to answer my question?"

"I don't know who she was having an affair with, O.K.? We didn't know each other all that well. There was a lot of crap talked about her. But I don't know any more than that. Have I annoyed you so much that you're going to arrest me on those grounds?"

"You haven't annoyed me," von Post said. His voice had become a little muffled.

"I'm glad to hear it. I hope that means you will now clear off and leave me in peace. I have to make breakfast for my dying mother in the morning: she has difficulty in swallowing now. It takes an age. The carers don't have time . . ."

They could hardly cram themselves into the car quickly enough. But they had not left the drive before Stålnacke exploded.

"Fucking hell! Stop the car! I need to shit! Christ almighty, I can't wait. Stop now or it'll be all over the back seat . . ."

He ran back to the house.

His colleagues watched in the rear-view mirror as Maja Larsson opened the door. There was a pause before she stepped to one side and allowed him in.

Stålnacke sat on top of the toilet lid. He didn't actually need to empty his bowels at all. After two minutes, he flushed the lavatory. Then he flushed it again. He washed his hands, and went out. Maja Larsson and her boyfriend were sitting at the kitchen table. He nodded to the man, then said to Larsson, "All your guesses were right."

She tossed her head to indicate that she could not care less, and stubbed out her cigarette on the inside of a jar lid, dropped the butt into the glass jar and screwed on the lid.

"He fixed it so that Martinsson was dropped from the investigation team. And we can do nothing about it. Anyway, sorry about all this . . ."

He gestured towards the kitchen.

"But you can be sure that we shall do everything we can to catch whoever did it."

Her mouth twitched, and she looked the other way.

"Thank you for letting me use your lav. I'm getting old, dammit! Constipated for a week, and then suddenly . . . Anyway, I'd better go."

"Wait a moment."

She was still looking away as she continued.

"She was having an affair with a married man who lives here in the village. As you know, you have to be careful about what you say to the police sometimes. Before you know where you are, the local kids are throwing stones through your windows. I expect you think I'm a coward. But who cares who she went to bed with? She's dead. She's not going to come back to life. And as for that jumped-up little prat who wants to use her to further his career prospects – do we really have to read in the newspapers about who she went to bed with? For Christ's sake . . ."

"Who was it?"

"I don't know. All I do know is that he works in Kiruna. And lives here in the village. And that he's married with children."

"I thought you were never going to come back," Rantakyrö said to Stålnacke when he got back to the car.

"Huh," Stålnacke said as he struggled with his seat belt. "It was a three-kilo dollop. Hell's bells. I've been out of action for a whole week – then suddenly: whoosh! You'd never believe how happy it made me. I was thinking of having the little blighter christened."

Von Post accelerated away, gravel clattering against the chassis.

Mella gave Stålnacke a knowing look. He nodded almost imperceptibly.

Krister Eriksson stood alone in his kitchen and held up his tin of chewing tobacco.

"I'm giving up," he proclaimed to the whole universe. "I've had enough. No going back to baccy."

He threw the tin into the rubbish bin under the sink, lifted out the plastic bag and tied it in a tight knot, then carried it out to the big bin by the car port.

Inside the house Marcus was finding it hard to settle down. He crawled about with the dogs and seemed able to carry on playing forever. Eriksson let him be. After all, it was when you went to bed that fear and horror started to prey on your mind. The same applied to adults as well. And the boy could sleep for as long as he liked the next morning.

It was not until after eleven o'clock that he came crawling up to Eriksson and announced that the Wild Dog was tired.

They brushed their teeth, despite the fact that the other dogs didn't need to. But then the Wild Dog made it clear that he didn't want to sleep in a bed under a duvet.

"The Wild Dog wants to sleep outside in the dog kennel," he said.

So Eriksson set up his winter tent in the garden, next to the dog kennel.

Then Eriksson and Marcus sat in the dog kennel with a torch. Vera, Tintin and Roy were scampering around them. The dogs were thrilled to bits to have company – and with the reindeer skins

Eriksson had laid out over the floor. The place smelled reassuringly of dog, and somewhat pungently of reindeer skin.

Eriksson read aloud from *The Little Prince*, lighting up the illustrations with his torch.

"The little prince was given a fox," Eriksson said. "Just as I got you, the Wild Dog."

"My life is very monotonous," the fox said. "I hunt chickens; men hunt me. All the chickens are just alike and all men are just alike. And, in consequence, I am a little bored. But if you tame me it will be as if the sun came to shine on my life. I shall know the sound of a step that will be different from all the others. Other steps send me hurrying back underneath the ground. Yours will call me, like music, out of my burrow."

"Can I have a look at the fox?" Marcus said.

Eriksson found a page with a picture of the fox, and Marcus placed his finger on it.

"Read some more," he said.

"Do you see the grain-fields down yonder?" the fox said. "I do not eat bread. Wheat is of no use to me. The wheat fields have nothing to say to me. And that is sad. But you have hair that is the colour of gold."

"You don't have any hair," Marcus said.

"No, but you have," Eriksson said, stroking a hand over the boy's blond hair.

Don't get too attached to him, Eriksson told his heart sternly as his hand caressed the boy's soft hair. He carried on reading.

"Think how wonderful that will be when you have tamed me! The grain, which is also golden, will bring me back the thought of you. And I shall love to listen to the wind in the wheat . . ."

Marcus looked again at the picture of the fox. Then they turned back to the page they had reached in the story.

The fox gazed at the little prince, for a long time.

"Please – tame me," he said.

"I want to, very much," the little prince replied. "But I have not much time. I have friends to discover, and a great many things to understand."

"One only understands the things that one tames," said the fox. "Men have no more time to understand anything. They buy things all ready made at the shops. But there is no shop anywhere where one can buy friendship, and so men have no friends any more. If you want a friend, tame me . . ."

Now Marcus was leaning heavily against Eriksson's side.

"Are you asleep?"

"No," the boy said, his voice slurred and sleepy. "Read more. The Wild Dog wants to hear more about the fox."

"What must I do, to tame you?" the little prince said.

"You must be very patient," the fox said. "First you will sit down at a little distance from me – like that – in the grass. I shall look at you out of the corner of my eye, and you will say nothing. Words are the source of misunderstandings. But you will sit a little closer to me, every day . . ."

Marcus had fallen asleep. He was breathing deeply. When Eriksson laid him gently down and zipped up the sleeping bag, he mumbled, "What happens next?"

"The fox tells the little prince a secret," Eriksson whispered. "But we'll read about that tomorrow. I shall be sleeping in the tent just outside the kennel. Vera will stay in here with you. Come out to me if you wake up during the night, O.K.?"

"O.K.," said Marcus, almost in his sleep. "The Wild Dog is just like the fox."

Eriksson sat still while the boy drifted off into dreamland. Then he crawled out of the kennel. Frost was taking possession of the grass. The night was dark but starry.

No, my friend, he thought. I'm the one who's just like the fox.

MONDAY, 24 OCTOBER

Anger was hurtling around in Martinsson's dreams, and eventually woke her up. Her mobile told her it was five o'clock – early, but not the middle of the night, at least.

But I can wake up whenever I like, she thought. And take a morning nap. I'm not going to work. They can go to hell.

Björnfot had simply taken away her investigation and handed it over to von Post.

What did he think she was going to do? Smile politely, lick her sores in silence and submissively take on his confounded tax case? Did he think she was stupid?

I'll never go there again, she thought.

The Brat was lying at the bottom of her bed, snoozing. When she moved he woke up and wagged his tail a couple of times. He was never angry when he woke up. She might just as well get up and light the stove.

The dog ran to the door and wanted to pee.

"O.K., O.K.," she said, putting on her shoes.

It was dark outside, the way it was only in late autumn, just before the first snow. A sort of decaying blackness that sucked up the pale light of the moon, the lights from all the houses in the village where people were living their lives and everything was continuing just as it always did, despite what had happened. The river was skulking in the background, silent and autumnally calm. All the boats and jetties were dragged up onto its bank, and the ice would form any night now.

The Brat disappeared into the darkness. Martinsson stood in the barely existent light from the lamp over the porch. She was restless and dying for a cigarette.

Tell me what I should do, she thought. Where I should go.

She suddenly heard the dog barking. A mixture of barking and growling. Fear, defence, warning. She could hear him scampering back and forth. Then a voice.

"Hello, Rebecka. It's only me. Maja."

The light of a torch became visible by the wall of the cowshed.

"There, there, little dog. Were you scared? I'm not going to hurt you."

The Brat circled around her until Martinsson called him. She walked together with him towards the torchlight. He was growling deep down in his throat. People who lurked around in the dark in his territory were not to be trusted.

"It's only me," Maja Larsson said again, shining the torch into her own face which looked very white with dark, ghostly shadows around her eyes.

She lowered the torch and the beam of light fell onto a mass of cigarette ends lying on the ground. The smell of cold smoke mixed with the autumnal scents of organic decay.

How long has she been standing here? Martinsson wondered.

"Forgive me," Larsson said. "I didn't mean to frighten you."

She greeted the dog and allowed him to lick her hands.

"Is it my fault? Am I the reason they're taking you off the case?"

Martinsson shook her head – then realised that she couldn't be seen in the darkness.

"No," she said.

Larsson had switched off the torch, put it in her pocket and lit a cigarette.

"I've been thinking about you," she said.

Her voice was deep and hoarse in a pleasant way. A real voice of the night. It was appropriate for the darkness.

Martinsson had released the Brat, who could be heard scuttling around here and there.

"And I've been thinking about your mum. It's as if she were with me all the time. Now as well – I dreamed about her. And I felt obliged to come here and wait for you to get up. I thought you would be up early, to let the dogs out. I'm sorry I didn't tell you that Sol-Britt had been having an affair. I don't know who with. But I obviously should have mentioned it even so. But I didn't want to get involved."

"That's O.K. They'd have taken me off the case even so."

"That prosecutor is a right bastard. He couldn't care less who murdered Sol-Britt, he only wants to . . ."

"Yes."

"Your mum—"

"Hang on," interrupted Martinsson in a pained voice. "I know you mean well, but I don't want to hear about her."

She had to stop talking. She had a pain in her throat.

What's happening? she thought.

"Just let me tell you this," said Larsson in a low voice. "If you give me five minutes, I'll promise to leave you in peace from then on. Then she might leave me in peace."

Martinsson said nothing.

"Your mum," Larsson began. "I know what they say about her here in the village. She rolled up here from Kiruna, pretty and well made-up. Started a relationship with your dad. Grew tired of him. Took you with her and moved back to Kiruna. They say it was her fault that he started drinking, no doubt you've heard about that. Then she moved to Åland to live with a new man, and left you here. Had children with her new bloke, then killed herself in a road accident."

"No," Martinsson said, "she was run over. She wasn't even in the car, she had got out . . ."

"Yes. Your younger brother as well. She had him in his pram."

"But I never met him, so . . ."

"I have to tell you. People say your dad was too nice before he met her, but the fact is that he was too weak. That's not the same thing. For instance, he sometimes worked for a haulage contractor in Gällivare: when it was time for him to be paid, they opened up a container full of tools that they were taking to a building site, and he was allowed to take whatever he wanted instead of being given any money. As you'll have gathered, the tools didn't belong to them anyway – Mikko realised that as well. They let him steal while they just stood there, watching. By Christ, he hated every moment of that. But he simply couldn't bring himself to do anything about it. Sometimes there was a wreck of a car that would be worth something if only somebody could fix this and that. Your dad was hopeless at mending cars – there were two old bangers rusting away in their garden. Your grandma despaired, but she was only strong in her home territory, and was incapable of asserting herself in the world at large. He was paid for that in diesel – the haulier could claim a tax rebate on the value of the diesel, but the payment to your dad was based on filling station prices. National insurance and pension contributions? You could forget that . . ."

Larsson lit another cigarette from the glowing butt of the previous one. The Brat was digging away like a madman by the cowshed wall; they could hear him squealing in excitement. Presumably a field mouse. No doubt it was a hundred miles away by now, but the scent was quite fresh, of course, and totally irresistible.

"And then he joined Sven Vajstedt's company," Larsson went on. "Sven had an excavator. Your dad took out a loan and bought a dumper truck. Sven was the one with the gift of the gab, and talked his way into setting up most of the jobs. Somehow or other, the costs were shared extremely scrupulously, but most of the income landed up in Sven's pocket. Your mum put a stop to all that. She severed the link between Sven's company and your dad and his dumper truck, and so he was able to do jobs off his own bat. She looked after the accounts, and would accept no payment except ready cash. She drummed up jobs for him as well – but the company belonged to your dad and his mother, and all the profits were ploughed into their house and garden. That was around the time when package holidays started to become popular. Your mum wanted to travel. But she got nowhere with that. Travel abroad? What was the point of that? . . ."

Martinsson said nothing, didn't move a muscle. Larsson chuckled.

"She liked dancing. And they actually met at a dance. But then he stopped going out dancing with her. And as for the talk about him starting to drink after she'd left him – he drank too much before then as well."

"I don't understand what you want from me," Martinsson said, her voice non-committal.

The Brat came running up to them and sat down beside Martinsson with a deep sigh.

He wanted his breakfast.

Larsson stamped on what was left of her cigarette.

"I just wanted to tell you this. I'm sitting at the bedside of my dying mother. Sometimes I want it to be all over as quickly as possible. So that I can get away from Kurravaara. And her. People often have good cause to be angry. And I know you have. But then, life is so blasted short. Cheers."

She strode off like an elk. Disappeared into the darkness. Martinsson had no opportunity to respond. But she couldn't have done anyway. Her voice was stuck fast in her throat.

What's going on? she asked herself. I've had enough of this. I must be out of my mind, she thought as she went back into the house. Why on earth did I come back here?

She saw traces of her dad in this house all the time. The spot on the door frame he used to hold on to when he pulled off his boots. Her mum engrossed in a weekly magazine at the kitchen table. Her grandma marching resolutely down the drive, always on the way to tell somebody off – children or animals, workmen taking a break, a neighbour desperate for a coffee.

If only I had somebody to hug me, she thought. Until it all blows over.

Perhaps she ought to phone Måns? – No, she wasn't in a fit state to talk to him. What would be the point of sobbing?

It wouldn't help, she thought. He cannot put me to rights. All those who could help are dead.

She checked her mobile. She had a text message. It was from Eriksson.

Ring me as soon as you read this, it said. *It's about Marcus!*

On Saturday, 8 August 1914, Managing Director Lundbohm is due to host a crayfish party. The crayfish are transported live from the Östermalm Market Hall in Stockholm, in wooden crates filled with ice and sawdust. Lizzie reads up in her *Hemmets kokbok* how to cook them, and she and the girls grimace as they drop them, still alive, into the largest of the copper cauldrons and watch them turn red as they die a horrific death. She serves them in large dishes with crushed ice.

Elina is one of the guests. She has sent off for a velvet bow tie to wear under her collar, and a long scarf, by mail order.

Lundbohm has invited people who are important in their different ways to the community. All their efforts will now be recognised and encouraged. He gives a welcome speech and calls them his friends. Less than a week ago His Majesty the King announced that Sweden will maintain strict neutrality, so people are no longer gathering in the streets in an attempt to discover the latest news, ascertain the facts and spread rumours. The war will not last very long, all reasonable people agree on that. And Kiruna – indeed, Sweden as a whole – will be able to earn money as a result of the war, Lundbohm predicts. Just as they did in the Crimean War.

There are about thirty guests squashed together round the long table in the dining room. Among them are the chairmen of the Provincial Education Authority and the Poor Relief Board. The head of the Northern State Railways is discussing with the local pharmacist the pointless panic buying of groceries, smoked and salted goods, conserves and macaroni. And flour. Especially flour. People didn't even act in such an idiotic fashion during the General Strike of 1909.

District Police Superintendent Björnfot is there with his melancholy wife, whose silent hatred of Kiruna and everything connected with it grows inside her body like a cancerous tumour. Elina tries to talk to her, but soon gives up.

The acting parish constable, a notorious ladies' man, spends the whole evening flirting with Elina and passing on shells and crayfish heads to his dog, which duly throws up a pile of vomit on Lundbohm's bearskin rug during dessert.

Old Johan Tuuri, representing the Lappish population, laughs loudly and swears that he has never eaten anything like these crayfish, waves some claws around, and puts on a little act with two quarrelling crayfish in the leading roles.

The vicar seems always to empty his schnapps glass in two gulps, and keeps refilling it, while the railway pastor complains about his stomach and sticks to beer.

The District Medical Officer seems to be worn out and in danger of falling asleep on his chair, but after his fifth glass of schnapps he rises from the dead and turns out to be an enthusiast of Bellman's drinking songs.

The mining engineers find it difficult to talk about anything but the mine – it seems their preoccupation with the black gold increases with each glass they empty.

Some businessmen and a haulier are also invited.

Entertainment is provided by the Kiruna Orchestral Society, and they are treated to a schnapps in the kitchen before staggering out into the night.

Manager-in-Chief Fasth, Hjalmar Lundbohm's right-hand man, gives a speech of thanks to his boss. By this time his party hat has slid down to the back of his head and his colourful napkin has ended up among the crayfish shells.

He is a corpulent man, herr Fasth. Fatty food and strong drink have shaped both his body and his temperament. He never smiles. His head and his body are a small sphere on top of a large one. He is not nervous like the police superintendent's wife, but neither is he tired and dejected like the medical officer. No, the mine's manager-in-chief is as forbidding as the creaking, squeaking, relentless midwinter. He is as hard as the iron in the mine. His private opinion of the police superintendent and Managing Director Lundbohm is that they are weak. He has no problem when it comes to treating people like dirt. He never hesitates to evict, dismiss, reject, lay off, punish or abandon anybody. The fear in the eyes of the poverty-stricken leaves him cold.

Despite his small size he is physically strong. Few can beat him at arm-wrestling – of those present the only ones who have ever done so are the police superintendent and the acting parish constable.

Now he churns out his thank-you speech while recalling resentfully that if it hadn't been for him, the managing director would never have been here at all. A so-called philanthropist who prefers to mix with poncey painters and sodomites and women with hairs on their chests like Lagerlöf and Key – for Christ's sake!

And all those journeys! Lundbohm can travel all over the world and improve himself while he, Fasth, has to make sure that life in Kiruna runs smoothly, the workers are kept under control, and people know their place. And that iron is produced.

And that little schoolteacher sitting opposite him. While he is talking, his gaze falls upon her breasts and her waist. She's a nice bit of pussy, no doubt about that. Too many ideas in her head, though. Still, that wouldn't be anything he couldn't take care of, if only he had the chance. During the course of the party he has noticed the looks exchanged by Lundbohm and the teacher. So that's the way it is, is it? What does she see in him? Money, of course. He'll find out how much she gets paid first thing tomorrow.

Lizzie sends the girls out to clear the table, and then serves hot apple pie with whipped cream. Apples do not grow this far north, and so these were also sent to Lundbohm in wooden crates, every apple carefully wrapped in newspaper.

Lizzie stands in the doorway and sees the way Fasth is looking at Elina. His eyes are listless, half-closed. His mouth is open. But there is something predatory in the background. Like a pike in the reeds in summer, ready to pounce.

As she serves a slice of apple pie to Elina, she whispers into her friend's ear.

"Make an excuse to leave the table, and come to the kitchen."

She intends to advise Elina to go home straight away. Fasth is a nasty sort at the best of times, and now he has had too much to drink. He's a danger to women.

But Elina doesn't come out to the kitchen. The schnapps has made her tipsy and talkative. Maybe she didn't even hear Lizzie – the party has become rather noisy.

When it is time for cognac in the drawing room, most of the women go home: but Elina stays behind. Fasth barely says goodnight to his wife when she thanks Lundbohm for an enjoyable evening and takes her leave. Fru Fasth makes no effort to take her husband home with her. Perhaps she thinks it will be good not to have to put up with him. Perhaps she will be relieved if he can find an outlet for his needs between the legs of some other woman.

Lizzie washes up, and races around like a madwoman with towels and cloths, in order to be finished by the time the last of the guests go home.

But when Elina is ready to leave, Lizzie hasn't finished her work.

174

The cognac glasses and the dishes of goodies are still in the drawing room, and must be taken care of and washed as the last of the guests stand around in the hall, thanking their host for such an enjoyable evening.

Lizzie watches as Fasth takes Elina by the arm and assures Lundbohm that he will personally make sure that she gets home safely. He leads her off into the night before any of the other guests has time to say a word.

Elina feels distinctly uncomfortable. Her arm is being held in a vice-like grip, and Fasth barely seems to notice when she stumbles as he strides out at what seems like breakneck speed.

The light nights of summer are no more, and she is alone with a man who stinks of strong drink, and is more or less dragging her along.

When they have passed Silferbrand's general store, he suddenly stops and pulls her into the back yard. It's as dark as a sack of coal next to the wall, while further away pale moonlight hints at the outline of barrels and wheelbarrows, a cart and some empty crates.

Fasth pushes her up against the wall of the woodshed.

"So," he grunts as she tries to protest. "Don't be difficult, now . . ."

He grabs hold of her breasts.

"No messing about, now. You give yourself to Lundbohm . . . And no doubt lots of others . . ."

His mouth slithers over her face as she tries to turn it away. He tightens his grip on her breast. The weight of his body forces her up against the wall.

"Once you've had a taste of a real man, you won't want anything else."

He takes hold of her chin and forces her mouth over his own, then thrusts his fat tongue inside it.

She bites his lip so that the taste of blood explodes inside her mouth.

He curses, and the hand that was making mincemeat of her breast moves up to his mouth.

She gasps for breath and shouts for all she is worth.

"Let me go!"

She shouts so loudly that everybody round about must have been woken up.

And her shout infuses her with unexpected strength. She thrusts Fasth to one side.

He is drunk, and perhaps that is why she is able to evade him before he has recovered his balance.

She runs out of the back yard like a fox pursued by hounds. She hears his voice behind her.

"Whore!"

Krister Eriksson woke up early. It was cold in the tent. Wild Dog Marcus had taken over his winter sleeping bag, and he was using the summer version. Tintin was lying beside him. She woke up when he stretched himself, and licked his face. By Christ, but it was cold. He simply couldn't lie here any longer. He would have to get up.

And he was dying for a wad of chewing tobacco.

Roy was lying over his feet. When he started moving, both dogs stood up and began walking around the little tent. They squeezed out through the opening and disappeared – no doubt having a morning pee somewhere in the garden.

Eriksson stuck his head out through the tent opening. He was pleased to note that the first snow had not yet fallen. He crawled out and peeped into the dog kennel. Roy and Tintin went for a stroll around it, sniffing away.

It was a simple little hut with no heating: he had made it himself in a single day. Hanging in front of the door opening were three plastic sheets. They did not keep the cold out, but they prevented it from drifting straight in. And the dogs could get in and out without any problems.

He folded the plastic sheets to one side. Marcus was lying there asleep, with Vera beside him. No doubt he wasn't freezing to death: Eriksson had placed a reindeer skin on the floor, and an extra blanket over the winter sleeping bag.

Vera woke up straight away and went out.

"Sorry about this, but it must be done," he said to the dogs.

Then he walked over to the rubbish bin and opened it. He reached down into it and dug out yesterday's rubbish bag. The dogs gathered around him, watching with interest.

"I know," he said as he unfastened the bag and took out the less than clean tobacco tin. "It's disgraceful."

The dogs accompanied him into the house for their breakfast. Eriksson inserted a large wad of chewing tobacco inside his lip, and started to make his morning coffee, even though it was only a quarter to five.

He took the cloudberries he had collected this year out of the fridge. He hoped Marcus liked cloudberries. To be on the safe side he took out a packet of blueberries as well. If he made some pancakes, jam would be good to have with them. He would invite Sivving and Martinsson to eat with them.

Assuming Marcus stays here with me today, he reminded himself.

He did his usual exercises: pull-ups, sit-ups, press-ups and knee-bends. Then he paid his various bills online and vacuumed the whole house – as he did every morning. The dogs shed vast amounts of hair.

Vera was sitting by the door, scratching at it: she wanted to go out. Eriksson checked the time: ideally the boy ought to sleep until he woke up. No doubt Vera would go and wake him. On the other hand, that would be the best way for him to regain consciousness.

Roy and Tintin were lying on the living-room sofa: they had no plans to go anywhere at all.

Vera wagged her tail and looked at him. He had the feeling that she understood. That this dog, who had watched her master being murdered, somehow sensed what the boy had been through. That she had taken it upon herself to help him recover.

"And I need your help as well," Eriksson said, letting her out.

He walked over to the kitchen window, from where he could see the dog kennel. Vera appeared from round the corner of the house and made her way towards the kennel.

Then she stopped dead at the entrance.

Why doesn't she go in? Eriksson wondered.

Vera barked. It was shrill and seemed full of alarm. Then she poked her head into the kennel and backed out again. Barked once more.

Something was amiss. Eriksson ran out into the garden in his stockinged feet. He knelt down in front of the entrance and folded aside the plastic sheets.

Marcus was lying inside, fast asleep. Just inside the door was a flaming torch.

Eriksson's stomach churned in horror. A flaming torch! Where on earth had the boy got that from?

He removed it immediately, turned it upside down and laid it on the lawn. It extinguished itself with a sort of sizzling noise. Then he pulled Marcus out of the kennel, sleeping bag and all.

He shook the boy.

"Marcus! Wake up, Marcus!"

His head was swimming. Good God! What if he had tossed and turned in his sleep and the sleeping bag had caught fire . . . ?

He didn't manage to think that thought through – he had been set on fire himself. When he was only a couple of years older than Marcus.

Why hadn't he woken up? Burning flames in a confined space can be lethal. He knew that. Every year campers died from that very cause. They lit candles in their caravans or bivouacs, or used mini-barbecues in their little tents and then succumbed to carbon monoxide poisoning.

"Marcus!"

The boy was lying limply in his arms. But then he suddenly opened his eyes and looked at him without speaking.

Eriksson was so relieved that he almost burst into tears.

He was pleased to see that Vera licked him good morning without a care in the world. Marcus tried in vain to lick her back.

"You must never have burning candles or flaming torches in a dog kennel," said Eriksson sternly. "You can set the place on fire! All the air can be burnt up! Where did you get it from?"

Marcus looked at him in bewilderment.

"Wuff?"

"This!"

He lifted up the extinguished torch and showed it to Marcus.

The boy shook his head

Eriksson suddenly broke out in goose pimples. He looked around.

At that very moment a young man appeared from nowhere. His hair was gathered up in a sort of bun at the back of his head, and his black spectacles were reminiscent of the sixties. He was wearing a white shirt and much too thin a jacket. Trotting behind him was a similarly young woman. She was wearing a hooded jacket and baggy jeans. They looked like the types who squat houses and throw paving stones at mounted police, Eriksson thought. Instinctively he hugged Marcus even more tightly. Got up, stood Marcus on his feet, still in the sleeping bag.

"Krister Eriksson!" shouted the young man. "Why is Marcus sleeping in the dog kennel? Is he a security risk? Don't you dare let him sleep inside the house?"

"Eh?"

The woman had produced a camera and was taking pictures.

Journalists.

"Get off my premises!" Eriksson said.

He turned Marcus's face towards himself as he shooed the intruders away

The man and woman retreated as far as the letter box by the

garden gate. They knew their legal rights. It would take much more than a police officer who looked like a alien from outer space to frighten them off. The woman continued taking pictures while the man shouted out a series of questions.

"Is he dangerous? Do you think he was the one who killed his grandmother? Is it true that he's going to be cross-examined by a forensic psychiatrist today?"

Eriksson was shaking with suppressed fury.

"Are you out of your minds? Get out of here NOW!"

He picked Marcus up in his arms, and shouted for Vera, who was circling round the visitors with unconcerned interest.

"Come here! Here, at once!"

Couldn't Martinsson teach her dog to obey the simplest of commands?

Marcus was kicking about in his arms, didn't want to be carried. He barked at the journalists as Eriksson carried him into the house.

"Wuff!" he yelled. "Wuff, wuff, wuff!"

Von Post had slept badly. He had dreamt that he had strangled his wife with a thin steel wire. She had been blue in the face, which was swollen up like a balloon about to burst. The wire had cut her skin, and blood had been trickling out. He had woken up abruptly, and was unsure if he had shouted out, possibly even disturbed the neighbours.

He could not understand why he'd had such a horrific dream. It must have been something he'd eaten. Or perhaps he was falling ill? In any case, it had nothing to do with that Maja Larsson, and what she had said about his father and his wife. Certainly not. Larsson was a totally insignificant person.

Now von Post was standing in the doorway of Martinsson's office. Alf Björnfot was sitting at her desk with all the documentation for today's criminal proceedings spread out in front of him. Ten fairly straightforward criminal cases, one after another. Each of them was reckoned to last about half an hour.

This is marvellous, von Post thought as he felt the uneasiness that had possessed him in the aftermath of the dream ebbing away.

Martinsson had reacted better – that is to say, worse – than he had dared to hope. She had created a scene worthy of an hysterical old crone, quarrelled with her boss and then refused to come to work.

And now the outcome was that he had taken over the investigation, and she had passed the audition for the role as a shit, a quitter and a neurotic. He found himself struggling not to sing and dance. No, he must keep a straight face.

"A lot on your plate, eh?" he asked his boss in a sympathetic tone of voice.

Björnfot looked up at him in annoyance.

"It was such a bloody shame that she took it so personally," said von Post, who by now was in a mood reminiscent of his childhood Christmases. "It's disgraceful that you should have to drive up from Luleå and leave all—"

His boss interrupted him with a dismissive gesture.

"Pfuh, I could wind up a clockwork soldier and send him in to do what's needed. She has prepared everything so damned well – spelled out details of the procedures, prepared lists of questions, and even written a draft of the pleas. I only need to learn it all off by heart."

The machinery inside von Post's head ground to a halt. The Christmas carols stopped. He should have checked up and thrown her bloody notes into the shredder. Shuffled the documents around.

"I think it's disgusting," he said with feeling. "It's dereliction of duty and grounds for dismissal. Anybody who does anything like this should be given an official warning."

He congratulated himself on having suggested so elegantly that if the boss did not give her an official warning it would be interpreted as favouritism. And an official warning was necessary before anybody could be sacked. Not that Björnfot would sack her. He was too daft for that. But it wouldn't be necessary. If she received an official warning, she would resign – he was almost certain of that.

"I've granted her leave," Björnfot said curtly. "And personally I'll be pleased if she forgives me and doesn't resign. Meijer & Ditzinger would be thrilled to bits and make her a partner if she went back to them."

Björnfot was looking pale, von Post thought. Ill. Sickly.

"Just say the word if there's anything I can do," he said with a smile.

That very second Olsson and Mella appeared in the corridor, red-cheeked and exhilarated.

But when they saw von Post, they fell silent.

Von Post beckoned them to come to him.

"We've nearly got him," Olsson said, handing over a sheet of paper.

They greeted Björnfot, but their hearts were not in it. Mella glared at him. Björnfot acknowledged them somewhat awkwardly.

"I've gone through the text messages from Sol-Britt Uusitalo's secret lover," Olsson said. "Her latest pay-as-you-go card was activated two weeks ago. The text messages sent during the day come from a transmitter in Kiruna, and those sent in the evening are from a transmitter in Kurravaara. Last Saturday there was one sent from Abisko."

"She was murdered on Saturday night," von Post said.

"But it's only an hour's journey from there."

"Maja Larsson, Sol-Britt's cousin, told Sven-Erik that Sol-Britt was having an affair with a married man who lived in Kurravaara," Mella said. She was still avoiding looking at von Post. "I can check that with Martinsson's neighbour, Sivving. He knows the village inside out. He'll know if there's anybody who fits that description, and might have a cottage or a flat in the Abisko region."

"Do that," Björnfot said. "Without delay."

He smiled at Mella. She turned on her heel, walked away a few paces, then made the call.

A bit of excitement won't do any harm, thought von Post, feeling pleased. Just think – that little dwarf might have an attack of hysterics. Could one hope for anything more exciting?

Björnfot turned to Olsson.

"I don't suppose you know where the card was bought?"

"Oh yes, of course. A so-called convenience store called Be-We's Provisions."

"Go and ask them if there's anybody from Kurravaara who's in the habit of buying mobile pay-as-you-go cards there," Björnfot said.

He stood up, put on his jacket and prepared to deal with Martinsson's petty crime cases – to lead the battle being fought by the citizenry at large against people who urinated in public places and rode mopeds without safety helmets, against shoplifters, drink-drivers and moonshiners.

"People round here keep an eye on what others are up to," he said.

Nobody spoke. They could hear Mella out in the corridor saying "yes" and "hmm" and "thank you, but now I really must . . .". Those phrases were repeated several times before she managed to put an end to the call.

When she came back into the room, everybody was looking expectantly at her.

Come on, out with it, thought von Post.

"Jocke Häggroth," she said. "Not somebody I know. An ordinary sort of bloke, according to Sivving. With a wife and two kids of school age. Works as a welder at Nybergs Mekaniska. And Sivving seemed to recall that this Häggroth's brother has a holiday cottage out at Träsket, which is just outside Abisko. And there were a couple more he knew who have fishing boats up there. They also have children, although they are grown up now. I made a note of their names: Tore Mäki and Sam Wahlund."

"But at this time of year surely the fishing boats will be beached and unusable," von Post said.

"Get passport photos of all three and take them to Be-We's," Björnfot said. "They might recognise one of them. Do that, and bring this Häggroth bloke in for interrogation."

Mella nodded.

"So we've got him," she muttered. "That was quick."

That was almost too quick, von Post thought. But still . . . Hip, hip, hooray!

He would be able to arrange a press conference that very afternoon. March into the room, sit down. The introductory words would be important. "I took over this case yesterday and it has been conducted very efficiently – which has produced results." No, not "which has produced results". Maybe "that's the way to produce results". More subtly devastating.

He hoped the secret lover was the father of small children. The newspapers always like that. It would produce good headlines.

Mella's mobile rang. The display said *Krister Eriksson*. She answered.

"Yes . . . yes . . . what the hell are you saying?"

"The children?" whispered Björnfot to von Post and Olsson.

Nobody spoke.

She hung up. Still holding the mobile in her hand, she turned to look at Björnfot.

"That was Eriksson," she said eventually. "He says somebody has tried to kill Marcus."

"Rebecka Martinsson said that I should talk to you."

Eriksson had come to the police station. Marcus was playing at wild dogs with Vera in the corridor, and von Post, Eriksson and Mella were talking quietly in Mella's office.

"I don't understand why you rang Martinsson at all," snapped von Post. "I'm in charge of this investigation."

"Here is the torch in any case," Eriksson said, handing it over in a paper bag. "I thought you might want to test it for fingerprints . . ."

"It could just as well have been the boy himself who took the torch into the kennel and lit it," von Post said.

He took the paper bag somewhat reluctantly.

"I don't have any torches at home. Where could he have got it from? And what has happened to the matches? Somebody placed it in the dog kennel while I was in the house."

"That was also brilliant – letting him sleep in the dog kennel," von Post said sarcastically. "Half an hour from now we'll be able to read about it in the newspapers as well: 'The Police in Kiruna keep a traumatised boy in a kennel'."

Eriksson said nothing.

"The lad must have seen something," Mella said, taking the paper bag from von Post. "Why else would anybody want to kill him? This is important. I'll be driving to the airport to pick up a colleague from Umeå, the one who's a specialist in interrogating children. She's due in at twenty past one this afternoon."

"Excellent," von Post said, wiping the palm of his hand on his trouser leg. "Will you look after him until then?" He looked at Eriksson and gestured in the direction of the corridor, where Marcus was crawling around in circles.

Eriksson nodded.

He left his colleagues and went out into the corridor. There was no sign of Vera or Marcus. A twinge of unrest deep down inside him made him increase his speed, but in one of the empty offices he found the boy sitting underneath a desk. Vera lay stretched out on the carpet.

Eriksson bent down.

"Hi there," he said softly. "How are things?"

Marcus said nothing. And avoided looking him in the eye.

"How's the Wild Dog?" he said. "Is he hungry or thirsty?"

"The Wild Dog is very frightened," Marcus said in a near whisper. "He's in hiding."

"Oh dear," Eriksson whispered, appealing to the gods to help him act wisely and cautiously. "Why is he afraid?"

"All the other dogs in his family are dead. Hunters came to chase after them and shoot them and dig holes for them to fall into and impale themselves, and there were other traps as well, they . . ."

"What did they do?"

Marcus said nothing.

"O.K.," said Eriksson after a while. "Is there anywhere where the Wild Dog can feel safe and secure?"

Marcus nodded.

"He's not so frightened when he's together with you and Vera."

"It's a good job I'm here, then," Eriksson whispered, edging a little closer. "Do you think the Wild Dog would like to jump up into my lap?"

The boy leaned towards Eriksson.

What on earth can I do? Eriksson thought, lifting Marcus up.

The boy wrapped his thin arms round Eriksson's neck as the police officer stood up.

What can one do with a little lad like this who has no adult left in his life? He tried to suppress his anger at the boy's mother who wanted nothing to do with him. But I know nothing about her. There's no point in my getting angry.

He sat down on the desk chair with the boy on his knee, and immediately felt his thighs becoming wet. There was a wet stain on the carpet under the desk.

"I'm sorry," Marcus said.

"No problem." Eriksson swallowed. "These things happen. You can lean against me if you like. We'll sit here for a while. Then we'll go and get some clean clothes for you. I'll carry you to the car if you like."

Eriksson leaned his cheek on Marcus's hair.

You don't need to be afraid, you little dog, he thought. I promise you that.

"You are strong, you can carry me," Marcus whispered. "Then the hunters won't be able to see me."

"No, they won't see anything at all."

Eriksson's eyes misted over.

"You can trust me. You don't need to be afraid. I'm incredibly strong."

Martinsson sat at her kitchen table, scribbling on the back of a brown paper envelope lying among the heap of unsorted mail in front of her. She had spoken to Eriksson on the telephone. He was convinced that Marcus had not produced and lit the torch himself.

"Do you want to know why?" he had asked. "It's obvious – where could he possibly have got the torch and matches from? But even more significantly: I'd put a blanket over him while he was asleep. He's such a little lad – they can never really snuggle down into the sleeping bag as far as they should and then arrange the blanket over the top of the bag. So I put the blanket over him and tucked it in carefully on all sides. That blanket was still tucked in just as I'd left it when I stuck my head into the dog kennel and pulled him out."

Never believe in coincidences, Martinsson thought. It was meant to look like an accident. Yet another accident.

She scribbled away on the envelope, drew rings, wrote in names, put crosses against the names of the dead.

Hjalmar Lundbohm was Sol-Britt's paternal grandfather. Her paternal grandmother, the schoolteacher, was murdered. Sol-Britt's dad was mauled and eaten by a bear a few months ago. She herself was murdered. Her son was run over – a hit-and-run incident three years ago. And now it seemed that somebody had tried to kill her grandson, Marcus.

The obvious conclusion to draw was that whoever murdered Sol-Britt knew that the boy had seen something. Something he had not yet told them about. That was the kind of situation that gave rise to rumours. But the fact that Sol-Britt's father had been killed and her son run over – those events had nothing to do with this business. Why should they?

People do die, she thought. We all die sooner or later.

Martinsson placed the tip of her finger on the circle in which she had written the name of Sol-Britt's son.

I'm going to check up on that hit-and-run. I've got nothing else to do, after all.

It is October 1914. The war is ravenous for iron and steel. The cold of autumn is biting deep into the mountain. The leaves on the hunchbacked birch trees are turning into gold coins, and the bogs are taking on a reddish tint.

The school day is over and Elina is hurrying to Lundbohm's house. He has been away on his travels for a long time, but now he is back in Kiruna. She tries not to run along Iggesundsgatan.

She has been longing and longing for him, but he has not even written to her.

The human heart is a remarkable thing, she thinks.

Then it dawns on her that she has forgotten her cardigan in the classroom. You scatterbrain! she tells herself.

Two hearts are searching for love. They find it. Abandon them-selves to love. Make love. Almost die in ecstasy. But she cannot cope with her next thought. That he has found somebody else. Had his fill of her love, fallen asleep, woken up and wandered off, keen to find somebody different.

That doesn't have to be the case, she assures herself. There can be no end of different explanations.

The whole world is arming itself. Managing Director Hjalmar Lundbohm exports iron ore to the U.S.A. and Canada. And of course also to the biggest armoury in Europe: Krupps, in Germany. Sweden is neutral, and sells goods to anybody who is able to pay for them. No doubt he has been working day and night. He has been away since August 14. That day church bells rang in Kiruna non-stop, just as they did in every other Swedish town. A message of defiance, to announce that Sweden was ready to defend itself against any possible attack. The sirens at the mine also sounded from morning till night. Several conscripts climbed aboard the train together with Lundbohm. The sobs of women and children mingled with the tolling and the laughter. Elina went down to the railway station to say goodbye. He was in high spirits. He said that he was likely to be away for a long time. But when he saw the look on her face, he promised to write. He promised.

Not a line. Her first reaction was Good Lord, this was not surprising. Some people were already calling the war a world war. But then she thought that if he was longing for her, if he really loved her, he would not be able to prevent himself from writing – he would spend the nights writing to her instead of sleeping. Then she thought that he could go to hell. Who did he think he was? And why should she wait? There were others. Almost every day she found letters outside the door of her and Lizzie's flat. All kinds of prospective boyfriends inviting her for coffee and walks.

The next time he comes back to Kiruna he will find her walking arm in arm with somebody else! And if he wants to meet her, she will be busy preparing her lessons so he can sit at home and mope.

She has tried not to worry about it, attended various clubs, and read a lot, of course. Lizzie often wants her to read aloud. "Please read something to me while I do the washing up," she says. She has even accompanied Lizzie to the Domestic Servants' Club, and to Salvation Army meetings to listen to the band.

Lizzie is glad of the company. Her fiancé, Johan-Albin, adores Lizzie, but he refuses to accompany her to the Domestic Servants' Club or to church. There are limits, he says.

*

But so much for all her intentions. Here she is, almost running along the street without a cardigan.

It is like what it says in the Bible. She is like the woman in the Song of Solomon. The woman who wanders around the city searching for her beloved, despite the fact that the watchmen beat her and mock her. "I will rise now and go about the city in the streets and in the broad ways. I will seek him whom my soul loveth." Over and over again she says: "I am sick with love."

That's the way it is. That's love. A sickness in the blood.

She slows down as she approaches Lundbohm's house. A pulse shoots through her when she catches sight of him. Like when a salmon trout prepares to pounce: a shooting pain that passes through her whole body. It is that treacherous love which resides inside her, that is what makes her heart beat faster. Then comes another pulse, but this time of fear: Manager-in-Chief Fasth is standing there as well, talking to Lundbohm. She hasn't seen Fasth since the crayfish party. Afterwards she had told Lizzie about what happened, and was duly warned: "Keep well away from him, I beg of you; he's dangerous." Standing a few paces away is Johansson, principal of the children's home, waiting his turn to talk to Lundbohm.

Fasth is the first to see her, as Lundbohm is standing with his back towards her. She walks towards them as slowly as she can, and only when she is up close does she acknowledge them with a slight nod of the head.

Lundbohm exclaims: "fröken Pettersson!", and all three touch the brim of their hats – well, not Johansson as he happens to be wearing a grey knitted cap, which he tugs at slightly awkwardly. But in any case, she has already passed them with her aching heart, which is pounding and thumping with both love and fear.

Now she has to restrain herself from running away.

Don't run, she says sternly to her body, and she can feel their eyes on her back. Don't run. Don't run.

*

Fasth alternates his gaze between Elina and Lundbohm. So that's how it is. She parades past like a streetwalker without a cardigan or a jacket in order to display her slim waist and ample breasts. And that mop of blonde hair. But Lundbohm – he just stands there in front of Fasth, waiting for him to continue talking. Does this mean the little affair is over? If so, the field is clear. Now that the wolf and the bear have eaten their fill, it's the turn of the raven and the fox.

Run, rabbit, run, he thinks, contemplating the swinging of her waist and bottom. Run, run, run.

That evening a messenger boy comes with a note to Elina.

My dearest Elina,

You hurried past so quickly that I didn't even have time to say hello. Perhaps the war has taken you from me. Perhaps your feelings have cooled, and perhaps you have even found somebody else. Even if that is the case, I would still like to remain your friend, and as a friend, invite you round for dinner this evening. Can you? Would you like to?

Your H.

She only sees the words "dearest Elina". Reads the word "dearest" over and over again. Then she hurries off to his apartment. Yes. She is sick with love. Even before dessert they find themselves in bed.

And she asks no questions. Do you love me? Are you fond of me? What is to become of us?

But she looks at him. He is sleeping as if somebody had hit him

194

hard on the head. If only he had chatted to her for a while, as they used to do. If only he had whispered that he loved her, and then fallen fast asleep like a child in her arms. No, he simply turned over on his back and fell asleep like a shot. She gets up and washes her private parts. Goes back to bed. Contemplates him a while longer. It's impossible to sleep.

Her thoughts are like gravel. She breathes in gravel with every breath she takes. Soon the whole of her is nothing more than a pile of grey slag from the mine. He doesn't love her. She means nothing to him.

In the end she gets dressed and goes home in the middle of the night. He sleeps on.

A layer of ice is now covering Lake Luossajärvi. It thickens quickly in the middle of a cold night like this one. It crackles and rumbles. The Lapps have a special word for this. *Jåmidit,* when the ice sings and rumbles even without anybody walking on it.

All the way home Elina can hear the sad singing of the ice in her ears; it is sobbing, crackling and sighing.

"Pretty sure," said Marianne Aspehult at Be-We's, pointing at the passport photograph of Jocke Häggroth. "Well, absolutely certain, in fact. He sometimes shops here, but I don't remember if he's bought a top-up card in the past week or so."

Mella looked around the shop. Very pleasant indeed. She had never set foot in it before, although it had been here forever.

Aspehult looked at the photographs of the two men who Sivving had said owned a fishing hut in the Abisko area.

"Well, it's possible that they also shop here now and then, but I don't recall having seen them. But I don't think . . . no."

Mella nodded.

"Thank you," she said.

"I really must ask you," Aspehult said. "Has this got anything to do with the murder in Kurravaara?"

Mella shook her head apologetically.

"No, of course not," Aspehult said. "Take a few goodies if you fancy anything. Or an evening paper."

People are so nice, Mella thought as she left the shop. Helpful and kind. Most of them don't spend their time killing their neighbours.

Then she rang von Post. It was time to bring in Häggroth for questioning.

Martinsson drove down to Jukkasjärvi. Sol-Britt's son Matti had been employed by the ice workshop linked to the Ice Hotel.

That was where they sawed up blocks of ice to use when they began building the hotel every winter, provided the sculptors with blocks from which they created their sculptures, and carved patterns into the ice in accordance with their instructions, using special machines. They also made drinking glasses out of ice, plates of ice, everything you could think of that could be used in the Ice Hotel when the tourists started arriving.

It was like an ordinary workshop: the sound was the same, the rasping and roaring of saws and drills. The big difference was the cold.

I ought to have brought my quilted jacket, she thought.

Martinsson eventually tracked down Hannes Karlsson. He was the one who had found Matti Uusitalo after he had been run over. The records of the inquiry were somewhat scanty, but it had said that they had been workmates.

Karlsson was working with a small saw. He was making five-centimetre-long polished crystals of ice.

When he saw her approaching, he took off his protective goggles and earmuffs.

"These will become part of a cut-glass chandelier – but instead of glass it will be made of ice. We make all the individual pieces with the ice we have in store. Then the artists and the interior decorators will apply the finishing touches. We're waiting for winter to come now, so we can build the hotel itself. When it's finished I usually move up to Björkis and work there when the skiing season begins."

He had a close-clipped black beard and was still suntanned. He looked strong, despite his thin, sinewy body. He regarded Martinsson with unconcealed interest.

He's one of those adventurous souls, Martinsson thought. Someone who drives dog teams and goes canoeing down waterfalls. One of those restless types.

"Let's go somewhere more comfortable," he said with a nod of the head that indicated he realised she was feeling the cold. "It's time I took a break anyway."

"It was a terrible tragedy," he said when they had installed themselves in the coffee room with a mug each. "It's three years now since Matti was run over and killed. Marcus was four. If Sol-Britt hadn't been there . . . And now . . . A terrible tragedy, as I said . . . How is he?"

"I can't really judge that," Martinsson said. Then she took a sip of coffee and continued. "One of the police officers is looking after him. Matti and you were workmates, is that right?"

"It certainly is."

"Can you tell me about . . . you know, when Matti . . . It was you who found him, I gather."

"Yes, of course. I thought you'd been asking Sol-Britt about that."

She waited patiently.

"What can I say? He died while he was doing his regular jog. Three mornings a week he used to run all the way from Kurra to Kiruna. He'd have a shower and get changed at my place – I lived in Kiruna at that time – and then he'd join me in the car and I'd drive out to Jukkas. In the afternoon, after work, he'd run back home from my place."

"Was it always the same days of the week?"

"Yep! Monday, Thursday and Friday."

Martinsson nodded encouragingly.

"What can I say?" he said again. "It was a Thursday. We had to finish work on stuff to send to the ice bar in Copenhagen, so we didn't want to be late. There was no sign of him. I got a bit impatient and rang. Sol-Britt answered. And she was worried because he'd set off ages ago and ought to have arrived at my place by then. I called work and told them I was going to be late, and then I drove all the way to Kurravaara. Still no sign of him. I drove back – and then I saw him: it was on that side of the road that he was lying. In the bushes. It was early summer, so the leaves were still quite small – if it had been high summer I'd never have seen him. He'd been sent flying quite a long way from the road. Why are you asking about this?"

"I don't know, I just have a funny feeling in my stomach." Martinsson made an attempt to laugh. "But maybe it's just something I've eaten."

"Maybe I've eaten the same thing . . . You know, I thought it was a bit odd. It was in the middle of a straight stretch of road. Broad daylight. And he was wearing a reflective jacket. But let's face it, there are drunks, and drivers as high as kites, and others who fall asleep at the wheel. I asked the police if they were intending to check all the cars in Kurravaara. They were; but you know what it's like in the villages – everybody knows which of the old blokes definitely shouldn't have driving licences but are out on the road anyway, half blind and half asleep. And everybody knows who drives into Kiruna at that unearthly hour in the morning, half past six – there aren't very many. 'Check up on the obvious suspects,' I said. There can't be all that many of them, I thought. But they didn't. 'If we have a suspect,' they said. But they just wrote it off. A hit-and-run accident."

He stood up and fetched some more coffee for both of them.

"I actually ferreted around in Kurravaara myself. I suppose I was in shock after finding him, but I didn't understand that. I took a few days' leave from work – Göran said I didn't need a sick note or anything like that. We were all in a bit of a state. And we thought about the young lad. I mean, everybody knew that Sol-Britt . . ."

He held a pretend glass in his hand and mimed emptying it in one gulp.

". . . and we thought that she wouldn't be able to look after him. We knew that his mother didn't want anything to do with him. Matti had a hell of a time with her. He thought she would want to meet her son now and then, you know – a week in the summer, at least. But no. She simply washed her hands of him. Her own bloody son. But Sol-Britt pulled herself together. Somehow or other. When the police had talked to me and it became obvious that they weren't going to lift a finger to . . . Well, I got into my own car and did the rounds in Kurravaara. I asked somebody I know down there about who sets off for work early, and who's not fit to drive a car but does so nevertheless. I checked at least ten cars. I was looking for a dent, or for a car that had been thoroughly washed and cleaned . . ."

"And?"

"Nothing. So I don't know. I suppose it was something I needed to do to get some peace of mind."

Martinsson said nothing. They sat in silence for a while.

But if it wasn't an accident, Martinsson thought. Everybody knew that he ran to Kiruna three mornings every week. If I'd wanted to kill him, I'd have done exactly what his murderer did. That way you avoid having the police poking around as well. If everybody thinks it was a hit-and-run accident, the police are not going to spend much time on it.

"Hello there!" Karlsson said in the end. He waved his hand in front of Martinsson's face. "Have you been on a trip to outer space?" He smiled.

"Yes," she said with a grin. "Thank you for your time. And thank you for the coffee."

"Are you any the wiser?"

"I don't know," she said with a shrug.

She stood up.

"Did you know he was related to Hjalmar Lundbohm?" Karlsson asked in an attempt to hold her interest. "Lundbohm was his maternal great-grandfather."

"Yes, I'd heard that. And the teacher Lundbohm had the child with – what does that make her? His maternal great-grandmother, I suppose – she was murdered."

"Oh dear, I didn't know that. Anyway, we shall be having a *surströmming* party at the inn on Friday – they serve excellent fermented Baltic herring. Staff and friends. A first-class live band. Would you like to join us?"

"Sorry, I can't," Martinsson said untruthfully. "My boyfriend's coming up to visit me on Friday."

And if I'm unlucky he might just do that, she thought.

Martinsson got into her car and started surfing through the radio channels. She stopped when she came across the Beatles' "While My Guitar Gently Weeps" on one of the frequencies. Just as she stretched out her hand to turn up the volume, Mella rang. Martinsson turned down the volume instead, and answered.

"I think we've got him," Mella announced, somewhat out of breath. "The bloke who was having an affair with Sol-Britt Uusitalo. I just wanted you to know. We're on our way now to search his house and all that."

"Good," Martinsson said.

She could hear that she sounded unhappy about it, but told herself that it was not Mella's fault.

"How did you track him down?" she said, mainly to show they had her support.

"We traced his pay-as-you-go top-up card to the place where he bought it, Be-We's. And then we saw that he'd been using his mobile in central Kiruna during the day, and in Kurra in the evenings."

"So he lives in Kurravaara, then," Martinsson said.

"Yes," said Mella. "Jocke Häggroth. "Is it somebody you—"

"No! I know next to nobody in Kurravaara."

Silence reigned. Both women were determined not to get angry. And both were wondering if they ought to say sorry, but decided not to.

"We had intended to arrest him at work," Mella said after a while. "But Sven-Erik rang and they said he was at home, ill."

"Ill, eh? No doubt he's in bed with galloping angst."

"Presumably. Anyway, we'll get him now."

"Good luck," Martinsson said. "And just so that you hear it from me first, I'm checking up on that hit-and-run accident. When Sol-Britt's son died."

"O.K. . . ."

It sounded as if Mella wanted to say something more, but she didn't.

"Thank you for ringing," Martinsson said in the end

"Oh, it was really . . . It was nothing."

"While My Guitar Gently Weeps" had come to an end on the radio.

Well, well, well, Martinsson thought. It won't do any harm for me to keep myself occupied.

She looked out at the hunchbacked birch trees that were stretching their spindly arms up towards the cloudless blue sky. Just a few yellow and red leaves were still clinging to them. Flocks of black birds were rising and spreading themselves out as they soared skywards.

Martinsson dialled Pohjanen's number.

Mella's Ford Escort shot along the road down towards Kurravaara like the ball in a pinball machine. With her in the car were Stålnacke, Olsson and Rantakyrö. They were on their way to apprehend Jocke Häggroth, who lived just outside the village, in Lähenperä.

Mella's colleagues exchanged glances. She was driving like a madwoman.

"Somebody might be coming the other way," Stålnacke said, but she did not seem to hear him.

"What about the kids?" Rantakyrö said.

Did she have no mothering instincts? Who would look after her youngsters if she killed herself?

District Prosecutor von Post had been left behind in his new Mercedes G.L.K.

"They are six and ten," Mella said, who thought he was asking about Häggroth's children. "Häggroth himself is fifteen years younger than Sol-Britt, but that's not a problem, of course."

"What gets into people?" she asked her colleagues.

Nobody answered. They were all too busy hanging on for dear life as the car flew round the bends.

"I would never have time to have a fling with somebody on the side. I'm only too pleased to get together with my old man now and then."

"But it doesn't have to be him, of course," she continued as the car left the main road and started bouncing along the dirt road.

The others instinctively pressed their feet down onto the floor and slammed the brakes on – to no effect.

It was a timber-clad house, painted red. Not far from the house was a barn and an adjacent cowshed. And a wooden smithy down by the shore.

The farm had been handed down from one generation to the next in Häggroth's family, but when his parents died he and his wife had clear-felled the forest, divided the ground up into lots, and sold them off.

So they were not short of money, according to the villagers.

It was his wife who answered the door. She had her hair gathered in a bun, dyed blonde but with dark streaks, and was wearing track-suit bottoms. A lot of make-up around her eyes, and all kinds of fuzzy tattoos crept out from underneath her wide T-shirt in all directions – roses, lizards, tribals and runic symbols.

"Jocke is ill," she said, looking over Mella's shoulder at the other three people clambering stiff-legged out of the car. "What do you want?"

Von Post drove in through the gate and parked quite a long way away from Mella's car. He stepped out, adjusted his long overcoat and brushed a speck of dirt from his paisley-patterned scarf.

"He must come with us even so," Mella said. "And you should put on a jacket and some shoes because we're going to search the house."

"Come off it," fru Häggroth said. "Who the hell do you think you are?"

But she put on a jacket that was hanging within arm's reach, and slipped her feet into a pair of boots as she shouted to her husband.

He looked like death warmed up. A pallid face, unshaven and red-eyed. Dark rings under his eyes. He said nothing when he saw the plain-clothed police officers. Seemed not to be surprised.

"We want you to come with us," Mella said. "Is there anybody else in the house?"

"No," said his wife.

Her eyes shifted between all the people spread out over her premises. Rantakyrö disappeared into the barn, Olsson into the garage.

"The kids are at school. Can somebody please tell me what the hell is going on?"

"Your husband had an affair with Sol-Britt Uusitalo," von Post said. "And now we want him to come with us and answer a few questions. And we shall search through your house."

Fru Häggroth laughed mirthlessly.

"What a lot of rubbish!" And, after a pause, she said, "You're lying."

She turned to look at her husband.

"Say that they are lying."

Häggroth looked down at the floor.

"Would you like a jacket?" Mella said.

The devil take von Post. Why did he have to mention that?

"Go on, tell them they're lying," Fru Häggroth yelled shrilly.

There followed a few seconds of eerie silence. Then she punched him on the chest.

"Look me in the eye, you bastard! And say that they are lying! Say something, at least!"

Häggroth raised his arm to protect his head.

"I need some shoes," he said.

His wife looked at him in disgust. She put her hand over her mouth.

"You fucking bastard," she said. "You little creep. That old bag . . . For Christ's sake. This can't be true."

Mella reached out for the biggest pair of shoes standing in the hall and placed them in front of Häggroth.

He put them on and walked cautiously through the porch. Mella prepared to catch him if he should fall over.

"I'm sorry," he said without turning his head.

His wife knocked over a chair standing in the porch.

"You're sorry!" she yelled. "Sorry?"

She grabbed hold of a ceramic pot that was standing upside down in a dish and serving as an ashtray, and threw it at her husband's back.

He stumbled, and took a step forward so as not to lose his balance. Stålnacke put a hand behind his back and led him to the car.

"Calm down," Mella said to Fru Häggroth. "Otherwise we shall have to—"

"Calm down?" Fru Häggroth screamed.

Then she caught up with her husband, who was about to get into the car through the door being held open for him by Stålnacke. She attacked him from behind. Threw herself at him and started scratching his face. When Stålnacke took hold of her she hung onto her husband's clothes and refused to let go.

Häggroth tried to protect his face from her blows.

"You bastards," she yelled when Mella and Stålnacke combined to tug her loose from her husband. "I'll kill you, by God I shall . . . Let me go! Let me go!"

"Calm down now," Stålnacke said. "If you calm down, I'll let you go so that you can be at home when your children come back from school. Think about that."

She stopped screaming immediately. Ceased struggling.

"Are you going to stay cool now?" Mella said.

Fru Häggroth nodded.

She stood with her arms hanging by her sides, and just as Mella closed the car door she said to her husband, "Don't you dare come back here. Do you hear that? Never!"

Then she ran off at high speed to von Post's new Mercedes. It was parked next to a wheelbarrow.

Before anybody could raise a finger she lifted up the wheelbarrow, held it at arm's length over her head, then threw it at von Post's car. It landed on the bodywork with a loud bang.

Then she turned on her heel and ran off into the trees.

They let her go. Von Post raised his arms. He slowly bent over the car, placing his hands on it as if to heal it. Then he yelled out, in a voice so strained that it broke, "Catch her, for God's sake! After her!"

"We'll do that another day," Stålnacke said. "You have witnesses, and it will be taken care of. We must search the house now."

At that very moment Rantakyrö whistled loudly. He was waving his hand to attract their attention. When his colleagues turned round he crept underneath the barn. When he emerged he was holding a three-pronged hayfork in his hand.

Von Post let go of his car and straightened up again.

Mella's heart missed a beat. Three prongs. What were the chances of that? Most hayforks only have two.

It must be him, she thought. We've got him.

When she turned back, her eyes met Häggroth's gaze. He looked at her vacantly, then his gaze focused on Rantakyrö, standing there with the fork in his hand.

You shameless swine, Mella thought. Häggroth crossed his arms over his chest, leaned back in his seat and stared fixedly ahead.

Martinsson was smoking a cigarette with Pohjanen on the wooden bench in the mortuary staffroom. Pohjanen was breathing in short gasps, as if his lungs were longing to take a deep breath, but were incapable of doing so.

From time to time he was afflicted by a persistent cough. When that happened, he would take a crumpled handkerchief out of his pocket and hold it up to his mouth. When he finished coughing he would contemplate the contents of the handkerchief before stuffing it back into his pocket.

"Thank you," he croaked.

"Eh? It was your cigarette," Martinsson said.

"Thank you for sitting here with me," he said. "Nobody else smokes with me anymore. They regard it as deeply immoral."

Martinsson grinned.

"I'm only doing it because I want you to do me a favour."

Pohjanen chuckled raucously. Then he handed her his cigarette butt. Martinsson put it into the ashtray. He leaned back and put on his glasses, which were hanging on a band round his neck.

"So, this character who was mauled by a bear . . ."

"Eaten by a bear. Frans Uusitalo."

"So he was Sol-Britt Uusitalo's dad, is that right?"

"Yes. He was reported missing in June. In September a bear was shot, and in its belly they found the remains of a human hand.

So the hunting team called in a few extra helpers and they searched the area. And found him."

"No doubt it was an appetiser. I didn't do the post-mortem – if I had done I'd remember it. It must have been one of my colleagues in Umeå."

"Hmm. There wasn't much left of him."

Pohjanen's eyes narrowed. Out with the handkerchief again. He cleared his throat into it.

"Hmm. What exactly do you want, Martinsson?"

"I don't know. It's just a feeling I have. No doubt the post-mortem took place on the assumption that he died a natural death in the forest, and that the bear found the body. Or that the bear mauled and killed him. But I'd like you to look at him a bit more . . . a bit more carefully."

"A feeling," Pohjanen muttered.

Martinsson has a feeling, Pohjanen thought. Pfuh! But she has been right before. Eighteen months ago she had had a dream about a girl who had drowned, and she had persuaded him to make tests on the water in the dead girl's lungs. Sure enough, they discovered that she had not died in the river where they found her, and that it had not been an accident.

A feeling, he thought, pushing his glasses up to his forehead and letting them slide down onto his nose again. We use the word carelessly.

More than ninety per cent of a human being's intelligence, creativity and analytical ability was based in the unconscious. And all those things people called gut feelings or intuition were often the result of an intellectual process which they hadn't the slightest idea they had been involved in.

And she's on the ball, he thought. Even when she's dreaming.

"And you want me to do it without . . ."

He made a circular gesture with his hand to illustrate formalities and bureaucratic procedures.

She nodded.

"I'm not even working at the moment," she said. "And I might well get the sack tomorrow."

Pohjanen made a rattling noise that was presumably a laugh.

"Yes, I've heard about that," he said. "Everything you do stirs up a hell of a lot of drama, Martinsson. But anyway, I'm afraid I can't do it. Not if he was found two months or more ago. He'll be buried by now, or burnt to a cinder."

"But you could ring your colleague in Umeå who did the post-mortem."

Martinsson took out her mobile and handed it to him. Pohjanen glared at it.

"I see, so the call has to be made right away, has it? You Kiruna girls are not exactly the patient sort, are you? I'm actually surprised that Mella hasn't been in to snatch Sol-Britt's post-mortem report out of my hands."

"They've found the bloke she was having an affair with, and are on the way to Kurravaara to arrest him and take him in for interrogation."

"So that's the way it is, is it? O.K., I'll do it. But younger colleagues aren't often thrilled when an old fart like me rings and asks them about the job they've done. They get nervous. But O.K., I'll do it. If you do something for me in return."

"What?"

"Invite me to lunch."

"Of course. Where would you like to eat?"

"At your place, of course. I eat lunch out all the time. I want some homemade food. And you don't have anything important to do anyway, do you? You can cobble something together for an old grave-robber like me."

He took hold of Martinsson's mobile and turned it over a few times.

"Is this one of those so-called touchscreens? You'll have to dial the number for me."

"When do you have to be back?" Martinsson wondered.

The colleague in Umeå had been unobtainable. But Pohjanen had left Martinsson's telephone number and been promised that his colleague would telephone him as soon as possible. Now they were on their way to Kurravaara.

"Huh. Not until tomorrow."

"That's O.K., then," Martinsson said.

They parked in front of her grey Eternit house.

Pohjanen clambered out of the car, leaned against it and lit a cigarette.

"You have a terrific spot here," he said, gazing out over the river, as blue as a jewel in the autumn sun.

Martinsson came back from the house with a fishing rod over her shoulder and an old Windsor-style chair in her hand.

"Put that fag out and come with me," she said. "We're off to the riverbank."

When they got there she tossed her coat into the frozen grass and attached the Rapala lure.

"If we don't catch any fish I have some slices of reindeer meat in the freezer."

"If I were younger I'd ask you to marry me," Pohjanen said.

He had flopped down onto the chair and lit another cigarette. He screwed up his eyes as he looked towards the setting sun that was spreading a pink glow over the river and the trees and the houses on the opposite bank.

Martinsson spread a blanket over his knees. The Brat had lain down on his feet, and sighed with boredom.

Pohjanen had with him a worn-out Co-op plastic carrier bag containing his belongings. A spare jumper, cigarettes, files, papers. He rummaged around in it and took out a hip flask.

"Would you like a drop?" he asked Martinsson.

She smiled in surprise.

"What is it?" she asked. "Methylated spirits?"

"You can bet your life it is."

"Ugh," she said, with feeling.

"None of your ughs. Try it."

She wound in the line and disappeared in the direction of the woodshed. Came back with a hip flask of her own and two plastic goblets.

Pohjanen couldn't conceal his delight.

"For Christ's sake, woman," he said. "You are a prosecutor. Do you brew your own moonshine?"

She shook her head. He asked no more questions. They each poured out a drink for the other.

Martinsson said that the methylated spirits wasn't at all bad. Pohjanen explained that the trick was to mix it with water and place it in an ultrasound bath so that the connections between the water molecules were broken down, enabling them to blend with the ethanol.

He emptied his glass in one gulp, and in turn praised Martinsson's moonshine. She explained that the trick was to keep the temperature at the right level, both on the hob and in the cooling stage of the distillation process.

Pohjanen nodded and held out his glass for a refill.

As the telephone started ringing, Martinsson felt a bite. While Pohjanen was talking to his colleague in Umeå, she reeled in three perch and a salmon trout.

*

If the forensic specialist in Umeå was put out at being asked about a post-mortem he had carried out, he didn't show it. Instead, he offered them a bone.

It was Lars Pohjanen who was asking after all. There wasn't a pathologist in the whole of Sweden who wouldn't bend over backwards to assist him in any way possible.

"I remember him very well," he said. "Hang on a minute, I'll check up in the computer . . . Yes, he was buried a month ago. But I still have a bone if you would like it. Yes indeed . . . You know, the old bloke was over ninety, but fit as a fiddle. When we were trying to identify him, the police didn't manage to dig up any X-ray plates for him – he had never been in a hospital. And he hadn't had any teeth for over twenty years, so there was not much point in trying to identify him via dental X-rays. I sawed a piece off his femur to send off for D.N.A. analysis, but it was slightly damaged and looked a bit odd: so I put it in the freezer and sent a different bit to the National Forensic Laboratory."

"What kind of damage?"

"Possibly the bear. I don't know. Would you like the bone?"

"Yes please, that would be kind of you. And by the way, you don't need to make a note of the communication anywhere."

"I see, so that's how it is . . . By the way, I don't know if it's of any interest to you, but one of the crackpots in the hunting team that discovered his body found the old boy's shirt not far away from the spot a week or so later. He rang and wondered if we wanted it. I said he should give it to the police – they're bloody useless anyway."

Pohjanen and his colleague from Umeå laughed loudly, like two arrogant crows in the crown of a pine tree.

Martinsson was standing on a rock in her best boots and turned to see what the noise was all about. The Brat lifted his head and barked.

*

"But you have to agree that it's very odd," Martinsson said to Pohjanen, who was sitting with his half-full fourth or fifth glass of methylated spirits. "It's very strange to have all those deaths in the same family." She took a sip out of her own glass and pointed it at the stove. "This is the way to boil almond potatoes. Look. You put them in a pan of cold water and just when it starts boiling you take it off the hot plate and let it stand for half an hour. Otherwise the potatoes will crumble. They're delicate little things."

She put down her glass and listened to the butter sizzling in the cast-iron pan. When she had put the fish in it, she picked up the potato pan.

"The only thing that's odd," said Pohjanen, whose tongue was having difficulty in keeping up with his words. "The only thing that's strange is that somebody didn't marry you ages ago."

Martinsson nodded vehemently and poured off the water from the almond potatoes. Then she whisked a little salt, black pepper and a knob of redcurrant jelly into the morel sauce. Pohjanen staggered as far as the refrigerator and opened two beers.

"You'd better take a taxi home," Martinsson said. "Or sleep here on the sofa."

They sat down opposite each other.

"But if you do sleep here, you must promise not to die."

Pohjanen filled Martinsson's schnapps glass. The methylated spirits was all gone, but Martinsson's hip flask was still half full. He nodded.

"That shirt . . ." said Pohjanen, mashing the potatoes into the sauce with his fork. He didn't bother to peel them, neither did Martinsson.

". . . We ought to take a look at it. I wonder if the police still have it?"

*

They ate all the fish. Pohjanen was still eating potatoes and sauce when Martinsson pulled herself together, rang Sonja the switchboard operator, and asked her about the shirt that had been found in the forest. When Sonja rang back Pohjanen had also finished eating. They were now sitting in front of the open fire, each with a beer. They had left the schnapps on the table.

"Have you been crying?" Sonja wondered. "Your voice sounds so odd."

"No, no," Martinsson insisted. "I'm fine."

It's time to put on a pan of strong coffee, she thought.

Sonja was able to explain that it wasn't in fact one of the hunters who had found the shirt, but somebody from Lainio who had been out picking berries. After the bear had been shot and Frans Uusitalo's body found, there had been masses of people wandering around the spot out of sheer curiosity. And one of them, this berry-picker, had found the shirt and contacted the police.

"Have you still . . . have we still got it?" Martinsson asked.

"No," Sonja said. "We didn't want to keep that filthy old thing lying around, good God no. But I've still got his number. I can text it to you if you like."

"Excellent!"

"Are you really sure you're O.K.? Have you got a cold?"

Pohjanen and Martinsson drew lots to decide who would phone the berry-picker. Martinsson drew the short straw. Pohjanen threw a tennis ball for the Brat while she was ringing. Rugs and chairs went flying in all directions.

"It was something I wanted to see with my own eyes – and so did lots of others," the berry-picker said to Martinsson. "And so I went to check out a bog not far from the scene, looking for cranberries. Last year I sold fourteen thousand kronors' worth of lingonberries and cranberries."

He fell silent. It dawned on him that he was talking to a servant of the law. He had not declared that income in his tax returns. He had opened his mouth and put his foot in it.

"Huh," Martinsson said. "I'll believe that when I see it. Still, very impressive. And then you found that shirt, you said."

"Yes," the berry-picker said, exhaling in relief and thinking that there are actually prosecutors who are human after all. "I had lots of plastic bags with me, for the berries, so I took a stick and picked up the shirt and poked it down into one of the bags. Then I called the police and asked if they wanted it. But they weren't interested. They said I should give it to the pathologist. And so I rang him. That was even harder than getting through to the telephone company. But he reckoned I ought to give it to the police. Bloody amateurs, the lot of 'em, if you ask me."

He fell silent again.

"Anyway, those are the facts," he said in the end, his tone of voice suggesting rebellion against those in authority.

"I don't suppose you still have it, do you?" asked Martinsson.

"Of course I've still got it," said the berry-picker grumpily. "Both the police and the pathologist know that I have the shirt. And then they suddenly decide that they want it after all. Huh, I suppose I'd better cough it up. Don't you think? It's in a plastic bag in my garage. Stank to high heaven – it drove the dogs mad."

Martinsson stood up, her legs feeling decidedly shaky.

"Don't touch it," she said. "I'll come and fetch it right away."

How do you defend yourself against men? Against Manager-in-Chief Fasth? He's like a beast of prey, like a wolf. And the only way to defend yourself against a wolf is to seek safety in numbers. As soon as you are alone, you are an easy catch.

Elina no longer goes to and from school alone. Every day she chooses a boy or a girl to carry their teacher's books home, so Fasth never finds her alone in the classroom, nor on the way home after a day's work. And she does the same in the mornings: she arranges for one of the children to fetch her.

One day when she comes home she finds Fasth standing at the bottom of the stairs. How long has he been waiting there for her? He has opened a letter addressed to her that somebody has left on the bottom step. He reads it without a trace of embarrassment, then hands it over to her. She cannot prevent her hand from shaking as she accepts the handwritten sheet of paper. She can see from the handwriting that it is not from Hjalmar Lundbohm, she gets as far as "fröken Pettersson, you don't know who I am, but . . ."

"Fröken Pettersson," he says. "Apparently one has to queue up to see you."

Then he notices the boy she has by her side.

"Run along home now," he says to him.

But Elina takes hold of the boy's hand and refuses to let go.

"Arvid isn't going anywhere," she says. "He's going to . . . practise reading aloud."

And she elbows her way past Fasth, holding tightly onto the poor little boy who is white about the gills. As she hurries up the stairs, Fasth manages to slap her bottom.

"Sooner or later, fröken," he says from behind her back.

And he really draws out the word "fröken". Cuts it to pieces until it means simply "unmarried hussy".

"Frööööken Pettersson."

The interrogation of Jocke Häggroth took place at a quarter past four in the afternoon of Monday, 24 October. Outside, the sky had clouded over and it started snowing. Large flakes that were in no hurry to tumble down through the blue twilight.

Von Post and Mella were the witnesses, and Stålnacke was the interrogator.

"Let Stålnacke conduct the interrogation," Chief Prosecutor Björnfot had told von Post. "He's the sort of person that people open their hearts to."

Now he was sitting there opposite Häggroth. Both were wearing striped shirts. Stålnacke scratched his large moustache.

"Are you alright?" he asked. "Can we begin?"

Häggroth did not answer. With a deep sigh, his tongue tucked into one corner of his mouth, Stålnacke switched on the tape recorder, a routine which involved him checking the battery and making sure it was recording the sound. He shifted his position on the chair. Grunted and panted a few times, and leaned his head on one side to stretch out any stiffness.

It's like having a bear in your house, Mella thought.

"Let's begin at the beginning," Stålnacke said. "Would you like to tell us all about it? About you and Sol-Britt? How did your relationship begin?"

Häggroth looked down at his hands.

"It was last spring. I'd had a row with Jenny. I suppose I was drunk. Not all that much, but still . . . I went round to Sol-Britt's house. Not that I really know her. We say hello if we meet somewhere. But I couldn't go to anybody we know, there'd be so much gossip. I couldn't take the car as I was over the limit. I just went out for a walk. I didn't know where to go. And I was cold, I hadn't taken a jacket with me. Then I found myself outside her house. It was pure chance."

He looked up at Stålnacke.

"I didn't kill her."

Oh damn, Mella thought.

"Let's take one thing at a time," Stålnacke said. "What happened next?"

"We just talked. Nothing more. I suppose I tried to get off with her – she had a reputation after all."

"What kind of a reputation?"

"That she would go to bed with more or less anybody. Folk . . . They talk such a lot of crap."

He exhaled, then breathed in greedily, as if his lungs were not getting what they needed.

"Ouch," he said, placing his hand over his jaw.

"And then?" Stålnacke said.

"Then? Not . . . oh hell . . . The next time I screwed her. And then we carried on like that occasionally. That's all there was to it. I didn't kill her. I don't . . . I don't know who did it."

He panted like a bull elk. Held his hand to his chin. His face had turned deathly white.

"Ouch," he whimpered again. "Bloody hell."

Mella and von Post exchanged glances. Stålnacke looked hard at Häggroth.

"How do you feel?"

"Not good. Damnation!"

His hand slid over his neck and landed on his chest. He leaned forward.

"Try and breathe calmly, my friend," Stålnacke said. "Where does it hurt?"

"In my face, here." He stroked his cheeks and nose. "Oh shit, shit, shit!"

He put his other hand on the table, as if to support himself.

Then he fell off the chair. Landed flat on his face.

Mella and von Post jumped to their feet.

"What the hell did you do?" von Post yelled to Stålnacke.

Häggroth was sweating like a pig and was already soaking wet.

"Call an ambulance," said von Post. "He mustn't die, for God's sake! An ambulance! Without delay. He's going to be arrested, dammit!"

Von Post rushed down the hospital corridor. He was furious. He ought to have taken charge of the interrogation himself. He knew that he should have been the one. He must stop listening to other people. Take control over that confounded police station.

He glanced over his shoulder at Mella, who was half-jogging behind him. He opened the double doors, walked through them then let go so that they smashed into her.

The dwarf unit, he thought, glancing back again. Special measures against goblins and trolls.

"Who killed her and wrote 'whore' on her wall?" he bawled, pressing the lift button over and over again, as if that would hurry it up. "Her boyfriend, or lover! Lesson one in the murdering of women. She dumped him! Häggroth was raving. Drank until his brain was like a lump of mouse shit. Then he took the hayfork and did her in. Staggered back to his pathetic farmhouse, slung the fork under the barn and went to bed. That's exactly what happened. All too predictable. That's how it always happens, for Christ's sake."

They stepped out of the lift. God, how he hated hospitals. A handrail ran all the way along one of the corridor walls. Occasional chairs outside the closed doors. An empty hospital bed on wheels. Some sort of so-called art hanging on the walls, slightly higher than the plaques with instructions to follow if the place needed to be evacuated. A green, highly polished plastic floor, reflecting the fluorescent tube lights.

They came to the locked door of the intensive care unit, and he kept his finger pressed on the bell button, demanding to be let in.

She's scared stiff now, he thought as he looked at Mella. There's a lump in that wobbly baby-belly of hers.

Häggroth was your archetypal femicidal maniac. Although the way he actually killed her was rather novel. A touch of the mad professor there, Jocke. Instead of bashing her against the nearest wall, or hitting her with a hammer, or cutting her up with a kitchen knife.

Nervous devils. Not to mention Stålnacke. He'd been on the point of tears when the ambulance arrived to fetch Häggroth.

And he had good reason to cry. Uncle Walrus would be well and truly in the shit if Häggroth died on them. Mella as well!

Von Post kept his finger on the bell button, swaying back and forth. Thank God he was in no way responsible for this catastrophe.

Out of respect for their long experience he had remained a passive observer. He hadn't said a bloody word!

It was just as well that he hadn't conducted the interrogation himself.

But what if Häggroth died without confessing? The investigation would be written off. And the whole pack of bloody hyenas would set about the police. Their interrogation methods would be questioned. The circumstances of his arrest would be splashed all over the papers.

He was surrounded by idiots. And they were always plotting against him. They couldn't even keep that Häggroth woman under control. How the hell could they allow her to vandalise his car and then run off into the woods? How the hell was that possible?

The duty doctor refused to allow the police access to her patient.

She positioned herself like a Russian border guard outside the closed door of his private ward. She ran her hand over her close-cropped dark hair and pushed up her aviator-style spectacles, which had slid down to the tip of her nose. Then she explained that Jocke Häggroth was conscious, but had probably suffered a heart attack. She used words like "morphine" and "low pulse rate" and "oxygen" and "beta-blockers", and concluded by saying that under no circumstances must the patient be exposed to stress.

A dyke, decided von Post in annoyance. So there was no point in putting on a smile and addressing her in a manly voice.

But a competent young lady as well, he thought when the doctor explained that yes, she heard what von Post was saying. The patient was suspected of the brutal murder of a woman. And yes, of course she was horrified by that: but she had no intention of risking her patient's life. They could continue with the interrogation when the patient's condition had stabilised. When would that be? Hard to say.

She stood there, the case notes under her arm. She didn't even come up to von Post's chin. The A. & E. DOCTOR on her identity disc shone into von Post's eyes like a searchlight.

"I want to speak to your superior," von Post said.

But that did him no good. The senior doctor was based in Luleå, and said on the telephone that he had no reason to doubt his colleague's assessment of the patient's critical condition.

He had no alternative but to return to the police station. How the hell could you do a decent job when everybody was conspiring against you on all sides?

Life became no kinder to von Post when he got back to the station. The inspector from Umeå who was supposed to be a specialist in interrogating children had spent the day wasting taxpayers' money.

She was in plain clothes. A large woman wearing layer upon layer of linen clothing, with thick grey hair gathered in a bun. Round her neck was a leather strap with a large ornament made of silver and wood, which von Post assumed was supposed to bring out the goddess in her.

Von Post eyed her up and down, and had the feeling that he also needed a dose of oxygen and beta-blockers and morphine.

Only the best studied law. And only the best of the best became prosecutors and judges. But evidently any old riff-raff could become a police officer.

"So he didn't say anything?" he asked.

"He doesn't remember anything," she said. "My guess is that he really has seen or heard something horrific. There is a gap in his story which suggests this. Why did he wake up? How did he get to the hut in the forest? Why did he climb out through the window?"

"I know all about the gaps," von Post said steadily. "That's why we brought you here. Surely it must be possible to find out what that memory is. By hypnosis or some such method, I don't know. Isn't that your job? We've flown you here. What the hell are we getting for our money?"

"My job is to talk to the boy. I've done that. But he doesn't say anything about the night of the murder. He can't. Or maybe he doesn't want to. He shall certainly not be hypnotised."

"So when can we interrogate him?"

"You can interrogate him as much as you like. But if you want to get out of him what he's seen, you must make him feel secure. That police officer who's been looking after him, Krister Eriksson. The boy is evidently living with him and pretending that he's a dog. Eriksson told me he would be able to carry on looking after him for a while. That's excellent. The boy has nobody else he can turn to, as I understand it. The more secure he feels, the better the odds that he will tell us something. And it's not usual for everything to come out at once. It tends to come out a bit at a time. And it doesn't come when we expect it to – very seldom when we're talking about the incident; when mostly he's busy with something quite different."

"Brilliant," said von Post. "We've paid all that money to be advised that we have to wait. Marvellous! Wonderful! It would be fantastic if only somebody, some time, would do the job they get paid for."

The inspector opened her mouth, but closed it again. She took out her mobile and looked at it.

"I must go to the airport now," she said, looking out at the falling snow. "We'd better leave plenty of time. Inspector Mella's going to drive me there."

Von Post made no reply. Why should he?

Give me a normal person who understands what people are saying, he thought.

"That prosecutor," the colleague from Umeå said to Mella while they were driving out to the airport. "He wasn't a very nice man."

"Hänen ej ole ko pistää takaisin ja nussia uuesti," said Mella sternly.

"I don't understand Finnish – what does that mean?"

"Er, well . . . That he's not a nice man. God, but it's really snowing hard now. We'll have to see if it settles."

The windscreen wipers swung back and forth. The headlights were reflected in all the flakes. It was like a white wall ahead of her, hard to see anything at all.

It's snowing. It's 14 April, 1915, and the snowflakes are fluttering down from a grey winter sky. Hjalmar Lundbohm has some very special visitors. Artist Carl Larsson's wife has travelled up with Anders Zorn and his wife, the architect Ferdinand Boberg along with fru Boberg, the sculptor Christian Eriksson and the illustrator Ossian Elgström.

Larsson himself has never been to Kiruna, but his wife Karin comes up occasionally with various artist and author friends. Trips to Kiruna are always such jollies.

Lundbohm has arranged some reindeer-racing for his guests. They are all wearing Laplander hats and riding on Lapp sledges. The weather could have been better: Lundbohm would have preferred some brilliant winter sun shining down on a delightfully snow-covered Kiruna, but not even he can control the weather.

Even so, the event is very successful. The reindeer race pell-mell along Bromsgatan, and the guests cheer and urge on their horned steeds.

Johan Tuuri and other Lapps join in the fun and run alongside at times, to keep the animals on the right course.

The winner is Karin Larsson. She laughs until she cries, the photographer Borg Mesch immortalises the moment as she stands there looking delightful, her Lappish hat askew and with a young Lappish boy standing proudly by her side. The reindeer belongs to his family and he has been skiing alongside it all the way, shouting encouragement.

Anders Zorn has fallen out of his sledge and wins the improvised prize for Snowman of the Day.

Everyone is so hot that they are boiling over, exhilarated and noisy. They chase one another and push each other off the trodden-down pathways – as soon as anybody leaves the path they sink down into the snow up to their waists. On the way back they try to engage in a snowball fight, but the temperature is below freezing and the snow is too powdery to make into snowballs. Instead they throw loose snow at each other until they are all completely white from top to toe.

Yes indeed, Lundbohm has every reason to be pleased when they get back to his residence for hot punch, a change of clothes and lunch.

Even so there is something gnawing away inside him. What irks him is the knowledge that he can join in and play one day, but not the next.

For instance, the Zorns held a masked ball last New Year's Eve, and he was not on the guest list. And when they throw parties out at the island of Bullerö in the summer, he is never invited.

He sees Karin Larsson laughing away, arm in arm with Emma Zorn, and the thought strikes him that if only he were married to a woman like that, sociable, artistic, happy and pretty and from a superior family . . . And just as he is gazing at Karin and thinking along those lines, they bump into Elina and Lizzie.

He feels rather ashamed when he sees Elina. It is partly her appearance, but also because his conscience is troubled: he hasn't been in touch with her. He has had so much to do. Because of the war he has travelled to the U.S.A. and Canada, and also to the Krupp works in Germany. It takes a special sort of person to deal with all these mixed loyalties. He has made sure that when ships take iron ore to the U.S.A., they bring back with them salted American pork for the workers in Kiruna. He has held his own with the Swedish government when they tried to confiscate the meat for feeding the Swedish military. He has not been able to spend much time with Elina. They meet when he is at home in Kiruna, but not so often. A few evenings, a few nights: but what he has longed for above all else is sleep.

Lizzie and Elina have been out in the forest, collecting firewood. They have to make the most of the opportunity now, before it gets warmer and the snow on the winter paths becomes soft and treacherous to travel on.

They are wearing their oldest and shabbiest clothes. Elina has borrowed a worn-out leather jacket from one of their lodgers; it goes down almost to her knees. She has a headscarf tied under her chin like an old lady. Lizzie has on a knitted jumper that is falling to pieces.

They have been sawing wood and are covered in bits of bark and sawdust. The hems of their skirts are stiff and heavy with snow.

Together, they are pulling a sledge laden with firewood.

Elina sees the elegantly dressed group and wishes the earth would swallow her up.

Lizzie curtseys.

"Well, hello there, fröken Lizzie!" shouts Boberg the architect, who has a remarkable memory for names and faces. "Are you going to cook that magnificent smoked reindeer fillet for us again this evening?"

"Oh, you remember it, do you?" says Lizzie with a smile.

She is not in the least embarrassed about how she and Elina look. It is only Elina who wants to die the death.

And Lundbohm doesn't even look at her.

Lizzie announces that they will have to survive that evening without her culinary skills.

"Today is my day off. And herr Lundbohm has arranged both food and staff from the Östermalmskällaren in Stockholm, so no doubt you will eat splendiferously tonight."

"You look as if you're working hard on your day off," Boberg says.

Lizzie explains that they have been collecting firewood, and not just for themselves. As they were going out anyway, they have collected some for a few neighbours as well, and earned themselves no less than seven kronor.

Elina's cheeks are blazing red.

"I'm dumbfounded," Boberg jokes. "Shall we not have the pleasure of seeing your delightful self this evening? Have I travelled all this way simply to eat Stockholm food? If I ask you nicely, will you come and make us some heavenly beestings pudding with cloudberry jam as a dessert?"

"You can beg until the second coming of Christ accompanied by the heavenly host, but I'm going to a dance with my fiancé this evening."

Everybody laughs apart from Elina and Hjalmar Lundbohm, but nobody notices that.

"Goodbye, then, girls," says Zorn, who has got snow inside his collar and is beginning to long for the promised punch.

The group moves on. Karin Larsson and Emma Zorn wave to Elina and Lizzie as one does to small children. Elina hears Karin saying "what a sweet little thing", and one of the men makes some comment that she can't catch, and everybody laughs.

Elina is embarrassed and angry. She puts all her strength into pulling the firewood over the last lap of its journey. She is angry with Lizzie as well, although she cannot really explain why.

When Lizzie asks what is wrong with her, she says, "He could have introduced me to them at least."

"As what?" Lizzie wonders.

She is not the sort to pass judgement, and she says nothing, but she nevertheless thinks that Elina is a goose. Starting an affair with a big shot like that. Personally, she has always steered clear of men with too much or too little money, and in the end chose a working man from the same social class as herself. A man who looks after himself and doesn't hit the booze. So that they can make plans for the future. There's nothing wrong with Lundbohm – as an employer! But this relationship can only end in tears, Lizzie can see it coming.

They keep silent all the way home. In the evening Lizzie goes out dancing with her Johan-Albin, but doesn't manage to have much fun.

Lundbohm's guests depart, but he makes no attempt to contact Elina.

Lizzie tries to persuade Elina to accompany her to the Baptist church, and to a lecture on phrenology that Borg Mesch is giving in Folkets Hus, but without success.

"You can't just sit here reading and reading," Lizzie says, genuinely worried.

After four days a messenger boy comes with a note from Lundbohm, but it is not an invitation to meet: it is just a quick couple of lines to say he has to go off on his travels again. He writes that he misses her, but that doesn't help much. He doesn't use any of the loving names he used to call her, such as "little bunny", "Puss-Puss", "my little fox cub". No, just "I miss you". But if he really missed her, surely they would have met? There is no getting away from that.

And it doesn't help that the whole of Kiruna is teeming with young men. She is lost. It is a different Elina who goes to school every day, somebody else who smiles and talks and behaves exactly as she always did.

The real Elina reads *Jane Eyre* and *Wuthering Heights*. And cries as soon as she is alone.

*

He comes back again in May. She receives another note. The same old story. He wants to meet her. A thousand times she has told herself that she certainly will not agree to see him. But that treacherous heart of hers somehow convinces her otherwise. Persuades her that the right thing to do is to see him. She washes her hair. Irons her best blouse.

She falls immediately into his arms, and there is no yesterday or tomorrow. She hasn't the strength to worry about anything, as long as she can feel his skin next to hers. And he seems to be just as hungry for her. It is like it was at the beginning.

"Are you angry with me?" he asks as she lies on his arm.

He has lit a cigar, which she borrows and takes a puff from.

"No," she says. "Why should I be?"

"I ought to have introduced you to my friends," he says. "It was just that I was so surprised. I hadn't expected to bump into you in the street like that."

Her mouth is full of "perhaps you should have invited me to be there as well" and "what exactly am I to you?", but she doesn't let them slip out. She doesn't want to start an argument. All she wants is to sleep here on his arm.

In the middle of the night she wakes up and is as hungry as a wolf. She sneaks into the kitchen, and goes into the scullery. She eats two cold boiled eggs, some soured whole milk, two sandwiches, yesterday's boiled salmon trout and some meatballs lying in a dish.

Then she takes down a cast iron frying pan from one of the hooks in the ceiling, sits down on a stool, and sucks it. Sucks the greasy, shiny black iron.

It was almost three o'clock in the afternoon. It was starting to get dark. And it was snowing for all it was worth. Not exactly ideal weather for a car trip. But Martinsson and Pohjanen wanted to go to Lainio to pick up that shirt, no matter what.

He offered to drive. He had not driven a car for a whole year now, and it would make a nice change. Martinsson made it quite clear that since at this stage he was barely able to get up from his chair, there was no chance of him driving a car.

In the end they agreed that they should take a taxi. It would be rather expensive, of course, but if they thought about it . . . In fact they didn't do any thinking but simply picked up the telephone and ordered a taxi. Pohjanen promised to pay the fare from his own pocket provided that Martinsson invited him to dinner again when they got back.

The taxi arrived. The journey took an hour.

The car took them right up to the front door. Nevertheless, they were soaked through after walking the few steps they had to take without shelter. The snow clung to their hair and found its way under their collars, stuck in their eyelashes so that they got snow in their eyes whenever they blinked. They were standing outside the door like two homeless snowmen when the owner opened it. They declined the offer of coffee, and the berry-picker fetched the shirt, which was wrapped in a plastic carrier bag. They were given an extra bag to tie round it in the hope of preventing it from polluting the car. They thanked him profusely for his help, and ran back to the taxi.

"It must have been something extremely important," said the taxi driver, eyeing the tightly tied plastic bag in his rear-view mirror. "A long drive there and back. And in this bloody weather."

But by then both Martinsson and Pohjanen were fast asleep on the back seat. They didn't wake up until they were back in Kurravaara.

Pohjanen handed his Visa card to the driver.

Now they were both as hungry as wolves. The Brat was pleased to see them, and parked himself beside the stove.

Martinsson fried some potato dumplings which they ate with melted butter, pork and lingon jam. They drank milk with it.

Then they spread newspapers over the table, produced their hip flasks again and braced themselves to try and puzzle out the story behind the late Frans Uusitalo's filthy, torn shirt.

Back in Lainio the berry-picker was beginning to regret what he had done. He had kept that shirt in his garage for months. He had made it clear to any police officer prepared to listen what he had done – but what had he done now? Handed over the bloodstained and torn shirt to a woman and a man who had more or less tumbled out of a taxi on his drive. They stank as if they had just come from a party at which the booze had been flowing freely – that woman wearing high-heeled boots that she could barely walk in, and the walking corpse who accompanied her. How could he be sure that they were in fact a prosecutor and a pathologist? He hadn't seen any identification documents.

If that pair of drunks lost the shirt, well: he was left sitting there with his arse on the waffle-iron. What the hell had he been thinking of?

It took a few hours, but in the end he got up from his television armchair and telephoned the police in Kiruna.

A woman answered in sing-song Finland-Swedish.

Could he please have a receipt for that shirt? That was surely the least he could ask for?

Sonja on the switchboard put him through to District Prosecutor von Post.

It is the end of May 1915. Fröken Elina Pettersson is walking home from the bandstand where there was a showing of the artist Isaac Grünewald's adults-only film about the one-step.

Critics consider the dance to be disgusting, a modern dance aimed at subverting healthy and natural happiness, and insist that everybody who feels a sense of responsibility for the young people of today, and expects to find culture and refinement even in popular entertainment, must condemn the showing of this film in family circles.

Grünewald, who dances with his wife in this cinematographic response, defends it passionately. This is a young person's dance, he maintains. Just like the tango. And obviously, everything new is obscene and unaesthetic. How obscene is modern art in general? he wonders.

Elina both one-steps and two-steps as she plods away. The snow is melting, and the ground cannot absorb all the water: the street is a river of mud.

The nights are still cold, so it is easier in the mornings: she can walk on the frozen mud, which crackles under her feet. But during the day the sun acts like a flamethrower. Shoes are stuffed with straw and newspaper and stand in the kitchen to dry, but are still damp in the mornings. The hems of her skirts are mud-stained. The lodgers reek of the cowshed, and bring so much filth into the flat that Lizzie tears her hair out.

Elina does not normally walk home alone, but on this occasion nobody else was going her way. Bearing in mind that it was light outside, and she didn't have far to go, it felt awkward to ask somebody to accompany her. Nor has she told anybody else apart from Lizzie about Fasth and his improper advances. People talk. And you end up being regarded as the guilty party, as always. Especially when the aggressor is a man like Fasth.

But just as she is passing the cemetery, she hears footsteps approaching rapidly from behind.

When she turns to look, Fasth has already caught up with her. Fear crawls down her spine.

The street is deserted. Only him and her. She starts walking faster, forges ahead straight through all the puddles without a thought for the welfare of her skirt or boots.

"Fröööken Pettersson," he says. "Why the rush?"

He puts his arm around her waist and tells her that she really must be nice to him – he is the one who pays her wages after all.

She tries to insist that it is in fact the mining company and herr Lundbohm who pays her wages.

Oh no, he tells her. Lundbohm doesn't stoop so low as to bother about such minor matters. Especially not now. He spoke to Lundbohm on the telephone earlier today, and he seemed to be having fun with a new girlfriend in Stockholm. Surely she didn't think that she was anything special as far as Lundbohm was concerned? Of course not. And besides, she's no doubt an emancipated woman. If she has urges, no doubt he can help to satisfy them.

He takes firm hold of her wrist so that she has to stop, and forces her hand down to the bulge in his trousers. His face is as red as a slice of raw meat.

"Feel that," he urges her. "It will make you . . ."

At that very moment somebody shouts, "Hi there!"

And there, thank God, is Lizzie's fiancé Johan-Albin, with a

238

friend. They hurry towards Elina, who is standing as if caught in a bear trap. Fasth has still not released her wrist; his grip is like steel.

"What's going on here?" wonders Johan-Albin when they come up to Fasth and Elina.

Elina is incapable of speech, but Fasth is.

"Off you go, boys," he says, without even taking his eyes off Elina. "This young lady and I are enjoying a little chat."

"Off you go now, on your way," he adds when the young men show no sign of moving.

But the two men merely take a step forward.

"Off you go yourself, Fasth," says Lizzie's fiancé. "I shall say that only once: after that it will be fists that do the talking."

Manager-in-Chief Fasth lets go of Elina's wrist.

"Alright, you can have her. She has an urge in her pussy, and she was so keen on me helping her to satisfy it."

Then he walks calmly away. Does not hurry at all.

The two men and Elina remain standing there, without saying a word. Only when Fasth is no longer in sight does Johan-Albin say, "Don't cry, Elina. We'll take you home now."

"Thank you," she whimpers.

"No need to thank me – I have no time for managers and similar types who boss you around."

And as they are walking home, he tells his tale to Elina and his friend. Elina has already heard about it from Lizzie, but she doesn't mention that – she does not want him to think that Lizzie has betrayed a confidence. Men sometimes do not understand things like that – the fact that women tell each other things. About themselves and about the people they love.

He tells them about his parents, who were poverty-stricken crofters outside Överkalix.

"And my dad was good with animals. He knew all about herbs that could cure illnesses in cattle. In people as well, but they didn't talk about that. How to stop bleeding. That sort of thing. And he was good when mothers were giving birth, brilliant at getting them out – calves, foals, babies. 'Oops! Look out there, give me a hand, Heikki – we'll lift her over this little lake. When are they going to dig proper drainage channels here? It's the same every spring when the snow melts . . .' Anyway, sometimes he wasn't able to get them out in one piece. When the calves were too big, or lying in an impossible position. That was always a hellish job, breaking up the unborn calf inside its mother without injuring her, then getting it out. But it had to be done. If a family lost its cow, they were ruined. That was the only time he ever drank heavily, after an incident like that . . ."

He shakes his head.

"People used to give him a bottle of schnapps as thanks for his efforts. He would find his way to an isolated hayloft and drink until he passed out. Didn't come back home until he'd sobered up."

Heikki comments in Finnish: "Voi helvetti."

"But what about managers and other bosses?" Elina says. She knows the answer already, but wants to help him to continue his tale.

"They had an assistant bailiff supervising all the crofters in the area. He was a German, and keen on Lappish girls."

"I'm sure you know," Heikki says to Elina, "Karl XII had a lot of German mercenaries in his army. After the war they couldn't return home – they had been fighting against their own countrymen after all – so they settled in Sweden and did what they were good at."

"They became executioners," Johan-Albin says, "and bailiffs. And their sons became executioners and bailiffs. And their sons . . . Anyway, all those eleven- and twelve-year-olds . . . They were only Lapps, so he could have his way with them. But when they became pregnant, their bodies weren't ready to produce children. And so my dad was called in. He was unable to save two girls. They died in childbirth. And then, after the second death . . ."

They are back at Elina's and Lizzie's home now. Elina invites them in. They will have to cook for the lodgers anyway, so it will be easy to accommodate a couple of extra guests. That is the least she can do.

Lizzie comes home shortly after them. She has a bucket of fish with her. It will be boiled burbot for dinner.

They tell her what happened to Elina. She listens while cutting the heads off the burbot, then skins them and guts them as if it is Manager-in-Chief Fasth lying there on the chopping board.

Then Johan-Albin continues his story.

"When the second girl died, Dad had had enough. He grabbed hold of that bailiff one spring evening and castrated him as one castrates a horse. Beat him unconscious first. Then nailed him to the stable door through his clothes. Split open his scrotum, turned it inside out and snipped off his balls."

He clenches his fists and has to pause for a few moments. Lizzie stands there with her hands soiled by the fish she has been cutting up, but looking as if she is about to hug him.

"The bailiff survived. But my dad was condemned to five years in prison. After two years he died of consumption. Mum couldn't take care of us children on her own – there were five of us. I was six years old. We were all put up for sale at a paupers' auction. I was bought by a Finnish charcoal-burner. But I could only take that for a year, then I ran away. I joined up with the navvies building the railway. I started as a so-called nail boy for teams of navvies. My job was to run back and forth with buckets full of nails and spikes that had buckled, take them to the smithy where they were hammered out straight, then take them back to where the action was. I've never been to school or anything like that. And now I've ended up here. As I said, I've no time for bailiffs and managers and types like that."

The atmosphere is hardly uplifting as they eat their dinner. Poverty is lurking around in the forests surrounding the mining town of Kiruna. Ready to swallow up any woman who loses an arm, a husband, or her virtue.

Virtue. Elina feels the food swelling inside her mouth, but she says nothing. Neither to the others nor to herself.

Von Post was going out of his mind.

"I'm going out of my mind!" he yelled at Sonja on the switch-board.

And when he pressed Sonja a little he discovered that as well as collecting a shirt that had been worn by Sol-Britt Uusitalo's father when he was mauled by a bear, Martinsson had also asked Sonja to produce records of the hit-and-run incident that robbed Sol-Britt's son of his life.

"Fucking hell!" he shouted as he hurtled up the stairs to Martinsson's office where Björnfot was writing judgments one after another after the day's proceedings.

"That woman," he said in a voice shaking with emotion, "that Rebecka Martinsson! She's interfering in my investigation."

Björnfot slid his glasses down to the bridge of his nose and looked at von Post. Then he slid them up onto his forehead again and continued writing while von Post gave a long and rather loud summary of what had happened.

"This is a matter for the personnel section of the Prosecutor-General's Office," von Post claimed. "She must be moved away from here."

"But if I understand you rightly," Björnfot said calmly, "it's not your investigation that she is getting involved in. She is looking into two accidents – the fact that those involved are related to your murder victim . . ."

"This is not O.K.," von Post snarled. "You can't defend her, and you know that full well. The Prosecutor-General should . . ."

Björnfot flung out his arms in an I-give-up gesture.

"I'll have a word with her," he said.

Von Post was incapable of speech. He was so furious that his mind was a complete blank.

But one thing was certain. He would talk to Martinsson himself. He had a lot to say to her.

Martinsson and Pohjanen had donned thin rubber gloves and were playing jigsaw puzzles with the shredded shirt. They succeeded in fitting most of it together, but half a sleeve was missing, and part of the back.

"What claws that bear must have had," Pohjanen said with admiration in his voice as he examined the edges of the various pieces of cloth. "It's as if somebody had cut it up with a pair of sharp scissors."

He lifted up part of the front of the shirt and held it towards the light. It was stained brown with mud and blood, but in the middle of it was an obvious hole.

"What do you think this is?" he asked.

Martinsson examined the hole.

"I don't know," she said, but her heart missed a beat. "What do you think?"

"Well," said Pohjanen slowly, "I think it's a bullet hole. That's what I think. And I think we should send it to the National Forensic Science Laboratory and ask them to test it for traces of metal and gunpowder."

"So the bear didn't kill him," Martinsson said. "It ate him, but it didn't kill him."

Pohjanen gave her a look that she could not really fathom.

"You and your dreams," he said in the end.

Then he shook his head.

"I'm . . ."

"As drunk as a lord," Martinsson said. "I reckon we should have a sauna – what do you think?"

It was Martinsson's grandfather, together with his brothers, who had constructed the wooden sauna on the riverbank. It was painted in traditional Falun red, had an entrance porch with wooden benches for two on either side, then a little changing room with an open fire, followed by a washroom with buckets, ladles and a washbasin – and then the inner sanctum: the sauna itself, heated by firewood of course, and with a window overlooking the river.

Both Pohjanen and Martinsson had grown up in environments where it was the done thing from time immemorial for men and women to sit naked together in the sauna without the slightest feeling of embarrassment. Bodies were exposed irrespective of their imperfections, their signs of ageing or of multiple births – one had no need to feel ashamed of anything in the sauna. The plumpness of youth in the right places, skin like flower petals – no-one gave such things a second glance.

Martinsson carried in buckets of water and lit the fires while Pohjanen purred with delight, drank beer and warmed up his rickety body in front of the open fire.

Then they entered the sauna itself. Martinsson was better able to cope with the heat, and sat on the highest bench. Sweat trickled down into their eyes, the water sizzled away on the hot stones, the steam rose up to the ceiling.

They spoke about all the things people always discuss in the sauna. That they ought really to have had birch twigs to beat themselves with – but that was not really possible at this time of year because there were no leaves on the trees. That this was the only way to become really clean – who the hell would want to splash around in water tainted by the filth of their own bodies in a bathtub? They talked about smoke saunas, and old relatives who could tolerate the heat of a real sauna; about their childhood sauna experiences, and how electric-fired saunas were an invention of the devil.

They scratched their skin and contemplated the grey deposits under their nails. They bowed their heads and groaned in a mixture of delight and pain when Martinsson poured more water onto the burning hot stones and the first of the hot steam hit their skins. Martinsson blew onto her hand, and as always was astonished by how hot that spot became in the area blown onto.

Martinsson went out twice into the darkness and snow and immersed herself in the wintry river. Pohjanen desisted, but declared his willingness to bathe in a hole bored through the ice if he was invited to a Christmas sauna later in the year. The Brat, who had been basking in front of the open fire in the changing room, followed Martinsson out, barking excitedly at her, and after failing to catch falling snowflakes eventually jumped into the water after her.

"What's the matter with dogs?" wondered Pohjanen with a laugh when Rebecka came back into the warm sauna with the Brat at her heels. "Why do they always have to shake the water off themselves when they're standing next to a human being?"

Eventually they felt they had had enough of the sauna, and made their way back to the house.

Martinsson contemplated Pohjanen's emaciated back.

I really do hope you'll come here for a Christmas dip, she thought. Please do live that long.

As Pohjanen took hold of the door handle, von Post turned in to the drive.

He got out of the car dressed only in his shirtsleeves. Pointed at Martinsson and yelled, "Damn you, Martinsson! Damn and blast you!"

Martinsson didn't say a word. She lowered her hands and let her arms hang loosely. The snow gathered to form a cap on her damp hair. Pohjanen walked up the steps to the porch, but the balcony overhead was an inadequate shelter.

"Do you think I don't know exactly what you are doing?" von Post bawled. "You know that we've arrested the murderer, but if we can't get the necessary forensic proof it will be a case based on circumstantial evidence. And now you are trying to cock it all up for me by inventing alternative motives . . ."

"I'm not inventing—"

"Shut your mouth! If there's the slightest suspicion that somebody is intent on murdering the whole family – her son, her father – you know full well that it will be impossible to nail Jocke Häggroth. You are trying to find alternative motives, alternative suspicions, purely in order to stop me from solving this case. You're prepared to let a murderer go free for no other reason than to do me down. It's scandalous. You're sick, damn you."

He raised his index finger again.

Pohjanen took an unsteady pace forward.

"Calm down, young man. Come in and have a drink, and you can hear what we've discovered. It's no secret."

Both Martinsson and von Post looked at Pohjanen as if he had just announced an arranged marriage, or that they should all sing "We Shall Overcome".

"You're out of your minds!" von Post snarled. "You think you can bugger me about, Martinsson, but you'll soon find out how wrong you are. I know the man in charge of personnel at the Prosecutor-General's office, and I shall tell him that you are a security risk for the investigation. A danger to yourself. Everybody knows you spent time in a psychiatric hospital. And now you're falling to pieces in this sensitive situation. I worry that you will abuse the means of compulsion that we have at our disposal. So the personnel unit will make sure that you undergo neuropathological tests in connection with your abnormal behaviour. I can assure you that it is a very degrading business. A sort of inquisition. And then you will be moved to a new post where you will be unable to cause any harm. A job in the legal department of the police – dealing with such matters as objections to parking tickets, or the granting of permission for officers to carry weapons."

He paused. Breathing heavily. Panting, as if he had been running up a hill.

The Brat ran up to him, wagging his tail, and dropped a pine cone in front of his feet. This was the Brat's role on such occasions: to defuse tension. To produce a cone from somewhere and suggest the playing of a game. A harmless little clown.

Von Post stared at the cone with a mixture of revulsion and incomprehension. Then he waved his hand at the Brat, as if to shoo him away. The dog picked up the cone and moved it a little closer to von Post. Looked up at him, ears cocked, as if to say: *Aren't I irresistible*? Pohjanen produced a strange, hoarse sound. Only if you knew him well could you know that it was a laugh.

"You're bloody stark, staring mad," von Post said. "The lot of you!"

He got back into his car without brushing off the snow, and drove away.

"What a prat!" Pohjanen chuckled as von Post's car disappeared from view.

He held out his hand and allowed the Brat to drop the cone onto it. Then threw it a couple of metres away.

"The man's a bloody psychopath. I pity the poor old man in the street if it's bastards like him leading the fight against crime."

Martinsson was watching the Brat fetching the pine cone.

She thought about von Post. He had stared at the dog as if he wanted to kill it.

"That dog," she said to Pohjanen when they had reached her kitchen and relit the fire in the stove. "Sol-Britt's dog. When I read the record of the interrogation Mella had with Marcus, he didn't say a word about the night of the murder. It was as if he didn't know what she was talking about. But he did say that their dog had gone missing."

"Really?"

With considerable effort she took out her mobile and rang Sivving. He answered immediately, as if he had been sitting by the phone waiting for a call. She felt a pang of conscience. She ought to have invited him to the sauna as well.

"I have a question," she said. "Didn't Sol-Britt use to have a dog? Do you know when it disappeared?"

"Yes, she did," Sivving said. "She posted lost notices all over the village. When can it have been? Less than a month ago. I've told you, haven't I: keep Vera on a leash! There are weird people around. Some go out of their way to run over dogs if they get the chance."

"Thank you," Martinsson said. "I'll ring you again later."

"Have you been drinking? You sound a bit jolly."

"Of course not," Martinsson said and hung up before Sivving could say anything else.

"It went missing about a month ago," she said to Pohjanen. "If I were planning to break into a house and murder somebody, I'd certainly make sure they didn't have a dog."

Pohjanen nodded.

"Yes indeed," he said. "The gangs who break into every house in a street in the middle of the night, when people are fast asleep in their beds, always miss out houses where there are dogs."

"If it really was Jocke Häggroth who did it . . ." Martinsson said ". . . if it was . . . Then he didn't do it on the spur of the moment."

The day after the incident with Fasth, Elina comes home at about three o'clock. Lizzie and Johan-Albin are sitting at the table. The lodgers are still at work. Johan-Albin is sitting with his head bowed, and Lizzie is holding his hands. She gives Elina a serious look. Johan-Albin is staring down at the table.

"What's the matter?" Elina asks. "What's happened?"

Johan-Albin shakes his head, but Lizzie explains.

"It's Fasth," she says. "He's sacked Johan-Albin."

"Not sacked," Johan-Albin says.

"No, he daren't do that because of the reaction there would be from the trade union. There's a lot of dissatisfaction simmering away everywhere just now, and Johan-Albin is popular. But Fasth has redeployed him. He was a loader earning six kronor an hour, and Fasth has now switched him to the stone crusher – three kronor an hour! That's barely enough to live on. And of course, we're meant to be saving for our future . . ."

"It just involves keeping an eye on things and making adjustments when necessary," Johan-Albin says. "They don't pay much for that kind of work. And Heikki's new job is emptying the shithouses in the resting huts."

Elina cannot even bring herself to enter the kitchen. She remains standing in the hall.

The stone crusher. The machine from hell that crushes the ore into small stones. There is no worse job in the whole mine. Workers are made deaf by the noise from the enormous screw-like auger that crushes the stones and spits them out into the wagons standing underneath. Their lungs become black as a result of the flying dust. And it is highly dangerous as well. The attendants stand around with their iron rods and prise away loose stones and slabs that get stuck in the screw. The rod can also get stuck and drag the operator down into the crusher, or spring back and give him fatal injuries. It can happen in a split second.

"I'm sorry," she says. "It's my fault."

Johan-Albin shakes his head again, but neither he nor Lizzie contradict her.

Lizzie's face, which is always so bright and cheerful, is full of worry. She gives Elina a stern look.

"You'll have to talk to Lundbohm."

Elina turns white.

Lizzie stands up and walks over to her. She adjusts Elina's scarf and strokes her cheek.

"You really must talk to him . . . no matter what. Don't you think?" she says quietly, her eyes roving over Elina's breasts and stomach.

Elina nods without speaking. Of course. Two women who sleep in the same bed. What can they possibly hide from each other?

"It's nothing you need to plan or to worry about," Lizzie says. "He's at home. Just go and tell him."

What shall I do? wondered Martinsson.

Pohjanen and the Brat had fallen asleep on the sofa in the little lounge. The fire had died down and the last of the small logs were glowing red in the darkness.

Von Post had succeeded in frightening her. Good and proper. Martinsson could not bear the thought of neuropathological tests. Some second-rater with his head on one side: "How do you really feel, Rebecka?" And some poor soul from the union who would have to hold her hand . . . Never. She might as well resign the next day.

But what would she do then? Everybody seemed to think that working in the solicitors' office in Stockholm was always there as an alternative. Måns thought so as well.

But that would finish me off . . .

The very idea of life in the office. The frenzied efforts of the trainees, pressure from the partners, the lawyers with children who simply couldn't cope with the lifestyle. Everybody always felt so ill. But superficial appearances were everything. And the money.

This is where I want to be, no question.

She felt the urge to talk to somebody. Much to her surprise. But who could she talk to about something like this? She still had a friend in the Stockholm office, Maria Taube – but no, Maria was about to become a partner. She was busy toeing the line. She had become one of them. She simply could not understand what Martinsson was doing in a prosecutor's office in the far north of Lapland.

Martinsson put on a jacket and went down the stairs. The Brat woke up and insisted on going with her.

Then she cycled to Maja Larsson's place. It had stopped snowing, but there was a layer of snow thick enough to make pedalling hard work. Sometimes the wheels spun round and round as the tyres failed to grip, but she managed it.

The Brat was rushing about, back and forth. As happy as a sandboy in all the snow.

Fröken Elina Pettersson is sitting in Hjalmar Lundbohm's study, plucking up courage. He calls the room his smoking room. She has always felt at home here. It smells of cigars, and in cold weather there is always a crackling fire in the grate.

One of the girls has just been in and added some more wood: the fire is now spitting and sizzling and spluttering and crackling, and before long it is blazing away. The flames are thrusting their way eagerly up the chimney.

The fireplace was created by Lundbohm's good friend the sculptor Christian Eriksson. The side columns are made of sandstone: one depicts two bear cubs climbing up it, and the other a female bear playing with her cubs. In the fireplace itself are three cast-iron plates with motifs from the interior of a Lapp tent, the centre one depicting a Lapp couple and the other two children playing, and a reindeer-herding dog.

Elina knows that it is when the fire has died down and only the embers are still glowing that the images really come to life. She and Lundbohm have often sat in front of the fire and said that the people depicted are them and their children, and joked about Lundbohm having lost such a lot of weight. Then he has suddenly become serious and declared that this is how he would like to live, free and unconstrained, close to nature. And she has talked about her love of that very freedom, how that was the reason why she became a teacher – so that she could support herself. Not be dependent on anybody else.

She recalls some of their first nights when he asked what she thought about marriage, and she said: never!

Freedom is simple when love is strong.

But now she is prepared to sacrifice that freedom. Now she wants him to go down on his knees before her. Or just say: "Shouldn't we . . ."

Her gaze wanders over what can be seen of the wood-clad walls, the top half of them covered by a tapestry from Jukkasjärvi; the mahogany furniture polished red, the table with its carved legs, the chairs with their high backs. It is a beautiful room. He was helped by his artistic friends when he planned it. It looks simple, but she knows better.

On the floor are a polar bear skin and a brown bear skin, side by side. Not long ago she was lying stretched out on them. Now she is sitting here, straight-backed, on the bench standing next to the wall, as if she is a representative of some worthy association or other, respectfully asking the managing director of the mine for a modest contribution to their activities.

She wants to live in this house as his wife. She wants to accompany him on his journeys. She and the boy, because she knows it is a boy. She wants to see America and Canada. And when she is unable to accompany him, she wants to be at home here, waiting for him, longing for him, borrowing his desk and writing long letters to him while the children run up and down the stairs and Lizzie sings out in the kitchen. She wants to. Oh, how she wants to.

But she is proud as well. She would never force herself upon him. But if, instead of proposing to her, he asked how much she wanted paying? What would she do then? When her fantasy conversation gets that far, her brain comes to a stop.

Now Lundbohm comes into his study, and apologises for keeping her waiting. Then he kisses her. On her forehead!

He sits down – not next to her, but on one of the chairs round the library table. He looks her in the eye, but she notices how his gaze soon shifts to the Stjärnsund clock in the corner.

Elina's heart sinks. Like a stone in black wintry water.

She asks if he has a lot to do, and he says yes, he certainly has. What she wants to talk to him about is like a living, silent being between them.

They talk about how the mining company, L.K.A.B., is providing the whole of Europe with steel. A lot of travelling, a lot of business. And things are not made any easier by all the newspaper articles and arguments about the political status of Kiruna. The agitators are still upset after the ballot in 1909. The people of Kiruna wanted the place to be a market town, in which case the local council would receive taxes paid by the mining company, and be able to build the necessary infrastructure. But the management of the mining company wanted Kiruna to become an urban district: that would mean that the company would pay taxes where its headquarters were situated, i.e. in Stockholm. A ballot took place in 1909. Voting was based on how much tax an individual paid – which meant that the more you earned, the more votes you had. Lundbohm himself had the maximum number of votes, a hundred, while an ordinary worker had just one vote.

Lundbohm voted as his superiors in Stockholm wanted, and the engineers and bourgeois of Kiruna voted in the same way as Lundbohm. And so Kiruna became an urban district.

The question is still being debated. Passionately.

"How can they call me a traitor?" he says angrily to Elina, and Elina assures him that deep down everybody knows he is on the side of the people.

But the mood is restless. People are indignant. That is what happens when so much in the rapidly growing town simply does not work. Protesters gather on every street corner. When the women are not holding meetings agitating for the right to vote, they meet to complain about such matters as water supplies. They wonder, very loudly, how it can be that there are only twelve water pumps in Kiruna, but no fewer than twenty-four alehouses.

Elina braces herself. She is afraid that he suspects something unpleasant is on the way. That he might suddenly stand up and claim that duty calls, and that the opportunity of speaking up will be lost.

"I miss you when you're away," she says, trying to force her voice to maintain a light-hearted tone.

"And I miss you," he says.

And taps her on the hand!

"But I'm an inconsistent person," he says.

She nods, for she has heard this before.

He is an inconsistent person. The opposite of what is called a well-organised person. Oh, when she lay on his arm and heard him say all that for the first time! Then his words made her feel almost frantic with happiness. "I can't," he had said then, "do like so many other people and adhere to certain regular rules and habits."

And now comes the speech about his personality once again. She forces herself to nod and smile as he delivers his – yes, his speech about himself.

Sometimes he works conscientiously, he tells her. At other times he is lazy and only works on and off. Sometimes he observes the obligations of politeness, makes visits and attends parties, answers letters and writes some himself; but at other times he lives the life of a hermit, declines invitations and neglects his correspondence completely. That is his nature. He will never be like most ordinary folk. He has to keep travelling, not only on business but also because the nomad inside him becomes too strong.

He looks down at his shoes as he talks. Not so long ago she lay on his arm, kissed him and said: "Never become like other folk."

Most folk, the rest of the world, were boring and colourless. She and Hjalmar were two burning torches in the snow.

But now, she feels, she is like other folk. Other women.

"What do you think about us, Hjalmar?" she asks in the end.

"What do you mean?"

"Have you thought about anything more than . . ."

She allows a gesture to conclude the sentence for her.

Now he is under pressure. She can see that. But she must have an answer now.

"I thought you were a free spirit who was satisfied with the way we conducted our relationship," he says.

When she makes no reply, he continues.

"I'm an old man. You don't want me."

But who doesn't want whom is perfectly obvious.

She braces herself.

"There are going to be consequences," she says.

He sits for a long time without saying anything. And already, during this unbearable silence, she knows she ought to stand up and leave. For if he still loved her he would not hesitate, would not need to think. He would simply embrace her.

He rubs his hand over his face.

"I have to ask you," he begins.

And she thinks: No, no, he mustn't ask her that. He simply must not.

"Are you certain it's mine?"

She stands up stiffly. Unsure if she should have a fit of temper, or burst out crying. Shame is clawing at her with its old-crone's fingers. It's the other people in her home village that are clawing at her. Pulling at her elegant blouse with their scratchy hands. Standing round her mother's coffin, and whispering about the girl who could allow her mother to work herself to death as long as she was able to go to that "college". Talking about girls who go out of their minds because of reading all those books. And end up in a mental hospital.

What had she been thinking? That she would be able to get away from them? Emancipated?! That is for heiresses and gentlemen's daughters. Strindberg's words spring into her mind. It is Jean who says in "Miss Julie": "Huh, it's that damned farmhand sitting on my shoulders."

A young crofter is sitting on her shoulders.

Lundbohm has caught sight of that young crofter. And he no longer wants her. He is looking so embarrassed. Panting like a locked-up animal.

"I shall go now," she says with all the coolness she can muster. "But there is one other thing."

And she tells him about Lizzie's fiancé being redeployed. She says it is most unjust, but mentions nothing about the role of Fasth – she simply cannot bring herself to do so, her feeling of shame is too great. He would no doubt ask if Fasth is the father of her child.

Lundbohm says it is none of his business to interfere in the way in which work is carried out and distributed. He knows that Fasth can be hard, but never unjust.

She curtseys and goes to the door. There is nothing more to say. He makes no attempt to talk her into staying. This is the last time they will see each other, but they are not aware of that. Elina cannot get out quickly enough – the tears are now flowing freely.

Lundbohm watches her leave, and thinks that if he had been the only one, she would have said so.

Elina walks home thinking: what shall I do? What shall I do? What shall I do now?

Maja Larsson was awake. Martinsson leaned her bike against the crumbling porch and looked in through the kitchen window. Larsson was sitting at the table opposite her boyfriend.

They could almost have been brother and sister, Martinsson thought when she saw them both in profile on either side of the kitchen table. Larsson with silvery-white hair in a thousand plaits, him with his mop of the same colour, which kept falling down over his eyes.

She knocked on the door. After a pause, Larsson shouted, "Come in!" She was now alone in the kitchen.

"Rebecka," Larsson said, beckoning her towards the kitchen table. "And a dog. How nice!"

"I'm sorry, I didn't mean to frighten off your friend – what's his name?"

"Huh, don't worry about Örjan. He's shy. Would you like some coffee? Or a beer?"

Martinsson shook her head and sat down.

"I'm sorry," she said. "Sorry for being so abrupt when you came to talk about my mother and all that. It's just that I'm . . . I don't know."

"I understand. Better than you think," Larsson said, shaking a cigarette out of the packet.

"How's your mum?"

"My little mummy . . . I keep thinking that she mustn't die until

260

I've learnt to distinguish between what I want and what I hope for."

"What do you mean?"

"Huh, it's so pathetic. I'm nearly sixty. But in here . . ."

She pointed demonstratively towards her chest, and looked Martinsson straight in the eye.

"In here is a little girl who wants her to say something before it's too late."

"What?"

"Oh, nothing much. 'I'm sorry,' perhaps. Or that she loves me and is proud of me. Or maybe: 'I understand that it wasn't so easy for you.' You know. It's so ironic. She left me and moved away when I was twelve years old because she had found a man who said: 'No children.' God, but I pleaded and promised that I wouldn't cause any trouble. But she . . ."

Maja raised a hand and whisked it around.

"I had to live with my aunt and her husband. He was . . . interesting. He glued decorations onto window ledges and sofa tables so that they were positioned just right. I assume they had some sort of financial arrangement with my mum in return for looking after me. She has spent all her life looking for men who loved her. And I . . . Well, I'm an old woman now, but lots of men have been mad about me. And I couldn't have cared less."

She tried to smile, but couldn't any longer. It turned out more of a grimace.

"What about him?"

Martinsson glanced up at the ceiling.

"Örjan. He came one day to read my water meter. And stayed on. Like a stray dog you take in."

She tickled the Brat under his chin.

"He knows that I don't believe in Love with a capital L," she said. "But it's good to have company. And he's good at distinguishing between what he wants and what he can hope to get. He wants us to live together and be together all the time, but he has the sense not to hope for that. He takes me for what I am. He doesn't hope that I'm going to change. He's satisfied. Kind. Calm. Those are grossly under-rated qualities in a man."

Martinsson couldn't help laughing.

"What's so funny?" Larsson said, lighting a new cigarette from the glowing stubb of the first one.

"My boyfriend, or whatever I should call him," Martinsson said. "Satisfied, kind and calm are things that come way down the list of his qualities."

Larsson shrugged.

"What's important for me doesn't have to be important for you."

Martinsson thought about Måns. About how restless he was when he came up to Kiruna. His disapproval. It was always "bloody cold" and "teeming with bloody mosquitoes". The winters were too dark and the summer nights so light that he couldn't sleep. The dogs were too filthy and too lively. It was too remote and too quiet. People were too stupid, and the water in the river was too cold.

She always thought that they had to think of something to do whenever he came. They couldn't just be themselves.

"I ought to stop hoping that he'll change," Martinsson said.

"One should always stop hoping that things will change," Larsson said. "Wanting something is a different matter, as I said. As is the case with my mother. I want her to do what I told you about – to take hold of my hand and tell me that she loves me. But I must stop hoping for it to happen. Because it never will. And when I stop hoping for it, I think I'll be liberated."

"How long does she have left? I don't even know what's wrong with her."

"Oh, I think she could pass away at any moment. Cancer of the liver. And now she has secondary tumours all over the place. She's being fed by a drip, but she's more or less stopped passing water.

So her kidneys aren't working any longer. And then . . . No, I need a beer now. Are you sure you wouldn't like one?"

Martinsson declined, and Larsson took just the one can out of the refrigerator. She opened it and took a deep swig straight out of the can.

Neither of them spoke for a while.

"My mum also went off with a new man," Martinsson said.

She could hear how negative that sounded.

"But I refused to go with her. She would send picture postcards now and then. *The apple trees here are in blossom.* So what? *Your little brother is the sweetest little creature you could possibly imagine.* Not a word about her missing me, or – you know? 'How are things with you?' You're right. Hope was what got at me most."

"That's what's so difficult," Maja said, contemplating her own reflection in the dark window. "Coming to terms with the way things are. What other people are like. What you are like deep down inside. You're sad. Annoyed. Scared. Happy and cheerful sometimes, if you're lucky."

"Yes," Martinsson said. "I ought to go home now. So that your poor bloke dares to come down from upstairs."

Larsson said nothing. Smiled somewhat wearily and drew at her cigarette. Martinsson found it hard to leave the peace and quiet that had taken possession of the kitchen. They sat there in silence together for a while longer.

Dead women, mothers, grandmothers – all of them sat down on the empty chairs around the table.

Maja Larsson's boyfriend stood in the darkness upstairs, watching Martinsson leaving the house and taking up her bicycle.

That bloody dog was digging around by the compost heap.

He heard her calling to it.

"Come on! Come on now!"

The dog was still scratching around. In the end she lay her bike down on the slope and went to fetch the dog. Pulled it along by the collar.

She had some difficulty in holding on to the dog and at the same time pushing her bike towards the road. The dog kept staring longingly at the compost heap as she dragged it along.

Clear off now, thought the man upstairs as he watched the dog. Otherwise you'll end up in there as well.

"Ninety-eight, ninety-nine . . . a hundred. Now I'm coming."

Krister Eriksson and Marcus were playing hide and seek. It was Eriksson's turn to seek, and he was wandering around the ground floor, yanking open wardrobe doors and shouting: "Gottya!" Only to add in disappointment: "No, by Jove, not there either."

Then he heard clearly a little voice upstairs say: "Go away, Vera, you're spoiling everything."

While he was looking, he sent a text message to Martinsson. *We're playing hide and seek. And you?*

He had to smile at himself, at his efforts to show himself in the best possible light in Martinsson's eyes. He had even been known to bake, purely in order to be able to send her a text message: "*Am baking fruit cake, v. good for me. And you?*"

He found Marcus in the bathroom.

"How can you make yourself as small as this?" he asked in admiration as he helped the boy to scramble out of the laundry basket.

"Again!" Marcus said. "Can we play outside?"

Eriksson looked out. It was dark. And late. With lots of marvellous new snow. The moon was licking the heavily laden trees with its silver tongue.

"Just for a short while. You said you wanted to go to school tomorrow."

They played hide and seek for a while, but there were not so many good hiding places. Then they threw snowballs for the dogs, but the snow was cold. They had to thaw it slightly in their hands before they could make it into balls. It made their fingers very cold. The dogs could hardly believe their luck to find their boss playing so much.

Tintin's fur suddenly stood on end, and her tail disappeared under her stomach. She started growling, pursed her lips and lowered her head. Eriksson looked at her in surprise.

"What's the matter with you?"

She barked towards the trees over by the cycle track.

Then all the dogs raced off towards the wire fence surrounding his garden as if they had been given an order. They jumped up at the wiring, barking frenziedly.

"Hallo," Eriksson shouted into the darkness among the trees. "Is there somebody there?"

But nobody answered. The dogs went back to the house.

"Come," Eriksson said, lifting Marcus up in his arms. "It's time to go in."

"But I want to lie down in the snow and become an angel," Marcus protested.

"Tomorrow, my little Wild Dog. Will you please do me a big favour and feed the dogs?"

When everybody was safely inside he locked the door and lowered the blinds. Somebody had been lurking in the darkness among the trees, watching them.

A journalist, of course, he told himself.

He ought to have taken his service pistol home with him. Never mind that it was against the rules.

Somebody had planted that torch inside the dog kennel.

But they had caught the murderer. He was in hospital.

It must be a journalist, he thought as he resolutely poured water into his chewing tobacco tin and slung it into the rubbish bin. This time he really was going to give it up.

"Tonight all the dogs are going to be sleeping indoors," Eriksson said to Marcus. "Do you know why?"

"No."

"Because they're going to be allowed to sleep in my bed. And that's the most luxurious thing they can possibly imagine."

"Wild Dog also wants to sleep in your bed," Marcus said.

It was quite hard to persuade Vera, Tintin and Roy to dare to jump up onto Eriksson's bed. He coaxed them and urged them to leap up and lie down. He could see what they were thinking as they put their heads on one side; he understood what their dark doggy eyes were saying.

Oh no, they said. We'll be in trouble. The bed is a forbidden area.

But they all jumped up in the end. Agreed that this was something they could easily get used to.

Years of strict training straight down the plughole, Eriksson thought before falling asleep with Marcus on his arm.

TUESDAY, 25 OCTOBER

Eriksson woke up before the alarm clock went off. He reached for his laptop, which was lying beside his bed. The internet editions of both *Aftonbladet* and *Dagens Nyheter* reported that the police in Kiruna allowed a traumatised child to sleep in a dog kennel.

There was no mention of the fact that he had been sleeping in a tent next to the kennel.

He got up and went straight to the kitchen, opened the cupboard under the sink and dug out his tin of chewing tobacco from the rubbish bin. He opened it and eyed the contents dejectedly.

Bloody journalists. And why had he poured water into his tin of tobacco? He emptied the contents carefully onto a piece of kitchen paper, and put it all into the microwave. After thirty seconds of maximum heat, the tobacco was usable again – albeit not of top quality.

"Don't tell her about this," he said to Vera, who seemed to think it might be time for breakfast. "If you do I'll never be able to kiss her."

At lunchtime a technician rang the Kiruna police from the National Laboratory of Forensic Science, and informed them that there was blood on the hayfork, and that it was Sol-Britt Uusitalo's blood.

"Excellent," von Post said enthusiastically. "And what about Häggroth?"

The technician explained that no fingerprints nor strands of hair from Häggroth had been found. They still had to do D.N.A. tests, but that would take a little time. The blood test was more straightforward, and the cold temperature meant that the blood quality was good.

She assured him that they were giving the case top priority, and hung up.

Now, thought von Post, as he drank the rest of his cold coffee and strode towards his Mercedes. If anybody gets in my way, I'll kill them.

The first person to get in von Post's way was the duty doctor. The patient's condition was still critical. Von Post walked purposefully down the corridor, and decided to speak in a low voice. Health-care assistants went swishing past them in Crocs and Birkenstock sandals, and he noted how young they all seemed to be.

A uniformed police constable was sitting on guard outside Häggroth's room, and followed their conversation with interest.

Von Post explained the situation to the doctor. He had technical proof which could force Häggroth to confess. Then he tried to pull her heartstrings.

"I have a young boy aged seven who has lost the only adult he has ever had in his life," he said.

He told her how little Marcus had presumably witnessed the brutal murder, but had suppressed all memory of it.

"I don't want to force that poor boy to remember what he doesn't want to remember," von Post said, his voice shaking. "With all due respect, I would rather put the murderer's health at risk."

The duty doctor was still listening.

"And personally I think it would be more stressful for Häggroth to keep the truth to himself. He was having an affair with the deceased, you see. It would be better for him to admit the facts. I'm not a psychologist, but that's my experience."

Then he threatened her, albeit while wearing silk gloves.

"The media are going to town on this – you've probably seen the headlines."

She nodded.

"They've tried to force their way in here," she said. "One of them offered me money."

"They'll soon find out that it's the murderer we have in here . . . And if they discover that we're not allowed to interrogate him . . ."

They'll have you for breakfast, my dear, he thought. And I'll have a job on the side as a waiter.

He flung out his hands in a gesture designed to signal that he would not be able to protect her in those circumstances.

"Give me a quarter of an hour," he said. "You can be present, and you may interrupt whenever you like. In fact, I'd appreciate it if you were present – it would feel safer."

"O.K.," she said. "I'll be present. A quarter of an hour."

Häggroth was in a room of his own on the first floor, so they could talk without being disturbed.

Von Post moved a chair up to the side of the bed and sat down. Outside the window the sun was shining down on a dazzlingly white Kiruna. He saw that the duty doctor, who was standing a short distance away, was keeping a constant watch on the various monitors showing the pulse curve, heartbeat and blood pressure.

Häggroth looked completely shattered, as white as death, his thin hair sticking greasily to his scalp, dressed in the county council's wonderful one-size-fits-all hospital gown. He had a towel over his legs and a loose-fitting plastic identity bracelet around his wrist. A drip from a bag on a stand was attached to his arm.

Von Post switched on the tape recorder and put it in his lap.

"I didn't do it," Häggroth said without emotion. "And I have—"

"Yes, yes," von Post said, interrupting him. "But the fact is that the hayfork we found under your barn is covered in Sol-Britt Uusitalo's blood."

I would really like to ask him some more questions, von Post thought. What the hell were you thinking of? Why didn't you throw it in the river? How bloody stupid can you get?

He didn't dare to glance at the monitors. He hoped the readings were constant. He waited for a while, then leaned forward and said softly into Häggroth's ear, "We shall find traces of you, it's only a matter of time. Fingerprints, a strand of hair, a drop of sweat, a fibre from your trousers. Nowadays . . ."

He rubbed his thumb against his index finger.

". . . all we need is a speck. Do you understand what I'm saying? Aren't you going to tell me? I think you would feel better."

"You're lying," whispered Häggroth. "I've never seen that hayfork before. It must have belonged to my grandfather . . ."

He bit his lip. Then he turned his head away. It was only when his body started shaking that von Post realised he was crying.

"Come on now," he said awkwardly.

Let's hope he doesn't get so worked up that the doctor starts making a fuss.

"The children," Häggroth whimpered.

"Yes," von Post said. "I understand."

The sobbing increased, and the damned doctor started fidgeting and clearing her throat.

"He must rest now," she said.

Von Post cursed to himself and switched off the tape recorder.

"It was me," Häggroth said suddenly.

Von Post immediately started the tape recorder again.

"I beg your pardon," he said. "What did you say?"

"It was me. I killed her."

Then he started whining and the doctor was there like a shot.

"That's enough now," she said. "You can continue the interrogation later."

Von Post floated out of the room, out of the hospital building, up, up towards the snow-covered trees, towards the cold blue sky.

Press conference, he gloated deep down inside. We've got him. And it was me who got the confession out of him.

Van Post got into his car and drove along Hjalmar Lundbohmsvägen towards the police station. When it had just stopped snowing, as was the case now, Kiruna really did look beautiful.

The mountain which harboured all the seams of iron ore had been transformed from a scruffy heap of gravel and slag into a terraced, white-clad alp. The row of yellow-painted wooden houses looked like something from a book by Astrid Lindgren.

He glanced quickly into the mirror before getting out of the car. A series of witty one-liners had already taken shape inside his head. It was going to be an absolutely brilliant press conference. And Martinsson could have her job back. My pleasure, my dear. You are welcome to spend your time prosecuting drivers who have exceeded the speed limit or the alcohol limit. That's fine by me.

He recalled the first time their paths had crossed. She had been one of those up-and-coming wannabes from Meijer & Ditzinger. Her overcoat had cost as much as he earned in a whole month. But now it looked very much as though she would end her days all alone in her old house at the edge of the village, eaten up by her dogs.

*

When he entered the police station Mella, Stålnacke, Rantakyrö and Olsson were standing in the corridor.

There was something wrong. He could see it immediately in their eyes. Serious and distressed.

"What's happened to your mobile?" asked Mella.

"Eh? I've switched it off. Forgot to switch it on again. I was at the hospital and—"

"We know. They've just phoned. Häggroth has jumped out of the window."

Von Post's stomach turned.

He must have survived, he thought. It was only the first floor.

But he could see from his colleagues' faces that that was not the case.

"How did it happen?" he asked.

Everyone looked down at the floor. Then up at him.

"Head first," said Mella. "He landed on the asphalt right outside A.&E."

Lizzie and Elina are lying on the sofabed in the kitchen. It's the middle of the night, but the sun never sets at this time of year and it is just as light outside as it was in the middle of the day.

They are whispering to each other. The lodgers are snoring and farting in the living room. Elina has been crying her eyes out.

"You must know of somebody," she says to Lizzie. "Somebody who can get rid of it."

Lizzie's heart almost breaks when she hears Elina talk like that. Her God is not worried about the fact that she and Johan-Albin have sex together. She is quite sure of that. And sure that on the whole, Christ shares her own views – that one should take responsibility for one's own home, not spend one's wages on booze, be fair and just, have compassion. And above all, one should not take another's life.

"We'll cope with it," she whispers to Elina. "We can move away from Kiruna, you and me and Johan-Albin. He and I can adopt the child if you like. Then you can carry on working as a schoolteacher. We can live together, all four of us. Or you can be his mum, and we can help to look after him. Being a schoolteacher isn't the only job there is, you know."

She hugs Elina and whispers that it will be alright, it will be alright, it will sort itself out.

*

And Elina does not do it. She does not have an abortion. She cannot bring herself to do that. She conceals her condition the whole of July. She does not get paid during the summer holidays anyway.

In August she is informed, as expected, that the local authority has appointed a new teacher to take her place.

She accompanies Lizzie, who works like a woman possessed all summer and autumn. Not so much in Lundbohm's residence, as he is away most of the time; but Lizzie's services are constantly sought after. She can bleach sheets and chop wood. It is Lizzie who begs Elina to accompany her, saying that her friend can take care of less strenuous work – and of course, she can read aloud!

While Lizzie is hemming towels or changing curtains for engineers' wives, Elina reads aloud from *Oliver Twist* and *Emma.*

Lizzie and the young maids who assist her all agree that it is so incredibly exciting to be able to work all day long and forget to eat. And how Elina can read! It's like going to the theatre.

Books! They mitigate Elina's torments. When she is reading she cannot think about Hjalmar, or the future.

The baby is bracing itself inside her, and pressing its head up against her chest so hard that she has to keep clutching her ribs. It's kicking so hard that you can see the impact marks on her stomach.

The engineers' wives and the other teachers – all of them women – ignore her when they meet in the street. But nearly all the people who live in Kiruna are young, working class, and they are hatching babies all the time. There are lots of bulging stomachs around, and not all their owners are married. There are other people to greet and talk to. She can go to political meetings and lectures, and even go to the Salvation Army with Lizzie to listen to the band, without being stared at.

There's always a way, Elina tells herself and the baby inside her. And Lizzie keeps an iron grip on her good humour.

"I can do the work of three ordinary women, you know that!" she says.

And she laughs. Even when Elina feels depressed and Johan-Albin returns from the crusher with blood in his ears. She laughs and drives the shadow of the managing director of the mine out of the kitchen.

On November 3 Elina gives birth to a baby boy at home in their kitchen. The midwife slaps him on the backside and says "lovely" and "as pretty as his mother".

They have decided that he will be called Frans. And Elina makes up her mind that he will be recorded as Frans Olof in the parish register. Hjalmar Lundbohm's second name is Olof, and the angels know how to read between the lines. They see what is important, and do not stop dead at the word "illegitimate".

It was ten to six. The press conference was due to start shortly. The journalists were thirsting for blood.

Von Post was pacing up and down in the corridor, mumbling, "This wasn't our fault."

What does he mean, our fault? Mella thought. We weren't the ones who interrogated the sick man in the hospital.

She phoned Martinsson.

"It's a bloody catastrophe," she said. "So unnecessary. His youngest was the same age as Gustav."

"Yes," Martinsson said.

Then she told Mella about the shirt.

"Pohjanen has sent it to the National Laboratory of Forensic Science. You must admit that it seems very odd. She gets stabbed to death, her son was killed by a car that didn't stop three years ago, her father was probably shot, and Marcus . . ."

She didn't go on.

"You know all the details."

"It was probably some drunken hunter who panicked," Mella said. "That wouldn't be the first time. Assuming it *is* a bullet hole. And then the bear dug him up out of his shallow grave."

"Mmm," Martinsson said.

"Häggroth confessed, Rebecka. It's a damned tragedy that he jumped out of the window, but he was the murderer. And he had no reason to kill her father or run over her son. Sometimes it's just coincidence."

"I know," Martinsson said.

"I must go," Mella said. "The press conference is about to start. What I really want to do is to hide away until it's all over."

"Where are you?" Martinsson asked.

"In the loo. But I really must go and join them. Goodbye for now."

Martinsson hung up. She drank her cold coffee, then read a text message from Eriksson.

We're playing hide and seek, it said. *And you?*

Yes, she thought. Hiding away. Hide and seek.

She put down her mobile.

She could just see them, Eriksson and Marcus. Eriksson doing the seeking. Marcus hiding. And Mella hiding in the loo.

Yes. And in Sol-Britt's house all the big cupboard doors had been opened. Somebody had obviously been looking for Marcus. Thought that he had hidden himself away.

"I can't make head nor tail of this," she said to the Brat, who was sitting at her feet and gazing longingly at her sandwiches.

"But I suppose what they say is right. Why should Jocke Häggroth be chasing after the whole family?" She tickled the Brat's neck.

"Do you want something from me? Didn't you have your dinner only ten minutes ago?"

Eh? the Brat said. *I don't remember that. But hunger is gnawing at my body like a field mouse.*

Måns Wenngren was sitting in his office at Meijer & Ditzinger's in Stockholm.

He was the only partner still in the building, but lights in offices occupied by trainees indicated that they were still ferreting away. Occasionally they would pad along the expensive carpets in the corridor to fetch a cup of coffee or a glass of water.

One of them appeared in his doorway to ask him a question. He noted that she had taken the trouble to refresh her lipstick before leaving her room, and wondered in passing if he ought to abandon all thoughts of Martinsson and ask this girl out to dinner.

But now, of course, he was risking something more than just a refusal. He was risking being regarded as pathetic. She might go to one of the other trainees and say: "For Christ's sake, what the hell did he think he was on to?"

He watched the press conference in Kiruna on his computer.

Bloody fools! How on earth could they give him the opportunity to jump out the window? Just drive off after he had confessed.

He took his Macallan from the bottom drawer of his desk and took a swig straight out of the bottle. Then he dug out some throat tablets and swallowed a handful.

Von Post was sitting there at the press conference, taking all the questions.

Måns pointed at him.

"You stuck-up bastard! That's my girl's place."

"We have a confession and a tragic death," von Post said. "From the police point of view, this case is now closed."

Lots of cameras lifted up in the air to get a good picture, lots of hands waving and people simply shouting out questions.

"Didn't you have him under surveillance? How could this happen?"

"Of course we had him under surveillance."

Von Post paused. Gritted his teeth so hard that his cheek muscles were stretched.

"Of course. But our man was in a hospital . . ."

He let that information sink in, then continued while looking directly at the biggest of the cameras.

"A murderer has taken his own life. It's tragic, of course. We shall have to live with that. And our thoughts are with his relatives and friends. But – and this is important: as I understand it the doctor responsible had not observed any indications to suggest that he was suicidal."

Neat, thought Måns: "A murderer has taken his own life."

"What form did this surveillance take?"

"It was based on the assumption that he couldn't run away because he was under arrest, and the doctor responsible for him did not diagnose him as suicidal. We had no reason to question that judgement."

He's a crafty bugger, thought Måns. Shoves the responsibility over onto a doctor as if it were second nature.

You could almost see the journalists craning their necks and preparing to follow a different trail.

Poor bastard, Måns thought. I hope it's a senior doctor with a thick skin.

The prosecutor continued wittering away. Måns poured himself a proper glass of whisky.

Von Post explained that the murderer had been having an affair with the victim. And a murder weapon found in the grounds of Häggroth's house had traces of the victim's blood on it.

So a suicide has lost all form of legal protection, has he? Måns thought. Von Post calls him a murderer, but he hasn't been found guilty. What happened to the concept of being innocent until found guilty? I thought Sweden was still a country governed by law. I was evidently wrong.

Måns fiddled with his iPhone. He didn't have the strength to listen any longer. It was just a load of crap.

He checked his text messages even though nothing on the display suggested that he had any. He checked his latest incoming calls, even though there was no indication that he had missed any. He checked his e-mails: nothing from Martinsson.

Then, without a second thought, he phoned Madelene, his first wife.

It occurred to him that perhaps it wasn't such a good idea, and he ought to hang up. But she answered.

She didn't sound as put-out as he had feared she might do.

The passing of time is making itself felt, he thought. She no longer has the strength to hate me for ever and a day.

"How are things?" he asked.

"Måns," she said with more warmth than he deserved. "So you're ringing mc. What do you want?"

One of the trainees passed by his door. She was wearing an overcoat and carrying a heavy briefcase. She waved and mouthed *bye for now*.

He gestured with his finger that she should shut his door, which she duly did.

"What happened to us?" he asked. "Why did we split up?"

At the other end of the line Madelene took a deep breath.

"Can't we just forget about that?" she said without rancour. "How are you?"

"I haven't been drinking, it's just . . ."

"Is it something to do with Rebecka? I saw that they had caught the murderer up there in the sticks, and that he had committed suicide. But it wasn't her case, was it?"

"No, it was that idiot of a colleague of hers. Fancy having to work alongside halfwits like that."

He contemplated his whisky. He didn't want to pour himself another one while he was talking to Madelene. She would hear what was going on. Her ear was well practised.

"I'm serious about Rebecka," he said. "I would like to marry her. I've never felt like that about anybody else but you. But it's so bloody complicated. Why does it have to be like that?"

He heard her sigh as a sort of answer.

"You know," he went on, "I don't feel restless. I want her to move in with me here. I want us to grow old together and that she just . . ."

"What?" said his first wife patiently, and he noted with a degree of gratitude that she refrained from commenting on the fact that he and Martinsson could never grow old together because Martinsson was so much younger.

"Or else she can go to hell," he said, in a sudden fit of anger.

"Yes, that's how you usually react."

"Forgive me," he said without a trace of irony in his voice.

"Eh? Forgive you what?"

"Forgive me, Madde, for all that you had to put up with. And you were a fantastic mother all the time. If you hadn't . . . well, I wouldn't have had any contact at all with the children today."

"No problem, Måns," she said slowly.

"They're doing fine, aren't they? They're living good lives."

"They're doing fine."

"Excellent. Goodbye!" he said abruptly.

And hung up before she had an opportunity to answer.

Madelene Ekströmer, formerly Wenngren, put down her mobile.

Her ex-husband had concluded the call as usual. Rapidly and unexpectedly. It had taken her years to learn how to cope with the way he hung up.

Then she went in to her husband, who was sitting in the Howard sofa with a pre-dinner drink in his hand and the family's fox terriers at his feet.

"Måns?" he asked without looking up from the television.

"Do you know what?" she said, kissing his forehead as a sign that this was where she was at home now. "He said sorry to me. He actually apologised. Am I awake? I think I need a drink."

"Good God," said her husband. "Has he got cancer or something?"

Mella endured the press conference at von Post's side. She felt on edge, and had a nagging headache.

So this was the murder investigation for which she had sold her loyalty.

She ought to have told him to go to hell. Go to hell, you jumped-up prat of a prosecutor, she should have said when they stole the investigation from Martinsson.

Björnfot was standing right at the back of the room, looking grim. She tried to convince herself that it was his fault – he was the one who had made the decision.

But that did not alter the fact that she ought to have acted differently.

"A murderer has taken his own life." Von Post managed to say that three times during his introductory address and the subsequent question-and-answer session. The words would appear in at least one headline the following morning.

And that poor duty doctor: they had already started hunting her down. Mella noted how many of the journalists present began tapping away at their mobiles when von Post insinuated that it was the hospital's fault.

A feeling of hopelessness was looming over her. Their job was to hunt down criminals. To feel exhilarated when they nailed them. Doing that would compensate for all the unsolved crimes, for all those who got away with their evil deeds, for their lack of resources, for the shortage of time, for all the women who were beaten up by their husbands and for all the cases that were shelved, written off, filed away.

But what they ought not to do was to make them jump out of windows. That made her feel ashamed.

Now The Pest was holding forth again. She liked that – von Post was The Pest. The investigation had been conducted in a highly efficient and professional manner, he maintained. You don't say, Mella thought. That's news to me.

At the very back of the room, behind all the journalists and photographers, a door opened and in came Sonja from the switch-board. Her blue-framed spectacles were hanging from her neck on a red cord. Her hair was gathered in a large bun, and her blouse was impeccably ironed.

She whispered for quite a long time into Björnfot's ear. As she did so, his eyebrows rose higher and higher. He muttered something by way of reply. Her shoulders rose up to the level of her ears, and she started whispering again. Then both of them stared at Mella.

Björnfot sat upright, then tilted his head diagonally backwards to indicate that she ought to come over to him.

Mella shook her head almost imperceptibly to indicate that she could not.

He nodded his head slowly, and gave her an I-mean-right-away-*now* look.

"Excuse me," Mella mumbled as she left the platform.

She could sense von Post's eyes on her.

Go to hell, you jumped-up prat of a prosecutor, she thought, and slunk out of the room with Björnfot and Sonja.

"What's this about?" Mella said.

"Well," Sonja said in her sing-song Finland-Swedish, "I didn't want to interrupt you, but I thought this couldn't wait."

She opened the door to the interrogation room. Then she left Mella and Björnfot to their own devices.

Sitting on the table was a man of about thirty-five. He was wearing a loose-fitting quilted jacket over a hooded fleece, old-fashioned green army trousers and boots. On his head was a home-made knitted cap. His facial stubble was such that within a couple of days it would deserve to be called a beard. He contrasted startlingly with the austerely furnished room with its little conference table and the blue-upholstered chairs designed to seat the general public. His eyes were as red as those of a white rabbit, and his face suggested that he was not unacquainted with an excess of alcohol.

Huh, Mella thought. A loony who wants to confess?

He looked at them with eyes that reminded Mella of all the occasions when, in the line of duty, she had been obliged to visit next of kin and inform them of the death of a relative.

"Are you police officers?" he said.

The moment he started talking it was clear to Mella that the man was not an idiot. Just a drunk. She introduced herself, and Björnfot.

"I just got home not long ago and heard about what's going on," said the man. "My name is Mange Utsi. Jocke Häggroth is a mate of mine. Or was a mate of mine, perhaps I should say. And he didn't kill Sol-Britt Uusitalo."

"Really?" Mella said.

"I can't understand what's going on. I gather he must have confessed, and then . . . But it's all bullshit. He can't possibly have done it. He was with me the whole weekend."

Von Post stood in front of Mange Utsi, legs wide apart and arms crossed, with a sceptical expression on his face. The press conference had gone as well as he could possibly have wished – and then this lunatic turned up. He eyed the bedraggled creature suspiciously.

"You're lying!" he said, and there was almost a trace of a prayer in his voice.

"Any chance of a cup of coffee?" Utsi said.

He looked dejectedly at the other police officers in the room.

"Why should I lie? Jocke's dead, for Christ's sake."

Mella, Olsson and Rantakyrö were leaning against the wall. Stålnacke was at home. When they rang from the hospital to say that Häggroth had jumped to his death, he had taken his coat and vanished without a word. He had now called in sick.

"Have you any witnesses?" von Post said.

"I thought I was supposed to be the witness," Utsi sighed. "And a Coca-Cola as well," he added as Rantakyrö left to fetch some coffee.

"He confessed," von Post said. "Why should he confess to having done something he hadn't?"

Utsi shrugged.

"Tell this man what you told me," Mella said.

"We drove off on Saturday morning. To his brother's cottage up in Abisko. And . . . well, we drank ourselves legless. You know how it is – sometimes you need to give your mind a good clean-out."

The officers looked at each other. What could there possibly be to clean out inside that man's head?

"Jocke drove back home on Sunday, late. And I've only just got back, and heard what had happened. I can promise you, we crept out of the sauna on our hands and knees on Saturday. He couldn't have driven home then, even if he'd wanted to. The neighbour called in as well, so I'm not the only one who can testify where Jocke was at the weekend."

"I have to ask you," Mella said. "What about his wife? What was their relationship like?"

Utsi blinked as if he had sandpaper inside his eyelids. He shook his head and gave Mella a meaningful look, begging her to take pity on him.

"All I wanted to say was that he couldn't have done it."

"Everything will come out into the open," Mella said calmly. "Tell us about it; it will make you feel better."

Rantakyrö returned with the coffee and a coke. Utsi took them eagerly and emptied both the can and the mug in just a few swigs. He belched, excused himself, and after a brief pause said, "She used to beat him up."

The police officers exchanged glances again.

"How often? How badly?" Mella said.

"I don't know. He didn't talk about it. We never discussed it. Sometimes when he had a black eye he would laugh it off by saying that she was bloody deadly with a frying pan."

Utsi looked down at the floor and pulled a face.

"That kind of thing just doesn't happen. You joke about it. But whenever you saw him with no clothes on . . . He was always covered in old bruises."

"Do you know her?"

"Well, not really."

"Did you know he was having an affair with Sol-Britt Uusitalo?"

"Yes, I was sometimes his alibi. But . . ."

"But what?"

"He always used to say he would never leave Jenny, even if he wanted to. For the sake of the children, and . . ."

"And what?"

"And because she would kill him. That's what he said."

Or kill Sol-Britt perhaps, Mella thought, and could see that the others were thinking the same.

"How do you think she would react if she found out he was having an affair with another woman?"

"She wouldn't exactly be pleased," Utsi said. "Not pleased at all."

"Bring her in," von Post said. "And if anybody squeals to the press, then . . ."

He ended the sentence by looking at all the others in the room, clenching his fist and crushing something invisible.

Bringing Jenny Häggroth in was like sticking an arm into a sack full of snakes.

A woman with eyes swollen from weeping answered the door and introduced herself as Jenny's sister. She turned and shouted into the house for Jenny.

Is this a job? Mella thought, trying not to look at the wet children's shoes and small quilted jackets hanging up in the hall. Turning children into orphans and collecting immigrant families when they are going to be ordered to leave the country. Bloody hell! I think I hate this job.

Olsson and Rantakyrö were standing behind Mella, ready to act if necessary. Nobody had spoken a word during the journey to Kurravaara.

Rantakyrö hopped from one foot to the other, raised his arms and put his hand over the back of his head. Then started scratching intensely.

Stand still, for God's sake! she thought angrily.

Jenny appeared in the hall: unwashed hair, tracksuit bottoms and hooded jumper. Eyes narrow with hatred.

"I'm sorry," Mella said, "but you must come with us."

"So that you can throw me out of a window?"

"Jenny, you must understand—"

"Listen here, you," Jenny yelled so loudly that she made the police officers and her sister jump, "don't you even dare mention my name!

Is that understood, you fucking police whore? Bloody fuzz filth! Shit heaps, the lot of you!"

Without taking her eyes off them, she smashed her fist into the hall mirror. It cracked, and several splinters fell onto the floor.

The officers stared in horror at the blood pouring out of the cuts on her hand.

"Jenny!" exclaimed her sister.

"You shut your gob!" Jenny bawled.

Then she shouted up to the upper floor.

"You kids! Come here! Now!"

Two boys appeared at the top of the stairs. The older one was wearing a cap, even though he was indoors, a large T-shirt and sagging jeans. The younger one also had a big jumper and sagging jeans, and was holding a games console. He tried to take hold of his brother's hand, but wasn't allowed to.

"Here," screamed Jenny, holding out her bleeding hands. "Put the cuffs on me. Go on. In front of my children. These are the bastards who murdered your dad."

"Can't you just calm down and come with us?" Mella said.

"Calm down? I'll mark you for life," Jenny said, taking a step forward towards Mella.

Mella raised her hands to cover her face, and then Jenny was onto her. Grabbed her hair with one hand and punched her with the other. Tried to hit her in the face but only made contact with Mella's lower arms, then tried to push the policewoman's face up against the broken mirror. The children and her sister started screaming.

Rantakyrö and Olsson threw themselves at Jenny and dragged her away from Mella. Jenny was spitting and kicking, managed to pull one hand loose and scratched at Olsson's face.

Olsson shouted: "My eye!" and put his hands over one of his eyes.

Rantakyrö rushed forward, hit Jenny hard and pushed her onto the floor. He forced her down and pulled her arms up behind her back, Mella helped to put on the handcuffs, and they dragged her out of the house while she, her sister and the children carried on screaming and shouting.

Olsson showed his eye to Rantakyrö.

"It's still there," said Rantakyrö grimly, massaging his right hand.

Then Olsson sat down in the driver's seat.

"Hey," Mella said. "This is my car."

"For Christ's sake, Mella," Olsson roared. "Get into the car and hold your tongue. The last thing we need now is for you to crash the car and kill the lot of us."

And so they drove off. And the police officers were just as silent as they had been on the way there.

But Jenny Häggroth was anything but silent. She never let up, all the way to the police station. They were whores and arseholes and monsters and lunatics. She would sue them and kill them and get her own back and they had better watch out.

Nobody told her to shut up. Mella looked furtively at her face. It was swollen up after Rantakyrö's punch, and that bleeding hand needed treatment.

When Jenny met von Post at the police station, she lost no time in making him aware of her opinion of him as well: it had much to do with his deviant sexual preferences. Then she announced, surprisingly calmly, "I'm not going to say a word until I have a lawyer present, and I want Silbersky."

They put her in a cell, and von Post said he would do his best to provide her with her chosen lawyer.

"After all," he said, leaning against the wall in the corridor, "she's under arrest on suspicion of murder. And in view of what has happened today, we must make sure we do everything in strict accordance with the rules. What the hell have you done to her?"

"Violent resistance," Mella said, nodding in the direction of Olsson, who was still bleeding from the wound over his eye. "And that's just the start."

"There were three of you," von Post said wearily. "Arresting one lone woman. It's one hell of a cock-up, you must realise that yourselves."

He looked at the clock.

"Do whatever you like. We can't interrogate her until she has a solicitor present. If Silbersky is able to take it on, he'll have to get the first available flight tomorrow morning. We'll meet here at eight o'clock."

He marched off.

"I don't know about you," Mella said to her colleagues, "but I'm intending to go to Landström's for a beer."

They sat right at the back in Landström's, and drank their first beer in silence. They could sense that people were looking at them. The news was out already. A talented troubadour was singing Cornelis Vreeswijk songs in another part of the premises.

After a while the alcohol had smoothed down the sharp edges of the awful day. They ordered well-hung beef and Baltic herring with mashed potatoes and crispbread.

Mella relaxed a little. It was good to unwind, and even better to receive compliments from Rantakyrö and Olsson, which increased in direct proportion to the amount of alcohol consumed.

"I swear to God you're the best boss I've ever had," Rantakyrö said.

"The only one he's ever had, but all the same," Olsson said, proposing a toast.

"The best you could ever ask for," Rantakyrö said, looking at her like a faithful dog.

"That's enough now, she'll get ever so big-headed" Olsson said. Then he became serious.

"Dammit all, I'm so sorry for today, Mella. I got so bloody het up."

"No problem," she said. 'I think it's the worst day I've ever experienced. Those poor kids . . ."

"Those poor police officers," Rantakyrö said. "When Silbersky sees her black eye he'll report me. I'll be charged with assault. And then I'll lose my job."

"If only Martinsson was still in charge of the case," Olsson said. "She's not impressed by upstart solicitors, and isn't scared by them either. That bloody idiot von Post will throw you to the wolves as long as he gets away unscathed."

"You won't lose your job," Mella said. "I promise you that."

Rantakyrö waltzed off to the bar.

Mella and Olsson listened to the troubadour, who was singing the Swedish version of "Hello Muddah, Hello Fadduh".

"It's beyond belief," Olsson said.

"You can say that again," Mella said.

"She beat him up. He confesses to the murder and then commits suicide."

Rantakyrö came back with an Arvo special for Mella, and tequila with lemon and salt for himself.

"My favourite," Mella said. "Like a baby's dummy, but tastier."

Rantakyrö licked some salt, knocked back the tequila and took a bite of lemon.

"Sho what do you shay," he said, with the lemon still in his mouth, like a monkey. "Do you think she'sh capable of killing shomebody?"

Mella couldn't help giggling.

Olsson sprayed beer from his nose.

And then they all burst out laughing uncontrollably. Tears

were running down their cheeks. People sitting close to them fell silent and stared. Olsson sounded as if he were crying. Rantakyrö clutched his stomach. Then they all managed to calm down for a few moments – before bursting out laughing again.

They laughed and laughed until their jaws ached.

People round about were giving them strange looks. But they could not stop.

Mella walked home on her own. She felt uplifted by the newly fallen snow that lit up the darkness. But it would take more than snow to make her feel happy. She was longing for her husband and her children. And she was thinking about Jenny and Jocke Häggroth's poor children. About Jenny holding out her bleeding hands so that the police officers could handcuff her.

She could have done it, Mella thought. But I wonder . . .

Winter arrives like a raging demon. Stormy winds pile up snow against the walls of buildings, thrash any poor souls who have to be out in the streets, batter them in the face, fling them down onto the ground.

There is no point in clearing away snow – the pavements are knee-deep again within minutes. Pedestrians have to plough their way through it as best they can, and can't see where they are going.

Householders build up their fires until the whole building creaks and crackles. Some people burn their furniture when they run out of firewood. Water trickles out of the walls of poorly built houses with inadequately dried wooden cladding. Opening outside doors is asking for trouble – snow forces its way in and the winds threaten to wrench doors from their hinges. All windows are caked with snow and ice.

Frans Olof is two weeks old, and Elina hasn't set foot outside the house since he was born.

But on the evening of November 18, it suddenly becomes calm. The roaring and rumbling from outside fades away. The wind lies down and goes to sleep. Kiruna is completely white and silent. The moon heaves itself up, fat and yellow.

Elina makes a bed for her little boy in the sledge used for trans-porting firewood. She really must go out and get some exercise.

Narrow paths of trodden-down snow have already been made by

people who had been aching to get out of doors at last. They are like the tracks of field mice in the deep snow. Some children are playing with a dog. Frans Olof is asleep in the firewood sledge.

Elina is lost in thought, then finds herself standing outside the school.

Her heart aches as she thinks about the children, and the career that she will never again be able to pursue. She wonders if the children miss her, if the new teacher has replaced her in their hearts without any problems. She wonders if the classroom looks the same as it did before, or if the new teacher has changed everything.

Nobody locks doors in Kiruna. Perhaps she should be so bold as to go in and take a look. It wouldn't hurt anybody.

She lifts Frans Olof out of the firewood sledge, still wrapped up in all his blankets, and goes into the school. The lower halves of the windows are all iced up, but enough moonlight penetrates the top halves for her to be able to see.

No, not much has changed. She concludes that the new teacher is lacking in imagination. She herself had changed at least a thousand things during her first week . . .

Feeling warm, she places the sleeping Frans Olof on the floor behind the organ, and unbuttons her winter coat. As she puts it down on the teacher's desk, she hears the outside door open and then close again. Then her blood runs cold as she hears the unmistakable voice.

"Frööken. Frööööken Pettersson."

When he appears in the doorway, his face is swathed in darkness.

"So this is where you are. Running around the town like a bitch on heat as soon as the baby is born. Obviously."

She is incapable of movement as he carefully locks the classroom door from the inside and puts the key in his pocket.

All she can think about is the baby. Please don't let the little boy wake up . . .

If he discovers the baby he will kill me and leave the boy out in the cold to die, she thinks.

She knows for certain that is what will happen.

She puffs and pants like an animal under stress as he grabs her wrists with his powerful hands.

She turns her face away, but he takes hold of her chin and forces his mouth over hers.

"If you bite me, I'll kill you," he growls.

He rips open her blouse and forces her down on her back over the desk. She whimpers as he squeezes her breasts, so tender after feeding her baby.

He seems to be provoked because she doesn't scream and cry, doesn't try to defend herself.

He punches her in the face.

It does not even hurt. She just feels warmth spreading over her face, and she can taste blood in her mouth.

She realises that he intends to kill her. That is what he is going to do. He hates her. He is incensed by her youth, her beauty, her affair with Hjalmar.

He pulls down her knickers and takes out his cock. She is still in a bit of a mess down there after having given birth. He forces himself inside her.

"There you are!" he shouts. "You like that, don't you, you bloody whore? Don't you? Don't you?"

He punches her. Bashes her head onto the desk. Rips out handfuls of her hair.

Blood is running from her shattered nose and down into her throat.

He thrusts and thrusts, and shouts out louder than ever.

Then his iron fingers clamp themselves around her neck. She tries to defend herself, but her arms are so weak.

The moon and the stars force their way in through the ceiling. The whole classroom is filled with light.

The little boy sleeps like an angel. When he wakes up and starts crying an hour later, there is nobody there – apart from his mother lying dead on the desk.

WEDNESDAY, 26 OCTOBER

The weather turned, and it became warmer. The snow turned into slush. The grey sky glowered at the miserable spectacle down below.

Jenny Häggroth lay on the bunk in her cell, staring up at the ceiling. When she was interrogated, she had suggested that the police should go to hell. Besides, she maintained, if she had known that Jocke had been unfaithful to her, she wouldn't have murdered Sol-Britt – she would have murdered Jocke.

Leif Silbersky didn't interrupt her. He said very little during the interrogation. He waited until later.

And then the lawyer who considered himself a class above everybody else really went to town. He held a press conference at the Ferrum hotel.

Björnfot kept to the sidelines. He did what he felt was necessary as a stand-in for Martinsson, and listened in silence as von Post complained about colleagues and solicitors and suspects and journalists. The papers were full of comments about "the horrific mistakes made by the police": "Now the children are orphans!", "An innocent man accused – Took his own life!"

The weather and the murder investigation, Björnfot thought as he put on his jacket. What a joke, the whole business.

At eight o'clock in the morning Eriksson dropped Marcus off at his school.

"I'll be here waiting for you at hometime," he said.

He sat in his car and watched Marcus running across the playground. Three older boys saw him, and made to follow him – but Marcus managed to disappear into the school building before the they caught up with him.

Trouble, Eriksson thought.

Two girls passed by the car, and he wound down the driver's window.

"Hi there! Excuse me!" he shouted. "Don't be afraid – I was burnt in a fire when I was a little boy. Do you know Marcus Uusitalo? He's in class 1B."

The girls kept their distance – but yes, they knew who Marcus was. Why did he want to know?

"His grandmother has been murdered," one of the girls said.

"I know," Eriksson said. "I'm a policeman. Those are my police dogs sitting in the cage at the back there. This lady in the passenger seat, Vera, is an ordinary civilian dog. But please tell me, is anybody being nasty to Marcus at school?"

The girls hesitated for a moment.

"Yes. Hampus and Willy and a few of the lads in 3A. But don't say that we told you anything."

"What do they do?"

"They hit him and kick him. Say things. They take people's money as well, if anybody has any. Once they forced Marcus to eat gravel."

"Who's the leader?"

"Willy."

"What's his surname?"

"Niemi. Are you going to put him in prison?"

"No."

But I'd like to, Eriksson thought, as he drove off.

There is a family grave not far from Katrineholm. Elina's parents and a younger brother are already buried there.

Lizzie says goodbye to the coffin at the railway station. It is one of the coldest days of the winter. The snow creaks and squeaks underfoot. Hoar frost forms wherever body heat seeps out through clothes – on eyelashes, on scarves close to mouths, at the bottom of coat sleeves.

When the coffin is lifted into the goods wagon, Lizzie sobs uncontrollably, and the cold air makes it painful for her to breathe in so violently. The tears turn into ice on her cheeks. Johan-Albin has to hold her tightly to prevent her from falling in a heap.

There are not many people present – a memorial service was held at the Salvation Army hall earlier in the week. There was not enough room for all those who wanted to attend. The murder of the town's former schoolteacher has aroused sorrow and gloom throughout Kiruna. There were articles about it in the national newspapers.

They close the doors of the goods wagon, but all Lizzie wants to do is to cry and sob. The cold is causing her agony in her feet.

"Come on, my lovely, it's time to go home now," Johan-Albin says in the end.

And he insists on her going back home with him. But when they get there they see Elina's trunk, and all her books, and her clothes that have been washed and ironed and mended and starched so that they look absolutely new. Lizzie starts sobbing again.

But when Johan-Albin has made coffee for her, given her some biscuits, and a little twelve-year-old girl comes from the wet nurse carrying Frans, she stops crying.

She holds the baby in her arms and he looks her in the eye, and wraps his little hand round her finger.

"I'm going to look after him," she tells Johan-Albin. "Elina has a sister, but she couldn't possibly take him on."

Johan-Albin listens intently and dunks his biscuit in the hot coffee.

"He has only me in the world," she says. "If you want to cancel our engagement, I won't hold it against you. You have never promised to become responsible for a little baby. And I shall cope. You know that."

She smiles bravely at him.

Johan-Albin puts down his tin mug, and stands up. Lizzie forgets to breathe. Is he about to leave her?

No, he sits down beside her on the kitchen sofa and puts his arms around her and the baby.

"I shall never leave you," he says. "Even if you have a score of babies with you in the nest. It's obvious that you will cope no matter what – but I can't live without my Lizzie."

Now she has to cry once more. And laugh as well. Johan-Albin has to rub his eyes – after all, he was sold at a pauper's auction as a young boy. Life has a lot to answer for.

They don't hear the footsteps on the stairs, and both of them jump when there is a knock on the door.

In marches Blenda Mänpää, one of Fasth's maids. She looks serious. And she declines the offer of coffee.

"I have to speak to you," she says to Lizzie. "About Elina. And Fasth."

Grey and gloomy outside. Martinsson took her third mug of morning coffee and stared grimly out of the window at what ought to have been winter. The Brat barked. Immediately afterwards she heard footsteps on the stairs.

Björnfot was standing outside.

Martinsson could feel the anger mounting inside her.

"Can we have a chat?" he said.

She invited him in with a shrug. They sat down at the kitchen table. The Brat jumped up and sat on Björnfot's lap.

"Do you think you're a lapdog?" Björnfot said. "Rebecka, my wife tells me I'm very bad at saying sorry. But I'd like to say sorry to you. It was wrong of me to take you off that investigation. But you know how it is, he goes around for years with a chip on his shoulder, and he badly wanted this case. So I just let him have it without thinking about it. I suppose I thought – or hoped, at least – that you wouldn't mind."

Martinsson realised to her surprise that all her anger and associated emotions were loosening up and fading away.

"Go to hell," she said in a tone of voice that suggested he was forgiven. "Would you like a cup of coffee?"

"Let's hope to God that we can find some trace of Jenny Häggroth on that hayfork," Björnfot said when he had been served with coffee and kangos biscuits. "But it's far from certain that we can nail her."

"No," Martinsson said. "That hayfork has been easily accessible to anybody at all, lying there under their barn. It would be perfectly natural if there were some traces of her prints on the fork. She might well have used it, after all. We'd have to find traces of her in Sol-Britt Uusitalo's house. Incidentally, von Post seems to think I'm trying to sabotage his investigation."

"Yes, I know that," Björnfot said. "But I had a word with Pohjanen, so I know what you two have been up to. And somebody shot Sol-Britt Uusitalo's father. The National Forensic Lab have let it be known that it was a bullet that damaged the bone you dug up. From the freezer in the forensic medicine depot in Umeå!"

"Pure chance. But there were traces on his shirt as well. Did Pohjanen tell you about that?"

"Yes. The poor bastard wasn't mauled by a bear. He was shot, then left out in the forest and was eaten up. What should we conclude from that?"

Martinsson shook her head.

"It all seems so improbable. But if somebody is trying to eradicate the whole family – who is there that could hate them that much? To be sure, Sol-Britt Uusitalo wasn't universally liked: but she wasn't hated, just despised. I shall pretend not to notice that you have my dog on your knee and are feeding him biscuits. Well, little Brat, are you going to go home to herr Björnfot's place and sit in his best armchair and gobble no end of biscuits?"

"Just one biscuit is nothing."

"But as far as he's concerned, ten biscuits are nothing."

"Perhaps there is somebody who hates Hjalmar Lundbohm's family," Björnfot said, trying to drink his coffee despite the efforts of the Brat who had changed position on his lap and started scratching at him with his enormous paw in order to suggest that Björnfot ought to be stroking him instead. "Frans Uusitalo was Hjalmar Lundbohm's son – but I expect you knew that."

"Yes. Sivving knows all about that sort of thing. But who

could possibly hate Lundbohm to that extent? It all seems so improbable."

"I don't know. But there are always loonies around. And Lundbohm wasn't the saint that a lot of people seem to think he was. I know for instance that there was a rock-blaster in the mine, Venetpalo, who discovered some iron ore deposits in Tuolluvaara. He reported the find to Lundbohm who promptly filled in a prospecting licence application in his own name. Then Lundbohm handed over the prospecting rights to a private company of which he was the managing director. Venetpalo got nothing. You can get angry for less than that . . ."

"How do you know about all that?"

"My grandfather was the district police superintendent for Kiruna at the beginning of the twentieth century, so quite a lot of stories have been passed down through generations of the family. And I also recall somebody called Venetpalo sending a letter to the editor of *Norländska Socialdemokraten* about the Tuolluvaara mine a few years ago. He seemed a bit on the dogmatic side – the type who could end up going over the top. I remember thinking that at the time, in any case."

"Yes indeed," Martinsson said. "Bitterness can persist for generations. I can have a word with that bloke. It's not much of a straw to clutch at, but I've got nothing else to do."

Björnfot looked at her in resignation.

"Does that mean you're not going to come back to your job?"

"I'll be back in six weeks' time," she said. "Provided von Post is back in Luleå by then."

Two muffled-up women turn up at the Kiruna police station. When they have brushed off all the snow and unwound themselves from their shawls, they turn out to be Lizzie Andersson, Lundbohm's housekeeper, and Blenda Mänpää, a maid working for Manager-in-Chief Fasth.

District Police Superintendent Björnfot is sitting at his desk. He is busy writing up the week's events in the logbook. Writing minutes and summarising interrogations are not among his favourite occupations, but today it's minute-writing weather. Outside, snowflakes are cascading down and glistening in the light from the streetlamps.

He is a broad-shouldered fellow with considerable physical strength, an impressive stomach and fists like sledgehammers. The mining company, which pays the wages of the police authorities in Kiruna, requires its servants of the law to possess "diplomatic skills and physical strength". In other words, the ability to separate troublemakers – of which there are rather a lot in Kiruna. Socialists and Communists, agitators and trades union activists. And not even religious enthusiasts can be relied upon: Laestadians[†] and other low-church preachers are always hovering on the edge of ecstatic fits and lunatic behaviour. And then all the young men – navvies and miners, little more than schoolboys, who flock to Kiruna from all over the

---

† Laestadianism is a conservative Lutheran sect, based predominantly in Scandinavia. It traces its roots to the teachings of Sami-Swedish botanist Lars Levi Laestadius, in the mid-19th century.

place. Far away from their mothers and fathers, they spend their wages on booze and you can guess the rest.

But at the moment, all the cells are empty. Thanks to the wintry cold, people are drinking themselves silly at home rather than brawling in the streets.

The superintendent has never wished as ardently as he does now that there was somebody in the cells. A week has passed since the murder of the schoolteacher Elina Pettersson, and nobody has said anything. Nobody knows anything.

The caretaker discovered her when he arrived in the morning to light the stoves in the classrooms, and to tidy the place up. It had begun snowing again during the night, so there were no footprints outside.

The snow the two women haven't managed to brush off themselves is now melting on their clothes, and they will soon be wet through. Their cheeks are rosy red. The police station has a very efficient tiled stove, and thanks to the superintendent a roaring fire is blazing away inside it.

It is Lizzie who speaks first.

"We've come about Elina Pettersson," she says, coming straight to the point.

Then she nudges Blenda Mänpää.

"Tell him what you told me!"

"I work for Manager-in-Chief Fasth," she says. "He is a pest as far as we girls are concerned. We always work in twos when he is around. We don't even go to light the stoves on our own if he's in the room."

"Is that so?" Björnfot says, beginning to feel uneasy.

"But after the murder of fröken Pettersson he has been calmer than he has ever been before. He hasn't made advances to any of us – he hasn't even slapped our bottoms. It's as if he has become . . . satiated. Satiated and satisfied. Do you understand what I mean?"

"No," Björnfot says, although a little voice inside him says he understands very well.

"This is a very serious accusation you are making," he says eventually. "Very, very serious."

"Yes," Lizzie hisses bitterly. "It is very serious. But tell him about that other business!"

"One of the maids was going to empty the ash from the tiled stove in herr Fasth's bedroom," Blenda says. "It was the day after the murder. There was a piece of a shirtsleeve lying in the stove. That seemed very odd. Why would a man want to burn his shirt?"

Björnfot says nothing, just sits there with his hand over his mouth, looking at them both. It is a very unusual gesture, most unlike him.

"And besides," Blenda says. "When he changes his shirt he always leaves the dirty one lying on the floor. That day he took a new shirt, but didn't leave a dirty one for washing. So it was obviously the shirt he'd been wearing the previous day that was in the stove. Do you understand?"

Björnfot nods. He understands very well.

Lizzie glares at him as if what she really wants to do is to set the whole of the world on fire. Blenda bites her lips and hardly dares look at him. It was very brave of her to come here. Fasth is the most powerful man in Kiruna – apart from Lundbohm, of course, but he is hardly ever in town, he's nearly always away on business.

The mining company owns everything. The company has built the town and the church. The company pays the wages of the police and the vicar and the schoolteachers. And Manager-in-Chief Fasth is the company.

In the end Björnfot takes his hand away from his mouth.

"I want to meet her," he says. "The girl who found the shirtsleeve in the stove."

"Yes, my great-grandfather, Oskar Venetpalo, was a rock-blaster. A simple man, you understand. He was tricked by Hjalmar Lundbohm. He discovered extensive slabs of iron ore in Tuolluvaara. But, you know how it is: he was one of those old-fashioned, loyal workers, and so he went to Lundbohm and told him about it. And Lundbohm submitted a prospecting licence application the very next day."

Martinsson was standing on Johan Venetpalo's porch, smoking a cigarette. Venetpalo was in a wheelchair, and was evidently pleased about the unexpected visit. The fact that she was a prosecutor did not seem to bother him.

"But my great-grandfather said nothing about it, of course," he went on. "Not a word. I know that he signed some document or other that said it was Lundbohm who had discovered the Tuolluvaara iron ore deposit. And then from time to time he received gifts of money from Lundbohm – but he never said why. Obviously both his wife and his children wondered what was going on. My granddad always used to say that his father had been swindled. But of course, he was employed by the mining company, and probably didn't dare stir up trouble."

"No, of course not."

"And Lundbohm was crafty. No doubt he ought to have submitted the prospecting application on behalf of the state, but instead he sold the rights to a foundry owner who in turn handed them on to a newly registered mining company. It was devilishly difficult for the authorities to kick up a fuss, so they drew up a contract with that newly established company – and Lundbohm became managing director of that mine as well, with an income of five thousand a year. That was a lot of money in those days. Why are you asking about this?"

"Just general interest. You know how it is, you catch on to something that fascinates you, and so you follow it up."

Venetpalo gave her a searching look.

"Is it because of her – Solveig Uusitalo from Kurravaara? She was a grandchild of Lundbohm's, after all."

"Sol-Britt. Yes, in a way. I'm not involved in the murder investigation, but you can't help but be interested in her background."

Venetpalo gave a start.

"I'm not a murder suspect, I hope?"

"No."

"It's true that families up here in the north can hate one another for generations. And if there had been any money around, no doubt we would have done so. If Sol-Britt had inherited a few million. But Lundbohm died as poor as a church mouse. And Frans Uusitalo was illegitimate, as they used to say in those days."

"Yes."

"But what's the point of hating and cursing one another? It doesn't make you any richer."

"You wrote a letter to the editor of a newspaper."

"Oh, you remember that, do you? You know, after all this happened . . ."

He gestured towards his legs.

". . .I hit the bottle for a year or two. My wife left me, and I was a bit fed up with the world at large. But you learn your lessons, don't you? If it's not one thing, it's another, as the girl said when she got a nosebleed. Maybe my great-grandfather did the right thing, holding his tongue and coiling in a bit of cash now and then. Anyway, do you think we're going to have a winter at all this year? Or are we just going to have Stockholm-type slush? This climate change lark is a real pain in the arse."

Martinsson smiled at the man in the wheelchair.

Your typical murderer, isn't he? she said to herself.

Follow the money, she told herself later when she had sat down in the car and switched on the engine.

But there was no money to follow.

She phoned Sonja at the police station switchboard.

"Am I right in thinking that there was no money to speak of in Frans Uusitalo's estate?" she asked.

Sonja asked her to hold the line a moment, and was soon able to report that there wasn't – barely enough to cover the funeral expenses, in fact.

"And do you know," Sonja began – but by then Martinsson had already said thank you and hung up.

Martinsson drummed her fingers on the steering wheel and checked her watch. Only five to nine.

"Not everything ends up in the official estate documents," she said to the Brat. "I suppose I'd better drive out to Lainio one more time."

Stålnacke had reported sick. Said that he had a bad cold – but everybody knew that it was Jocke Häggroth who was haunting him with his shattered skull under his arm.

Eriksson drove round to visit him, and rang the doorbell. Stålnacke opened the door and two cats stuck their heads out, took note of the soaking wet conditions and decided to go back to the sofa. Stålnacke was dressed, shaved and combed.

Good, Eriksson thought.

It was tidy and cosy inside. Potted plants in bloom, and framed school photographs of grandchildren on the walls.

Those were the kind of things that were only to be found in houses overseen by a woman, Eriksson thought. In the homes of single men like himself you're only likely to find weeping fig plants with hardly any leaves left, or bayonet lilies in ugly pots with soil as dry as snuff.

Eriksson reported on Marcus, about how he was being bullied by older schoolmates.

"I spoke to both the headmaster and the school welfare officer after I'd dropped off Marcus. Oh yes, they both said, there had been a spot of bother now and then, but they had 'intervened directly'. And 'spoken to all those involved'."

"And a fat lot of good that would have done, no doubt," Stålnacke said, recalling his own depressing feeling of impotence when his daughter Lena had been frozen out by her schoolmates. She had become thin and sickly, with constant stomach ache. Hadn't wanted to go to school. She was grown-up now, but until she had transferred to another school it had been pure hell.

"I want to have a chat with that bully's parents," Eriksson said. "That's the least I can do for Marcus. It's people like that who protect their young gangsters no matter what the little swine get up to. And scare folk. I thought we could put an end to that. And I'd appreciate it if you would come with me."

"Why?"

"It would be better if there were two of us. And you could be a witness to prove that I hadn't threatened the bastard of a father."

Stålnacke grinned.

"I see, so that's how it is, eh? I'd better come along to make sure you don't murder anybody."

"Yes, please do that."

"Did you say they were called Niemi?" Stålnacke said. "Maybe we should ask around a bit before we pay them a visit."

"There you are, you see," Eriksson said with a smile. "I knew you would be useful."

The maid who found the shirtsleeve in the stove in the manager-in-chief's bedroom lives on the island with her mother and three siblings.

It is the mother who opens the door. She has large, frightened eyes, and there is something more than just fear in her gaze. Resistance.

The police superintendent has to stoop in order to get through the entrance door, and is barely able to stand upright in this little hovel.

He explains why he has come, and Lizzie and Blenda, who have accompanied him, urge the little girl to tell Björnfot what she saw.

The maid doesn't say a thing. Her two small sisters are sitting on the floor, and they also say nothing, stare in silence at the strangers. The mother starts clearing up after the evening meal, just simple wooden bowls and spoons: they have eaten barley porridge without even a dash of milk. She says nothing, but keeps a wary eye on her daughter and the visitors when Björnfot starts trying to coax the girl to speak up.

She is so unwilling to talk that at first he thinks perhaps she doesn't understand – maybe she only speaks Finnish? Or perhaps she's not right in the head? Is she an idiot? Someone who can only cope with the simplest of tasks – chopping firewood or rinsing washing?

"So you are Hillevi," he says, but receives no answer.

"You work for herr Fasth, is that right?"

Not a word. She merely tightens her lips.

"Puhutko suomea?" he asks in stumbling Finnish.

Then Blenda intervenes.

"What's the matter with you?" she snaps at the girl. "Tell him about the shirt!"

"I was mistaken," the girl says. "It wasn't a shirt. It was just a dirty rag one of the other maids had thrown into the fire."

She speaks quickly, as if reciting something she has learnt by heart, and glances furtively at her mother.

"Perhaps you had better come with us to the police station so that we can discuss this matter properly," Police Superintendent Björnfot says.

He tries to sound authoritative, but he can hear that his voice lacks its usual power.

The girl squeals in horror, and her mother catches his eye and stares hard at him.

"It's two months now since my Samuel was killed in a rock-blasting accident," she said. "He was keeping the dynamite warm and ready for the blasters. The mining company guarantees work for widows like me, so I work as a cleaner in the lodging houses used by unmarried men who work in the mines: I get forty kronor a week for every man I clean for. And a bit extra if I do his laundry as well. And Hillevi was given a job, working for Fasth. Between us we earn just about enough to keep our heads above water. If it weren't for what the company has done for us, and not least Manager-in-Chief Fasth, well! . . . I'd have had to sell off the children at a pauper's auction."

The working blouse she has on is so worn that it is almost transparent.

"I'm well aware of who fröken Pettersson was," she says, looking

316

at them in desperation. "Like a ray of sunshine from the heavens above. But . . ."

"I understand," Björnfot says.

He withdraws sadly into the falling snow. Trailing behind him are Lizzie, who is crying her eyes out, and Blenda, who is as silent as the grave.

"It's not right," Lizzie sobs. "It's not right."

"What do you expect me to do?" Björnfot says in annoyance. "Accuse the manager-in-chief of murder because he didn't smack the bottoms of his servants? I haven't got a credible case to argue. Even if that poor little girl were to dare to tell a jury what she saw, it wouldn't be enough."

Lizzie tries to stop crying, but the tears just keep on flowing. She sounds like an injured animal. Björnfot can't bear to listen to it.

"I shall be sacked," Blenda says. "Why? For nothing."

Police Superintendent Björnfot walks back to the police station, and spends the whole evening glowering at the empty cells while the tiled stove cools down.

Lizzie spends the night on the sofa bed, staring up at the dark ceiling.

I can't bear this, she says to her God, clasping her hands so tightly that her fingers turn white. I can't bear the thought of him getting away with this unpunished. It's not right.

Ragnhild Lindmark worked for the home-help service in Lainio. She welcomed Martinsson into her home, and did her best to answer the questions put to her.

"But I'm afraid you're not going to get any coffee," she said. "I was forced to give it up several years ago. You can probably understand how much of the stuff one had to drink in the houses of all those old folk. I'd poisoned myself by the end."

A canary was perched on the curtain pole, and occasionally sang. The whole of the window-ledge was covered in small glass figures. Outside everything seemed quiet and peaceful in the dull, misty weather. Ragnhild made some green tea and explained to Martinsson that the water shouldn't boil, and the tea shouldn't brew for too long.

"I buy it on the net," she said when Martinsson politely expressed her appreciation.

"You used to look after Frans Uusitalo, is that right?" Martinsson said.

"Yes – ugh! What a horrible mess that was! I told him over and over again that he should tell me when he was going to go out into the forest – he could fall off his bike or goodness only knows what else could happen, and it would help if I knew where to go looking for him. But you know what old men are like. He was in incredibly good shape. Over ninety years old, just imagine that! Why are you wondering about him?"

"I'm just looking a bit more closely into his death. Do you know if there was anybody who had a grudge against him?"

"No. What are you getting at? He was mauled by a bear."

"Can you remember if anything unusual happened shortly before he disappeared? Something outside his normal routine. Did he seem worried at all? Anything odd?"

"Eh? No. As far as I can recall, everything was exactly the same as usual. What do you think might have been worrying him?"

Martinsson did not know what to say.

What indeed? she thought.

"There's something about his death that doesn't add up," she said eventually. "Did he have any money?"

"As far as I know he had just about enough to pay for his food and his electricity bills."

Lindmark thought for a moment, then said frankly, "I don't know why you are asking all these questions, because I didn't know him all that well. But he did have a girlfriend here in the village. He was handsome, it has to be said. Tall, and he still had lovely curly hair. She lives only three houses away. Over there. A brick-built house. There is only one. Her name is Anna Jaako. Would you like to borrow an umbrella? We're in for some wet snow, not much more than sleet. But I shouldn't complain – it means I won't have to dig out all the old men and women on my list. It's not part of the job, but you have to do it even so, of course. Good Lord, last winter they'd never have got out at all if me and my old man hadn't cleared the snow away for them. It snowed practically every day."

I am out of my mind, Martinsson thought as she walked over to Anna Jaako's house. I don't even know what I'm looking for.

Anna Jaako was at home, and invited Martinsson in for coffee.

She accepted, and drank it as slowly as she possibly could in order to make sure that Anna didn't offer to top it up.

She was pretty. Looked like an elderly ballerina. Her hair was glistening white, tied up in a trendy ponytail.

"I don't think he was mauled by a bear," said Martinsson, who had made up her mind to throw caution to the wind.

They were only going to have a chat after all, so she might as well say what she thought, and hope to get some frank comments in return.

"I think he was shot, and that the bear ate him later."

Jaako turned a little pale.

"I'm sorry," Martinsson said.

Jaako gestured dismissively with her hand.

"No problem. I'm not as fragile as I look. But who would want to shoot him?"

"It could have been a mistake," Martinsson said feebly. "A hunter, for instance. Who didn't even see him."

"Isn't that rather unlikely?"

Very unlikely indeed, Martinsson thought. Especially in view of the fact that he was shot in his leg and his chest.

"I don't really know what I'm fishing for, to be honest," Martinsson said. "Could anybody have had a reason for wanting to kill him? Did anything special happen shortly before he disappeared?"

"No," Jaako said. "Not as far as I can recall. And he didn't have any money. But he could dance. We used to dance here in the kitchen."

The memory of that seemed to inspire her.

"If you remember anything, please give me a ring," said Martinsson, writing her telephone number down on the back of a receipt she happened to have in her handbag.

Anna Jaako looked at the receipt and read the number out aloud.

"I don't suppose it's important," she said, as if arguing with herself. "It was several years ago."

"What was?" Martinsson asked.

"The only thing I can think of. As I said, it was three years ago," Jaako said. "I remember that because I was just about to celebrate my seventy-fifth birthday. Anyway, he was Hjalmar Lundbohm's illegitimate son – perhaps you didn't know that."

"Yes, I do know," Martinsson said.

"His mother – although she wasn't his real mother, but the one he grew up with – was Lundbohm's housekeeper. And she was so angry with Lundbohm. And so he sort of grew up with the conviction that Lundbohm was a prat. Or really did, in fact, not sort of. She didn't tell him about his real parents until his foster father had died, and by then Frans was more than twenty. Anyway. Three years ago he found some old documents in a box with ancient photographs and school reports. There was a letter from Lundbohm in which he wrote that he had left some shares to his son Frans Uusitalo. He had been given his stepfather's name. And Frans joked with me and said that we could now book a cruise, because we were going to be rich. Wealthy. That's the word he used. Wealthy."

"Really?"

"But I suppose nothing came of it, because he never mentioned it again. I think his daughter looked into it, and established that the shares were worth nothing. But it was nice to be able to look at them. Nowadays shares only exist in computers."

"Three years ago, you said?"

"Yes."

And Sol-Britt's son was run over three years ago, Martinsson thought.

"I'm sorry," Jaako said, wiping her eyes that were suddenly filled with tears. "But I miss him so very much. If anybody had told me when I was your age that I would meet the love of my life when I was over seventy, I would have killed myself laughing."

She looked hard at Martinsson.

"You have to make the most of love when you find it, you know. Before you know where you are, you've experienced it for the last time. And everything else is meaningless."

You have to keep working so as not to go out of your mind. Lizzie has cleaned the flat several times, scrubbed the floor and the ceiling in the kitchen, washed and ironed the thin linen curtains and painted the cupboard doors in the kitchen blue.

"Are you mad?" her neighbours ask. "Washing the curtains in the middle of winter! Haven't you got enough to do with all the mining clothes?"

She has decided to make real potato dumplings. She has cut up the pork and the bacon rind, added cornflour and grated potatoes and shaped the result into grey balls. She drops the balls into the big cauldron of boiling water, and the whole kitchen fills with steam. It's like a sauna in there.

She hears a noise behind her, and for a fraction of a second she thinks it is Elina.

When she turns round she sees that it is in fact Manager-in-Chief Fasth.

His eyes are like the points of knives in his red, fat face. He peers quickly into the living room to make sure that he and Lizzie are alone in the flat.

"Fröööken," he says.

His voice is rough. She feels frozen to the bone by the sound of it. As when she has been rinsing washed clothes in winter and can't stop shivering, despite making a roaring fire in the stove during the evening.

"My fiancé is due at any moment," says Lizzie.

She regrets that straight away. The words sound so pitiful. She can't resist glancing at the kitchen knife.

He snorts scornfully.

"I don't give a fuck about all your boyfriends. Just listen to me. Tongues are wagging in Kiruna. About that whore Elina Pettersson and me. And the owner of the tongue that is wagging the most is Busy Lizzie Anderson."

"Yes, you have threatened your maids so that—"

"The next time you interrupt me I shall punch you in the face. That's the whore's baby, isn't it?"

He nods at the basket in the corner where Frans is lying asleep.

"If you utter so much as a word to the superintendent of police, or the managing director when he comes back from his travels, or to any other living person, I shall take that baby away from you. I shall tell the Child Welfare Committee about the dissolute life you lead – living here alone with four men, right? Plus an extra fiancé. Before there were two of you to share them all, but now you have to satisfy them yourself."

He pauses and gives Lizzie such a contemptuous look that she feels bound to cross her arms over her chest.

"Who do you think they will listen to, you or me? I'll take over the boy as a foster child. He'll get a regular good hiding, I can promise you that. Every day. Only the cane and the belt can overcome the inheritance left him by his loose-living mother. Now you may answer. Is that what you want? Answer me, I said."

Lizzie leans against the edge of the cooker. All she can do is to shake her head.

"Right," he says. "Not a word shall pass your lips. And you can pack your things together and move out of Kiruna. I'll give you a month, no more. And I warn you, I'm not the patient type."

Now she is incapable of standing up any longer. She sinks down onto the stool standing by the cooker.

Fasth leans over her and whispers into her ear.

"She enjoyed it, that schoolteacher. She begged and pleaded with me to continue. I was forced to strangle her to shut her up."

Then he disappears down the stairs.

The cauldron with the dumplings boils over, but Lizzie is incapable of moving it aside. She can't even stand up. When Johan-Albin arrives shortly afterwards to eat, she is still sitting there on the stool, Frans is crying in his basket, and the potato dumplings are burnt and stuck to the bottom of the cauldron. Water is running down the windowpanes.

Martinsson rummaged around among Sol-Britt's belongings. She had phoned Björnfot to check that the warrant for searching the house was still valid.

"I don't want that added to the list of accusations when von Post drags me up before the neuropathological crowd," she had said.

"If he tries anything like that, I'll make sure he spends the rest of his working life dealing with unpaid parking fines," Björnfot had growled.

What a lot of stuff people accumulate during their lifetime. Martinsson could feel the dust irritating her nostrils. Photographs, letters, copies of income tax returns, insurance documents, invoices, special mail-order offers from ten years ago, and God only knows what else.

When she found a letter from Sol-Britt's boss concerning her drinking habits, Martinsson was overcome by moral considerations and was forced to pause and go out with the Brat.

"But what I'm doing doesn't hurt anybody," she said to the dog, who was scampering around in the wet snow and leaving lonely-hearts messages on every tree trunk. "I'm just poking my nose around. More or less like you."

Her mobile buzzed in her pocket. It was Eriksson.

"Hi," he said, and his voice sounded so mellow that she couldn't help but smile. "I was wondering if you could take Vera. I'm

326

going to have words with the parents of some hooligans who have been bullying Marcus. I rang Maja and she said they were going to borrow a friend's cottage at Rautasälven, and that Marcus could go with them and do some fishing. So that fits in very nicely. It will be fun for him. They're only going to be there for the day."

"You can leave Vera at my place," Martinsson said. "I'll be home soon. Then I can go and fetch Marcus as well. The key is under the flowerpot in the porch."

Eriksson sighed audibly at the other end of the line.

"Under the flowerpot. . . Why bother to lock the door at all if you leave the key under a flowerpot? It would be the first place anybody would look. Either there or under the shoes that for some inexplicable reason are standing out in the cold."

"I know, I know," said Martinsson. "But isn't it great? When Grandma was alive the tradition was that nobody ever locked the door. And if you went out you left a broom outside the gate so that any visitors hoping for a cup of coffee wouldn't need to walk all the way from the road to the house in vain. It was obvious that there was nobody at home."

"O.K., I'll let the dog in and leave the broom outside the gate," Eriksson said with a laugh, and hung up.

Martinsson went back inside and continued searching through Sol-Britt's belongings. She eventually found what she was looking for. A large brown envelope containing three documents marked SHARE CERTIFICATE. And a letter in old-fashioned handwriting, somewhat shaky.

An old man, she thought, her heart pounding.

"Dear Lizzie," the letter began.

But she decided to postpone reading it, and in any case, the handwriting was not easy to interpret. Instead she telephoned Måns. He answered almost immediately, and sounded so happy. Her bad conscience gnawed at her, but she didn't have time for lovey-dovey talk.

"You know all there is to know about company law and shares and bonds," she said. "I need your help."

Lizzie wakes up during the night and speaks to God. It makes no difference how hard she works. She simply can't sleep. She tells her Good Lord that she can't cope. She lies there, staring up at the dark ceiling, so full of hatred. All she can manage to do is pray. She can't think of many words, just: *Help me, God, please help me.*

She tries to banish from her mind's eye the image of Elina's blonde head. Of Elina and Fasth. Of Elina's blood-soaked blouse the verger had given her when she went with clean clothes to the church where Elina was lying in a remembrance room before the funeral.

Help me, God, she begs. I want to kill him. Why should he be allowed to live? It's not right.

She is scared as well, all the time. She wants to leave Kiruna this very moment, for who knows what Fasth will do next? He might suddenly take Frans away from her. Johan-Albin promises that they will move away, but first they must find work in another town.

She thinks about what she will do if Fasth so much as looks at the boy: she will smash his fat skull with the poker, hit him again and again . . . How she wishes she had poured the boiling water and potato dumplings all over him.

Help me, she prays again. Help me. Dear, sweet Jesus.

Stålnacke, Eriksson and Marcus got out of the car when the dirt road petered out. In the middle of the forest. They could hear the sound of the River Rautas in the distance.

"Rebecka and Vera will soon come to collect you," Eriksson said to Marcus. "And I shan't be away all that long."

"But I want to go with you," Marcus said, grabbing hold of the sleeve of Eriksson's jacket.

"I'll be as quick as I can," Eriksson promised.

The snow was still lying on the path through the trees, trampled down. It was like walking along a narrow street covered in ice. Water was dripping from the trees. On the ground at either side of the path there were only occasional patches of snow left. They tried to tread on stones and clumps of lingon stalks sticking up through the ice, so as not to slip and fall.

But it was looking a bit brighter now, Eriksson thought, although he didn't dare to take his eyes off the path for more than a few seconds. The clouds had lifted and were thinning out.

A wooden staircase led down to a bog, and the path over the bog was a sort of bridge made of wooden planks.

But it was almost impossible to make progress. The steps were extremely slippery, and the wooden bridge over the bog was covered in a layer of ice, turning it into a skating rink.

"Talk about style and grace," Stålnacke mumbled. "I'm walking as if I've just shat myself. This is a death trap."

Then he shouted to Marcus.

"Mind how you go, mi'lad!"

"Kids," he muttered to himself. "Those were the days."

Thanks to the sense of balance and lack of fear typical of a young boy, Marcus was already a long way ahead of them, bending his knees and stepping out boldly.

At the far end of the bog, at the edge of the trees, a man appeared on the wooden bridge. He raised a hand in greeting.

"Marcus?" he shouted.

Stålnacke and Eriksson stopped, and waved back cautiously.

"I can take him from here on," the man shouted. "Maja is back there by the cottages. It's so damned slippery everywhere. You can go back now!"

"Aha, it's her bloke," Stålnacke said to Eriksson. "Örjan, I think his name is. He was there when von Pest dragged us all out to interrogate her. Or was it von Post? Von Pest is better . . . You should have been there. Bloody bastard of a prosecutor. Anyway, let's turn back. I'll be grateful if I get back to the car in one piece."

"Bye, then," Eriksson shouted. "Max an hour. Say hello to Maja and thank her."

They turned and made their way back to the steps with considerable difficulty. The man at the edge of the forest beckoned to Marcus.

Marcus went slowly towards the man with the mop of hair. Deep down inside he was talking to the Wild Dog. Vera will soon arrive. And Krister. And Rebecka. They'll soon be here. And fetch me. Soon.

The man said hello to him, turned on his heel, and Marcus followed him. Now and then he turned to look at Eriksson and Stålnacke, but before long they were no longer in sight. The wooden bridge over the bog came to an end, and the path continued through the trees. Now he could hear the sound of the rapids. He tried to step on bare ground whenever possible – there was sometimes ice under the patches of snow, and it was easy to slip and fall.

"You go first," the man said.

Marcus walked quickly ahead.

The trees began to thin out as they approached the river, and he saw a woman with white hair standing on the bank. She was about a hundred metres ahead by an upturned boat, hacking away at the oars that were frozen fast to the ground.

She was chopping away at the riverbank with a spade.

Holding the spade in both hands, and chopping away. Again and again.

Marcus stopped dead.

He had seen that woman by the boat before. Then. When he was standing at the top of the stairs and looking into his grandmother's bedroom. He hadn't seen the person's face, because whoever was with Grandma had worn a balaclava. The kind of woollen headgear you wear when riding a snow scooter, with holes for the eyes and mouth.

But now. He recognised the body. The arms, hacking away over and over again.

Stabbing his grandmother. And he had been a coward and run away. He hadn't rescued his grandmother. He crept back down the staircase and opened the window even though his hands were shaking. Jumped out of the window and started running. Ran through the forest. Then Krister had arrived. And Grandma was dead.

Now. Now the murderer was going to capture him.

He heard his own hoarse voice screaming.

He screamed as loudly as he could, and tried to run away. But he couldn't.

The man behind him had lifted him up. Holding onto his arm and jacket. Marcus's feet were running in the air.

"Shut up," the man grunted.

"Krister!" Marcus screamed as loudly as he could. "Krister!"

Then a tree came flying towards him.

And everything went blank.

Eriksson and Stålnacke did not hear any screams. They were in the car, on their way back to Kiruna. Two knights in shining armour who were going to make sure that Willy Niemi, aged nine, stopped bullying Marcus Uusitalo, aged seven.

Manager-in-Chief Fasth marches through Kiruna. He is a sort of living plough. People move out of his way, greet him curtly, raise their caps, curtsey, glance furtively at him.

It does not worry him in the least that people are afraid of him. On the contrary, he welcomes it. People's hatred only makes him stronger – it is like steel hardening in the fire.

And in fact he has no problem with what the people of Kiruna suspect, but cannot prove.

He forced that upstart fröken down on her knees, and now he has the whole population of Kiruna on their knees.

The only person with any power over him is Managing Director Lundbohm. But Lundbohm is a fool. Fasth has written to him about the tragic event. Explained that an investigation concluded that she had had several lovers, had given birth to a child, and that quite a few men could possibly be the father. But that the murder is unsolved, and likely to remain that way.

Lundbohm did not reply. Fasth expects to see very little of him in Kiruna in future. So much the better.

But now Fasth has other things to think about. The stone-crusher at the mine is out of order, and he is marching through the town like a ruler infuriated by the incompetence of others.

Some bloody minder who can't do his job. What is the point of mining ore if you can't transport it to where it is needed? None! The ore must be crushed and loaded onto railway wagons.

Normally you can hear the noise made by the stone-crusher from a long way off, the gigantic grinder that smashes up the large blocks of iron ore. But now silence reigns. The men are sitting around, smoking, but they soon get to their feet when they see the manager-in-chief approaching.

One of them tries to explain the situation.

"A large block of stone has got well and truly stuck."

But Fasth is not there to partake in a conversation over coffee. He shoves the man to one side and snatches the iron bar from him.

They all follow him like a school class. The crusher is a sort of enormous rolling pin with spikes sticking out from a screw-shaped jacket of steel. It normally spins round like a propeller, crushing the stone into smaller and smaller pieces which fall down onto the railway wagon waiting beneath it.

Fasth jumps down into the crusher.

"This is your job, for Christ's sake," he snarls.

He forces the iron lever under the block of stone that has stuck fast.

"You're a load of bloody women," he grunts. "Every one of you a soppy little fröken. You'll have your wages docked as a result of this."

The word "fröken" runs through the assembled spectators like a wave on a beach. They don't even need to look at one another. They are all thinking the same thing. It's as if she is standing there beside them. Eyes gleaming and cheeks glowing.

They glance unobtrusively at Johan-Albin – he knew her, after all. He's engaged to the housekeeper she used to live with.

Down in the crusher Fasth snorts like a bull as he struggles with the block of stone. It doesn't want to budge. But he is determined to teach that gang of namby-pambies up there a lesson.

"Does any of you even have a cock?" he asks, as he throws up his jacket.

Then he gets to work again with the lever.

The youngest member of the team picks up the jacket, and looks around for a place to hang it up.

And then everybody's eyes fasten on the same thing at the same time.

The main switch. Nobody has turned it off.

They exchange looks. Nobody says "voi perkele" and rushes forward to switch off the electricity. The young man with the jacket folds it neatly over his arm.

And then Fasth manages to prise the block of stone loose.

There is a roaring sound as the crusher starts revolving. Stones smash up against steel and all hell is let loose.

The stones under Fasth's feet sink down like quicksand. The crusher seems to gulp him down. In the twinkling of an eye the whole of the lower part of his body has vanished.

They don't even hear him scream. They just see the look of surprise and horror on his face. His gaping mouth. Any noise he makes is drowned out by the deafening roar of steel smashing against stone.

It is all over in a few seconds. The crusher swallows Fasth up and grinds him to bits together with the stone, reduces his body to scraps of flesh and bone and spits out the remains onto the railway wagon below.

Johan-Albin switches off the electricity supply, and silence falls. Then he spits down into the crusher.

"Ah well," he says. "We'd better fetch the police superintendent."

Måns called Martinsson back almost an hour later.

"Are you quite sure it says Share Certificate Alberta Power Generation?"

"Yes," she said. "I'm holding them in my hand."

"How many shares are we talking about?" Måns wondered.

"It says: 'Representing shares 501–600' on the first certificate, '601–700' on the next one, and '701–800' on the third."

"Good God, Rebecka. Does it say anything on the back about the transfer?"

"Just a moment, I'll have a look . . . 'Transferee' and '4 March 1926, Frans Uusitalo'. A bit further down it says 'Transferor, Hjalmar Lundbohm'. So, what does it all mean?"

"The company still exists. It's an incredibly big hydroelectric company based in Calgary. There have been a lot of new issues. In the early days those shares comprised a tenth of the value of the company. Now it's one ten thousandth of the whole value."

"What does that mean?"

"They're still worth quite a lot."

"How much? Shall I put them in my inside pocket and take the first flight I can find to South America?"

"Yes, you would certainly have been justified in doing that – had it not been for a deed of transfer on the reverse side."

"Meaning what? How much? Come on, Måns, explain yourself."

"What I'm saying is that those share certificates are worthless as far as you are concerned."

"But . . . ?"

"But for Frans Uusitalo, or his heirs, they are worth about ten million."

"What? You're joking!"

"Canadian dollars."

There followed a few seconds of silence. Martinsson took a deep breath.

So Sol-Britt Uusitalo was rich, she thought. She lived in a broken-down old house in Lehtiniemi, weighing up every krona she spent. And she had no idea . . .

"You can't steal share certificates," she said. "Because they spell out who owns them from generation to generation."

"Did her father have any other heirs?" Måns said.

"I'll ring you later," Martinsson said.

"What does that mean?"

"Thank you, Måns. Thank you – clever, handsome Måns! I love you! But for Christ's sake . . . I'll ring you later!"

"Don't do anything silly now," Måns said.

But Martinsson had already hung up.

"I tried to tell you this when we spoke not long ago," Sonja said when Martinsson rang. "But you were in such—"

"Yes, I know!"

"That's all very well, but there you see."

"I'm sorry. I'm listening now."

"He had a son as well. Older than Sol-Britt. With another woman. But there wasn't even enough money to cover the cost of the funeral in his estate."

No, there wouldn't be, Martinsson thought. But she said, "So Sol-Britt had a half-brother, did she? What was his name?"

"Oh, come on! How on earth could I remember that? Do you want me to check?"

"Yes, straight away," Martinsson said. "I want the whole family tree."

The Niemis' house was situated a bit further down the creek in Kurravaara. Fru Niemi let in the police officers who wanted to speak to her and her husband. She was scared stiff at first, but they assured her that nothing had happened to any of her children or relatives.

She was in her thirties, tall and slim. Her hair was dyed blonde and close-cropped at the back, but her fringe was long and the hair in front of her ears hung down as far as her mouth. She had several rings through her left ear, and one through her nostril. Her mouth was busy chewing gum, and she kept an eye on the television in the kitchen: somebody was advertising a miraculous vegetable peeler that would transform the purchaser's life and make their children beg to eat carrots and cucumber.

Stålnacke and Eriksson sat down, and fru Niemi shouted for her husband. He appeared in the doorway and introduced himself as Lelle. He was as blond as his wife, with muscular arms. His nose seemed to have been broken at some time, and gave him the appearance of a good-looking but somewhat worse-for-wear boxer.

"Police," fru Niemi said curtly.

"Yes, but we're not here on official business," Eriksson said.

"Can we offer you anything?" Lelle wondered, smiling as if they were two childhood friends who had come to visit him. "Coffee? Light beer?" Eriksson and Stålnacke raised their arms in a gesture that said *no thank you*.

"We've come about your boy Willy," Eriksson said, "and another boy at the same school. Marcus Uusitalo."

The smile faded immediately from Lelle Niemi's lips.

Too late now for a beer, Stålnacke thought.

"Not all that business again, surely," Lelle Niemi said.

Then he shouted upstairs.

"Willy, come down here!"

There was a sound of footsteps on the stairs, then young herr Niemi appeared in the doorway. His father ushered him in so that the boy was standing in front of him.

"If you're going to start going on at me about bullying, the lad should hear what you have to say. Because he's the one you're going to accuse, I take it?"

"Do you want me to address him or you?" Eriksson said.

"Talk to Willy direct. That's the way I've brought him up – matters are always discussed directly with the person concerned. Isn't that so, Willy? Eye to eye. No beating about the bush."

Willy nodded and gritted his teeth.

"You and your mates," Eriksson said to Willy, "I want you to leave Marcus Uusitalo in peace. Steer well clear of him."

"But what the hell," Willy howled. "I haven't done anything. I've said already, I haven't done anything. Tell him, Dad."

"It's alright, Willy," Lelle Niemi said, placing his hand on his son's shoulder. "I hope you're not going to call my son a liar."

"He is a liar," Eriksson said. "And a bully. I feel sorry for you, Willy. Because that's the kind of thing you learn at home. In one way or another. But now I'm going to make you stop bullying him. I'm glad to be able to do that – I'm concerned about Marcus's welfare."

"What the hell are you on about?" Lelle Niemi snarled. "That Marcus Uusitalo has serious problems. His mother abandoned him. His father was run over and killed about a few years ago. His grandmother . . ."

He finished the sentence by whistling and making a gesture with his thumb against his mouth suggesting that she was a boozer.

"And now she's been murdered and it's all over the pages of *Expressen* and the rest of the media. It's all very tragic. But for Christ's sake don't drag my son into it."

"Quite right," fru Niemi burbled. "I don't understand why you are chasing up Willy. It's harassment."

"I know what you and your mates have been doing," Eriksson said to Willy. "You've been hounding him ever since he started at nursery school. Calling him a cunt or a queer, throwing snowballs with stones inside, putting dog shit in his rucksack, knocking him over whenever you walk past him. It's gone far enough."

Willy shrugged.

"I don't know what you're talking about."

"Have the police nothing better to do than harass law-abiding citizens?" Lelle Niemi wanted to know. "Shouldn't you be out chasing thieves? It's time you were on your way. We've nothing more to say."

"And stop pestering ordinary people," fru Niemi said, looking at Eriksson without attempting to disguise her disgust.

Eriksson returned her gaze until she was forced to look away.

"But the fact is," Stålnacke said, breaking his silence, "you're not ordinary people. Lelle Niemi, you have been on sickness benefit for the last two years."

"Whiplash injury," Niemi said.

"But you are still working as a painter and decorator. On the black market."

"This is slander," fru Niemi whimpered. "I thought that was against the law."

"What the hell are you talking about?" Niemi said.

"That's a nice swimming pool you have," Stålnacke said calmly. "And two new cars in the drive. If we were to check your Visa card

I'm sure we'd find Christmas trips to Thailand and goodness only knows what else. Can that be right? How can you afford all that on your sickness benefit and your wife's part-time wages, especially as you have three kids as well? It's the kind of thing the fraud squad would be very interested to hear about."

"And I think we'd find an awful lot of paint bought using your credit card," Eriksson said.

"There's never any problem in finding witnesses in cases of this sort. People are surprisingly honest and talkative as long as they don't end up in court. It's not a serious crime to employ a painter and decorator on the black market now and then. But what you are doing, well . . ."

The Niemis said nothing. Young Willy looked anxiously at first one, then the other. The T.V. was showing a somewhat past-it Hollywood celebrity peeling a cucumber with religious fervour.

"If you ask me, there's a hell of a lot hanging over your heads," Stålnacke said. "Drawing sickness benefit when you are perfectly fit to work is gross fraud. And on top of that you're trading on the black market. Serious tax crime and false accounting."

"Jail," Eriksson said. "Several years. And when you come out again after the state has confiscated your mansion and you're trying to make ends meet in a poky little flat, and it's time to pay back all the tax you owe, you'll find you're not allowed by law to run your own business, and so you'll be a wage slave living on the breadline."

"You are not an ordinary person," Stålnacke said in a friendly tone of voice. "Ordinary people slave away and pay tax so that your boy can go to school, so that you can have an asphalted road to drive your car on. And they pay your sickness benefit. You're nothing more than a parasite."

"But still," Eriksson said. "What I'm more concerned about is Marcus Uusitalo. I'm not going to tip off my colleagues in the fraud squad provided you instruct this young man to leave Marcus

Uusitalo in peace. And the same applies to your mates, Willy. Leave Marcus alone. Totally. And absolutely."

"But I haven't—" Willy began.

"Hold your tongue," Niemi said. Then he added quietly, "You heard what the man said. Leave him alone."

"We'll be off now," Eriksson said, getting to his feet. "But you'd be well advised to discuss all this pretty seriously among yourselves. About how you want things to be. Because you only have half a chance. Just one look, one word, and I'll ring them. I'm not the patient type."

"Have we made the world a better place now?" Stålnacke wondered as they walked away from the house.

They could hear fru Niemi shrieking, and her husband bellowing back, although they couldn't make out the words.

They got into the car. Eriksson was going to drive Stålnacke home.

"No," Eriksson said. "Those kids will only find somebody else to kick around. But we've made the world a better place for Marcus. And that's good enough for me today."

When Manager-in-Chief Fasth is accidentally killed in the stone-crusher, Hjalmar Lundbohm is obliged to return to Kiruna.

Lizzie takes the opportunity of resigning. She has done it lots of times while lying awake at night. Called him a coward. Told him straight that if he had accepted his responsibilities, Elina would still have been alive. That it happened because he had turned his back on her.

But now she stands there in the kitchen and listens as he tells her how many guests there will be for dinner – engineers and their wives.

When he has finished talking she curtseys. It is enough to drive her mad. There was never any question of her curtseying when she rehearsed her resignation speech during the sleepless nights. The managing director was always shattered by his feelings of guilt. And she was always ruthless. Stood there in front of him and unleashed a series of truths like an avenging angel.

But now she is unable to utter a single word about Elina. All she says is that Johan-Albin has got a job in Luleå. He doesn't mention her either, although just for a second he seems to have something on his conscience that must come out.

But the moment passes and the telephone rings. He hurries to his study. It occurs to her that if that confounded telephone had rung during his mother's funeral he would still have dashed off and taken the call. She returns to the kitchen and starts ordering the maids

345

about with such fervour that they scurry around like frightened mice, dropping things, hardly daring to breathe without asking her how she would like them to do it.

She is furious deep down inside because Lundbohm did not even ask about the boy.

But there again, perhaps it is as well that he did not. What if he had in fact taken on responsibility for the child? Who would have looked after the boy then? Some housekeeper?

Nevertheless, she thinks as she allows the white sauce to burn at the bottom of the pan: he ought to have asked how the boy was!

It is late evening. Lundbohm is in the courtyard of his official residence, all by himself, smoking a cigar. He has donned his large wolfskin coat and accompanied his guests on the first stage of their walk home.

It has been a very pleasant evening – almost disgracefully pleasant, bearing in mind that Manager-in-Chief Fasth has not even been buried yet. Nobody so much as mentioned his name during the course of the dinner. When Lundbohm said a few words and proposed a toast in his memory, everyone raised their glasses in appropriate silence: but they were all keen to talk about something else the moment their glasses had been set down on the table.

Perhaps I'm the only one who will miss him, Lundbohm thinks as he gazes up at the pole star as usual.

Fasth was a tough customer, and widely disliked. But he did his job, and did it well.

And mine too, Lundbohm admits to himself. He took care of all the things I prefer to have nothing to do with – discipline, rules and regulations, bookkeeping.

And now Lundbohm has lost his housekeeper as well.

He tries to erase Lizzie's expressionless face from his memory. She is always sunshine itself, just like . . .

Elina.

But he is not going to think about Elina. He must not. Nothing can turn the clock back. What is done cannot be undone.

Pegasus, Taurus, the Charioteer – they all stare coldly down at him. He stands alone in the wintry night, and feels so shatteringly lonely. The words of the Bible float into his mind: *When I consider thy heavens, the work of thy fingers, the moon and the stars, which thou hast ordained; What is man, that thou art mindful of him? and the son of man, that thou visitest him?*

I am nobody, he thinks, and suddenly feels just as lonely as he did during those early years in the infant school. Even then he was an overweight dreamer, without friends.

And now – if I didn't have the mine, and this home? Who would I be then? The whole world knows the managing director of the mine. But who knows Hjalmar Lundbohm?

Elina, he thinks. Did she really love me? Did she? All those men who regularly turned their heads to look at her. All the letters they used to leave outside her door.

He recalled her skin. Her body. His own surprise at the beginning – because she really did seem to want him. Even though he was old enough to be her father.

He has difficulty in breathing, drops the cigar in the snow. He suddenly feels afraid of falling. And not being able to stand up again.

It's just that I'm tired, he tells himself. This is nothing. It's just that I've been working too hard.

He staggers indoors, arms outstretched in order to keep his balance.

Once inside, he flops down onto the bench in the hall.

The boy – obviously it could be his. But she didn't confirm or deny it when he asked. And how would he be able to look after him?

The lad needs a mother. And he knows that Lizzie and her fiancé have taken him to their hearts.

That is the best thing for him.

The house is so quiet. There is nothing in his bed apart from his hot-water bottles.

He shuffles slowly up the stairs to his bedroom. Muttering to himself on every step: best thing for him, best thing for him.

Ten million, Martinsson thought as she drove home. The share certificates were in her handbag on the back seat.

Canadian dollars, she thought as she stood at a loss in her kitchen, the share certificates in her hands. Eventually she placed them right at the bottom of the pile of invoices lying on her desk.

"I shall go and fetch Marcus," she said to Vera and the Brat. "You can wait here."

But when she opened the front door, Vera took advantage of the opportunity to sneak out.

"Huh, typical," Martinsson said as she opened the car door. "You never pay any attention to what I say, do you? So you are going to come with me and fetch Marcus, are you?"

Vera jumped in and sat down on the front passenger seat. Martinsson could hear the Brat yapping away inside the house.

She drove along the dirt road until she came to the path leading to the River Rautas.

The last of the daylight was fading away. The sky was dull blue. The moon shone out through narrow gaps in the clouds. Drops of moisture trembled on tree branches. Patches of snow here and there shone like polished mirrors.

The path was slippery, and you couldn't see where you were going. The wooden bridge over the bog was even worse.

Vera scampered along, digging in her claws, but both she and Martinsson slipped several times. Tumbled down into the mud.

When they reached the far side of the bog, Vera's stomach was soaking wet, and Martinsson was wet up to her knees.

Her boots were sliding in all directions. Her toes were icy cold.

The cottages on the riverbank were shrouded in darkness. Abandoned and empty. Boats were lying upside down on the riverbank. Tarpaulins were spread over bicycles and sandpits and garden furniture.

Martinsson wondered which of the cottages Larsson was renting.

"Ah well," she said to Vera. "Come on."

Vera sneaked off into the trees. Martinsson kept going until she saw a light in one of the cottages. She knocked on the door.

Maja Larsson opened it.

"Good heavens," she said when she saw Martinsson's soaking wet legs.

She produced a pair of dry skiing socks, and put the coffee on the stove.

Martinsson massaged her feet, and felt the pain as the cold slowly faded away.

"Örjan and Marcus went upstream to do some fishing," Larsson said. "Let's hope they don't slip and smash their skulls in the dark. They ought to be back any minute now. Why not take off your jeans while you're waiting? Would you like a sandwich with liver pâté?"

"Yes please. I haven't had any lunch. Did you know that Sol-Britt had a half-brother?"

"What? No, I didn't. She always used to say that it was lucky I was around because she didn't have any siblings. Hang on a minute, I have to count in order to make sure that your coffee isn't too strong. Örjan always says that the spoon ought to be able to stand up in the cup of its own accord . . ."

"So she didn't know about it?"

Larsson switched on the coffee machine and produced a loaf of bread from a plastic bag. She seemed to be thinking hard as she made the sandwich. She cut the bread slowly into exactly identical slices. Then spread the butter and liver pâté as if she were painting in oils.

"No, I suppose I ought to be absolutely astounded. But then, all families have their secrets, don't you think?"

She placed the sandwiches in front of Martinsson.

"She said nothing to me. But she must surely have known about it. After her father's death, in any case."

Martinsson's mobile rang. Maja turned away and collected two coffee mugs from a cupboard. Martinsson took her mobile from out of her overcoat pocket. A text message from Sonja.

Sol-Britt Uusitalo's half-brother. I'll send his name, personal identity number and passport pic by e-mail.

Martinsson opened her e-mails.

Örjan Bäck, 19480914-6910.

Martinsson stopped breathing. It took several seconds before the passport photograph appeared. She recognised that mop of fair hair.

"How did it happen?" she said, trying hard to make her voice sound the same as normal. "How did you and Örjan get together?"

Shit, she thought. Shit, shit, shit.

"He came to read my water meter last spring," Larsson said, putting the mugs down on the table.

"I thought homeowners read meters themselves nowadays, and sent the readings to the company?"

"Yes, I'd done that in fact, but they had some kind of computer glitch, and a lot of data simply disappeared out of the system. Anyway, Örjan came to read it. And I had a rotten tree that was threatening to fall down on top of my shed. He offered to cut it down for me, and things just went on from there. Why . . ."

Martinsson stood up.

"Marcus!" she exclaimed.

Larsson had picked up the coffee jug, but put it back down on the table.

"Good Lord, Rebecka," she said. "What's the matter with you?"

"I don't know how to put this," Martinsson said, "but Örjan, he's—"

As she said that there was a sound from inside the hall cupboard. A choking sound.

Larsson jumped back in horror, as if she had just seen a snake. She uttered a brief yelp of surprise.

Martinsson took a couple of quick paces forward and opened the cupboard door.

Marcus fell out. His knees were pulled up towards his face. He was trussed up with gaffer tape, round his wrists and feet, round his body and over his mouth.

He looked up and stared wide-eyed at Martinsson.

Martinsson bent down to remove the tape from over his mouth, but she couldn't: it was stuck fast.

A sudden thought flashed into her mind.

But . . . This was not possible. Because Örjan . . .

Marcus's gaze switched to something behind her head. And at the same moment she felt fingers of steel around her neck.

Larsson was astoundingly strong. She grasped Martinsson's neck with one hand, and grabbed tight hold of her hair with the other. Then she hit Martinsson's head against the doorpost. Martinsson raised her hands to defend herself, but before she had lifted them as far as her face, her head hit the doorpost for the second time. After the third thump, her vision started to turn black at the edges. It was as if she were looking at Marcus through a keyhole. She did not feel the fourth thud against the doorpost. She had a vague feeling of her legs disappearing from underneath her. Her arms became helpless.

Then she fell. On top of Marcus.

One evening in August 1919, Hjalmar Lundbohm bumps into Police Superintendent Björnfot. They decide to have dinner together, at the Railway Hotel. They start with cheese, butter and pickled herring, with a shot of schnapps and a lager chaser; then Lübeck ham with spinach and eggs and more schnapps; and they round things off with soured whole milk, coffee and cognac.

By the time the whisky appears on the table, they are both distinctly merry: but they are sturdy, upright gentlemen and can handle strong drink better than most, and so they continue beckoning to fröken Holm, who is their waitress. They drink and they smoke.

They talk about the war, which has finished at last. About how times have changed. Lundbohm sighs about the way in which the new board of directors at the mine keep poking their noses into everything: they want to be kept informed and consulted over every little detail.

"I'm a man of action," he says. "If something needs doing, I do it, no messing about."

It is a different world now. The jazz bacillus is everywhere. Votes for women. Civil war in Russia. And time is running out for the managing director of the mine. Herr Lundbohm will celebrate his sixty-fifth birthday next spring. They wallow in memories.

In the end Lundbohm brings up the subject of Elina Pettersson. He tells the police superintendent it's no secret that he and the schoolteacher were more than just good friends for the year before her murder.

Björnfot becomes very quiet indeed now, but Lundbohm doesn't seem to notice.

"But then, she had several lovers," he says, and pauses. When Björnfot looks puzzled, he goes on.

"I know about that. The investigation made that clear. There were several possible candidates for paternity."

"What investigation?"

"Yours! Your investigation! Manager-in-Chief Fasth told me about it before he . . . Well, that was also a tragedy. We've certainly had our trials and tribulations, haven't we?"

Police Superintendent Björnfot says nothing. He says nothing and shakes his head slowly. Stares at his glass of whisky, seems to hesitate, but then decides to speak up, come what may.

"No, as far as I'm aware she never had any other lover. But I'm absolutely certain that it was Manager-in-Chief Fasth who killed her."

Lundbohm shudders. Like a dog shaking itself free of water. Wonders what the hell Björnfot is talking about.

And the superintendent of police looks at the managing director of the mine and thinks: he didn't know. He really didn't know.

Then he tells his friend the whole story. About the shirtsleeve in the stove. About what the maids have said.

When he has finished, he expects Lundbohm to say something, to react in some way.

But Lundbohm just sits there with his eyes and mouth wide open.

In the end Björnfot becomes uneasy.

"Herr Lundbohm," he says. "Herr Lundbohm. Are you alright?"

But Lundbohm has lost the ability to speak. Nor is he capable of standing up. Björnfot calls to fröken Holm. One of the girls in the kitchen runs to fetch the doctor while they and a few customers who are still present combine to carry Lundbohm down to fröken Holm's bed.

"He's not drunk," Björnfot shouts. "I've seen him drunk, and he's not like this. Look at him! He's trying to speak!"

The doctor arrives, but by then Lundbohm is able to walk, albeit with difficulty, and to speak again.

The doctor suspects nicotine poisoning and heart problems. And he comments that drinking in moderation never did anybody any harm.

"And that applies to the police as well!"

Martinsson slowly recovers consciousness, and hears somebody shouting. Her head is riven with pain, and when she gasps for breath she discovers that she cannot breathe in through her nose. It feels as if somebody has deposited a large lump of clay over her face, over her nose, and blocked all her airways.

She doesn't move – the urge to vomit comes darting up from inside her.

Somebody is shouting over her, in the darkness. A man.

"No, no," he yells. "This wasn't what we agreed."

She is lying in such a strange position, her legs stretched up behind her back, and her hands behind her back as well.

At first she has the vague feeling that she has been split into two pieces. Broken her back.

Then she hears a woman's voice. Maja Larsson.

"Shush, this is the last one. It's all for you, my darling. Just keep calm. If you could move her car—"

"No, I'm not going to do anything. This has nothing to do with what I promised. I'm not doing anything."

"Alright, alright, I'll move it. I'll take care of everything. Keep calm. Sit down. Stop marching up and down. Keep calm."

No, her back isn't broken. She's been trussed up. And she has a splitting headache. She tries to hold her breath and listen for any trace of Marcus.

Lie still. Don't throw up. Don't move. If you do, Larsson will start smashing your skull again.

She hears the sound of a bottle being placed on the table. And something else. A glass?

"Here you are," Larsson says. "Just keep calm. I'll soon be back."

"What are you going to do? Where are you going? You mustn't leave me alone."

"I'm going to move her car. I'll put the boy in the boat and overturn it. The simplest drowning accident anybody could possibly imagine. I'll fetch a tarpaulin and some weights for her."

"I don't want anything to do with this. You promised."

"I'm sorry. But you don't need to do anything."

A somewhat muffled voice now. As if she is pressing her mouth against his hair.

"Keep going – it'll soon be over. And then everything will be yours. You'll be able to travel to wherever you like. Do whatever you like. For the rest of your life. And if you'd like to have me there with you . . ."

"Of course I would. You must come with me."

". . . then of course, I'll be there."

Steps over the floor. Then the door. Opened. Closed.

The sound of the glass as he slides it towards himself. The sound of the metal stopper when he opens the bottle. The sound of liquid being poured into a glass.

Has she gone now? wonders Martinsson. Is he on his own? Yes, he is.

If only I could understand, she thinks, struggling so as not to sink into oblivion again. It is like a heartbeat inside her, a sort of murky liberation. Fractions of a second that are not throbbing pain. Her body longs to give way. To sink into that oblivion.

No, she says to herself. And she says aloud to him, "She'll kill you."

As she says that, she opens her eyes.

Maja's boyfriend is sitting at the kitchen table. He gives a start and stares at her.

"Örjan," she says – her voice is hoarse as a result of her blocked nose, and she makes a supreme effort to spit out onto the floor slime and blood that would prefer to be sliding down her throat. "She'll kill you."

"Rubbish," he says. "Shut your gob, or I'll smash your skull in."

Martinsson is gasping for breath.

"My skull is already smashed," she manages to say. "This isn't what you had bargained for, surely? Killing a child."

He thumps his fist down onto the table, in time with his roaring.

"Shut up! Shut up, shut up! She's doing all this for me. For my sake! So why should she want to kill me? She wouldn't get an öre if she did that."

He slides his glass to one side, raises the bottle to his mouth and gulps down large amounts of Jägermeister.

"Cousins don't inherit," he says, as if he is repeating something he has learnt by rote. "Sol-Britt and Maja were cousins."

"No," Martinsson says. "But aunts inherit. And Maja's mother is Sol-Britt's aunt. Think about that. If Sol-Britt had survived, you would have inherited half of it. And half of it is a lot of money, But Maja wouldn't have got anything at all. She was patient to start with. It's three years since she ran over Sol-Britt's son."

"That was an accident; she had nothing to do with that."

"Oh, come on, Örjan. I think she had. But she had time to spare then. It was supposed to look like an accident. But then, all at once, it became urgent. How did you meet?"

"What's that got to do with you?" Örjan says, wiping his forehead and his upper lip with his sleeve.

We don't have much time, Martinsson thinks. Maja will soon be back.

"I think she set her sights on you," she says, perhaps a little too quickly. "It wasn't an accident. She told me that you came to read her water meter. So that she could claim that you took advantage of her. Made use of her so that you could get access to Sol-Britt and Marcus. But think for a moment. Why had it suddenly become so urgent? She killed Sol-Britt's father only a few months ago, and then Sol-Britt herself, and now Marcus is in more than a bit of a mess. Do you know why it suddenly became so urgent?"

Örjan Bäck says nothing. He strokes his mop of hair back and glares at Martinsson. There is something in his look now.

He's scared, Martinsson thinks.

"Maja's mother is dying," she says. "That's why it's become urgent. Maja thought along these lines: if you and Sol-Britt and Marcus are out of the way, Maja's mother will inherit the fortune. Aunts inherit. Her mother has cancer of the liver. Not much time left. It could be a matter of days. A few weeks at most. Maja is feeding her very patiently. Do you understand now? Maja thinks that once you are all out of the way, her mother will inherit all Sol-Britt's worldly goods. Then her mother will die, and everything will go to Maja. She wants it all."

"That's just a load of . . ."

Örjan's voice is a mere whisper.

"She would have killed you already if she hadn't needed you. I think you are her reserve plan."

"She loves me," Örjan says, wrapping his hand round the empty glass on the table.

"I understand," Martinsson says, closing her eyes for a few seconds. "I thought she really liked me as well. She knew my mother. Or says she did at least. Very odd. We became great friends. Incredibly quickly."

A pang of pain shoots through her back and head. What if she is bleeding? Inside her head . . .

"I think her plan is to blame you. She must have been very

surprised to discover that you existed. Perhaps Sol-Britt told her. But this business, getting rid of me and Marcus – there will be no way of hiding what has happened. There are traces of my blood here that will never go away. The tiniest strand of hair will be enough. And it will be obvious from an examination of Marcus's body that it wasn't an accident. I think she will fetch something from the house that you've touched. A spade, a crowbar – anything at all. She will kill Marcus and me with whatever it is. Then she will kill you and say it was self-defence. She wanted you to move my car. Because you refused, she will put something of yours inside it. Something with traces of you on it. Sweat. Hair. D.N.A.

Örjan holds his head in his hands. Then he stands up and goes to check on the hat rack. Looks around, on the floor and the table.

Then he stares hard at Martinsson.

"She's clever," Martinsson says.

He nods.

"Frans Uusitalo," he says. "She took an elk-hunter's gun from his cottage. And put it back again when she had finished with it. I always thought that . . ."

He wipes his face with his sleeve again.

". . . That she was too good to be true. Pretty and clever."

Cold-blooded, Martinsson thinks. He's a bloody fool as well. But everybody wants to stay alive.

"You haven't done anything," she says. "Cut me loose. You don't want to get involved. That's what you said."

Örjan sways from side to side, like a child in a cradle.

"What shall I do?" he says. "What shall I do?"

"You won't be able to bear the killing of Marcus," Martinsson says. "But you're innocent, Örjan. And you're already a rich man. Those shares are worth several million. Half of them are already yours."

"Fuck," he says pitifully. "Fuck, fuck."

And while he continues to swear, he fetches a knife from the kitchen drawer and cuts the gaffer tape from her legs and hands.

She makes a big effort to get up on all fours. Everything is flickering in front of her eyes. Especially on the right. She can't see properly with her right eye.

She struggles up onto her feet, leaning against the wall. Now she can see Marcus. He has been lying behind her.

He looks her in the eye – thank God, he looks her in the eye.

"Cut him loose as well," she begs Örjan.

As she does so, there is a pinging noise from his mobile. He stares at it.

"She's coming," he says.

Twilight is approaching. Lundbohm loses everything. He loses all his wealth. He has cashed in his shares and used the proceeds to buy more shares, but those shares fall drastically in value and the end is already in sight. By the spring of 1925, he owes four banks and one private citizen a total of 320,000 kronor. He is forced to hand over all his shares and an advance on his pension to his creditors, and to pawn all his art collection.

His health deteriorates. Attacks of dizziness become more and more frequent. He loses his memory, and is crippled with pain.

He loses his friends. He can no longer invite guests to high-class dinner parties, and he lives in poverty with his brother Sixten. The tone of the letters he writes is whingeing, and they are mostly about his aches and pains, his bad knees, and the fact that his doctor has forbidden him to eat and drink anything but vegetables and mineral water.

Replies to his letters are brief and rare. Often no more than a picture postcard.

Twilight is approaching. But there is one thing he must do. One thing, before darkness finally falls.

Martinsson takes hold of Marcus's jacket and drags him out of the house. How far away is Larsson? With a bit of luck she might have been on the other side of the bog when she texted Örjan.

If Martinsson heads for the bog and the bridge, she will risk bumping into Larsson, so that is out of the question. Maybe she can walk through the trees, following the rapids upstream and then branch off towards the main road, thus skirting round the bog.

It is dark, but far from pitch dark. The moon is shining all too brightly in the starry sky. All the patches of snow glisten like pools of molten tin. It is possible to see too far. It will only be a few minutes before Larsson comes out looking for her among the trees.

Having to take Marcus with her means she is going too slowly. She walks backwards, dragging him along purely in order to get as far away from the house as possible. It is hard work. Her legs are already shaking, and there is a pounding inside her head like a sledgehammer hitting an anvil.

She is grateful for the noise from the rapids. It drowns the sound of her footsteps, when twigs crack and crackle under her feet, and her panting breath.

She takes special care to avoid the patches of snow – she must not leave any tracks. If she can just get a bit further into the forest, she can hide herself somewhere and send a text message for help.

She peers towards the path – and there, only a hundred metres away, she sees the light of a torch flickering between the trees.

Ten paces of dragging, then a few seconds to get her breath back. Calm down, calm down. Ten paces of dragging. Getting her breath back. Moving as far away as possible. Now she is in among the tall pine trees. They are black and straggling, casting long moon shadows over the moss. She is quite well hidden by the trees now, and Larsson has not reached the house yet.

Something suddenly moves in among the shadows. Fear stabs at Martinsson's midriff, but she doesn't scream. And it only takes her half a second to realise what it is.

Vera.

The dog comes waltzing up. She sniffs at Marcus, then joins them as if they are enjoying a stroll through the woods like on any other day.

Good Lord, she had forgotten about Vera. She can't possibly hide both a child and a dog. Vera won't even lie down when ordered to do so.

"Hop it," she whispers hoarsely to the dog, letting go of Marcus with one hand so as to be able to shoo Vera away.

Vera stands still, and stares at the cottage.

Martinsson cannot hear anything – but she can see something. The light of a torch shining in all directions.

She drags Marcus a bit further away. Vera follows them.

She looks over her shoulder to see where she is going. Drags Marcus over the undergrowth, avoiding rocks and stones. Looking for a place where she can hide. A dip where she can pull moss and undergrowth over them. A pine with low branches. Anything at all, anywhere at all.

She glances over towards the cottage. The torch is shining around in circles. Then it moves a little closer towards Martinsson. Shines around in circles again. Then moves a few more paces in Martinsson's direction.

It takes some time before the penny drops. Vera walks over the patches of snow. And Larsson is following the dog's tracks. It takes some time to find the next patch of snow with paw-prints, but it's still quicker than Martinsson can move with Marcus.

Martinsson looks at Vera, and struggles to avoid bursting into tears.

Go away, you stupid bloody dog, she thinks.

But Vera doesn't go away. She follows them. Walks over the wet snow. Leaves paw-prints.

Martinsson sinks down on one knee next to Marcus. Her strength is ebbing away. They haven't a chance. They are not going to escape. She might just as well lie down and wait for the darkness to come.

"I'm sorry," she whispers to Marcus. "I can't cope with this."

She digs her mobile from out of her pocket. She holds it low down, not sure about how much light from the display can be seen from a distance. "cottages rautas" she writes, "danger beware maja". Then she sends the message to Eriksson, and to Mella.

She tries to loosen the gaffer tape from around Marcus's feet and hands, but it is impossible to shift. But she does manage to slide the tape over his mouth down a little, so that he can breathe more easily.

She tries to think. If she can hide Marcus . . . Cover him up with twigs, and continue alone with Vera . . . She won't have the strength to continue for much longer anyway. She even wonders if she will be able to stand up again. Maja will catch up with her. And then Vera will lead Maja to Marcus – she's only a clueless mongrel after all.

It's not possible. It's just not possible.

Or . . . Yes, there is a way. An absolutely terrible way.

"Come here," she says to Vera, and looks around for something hard: a stone, a branch.

There. A thick branch.

She picks it up and calls to the dog again.

"Come here, old girl," she says. And Vera comes to her.

Lizzie strolls home from church one Sunday in March 1926. Frans Olof is ten years old. He seems so mature as he walks along beside her, linking arms with her. Johan-Albin would not dream of setting foot inside the church, but Frans always accompanies her, even if he does not seem to appreciate a good sermon or the marvellous music that accompanies services at the Salvation Army citadel.

Perhaps it is the walk through Luleå that attracts him most. An occasion when they have time to chat to each other about this and that, just the two of them. Or perhaps because they sometimes go to Café Norden after the service. Or maybe it is just that he senses how much it means to her. That it boils down to love.

As they approach their house in Lulsundsgatan, they see a man standing outside it. It takes a while before Lizzie recognises him, despite the fact that he seems familiar the moment she sees him. Then it dawns on her that it is Managing Director Lundbohm. He has aged. His face seems to be hanging down from his body, and he is clinging to the gatepost like a very old man.

The sight of him makes her heart leap. Maybe she squeezes Frans's arm, because he turns to look at her.

"What's the matter, Mum?" he says.

But she cannot answer because they have now arrived at the entrance door, where the man is standing.

*

Lundbohm takes a few careful steps forward. He is afraid of being overcome by dizziness, and falling down. A flock of house sparrows has assembled in a bush close by him, chattering away.

He tries to keep calm. But that is not easy when he sets eyes on the boy. He is a living image of his mother. His head is covered in a mass of blonde curly hair. Lizzie is so meticulous, but she has not kept the boy's hair short – understandably: he looks like an angel.

And he also looks like his father. It is mainly his eyes: the outside corners of his eyes are much lower than the inside ones, giving his face a melancholy expression.

"Hello!" Lundbohm says. He stops short because he is on the point of saying "Hello, Lizzie": but she is no longer his housekeeper, and he can't remember her surname.

Lizzie manages to produce a curt "hello", and the boy bows his head in acknowledgement.

"Well, well, my lad," Lundbohm says, "I used to know your mother . . ."

The boy looks hesitantly at Lizzie.

"What does he mean?" he wonders.

"He doesn't mean anything," Lizzie snaps, staring Lundbohm in the eye. "He's old and sick and no doubt he's no longer surrounded by friends and admirers like he used to be, now that he's no longer the managing director of the mine. Am I right? And now he wants something that he's never bothered about before."

Lundbohm cannot bring himself to respond. He is holding a fat envelope in his hand, and now he presses it against his chest.

"Coming here!" Lizzie snarls. "After all these years!"

She catches her breath. Now at last she can say what she's always wanted to say! Her legs are rigid – she feels no urge to curtsey.

"Do you know what?" she says. "I thought about you today. The pastor's sermon was about greed, about Moloch, the idol to whom people sacrificed children in order to become rich. I sat there in the pew, thinking. Thinking that we all know the sort of person who does that. People like you! Just like you! Thinking that money is the root of all evil. You craved the limelight. Artist friends, aristocratic men and women. But all that brilliance has crumbled away and become no more than gravel in your hands. And now you must face up to your sins. To the way you abandoned her! Face up to the facts! She loved you! And you thought she was a nice bit of skirt – but not good enough for you! Not as eminent as fru Karin Larsson."

Lundbohm has to acknowledge his guilt. He has been found out.

Karin Larsson was often a guest of his in Kiruna. Her husband Carl, the great artist, never accompanied her. And for a while Karin's letters to him were so affectionate. "I sometimes think you are the only person in the whole world who can understand me," she once wrote. He read that sentence over and over again. But then relations between Karin and her husband Carl improved, and now she hardly ever writes, although Carl has been dead for many years. If he ever complains about this, she always says she has so much to do for her children and grandchildren.

"It's true, isn't it?" Lizzie screeches, so shrilly that Frans looks horrified and whispers, "Mother," and tugs at the sleeve of her coat.

"I was so terribly fond of her," she goes on. "Her voice when she read aloud to us. Her way with the schoolchildren. And the way in which she never made me feel like a maid."

"I have never treated you in a way that could suggest you were somehow inferior," Lundbohm insists. "And as for her . . ."

Neither of them mentions Elina by name. The boy looks wide-eyed at first one of them, then the other.

"You made her feel like something much worse," Lizzie says, interrupting him. "You left her in the lurch with . . ."

She looks askance at Frans, and prays to God that he will not understand.

Lundbohm's face is as grey as burnt paper. Lizzie has fallen silent. Then Lundbohm looks up.

"Does your pastor ever preach about forgiveness?" he asks quietly.

When Lizzie doesn't reply, he hands her the envelope.

"Here! I'm a ruined man, destitute. But they didn't take quite everything. These are shares in a foreign company, so nobody knows—"

"I don't need anything from you! Johan-Albin and I have worked hard, and we have managed so far."

So Lundbohm offers the envelope to Frans, who takes it as bidden when the man waves it in front of him.

"Go away!" says Lizzie firmly. "Just clear off! There is nothing here for you. Have you understood that? Don't you think you've done enough harm? Be off with you!"

Then she disappears through the front door with the boy.

Lundbohm walks over the street to the taxi that is waiting there to take him back to the railway station.

So there, my heart, he says to himself when the driver has shut the door behind him. Now you have done all I've asked of you. Just carry on beating long enough for me to get away from here. Then I shan't ask any more of you. All I want is to have my time over again. And if I can't have that, then too bad.

Lizzie takes the envelope as soon as they are inside the house. And she answers "nobody" and "nothing" to Frans's questions about the mystery man. Then she tells him that he must not say a word about what has happened to his father.

Once they are inside the flat, she opens the envelope. It contains

a letter from Lundbohm, and three sheets of paper headed SHARE
CERTIFICATE – ALBERTA POWER GENERATION.

She lights a fire in the stove, and intends to burn it all up – but
first of all she puts on some water for coffee. Then she hears Johan-
Albin's footsteps on the stairs. She takes the envelope and hides it in
among the papers on the desk.

And that is where it stays.

Martinsson kneels there among the trees, crying her eyes out. She is holding Vera's collar in one hand, and has the branch in the other.

The moon is like a cold, white goddess in the black sky. Not too far away, the light from the torch is shining in circles over the lingon shoots and heather, the snow and the tracks made by Vera. Larsson is finding her way methodically towards where Martinsson is hiding.

It's Marcus or Vera, Martinsson thinks. And I have no time to lose.

She has laid Marcus down beside her, and turned him away. This is something he must not see.

"My lovely little girl," she says to Vera in a soft, hoarse voice.

She presses her battered face against Vera's head, rubs her forehead against the dog's silky skin, against her soft ears. She kisses Vera on the nose – although it's not much of a kiss, her mouth is too cracked and sore.

Vera allows herself to be held. She can't slink off when Martinsson is holding on to her, but she doesn't even try to. Just sits there submissively.

"I'm sorry," whispers Martinsson with a lump in her throat. "You are the loveliest dog I have ever come across." She swallows.

On three, she thinks. One . . .

Perhaps he is waiting for his dog, that strange, solitary madman who owned her in the first place.

Two . . .

Now they can roam around in the wilds again. She can picture Vera running round and round him, barking in doggy delight.

Three. Martinsson hits with all her strength on the precise spot where Vera's snout sticks out from her head.

You were never my dog in that sense, she thinks. But I love you even so.

And Vera becomes heavy in her hand, sinks down onto Martinsson's feet, her paws twitch slightly. Martinsson lets go of the collar. She ought to hit her again, but she cannot. It is simply not possible.

The branch falls out of her hand and she digs her fingers into Vera's fur.

Let go now. Away you go. Away you go, now.

She will cry later, not now. Not now. Up. Up on your feet.

She takes hold of Marcus, and the pain she feels in her head and face is a blessed relief now as she drags him between the tree trunks and over the moss and the undergrowth. Lifts him over roots and low branches.

In the end her legs and arms are trembling. She simply cannot go on, she hasn't the strength to drag him even one more metre. She pushes Marcus under a fir tree, rips off twigs and small branches and covers him almost completely.

"You must keep absolutely silent," she whispers into his ear. "No matter what she says. Don't say a single word. The police will soon be here to rescue us. Krister. O.K.? We're waiting for Krister."

She thinks she sees him nod his head in the darkness.

Should she move away from him? But if she does, he might get scared and give himself away. She can't make up her mind. Nor does she have the strength. She tumbles down into the undergrowth.

In her mind's eye Vera is still running around. Scampering along a dry, dusty country lane, crouching slightly as usual. She slinks down into a ditch, comes up again. The sun is shining and Vera scuttles over a meadow which is covered by a veil of midsummer flowers, buttercups, red clover. It is almost impossible to see more of her than that ear sticking straight up.

How can one love a dog as much as I love her? Martinsson thinks. I hope you felt free when you were with me.

Then her thoughts and her tears trickle away into the cold moss.

Marcus the Wild Dog can feel that Martinsson has stopped shaking. She has been crying, but now she has stopped. He moves his arms, and now he can disentangle them from his legs. But his wrists are still taped together. The Wild Dog has sharp teeth. It finds the edge of the tape, and soon it has worked its paws free.

Now he hears the voice, despite the loud roaring from the rapids. She – Larsson – is quite close now. He has to hold his paw over his mouth. The light from the torch is sweeping back and forth over the ground. He pulls Martinsson's dark-coloured scarf over her white hand and face. Now they are almost invisible.

"Rebecka!" Larsson shouts, shining the torch in all directions. "I didn't think you were capable of that. So cold-blooded."

The torchlight moves further away. The Wild Dog doesn't dare to follow it with its eyes, but it doesn't dare to keep its eyes closed all the time either.

The voice is coming out of the darkness. What he sees most of is the torch. Sometimes it is shining directly at him and Martinsson. Then he hardly dares to breathe, although she is a long way away. Sometimes he can see her clearly in the moonlight. She is like a ghost.

"Rebecka," she shouts. "We can share it. You are Virpi's daughter. I would never . . . Surely you understand that?"

The torch continues to shine. For a while it is a long way away, but then it comes closer again. She starts shouting again. Now she is shouting to him.

"Marcus? Wild Dog! I'm worried about Rebecka. Is she with you?"

The torch is back where they left Vera. Now she is walking in a circle. Then a larger circle. She shines the torch behind rocks and under pine trees.

"Has Rebecka fainted?" she shouts. "Is she bleeding? She might die if she doesn't get to a hospital."

Now the Wild Dog is very scared.

"It's all your fault, Marcus," she shouts.

Maja sounds so angry. The Wild Dog looks at Martinsson. She keeps fainting, over and over again. She might die.

Should he shout? Martinsson said he ought to keep quiet, but she hadn't fainted then.

He opens his mouth to shout, but no sound comes. He has promised, after all.

And then, just when he is so scared that he can hardly stop himself from crying, he sees a very large lamp some way away in the trees. Two lamps. Three.

And then he hears Krister's voice.

"Marcus!" Eriksson shouts. "Rebecka!"

Maja's torch is extinguished and she disappears into the trees.

Marcus caresses Rebecka. Everything will be O.K. now. He won't say a word. The Wild Dog has played hide and seek with Krister before. And Tintin is no doubt with them. They will soon find him. And then everything will be alright.

Hjalmar Lundbohm dies in the morning of Easter Day, 1926. The doctor has been to visit him the evening before. He listened to Lundbohm's heart and his fast, irregular breathing. And said that there was not long to go now. Lundbohm did not wake up during the brief visit.

When the doctor left, Sixten returned to the armchair they had placed beside the bed. He held his brother's hand for a while. Then he read a few pages of his book. Fell asleep as he sat there. The book fell to the floor.

At half past four in the morning, Lundbohm opens his eyes for the last time. Sixten is asleep in the armchair. His head is drooping like a faded flower. His glasses are on his knee.

Elina is sitting on the edge of the bed. She bends down over Hjalmar and kisses his face.

Then she stands up. He stretches his hands out to her like a drowning man. She must not leave him.

"Come now," she says, and gives him a slightly surprised smile, as if she is wondering why he is lying there.

And then he steps out of his body, with no difficulty at all.

As soon as he takes a pace forward, he is no longer in Sixten's home.

It is early spring. The sun is shining over a snow-covered Kiruna.

She is walking a few metres in front of him. Her fair hair is constantly working its way free from the bun in which it is tied.

He hurries to catch up with her. She turns her head and smiles at him. There is no sorrow in her, no hatred, no disappointment. Nevertheless, he has stabbing pains in his chest.

"I'm sorry," he says. "Please forgive me, Elina."

She stops and looks surprised.

"What for?" she asks.

And he realises that she doesn't remember anything. He turns, as if the memory is something he has dropped out of his pocket and might be lying on the pavement behind him. But there is nothing there.

Then there is just snow and sunshine and a laughing schoolteacher with whom he has linked arms, and whom he will never let go. And the glories of spring that are lying underneath all the whiteness, waiting to burst forth in their full majesty.

Anna-Maria Mella went out into the hospital corridor to fetch another cup of coffee. When she got back, Martinsson had regained consciousness. She was lying in bed with a drip in her arm, staring up at the ceiling light.

"Hello," Mella said cautiously.

Martinsson turned her head slowly to look at her. Her eyes were as black as a winter night when she fixed her gaze on Mella.

"Marcus?" she said.

"He's fine. That Örjan knocked him out at the very beginning, so he'll be here in intensive care for tonight. But that's just so that they can keep an eye on him. He's asleep."

Mella sat down on the edge of Martinsson's bed, and stroked her colleague's head as she usually did with her children when they were ill.

"Can you speak?"

"Maja?" whispered Martinsson.

Mella took a deep breath.

"Tintin tracked her down," she said. "She ran off through the trees, but we commandeered a quad bike from one of the cottages, and caught up with her quite quickly."

Martinsson nodded. She knew the score. She had seen Tintin perched on a bathroom mat so as not to slip on the platform of a quad bike, pointing her nose in the direction the driver ought to follow.

"When we caught up with her she ran down to the river," Mella said. "And swam out."

She looked down at her coffee and pulled a face.

"You can guess what happened. Strong currents and below freezing. She didn't survive. Her body ended up twenty metres downstream. Tintin found it right away."

Mella took a swig of coffee. Thought about how she had stood there on the riverbank with her hand on her service pistol while Eriksson attempted cardio-pulmonary resuscitation, determined not to give up. Moonlight. Wet rocks glistening. The black river water. Stålnacke reporting by telephone that the ambulances had arrived with stretchers and that Martinsson was alive.

"Do you have the strength to say what happened?"

"There's an inheritance," Martinsson said, clearing her throat. "From Frans Uusitalo. Old shares that Hjalmar Lundbohm gave him. They are in Frans's name, so they are only of value to him or his legal heirs. I can't be certain, but I can well imagine that Frans Uusitalo or Sol-Britt asked Maja Larsson to look into it and find out if they were worth anything. Or perhaps she offered to do so."

"And were they?"

"Several million."

Mella whistled in astonishment – or perhaps it was mostly a blowing without sound.

"I think," Martinsson went on, "that Maja said they were worthless. Then she decided to be patient. Worked out how to ensure that all the other heirs would have accidents. Left quite a long time between them. Then she discovered that Sol-Britt had a half-brother. Perhaps she intended to kill him straight away, but then it occurred to her that she could save him until last, so that he could be the perfect scapegoat if anything went wrong, and if the police discovered that all the deaths were not in fact accidents."

She paused. Her tongue was sticking to the roof of her mouth.

Her head no longer felt as if it were about to burst. She wondered what medication they had given her. Mella stood up and fetched her a white plastic mug of water.

"Maja couldn't inherit Sol-Britt's fortune; they were only cousins. Cousins don't inherit. But if there are no children or grandchildren, and no siblings nor children of siblings, then an aunt can inherit. Maja's mother was Sol-Britt's aunt."

"So she started with Sol-Britt's son."

"Yes. And then there was no great hurry. Until her mother got cancer of the liver, and so she suddenly needed to get a move on. She shot Frans in the forest. Stole a rifle from a hunter's cottage, and then returned it to where she had taken it from. Örjan told me about that. Is he . . . ?"

Mella shook her head.

"No, he's O.K. He's talking away – Stålnacke noted it all down. What do you think? Complicity in murder? Protecting a criminal?"

"In any case complicity in attempted murder, in connection with Marcus," Martinsson said. "And Grievous Bodily Harm. He won't get away with that."

"I don't understand Maja," Mella said. "She seemed to be, I don't know, such a pleasant person. And she dropped von Pest in the shit."

Martinsson said nothing. She was thinking about her own conversation with Maja.

I wasn't even a person as far as she was concerned, she thought. We were all simply obstacles, or tools. We had to be eliminated, or used.

"She must have been overjoyed when she discovered that Sol-Britt was having an affair with Jocke Häggroth," Mella said. "It would have been dead easy to borrow Sol-Britt's mobile and send a text message to her own, saying that she was going to break it off. And then erase it from Sol-Britt's mobile. She knew that we would dig out all her messages, including the erased ones."

They said nothing for a while, and both of them thought about Larsson. Larsson stabbing Sol-Britt over and over again with the hayfork, to make it look like a frenzied attack by a madman. Larsson writing WHORE on the wall. Larsson searching for Marcus – opening all the cupboards. Putting the hayfork under Häggroth's barn.

"She probably never thought it would have been possible for him to escape through a first-floor window," Mella said, gulping down her coffee.

Much better than the stuff we get from the vending machine at work, she thought.

"We're going through her mother's house with a fine-tooth comb now. They've been at it for three hours already. We found a plastic sack in the compost heap containing the body of a dead dog."

"Sol-Britt and Marcus's dog," Martinsson said.

"And then she put the burning torch in the dog kennel while Marcus was asleep there," continued Mella. "A perfect accident."

"Yes," Martinsson said. "She didn't know."

"Didn't know what?"

"That she had already lost. When Marcus outlived Sol-Britt, that was curtains for Maja. Her mother would never have inherited Sol-Britt's fortune. What counts is the time of death, not the time when the estate of the deceased is distributed. An aunt is a third-in-line heir. She can only inherit if there is no first- or second-in-line heir alive when the person whose estate is to be distributed dies. Marcus became Sol-Britt's heir the very second she died. If Maja had killed him later, it would have been Marcus's mother in Stockholm who inherited the fortune. Marcus would have to have died simultaneously with Sol-Britt or before her for Maja's mother to inherit. She cocked it up."

And now she's dead, the cold-blooded lunatic, Martinsson thought. So I can't even tell her that.

"Why did she kill Vera?" Mella said.

Martinsson did not respond. She rolled over onto her side and with considerable difficulty sat on the side of her bed.

"My clothes?"

"They want to keep you in overnight, for observation," Mella said.

Martinsson peeled off the tape over the cannula conveying the drip into her arm, and pulled it out. She stood up somewhat unsteadily and walked over to the wardrobe.

"They can go to hell," she said.

"The Brat is at Eriksson's place," Mella said. "Eriksson wanted to stay with Marcus, but the nurses insisted that he should go home. They promised to ring him the moment Marcus woke up."

Martinsson got dressed. She avoided looking at herself in the mirror. Avoided looking at Mella.

"Let me drive you home at least," Mella said.

But Martinsson made a dismissive gesture and walked out of the door.

Mella took out her mobile and rang von Post.

It took her five minutes to report on the events of the last few hours. Von Post said not a word from start to finish. Mella broke off twice to make sure he was still there. She asked if he wanted to be present at the press conference the next morning, but he declined.

When she finished what she had to say, he said not much more than assuring her that he would be in touch the following day, then hung up.

Mella sat there for a few moments with her mobile in her hand.

She had expected him to be furious because she had not phoned him sooner – when she received the text message from Martinsson and drove down to Kurravaara with Eriksson and Stålnacke.

In a way she would have felt better if he had read the riot act.

What is he doing now? she wondered. Torturing a cat? Burning himself with cigarettes?

She rang Robert and asked him to collect her. Her Ford could stay in the hospital car park. It had started snowing again, but the car would just have to get snowed in. Something to worry about tomorrow.

Mella's husband was waiting for her at the entrance to A. & E. Journalists were already encamped outside the main entrance.

"My darling," he said when she had sat down in the passenger seat.

She leaned towards him and let him embrace her.

"Do you know what I want?" she asked as he caressed the back of her head as only he could.

"To hurry back home and make another baby?"

"Not this time, for a change. I want to find a friend. I hope to make friends with a girl. If I can."

Von Post did not torture a cat. Nor was he the type to burn himself with cigarettes. If he'd had a personal life coach, no doubt the coach would have told him that there was something he could learn from all this.

But von Post stood there with his mobile in his hand and had no intention of learning anything at all.

This just isn't happening, he thought.

The light from the street lamps was pouring in through the windows, and he unfastened the cords and let the Venetian blinds fall with a thud. He took two Zolpidem tablets and washed them down with three large glasses of whisky. Then he fell asleep on the sofa with his clothes on.

*

Eriksson was sitting at his kitchen table. It was almost midnight. The doctor at the hospital had given him some sleeping pills, but he did not want to take them. They had promised to ring as soon as Marcus regained consciousness, and he wanted to be awake when that happened.

He tried to convince himself that he would just have to reconcile himself to things that he could not change.

But he could not stop thinking about Marcus. He had sat on the edge of his bed at the hospital, holding his hand until he fell asleep. Then the doctor had insisted that he go home. "You must also get some rest," she had said.

All human relationships are transient, he told himself.

But that did not help.

He looked out at his dark garden where not long ago he had lain in the dog kennel, reading aloud to Marcus.

As soon as his mother hears that he is rich, he thought, she'll take the first available flight up here and come to fetch him. I must be happy. Happy for every minute I still have with him.

His train of thought was interrupted by the dogs starting to bark and running to the door.

Martinsson was standing outside.

She looked awful. The light over the door made her eyes look like holes. Her nose was blue and swollen. Her upper lip as well. They had stitched over her eyebrows.

"I've come to fetch the Brat," she said stiffly. The whole of her face was struggling to prevent her from bursting into tears.

"Oh, Rebecka," he said. "Come in."

She shook her head.

"No," she said. "I just want to go home."

"Vera?" he said. "What happened?"

She shook her head again. And something inside him suddenly caused him so much pain that he burst out crying.

"She left a trail," Martinsson said in a voice that threatened to break. "Maja would have found us."

Although he was the one who was crying, he wanted to hug her. To hold her close when she was so very sad.

She stood out there in the feeble light from the lamp over the door. Her chest was heaving as if she were out of breath.

"Marcus is still alive," he said eventually. "Come in for a moment, my dear."

"It doesn't help," she whispered. "It doesn't help that he's still alive."

She leaned forward. Pressed her clenched fist to her midriff as if to prevent the tears from forcing their way out. She held on to the rail. A long, agonised wail forced its way out. An anguished cry, of the kind that shatters a person, forces her down onto her knees.

"It doesn't help," she sobbed.

Then she looked up at him.

"Hold me tight. I must . . . Somebody must hold me tight."

He took a step forward and wrapped his arms round her. Rocked her from side to side. Held her tight. Mumbled into her hair.

"There, there. Cry now. Cry away."

And they both cried.

The dogs came out and stood round them. The Brat forced its nose in between Martinsson's knees.

She looked up at Eriksson. Sought after his mouth with hers. Cautiously, as it was so tender and painful.

"Have sex with me," she said. "Fuck me all ends up so that I can forget about all this."

He ought not to. He should say no. But she had her arms around him – how could he possibly thrust her away? His hands roved around inside her overcoat and under her jumper. He pulled her into the hall.

"In you come," he said to the dogs, and managed to close the door behind them.

Then he took hold of her hands and walked backwards up the stairs, leading her up. Her tears were dripping down onto his hands. The dogs followed them, like a sort of bridal procession.

He laid her down underneath him on the bed, and didn't want to let her go. Couldn't let her go. He caressed her. Over her skin and her small breasts. She wriggled out of her clothes and told him to get undressed. He did so. Lay down on top of her, expecting all the time that she would suddenly say "Stop!"

She was so soft. He kissed her hair and her ears and the side of her mouth that wasn't so tender. After all, he hadn't indulged in any chewing tobacco.

She did not say "Stop!" She guided him inside her.

This is all wrong, he thought. But he was away on cloud nine.

Afterwards he fetched a glass of water and one of the sleeping pills he had been given by the doctor.

"What about Marcus?" she asked when he came back. "Will his mother want to take him on now that he's rich?"

"I don't know," he said, handing her the tablet. "Here, take this. Sleep now."

"She'll want the money," Martinsson said. "She hasn't even wanted to see him. But now . . . That bloody woman. Of course she'll want to have him now."

She fell silent when she saw his sorrowful eyes.

"Would you have been prepared to look after him?" she asked.

"Yes," he said softly. "Ever since I first found him. I can't explain it. But I was allowed to take care of him for a few days. Now . . ."

He shook his head sadly.

She sat up.

"Get dressed," she said. "I'll ring Björnfot and Mella."

Mella, Martinsson, Eriksson and Björnfot met in the latter's little flat that he used when he was in Kiruna. It was in the middle of the night – half past one, to be precise.

They sat in a room that had both a dining area and a small three-piece suite, and warmed themselves up with a cup of tea. Björnfot's tracksuit was draped over the back of the sofa, and in the bathroom there was a special stand in which his skis were fixed, ready for waxing. It was obvious that at least somebody was longing for snow.

"You're out of your mind," Mella said to Martinsson.

"She left him when he was one year old," Martinsson said. "And she never even wanted to see him in the school holidays. I want those share certificates to disappear."

Björnfot opened his mouth, then closed it again.

"We can lock them up in a bank vault," she went on. "He can have them when he's eighteen. I promise to keep an eye on the company and make sure that they don't plan any new share issues, or anything else that could affect the value of Marcus's certificates."

"Örjan knows that they exist," Mella said with a yawn.

"That they existed! But – oops, Sol-Britt must have thrown them away," said Martinsson. "Under the impression that they were worthless. If Marcus's mother wants to take care of him, then that's fine – but she must want to have him without any financial reward."

"She won't want to in that case," Mella said.

She turned to Eriksson.

"But are you really willing to take care of him? Believe you me," she said, "looking after a youngster involves an awful lot of work. And he's been through quite a bit."

"Yes, I'm willing," Eriksson said. "And I don't want his money. We can burn those share certificates."

"Nothing is going to be burnt," Björnfot said. "Besides, what is there to burn? I've never seen any share certificates."

"Nor have I," Mella said. "Can we go to bed now?"

"Yes," Martinsson said, being careful to avoid looking Eriksson in the eye. "I suppose we can."

THURSDAY, 27 OCTOBER

Von Post woke up with a stab of pain in his chest.

Hell and damnation, he thought as he reached for the telephone. Björnfot responded after the first ring. Von Post looked at the clock. Yes, of course he would be awake – it was just gone eight, after all.

"Jenny Häggroth!" von Post said. "I take it she isn't still locked up in the cell at the police station?"

"Well," the Chief Prosecutor said ponderously, "if you, in your capacity as leader of the investigation, haven't issued an instruction to release her, she's no doubt still there."

"But I . . ." began von Post, searching desperately for some way of escaping from the tight corner in which he was trapped, "I wasn't even informed yesterday."

"Hmm," Björnfot said even more ponderously. "I spoke to Mella a short time ago, and she said she rang and reported to you last night. No doubt that conversation will be noted in both of your mobile phones, so perhaps you might like to devote a little time to adjusting your memory."

"I'll call them and instruct them to release her immediately," von Post said. "There's not really a problem. After all, it was only last night that—"

"With Silbersky as her defence counsel? You can't assume that. When the reason for holding somebody under arrest or in custody no longer applies, the unlawful deprivation of liberty must cease immediately. Immediately. Not a few hours later. And definitely not the following morning."

Von Post groaned audibly. That hook-nosed swine will have him for breakfast.

"I shall be found guilty of professional misconduct," he snarled between his teeth.

Judges and prosecutors were sometimes found guilty of professional misconduct. If they forgot to subtract days already spent in custody from a prison sentence, or in some other way deprived a person of his or her freedom illegally. The result would not be the sack, but a significant loss of prestige. It was the kind of thing that colleagues chirruped on about behind one's back for ever and a day.

"Rebecka Martinsson will sit in the public gallery eating popcorn," he said.

"I find that difficult to believe," his boss said, while thinking to himself: but I might.

Martinsson woke up and looked straight into Eriksson's eyes. How long had he been lying there, waiting for her to wake up? Lying at the foot of the bed were Tintin, the Brat and Roy, slowly waking up.

"Hello, my lovely," he said. "How are you feeling?"

She moved the muscles in her face. Stiff and swollen.

"Come off it," she said. "You are calling me lovely because you want to make love to me again. Dogs in your bed?"

He sighed.

"I know. It's your and Marcus's fault."

Martinsson reached for her coat that was lying on the floor, and took out her mobile. Three messages and five missed calls from Måns.

There's something wrong, she thought, when you don't want to ring your boyfriend. When you don't want to talk. When you just feel under pressure. And maybe there's something amiss when you have sex with somebody else.

"I'm going to dump Måns," she said to Eriksson.

He stroked her hair.

Yes, he thought. Yes!

But he actually said, "Don't make any big decisions now."

"O.K.," she said.

"Make small decisions. I'm going to fetch Marcus from the hospital. Would you like to have breakfast with us?"

She smiled. Tentatively. It caused her too much pain in her face and in her heart. One little decision at a time.

"Yes," she said. "I'd love to have breakfast with you."

THE AUTHOR'S THANKS

I stumbled and fell. The book came adrift and ran off into the trees. My thanks to all of you who helped me back up onto my feet – you know who you are. For a while I thought the book was lost forever, but it came back in the end, my beloved little devil.

Hjalmar Lundbohm actually existed – but the whole of his relationship with Elina is invented, of course. I make things up and tell lies, that's my job. I make a mess of Martinsson's face, and kill dogs.

There are so many people I would like to thank, but on this occasion I must make special mention of the following:

My publisher Eva Bonnier, and my editor Rachel Åkerstedt for your strict but loving assistance, and all the lovely people I have contact with at Albert Bonniers publishing house and the Bonnier Group Agency.

Eva Hörnell Sköldstrand and Sara Luthander Hallström who read my text and encouraged me. Malin Persson Giolito! "Read it with a knife in your hand," I said, and she produced a machete! My mum and dad, who are mainly to thank for my culture, my origins and my feeling for the part of Sweden where I grew up.

Curt Persson, county custodian of antiquities for Norrbotten, who so generously passed on his vast knowledge of Kiruna around the time of the First World War, and of Hjalmar Lundbohm. Kjell Törmä who allowed me to use his story about when he gave up chewing tobacco, but ended up by drying out wet tobacco in his microwave. Cecilia Bergman, who I ring non-stop with questions about the work of a prosecutor, and how the law works. Professor Marie Allen at the Rudbecklaboratoriet in Uppsala, who has such fascinating stories to tell about bones and blood that one is tempted to change one's profession. Chief Medical Officer Peter Löwenhielm, who has helped me with my dead bodies. Niklas Högström, who instructed me about shares in the old days. Jörgen Wallmark at the Ice Hotel in Jukkasjärvi for showing me around the workshops there. Any errors in the book are entirely my responsibility, because I forgot to ask, misunderstood what I was told, or made things up so that they fitted better into the story.

Stella and Leo. Now the book is finished! I know you have been longing for that to happen! Ola, my arctic fox: my love and thanks.

And for those of you who wonder about the meaning of "Hänen ej ole ko pistää takaisin ja nussia uuesti", I would translate it roughly as follows: "All you can do is put him back again and fuck him once more". In other words, "He is so awful that you have to recreate him". My grandmother used to come out with statements like that. The fact that she was a deeply religious Laestadian was no obstacle – language used to be a bit more spicy up in Tornedalen.

Åsa Larsson

UNTIL THY WRATH BE PAST

Translated from the Swedish by Laurie Thompson

In the first thaw of spring the body of a young woman surfaces in the River Torne in the far north of Sweden. Rebecka Martinsson is working as a prosecutor in nearby Kiruna. Her sleep has been disturbed by haunting visions of a shadowy, accusing figure. Could the body belong to the ghost in her dreams?

Joining forces once more with Police Inspector Anna-Maria Mella, Martinsson is drawn into an investigation that focuses on old rumours about the disappearance of a plane carrying supplies for the Wehrmacht in 1943. Shame and secrecy shroud the locals' memories of the war, with Sweden's early co-operation with the Germans still a raw wound. And on the windswept shore of a frozen lake waits a killer who will kill again to keep the past buried forever beneath half a century of silent ice and snow.

MACLEHOSE PRESS

www.maclehosepress.com
bscribe to our quarterly newsletter

Åsa Larsson

THE BLACK PATH

Translated from the Swedish by Marlaine Delargy

The frozen body of a woman is found in a fishing hut on the ice near Torneträsk in far northern Sweden. She has been tortured, but the killing blow was clumsy, almost amateur.

The body is quickly identified, raising hopes of an open-and-shut case. But when a six-month-old suicide is disinterred, Rebecka Martinsson and Anna-Maria Mella find themselves investigating shocking corruption at the heart of one of Sweden's biggest mining companies – one with powerful enemies of its own . . .

Set against a haunting, icy backdrop and packed with suspense, *The Black Path* is a menacing and evocative crime novel, replete with the complex psychological insight that is Larsson's gift to the genre.

MACLEHOSE PRESS

www.maclehosepress.com
Subscribe to our quarterly newsletter